Blossoming
A Novel

Sade Katarina

To my parents Henri and Nina,

Thank you for believing in the big dreams of your little girl.

Thank you for teaching me about love.

"My imagination makes me human and makes me a fool; it gives me all the world and exiles me from it." ~Ursula K. Le Guin

A Note From The Author

Hello there, my darling reader. If it is alright with you, we will be going on this journey together. You are, after all, taking a stroll through my imagination (and I'm so happy you're here!). Perhaps imagine me telling the story *to* you, so that this way, we can discuss our musings together. A book club, you and me. What do you say?

I promise it'll all make sense, very soon. Now, would you like some sweet tea?

Prologue

As I child, I longed for hurricanes. I knew they were dangerous, and yet there was an alchemy in the adrenaline. Dad boarding up the windows, sounds of whipping wind and rain, stark stillness of a house where the lights have gone out, the sliver of calm in the eye of the storm as we wait for the worst, still yet to come. I prayed for a category two; school days canceled, but no roofs ripped off. I hoped to brush against the edge of disaster, but to be spared by it... only just. The world you are entering is set in a society shaped by this peculiar euphoria, always wishing for a 'barely made it moment'.

The small towns you've never heard of, but that we've never forgotten.

CHAPTER ONE
Welcome to Weston Hills

Cows... lots of cows—Sadie Bexley wrote down her observations in her journal, the light blue one with the velvet cover—*smells like manure.* Though, the way her father's red Chevy trekked down the pothole-ridden highway made it impossible to report anything legible, and she had in fact written *smells like manuel.*

She continued her sulking in the backseat, her cheeks tired and scrunched on the glass, but just as uniquely buxom, like she'd stuffed a few marbles in her gums or had her wisdom teeth removed yesterday. She'd heard people who hadn't paid attention to her name reference them, so they must be somewhat defining and memorable. Sure, her friends got corset waist or legs-for-days, while she got ample cheekbones (and this is pretty symbolic overall).

Slivers of intimate tangerine light flickered through mosaic branches of orange trees, endlessly green backroads of them, with parked tractors and barbed wire fences. Meaning, they'd arrived at their new home (or lack thereof). 'Welcome to Weston Hills, Where Our Porch Is Your Porch' a rusty sign read with a congested row of scrappy starling birds perched on top, an unsightly canvas of white dressing below.

Sadie groaned, already smelling the deviled eggs, then ran a delicate index finger across her mood ring that had been stuck in a murky brown all week. Disgusting, lousy, miserable *brown.* The color of dead things, and dirt.

Her dad was Henri Bexley: an entrepreneurial-spirited, Tim McGraw look-a-like with a love for tools and productivity hacks —he'd been going on about shoe horns from Arizona to the sunshine state panhandle—and a tendency to sleeve his big heart behind some, mediocrely funny, humor. He slacked in the driver's seat now with a hand loosely on the wheel, tapping, before turning the volume nob all the way up and singing Lady A's 'American Honey', loudly and off key.

Margot, an exemplary template of a mom, laughed at her husband's misplaced confidence before leaning subtly seductive from shotgun to caress a hand down his strong thighs. She was a strikingly cultivated woman with a regal essence and a deck of oracle cards in her purse at all times; an artful balance of tender and tenacious. And she was breathtaking in such an organic way, it could make other women quite bitter; the only beauty enhancing a touch of red in her dark elbow-length waves, and even then she'd used natural henna.

The couple flirted in tiny confidential glances as Sadie immortalized each one in her journal, smiling and swirling a fibril of gold hair in delight. She did this often. Maybe these are things other people's kids don't notice, only scoff and make grossed out faces about, but Sadie would purposely linger when she could, just for that tiny glimpse of magic. It was fascinating to witness: her father's direct simplicity in her mother's fiery warmth and how true love laced those two together so silkily it felt mythic. Mythic wasn't far-fetched for Sadie, but expected.

After all, she'd grown up seeing an equally eloquent devotion in her late grandparents, and in second grade, decided it must run in her family—*epic loves*. She'd practically made it her life's purpose to continue the tradition of fabulous ever after, practically running into walls to keep her eyes at-first-sight ready, practically making herself sick with anticipation of forever. In other words, Sadie Bexley was highly *im*practical. An optimist, as young girls tend to still be.

That candy cane optimism was tested as she turned again to the window: *Um, was there a bullet hole in that stop sign?*

Ramshackle mobile home communities sat cluttered on every

2

corner, wild chickens grazed overrun yards, a disintegrating spring mattress rotted outside a Dairy Queen. They passed a Walmart with a McDonalds inside, then a few gun shops, a Super 8 Motel advertising hourly rates. A group of shirtless preteen boys raced ATVs along the road, tossing empty Monster energy drinks in ditches, aiming BB guns at a 4x8 plywood sign outside a windowless bar that read 'No Shoes, No Shirt, No Problem'; all of which *was* a problem. It was all chain places and old church bells and ugly weeds full of gnats. The ground was so sopping, it was sinking in on itself. It was exactly ninety-eight degrees. This was central Florida, indeed.

The Chevy screeched to a halt at a red light on Main Street, definitely an improvement with pleasurably old-style storefronts, healthy roads, and a white gazebo on a patch of plush grass in the center.

A group of the town's most recognizable football boys were gathered on the sidewalk, parallel to the light. They were in board shorts, Polo shirts or Under Armour ones, backwards Bass Pro Shop caps, tall Nike socks and slides. Pronounced farmer's tans and sun-kissed highlights kept them certifiably southern, from summer conditioning and skim boarding on the Pretty Pond streets that flood instantly after noon storms. While the rest rowdily tossed a football and disturbed the peace, there was one ruminant outlier. Sadie fixated on him as he lagged behind and smoldered gorgeously over a half-eaten Slim Jim. He looked moody and dangerous, and she hoped he was.

Brooks Holden had rich brown eyes with a vacancy one can't help but wonder about, crew cut hair, tallish build and athleticism beyond reason. He exuded status in that illogical way that makes you forget cool guys are just people too. His unsociable charm was just withdrawn and mysterious enough to leave you enticingly unsure, space to wonder…

Wonder, ambiguity, possibility: they're like little life-line candies for impractical girls with expectations to broaden, the girls who write grand stories in their head. And perhaps the boys like that. Perhaps they need someone to expect grand things from them, for themselves to believe they're capable of it.

When Brooks turned to catch the football, his tough brown eyes caught the sensitive green ones through the window, and he missed, stumbled, toppled over a fire hydrant with fascination and shock rumpled on his face. It was almost nothing, merely two strangers passing in the daybreak of an August morning, and yet Brooks' eyes glinted in concentration as if... he recognized... *her*...

Sadie felt it too, but not for any particular reason. She was merely stellar at assigning meaning to the meaningless. The light turned to 'go' as the truck jolted her vision. Suddenly, the tangerine light and everything under it was much more acceptable.

For the rest of the drive, Sadie mentally counted the abs under mystery hunk's gray Under Armour, noticing her mood ring refashion to soft lavender, her skin a roasted pink. Then her phone buzzed luridly between her legs, at the very *top* of her legs, continuously, relentlessly—the girl's group chat going off about the San Fernando Valley La Croix shortage—which was around the time she made the discovery that her leggings were of one-ply material. Definitely thin. Basically tights.

"Can we turn the air up, please?" Sadie chimed desperately, fanning her plump cheeks, before leaning forward and turning it herself.

About two bumpy miles later, the Bexley family had reached a wooded dirt road overgrown by gnarled roots and leading up historic HeLeup Hill; a hyperbole in itself considering they were still barely above sea level. Regardless, the bewildering conjunction of valleys, farmland and multitude of lakes was known as the roof of Florida.

Sprawling live oaks with octopus limbs opened to a clearing where an endearing yellow house sat at the base of a pond. Also, a beautifully framed carport and a separate shed with a roof that needed fixing. It was a southern heartland Sadie had known for summering with Grandma Ida and Grandpa Lance when she was still too young for fits over missing social events. The remaining twelve acres were encompassed by a labyrinth of orange groves spreading infinitely in every direction, like rays of a sun. Her private world, Sadie recalled, where her 4-year-old self had played forest fairy with a talent for mud soup and befriending snakes. "Red touches yellow, kill a fellow. Red touches black, friend of Jack," grandpa would sing-song before she'd run out to warn her about venomous snakes. Then she'd come back with earth-stained feet and a black widow in her picnic basket named Charlotte. "Friend of Jack!" Sadie would gaily repeat and point to the spider. He hadn't entirely thought that one through.

It'd become clear early in her life that Sadie was adept at following the rules. Moreover, finding the loopholes others were too distracted to notice…

"There she is." Henri stared up sentimentally at the semi-rotten cottage he'd too long ago abandoned, half waving at the dark-haired caretaker of the groves engaged over a supersize lawnmower.

Margot allowed him a moment alone, before sneaking up and wrapping both arms around him. "It's perfect."

"It will be with you in it." Henri leaned low for a kiss.

Back at the truck, Sadie ejected her stiff body and shook out her legs to make sure the lack of blood flow hadn't left any permanent damage. Eventually, she meandered up to the decaying house as more childhood memories slowly resurfaced.

"What do you think, honey?" Margot asked far too happily, teetering in her faux leather clogs.

Sadie had been shipped there every July from age five to eleven so it wasn't entirely foreign, although the aquatic climate had severely dinged the paintwork and gutters, the welcome mat was covered in crunchy leaves, there should be a fresh magnolia wreath on the door, and her grandparents.

"What do *I* think? Hmm, let's see." Sadie smacked her lips then pushed them out to a surly Brussels sprout floret. "You drag me across the country for no good reason, away from my friends, my school, civilization, to live… here? I say it's humid and I'm sticky and I hate you!" She marched back to the Chevy and slammed the door, only hating *herself* for what she'd said.

The words rang stark to say the least, because Sadie, viscerally agreeable, had always been an anomaly of sort. She'd never been grounded, never had her phone taken, never heard as much as a 'no', unless she gave the code nose-flick signal to say she *wanted* a 'no'. Like that time she'd been invited for car camping in Joshua Tree with Becks and her older and hairier boyfriend (and a baggie of wacky mushrooms). One flick to her right nostril and she'd peacefully spent the weekend finger-painting portobellos instead.

Despite her being in her prime years of feminine unrest towards womanhood, they'd never done the blowouts to lead to something like the H-word. Neither parties saw it coming.

"We did this to her." Margot weakly sighed as she watched her daughter through the glass. "She's completely right."

"You know she didn't mean that." Henri pushed back a henna strand to reveal the onset of her tear, and it made him wince. "This'll all pass, real soon. I'm sure of it."

"She's not the rebellious type," she reminded.

"Then maybe this a good exercise. Hm? Thicken her skin abit."

Margot's brow raised a little humorously. "Don't tell me you're planning on putting our daughter in some cow-country boot camp?"

"Imagine that." Henri did, and laughed. "No, no. I'm just sayin' things are different here. Everything ain't so buffed out and pretty like it is back home. We need to show her some real world for a change, out of that bubble of vegan, free-spirit, woo-woo." He watched her ball a hand on her hip. "You know what I mean."

"I always do." She nudged him lovingly. "And I thought you liked my woo woo."

"Woo woo is startin' to have a different ring to it, *ain't* it?"

Margot's chin shook in playful scorn. "You did warn me the outdoors made you tender."

"Amongst other things." When Henri went to kiss her again, he noticed the cloud of guilt had come back and swathed her sullen. It pained him drearily, but he'd been prepared for this. That Sadie would have a hard time adjusting and Margot would inevitably want to baby her, and in the end he'd be to blame.

This was, after all, his idea. All those nights telling Margot about the place where *the sky splits wide open on all sides, the cost of livin's fair and gettin' into a car that's been sittin' in the sun is a warm hug you grow to cherish.* He'd convinced her returning to his hometown was the reset he needed, but the truth…

Henri Bexley had left for a reason, stayed away for that same damn accursed reason. He swore he'd never come back. This wasn't his choice, nor would it be theirs.

"Darlin', look at me," Henri pleaded, cupping her always understanding face. "This is goin' to be good for us. No, better than good! Those girls Sadie was spendin' time with, her *friends*, well they never felt right. Not for her. Next week she'll be talkin' Twilight with someone new and forget all about Hex or Twex——"

"Becks."

"The one with the playboy bunny tattoo?"

"That was Sharpie I think, but yes. She was a straight-A student, you know."

Henri shrugged, as if he'd just proven his point. "So was I." Then taking her hand, he nibbled the tops of her fingers, continuing up her arm all the way to her earlobe. "I love the hell outta you, and I know we can do this."

Margot couldn't help but give in to Henri's impassable charm, knowing how it derived from a rare selflessness few men truly ever attain. It was his sexiest quality, she decided then, backed by a unanimous consensus amongst any woman who'd ever consented to it. *Women*, who were now all within a ten-mile radius.

"I love you too." She tugged him towards the door. "So, are you ever going to show us our new home… or am I going to have to break in?"

Henri chuckled rabidly. "After you, my lady."

Sadie observed their spinning dance inside, this time less inspired by the parade of affection. She punched the seat and yelped at the pang, before deciding she'd write an angry poem to deal. But she got distracted by swaying: heaps of gray spindling vines clothed around thick branches above. *Moss*, she recollected from years ago, and gasped with a mesmerized ogle as if it were the eighth natural wonder of the world, instead of parasitic tree hair full of chiggers.

The more she looked, the more she saw. Thousands, maybe even millions, of prevailing tangles acted as a jungle gym for squirrels. The moss appeared in constant motion, alive in the same way as coral reefs, but more eerie and bizarre, unexpectedly beautiful. She'd thought so when watching her Nicholas Sparks flicks with similar settings, usually after her friends had already passed out to 'Sex And The City' reruns. This unexpected relation planted a pretty seed in her mind: that this place, obscure and quaint and entirely budding with potential, could be like those movies. Maybe.

And by maybe, she of course meant *absolutely*.

Sadie allowed her eyes to fall closed and her embellishing conscience to drift into daydream, and as she did, the scent of sun-dried linens and cinnamon beguiled her senses, transporting her back to the bad-boy with brown eyes.

About five miles down the road, the Holden family had gathered for Sunday breakfast. A weekly routine typically followed by a morning of worship and an afternoon of ESPN; a common and sacred ritual amongst locals (with the exception of the Patels, but they owned a superb restaurant in town so most people didn't complain). Faith and football: those were the rules.

Brooks kicked off his Nikes on his way in and followed the scent of Aunt Jemima syrup to the kitchen.

The house was immovably on the ground, making it a lavish step up from the majority. It was clean, minus the never-ending cycle of empty water bottles, and that despite the army of Glade plug-ins, the stench of sweaty socks never budged. With a 75-inch flat screen and surround sound system, the Holden house was a crowd favorite three to four days out of the week.

Kelly Holden in high gear (her only gear) hovered over the stove, flipping pancakes with one hand and sipping Folgers classic roast with the other. She was wearing a red robe with the words 'I heart the coach' hand-stitched on the back, a sandy toned ponytail bouncing at her peak. In her busy body dashing all over,

it appeared Kelly was thriving as a southern wife and mother—
that's all she ever wanted to be—only lately, her busy body just
needed to keep busy.

"There he is!" She beamed at Brooks, grateful he'd decided
to join them. "You'd think with how much we pay for your phone
bill you'd at least have the sense to answer your mother's calls.
Hm? What are you doin' up, anyway? Reckoned you'd be snorin'
past noon with it bein' the last day of summer break." She
flipped the batter masterfully.

"Ha ha," Brooks answered, leaving out the part where he
hadn't gone to sleep at all. "And miss out on family breakfast?
Never."

Brant Holden sat dominant and dense at the head of the
table, only barely glancing up from the sports section of his Paw
Print Press. His strictly clamped lines kept unemotional like rock,
but undeterred by his frigidity, his chiseled looks had aged like
fine wine. Meaning, the beers hadn't yet coated his midsection
like they'd done to the rest of the starting lineup of his class.
Brant couldn't even make a run to the local Publix without
someone's wife *accidentally* ramming their cart into his, casually
mentioning they'd started a small business (as they adjust their
Arbonne visor). He didn't always entertain the chatter, his
wedding band constricting at his finger, but if he did it was only
to feel young again. Relevant again.

Brant scoffed at his wife's comment, to most of them, before
saying, "Sleepin' in? Not my boy. We Holden men are go getters,
ain't that right son?" He leaned to give Brooks' shoulder a good
squeezing, but was side stepped.

"Sorry old man, can't risk you messin' with my mojo. Ha ha."
Mojo? Brooks cringed.

"Good call, good call. That arm of yours is gon' give us an
undefeated season this year. I can feel it in my bones!"

Duke, the younger Holden brother and backup to Brooks,
picked at his grits nearby.

"A little rest now and again might be good for you boys.
Football will still be there when you wake up." Kelly slid them a
bowl of freshly cut strawberries they probably wouldn't touch.

Brant shot her a 'are we done' look, then leaned gamely on the table. "You two ready for practice today?"

"Uh, yeah." Brooks tediously smeared his syrup. "But you know, I really don't think we need it, dad. Baseball isn't until—"

"Don't need it?" Brant laughed, which usually meant the opposite of what God intended it to. "And you don't think that's somethin' your coach is damn well capable of decipherin' for himself? Not *needed*!" He laughed harsher. "Well shucks, maybe I should find a more entertainin' way for you boys to piss the day away. Is that what you're sayin'?"

"No sir."

"How about we go to Disney World? Or better yet, drive up to Homosassa Springs to see that Monkey Island everyone loves so much. Maybe even join 'em for some sunbathin' and hiney scratchin. Does that sound better to you?"

"No sir."

"Then I expect to see both of you boys warmed up at Ogilbee Park before that clock hits twelve. You hear what I'm sayin'?"

"Yes sir," the brothers spewed in militant unison, though Duke wondered if his dad would notice if he didn't show up. He didn't the last time.

Brooks' jaw audibly locked and grinded, which didn't help the molars already chipped from the same pressure. But this time, the reasons were far more hellacious than his father being a dick. "Excuse me." He stood. "Thanks mom. Breakfast was nice." It wasn't, but he felt she'd needed to hear it from at least one of them.

Down the hall, Brooks passed that celebrated wall of framed photos: him and Duke in the same number and color football jerseys, marking every year since they were five. In the first one, their cheese-ball grins were galactic. From then on, deteriorating.

Once through the bathroom door, Brooks fell limp against the wall with a crystallizing pain he hadn't yet accepted. It'd happened hours ago, and it was only getting worse. After a few moderated breaths, he lifted his shirt and looked in the mirror. He gagged twice before throwing up in the sink.

A yellowing purple bruise traced his shoulders to mid-back, flakes of dried blood peeled off the skin, the entire right side of his body ruthlessly swollen. After wiping his chin, he manned up, forcing the limp appendage into excruciating rotations to test the range, and as a result, Brooks shrank up like a disheveled and dizzy slinky. It was so bad his eyes went black and starry, as if having the wind knocked out of him on repeat.

A nearly empty tube of Icy Freeze eyed Brooks from the cabinet, and he fumbled for it, using his elbows to squeeze the last bit. He lathered it extra gently, but if he hadn't been staring at his palm the whole time, he'd have sworn it was the edge of a buck skinning knife buttering his bruised flesh. At one point, he wondered if it were normal for a wound such as this to have gained the odor of rotting meat.

"God, please. *Please.*" Brooks stopped lathering. He connected his hands in prayer. Before the quarterback could remember what it felt like to cry, he was. "Please."

A surge of nausea took him back.

It was around midnight, deep in the woods where the trees huddled a prairie. Rain poured in buckets on the field. The rival teams, Weston Hills and Orville, had gathered for the annual unofficial kickoff: an aggressive off-the-clock game known as the 'Dogfight'. No coaches, no padding, no rules.

In that homestretch, Brooks had it. The ball was safely tucked in the molded nook of his bicep, where it belonged. He was mere feet from the makeshift end zone. He was already smiling in triumph. But then… he no longer had it.

He no longer had anything.

Cameron Dickson t-boned into Brooks and both players collapsed in a violent buckle. Liquid heat flooded Brooks' spine with vicious rush. Face buried in the mud, he screamed but was deaf to it, the ringing in his ears drowning it out. He watched as the rival team took flight into the woods.

His two best friends arrived at his side, untying his shoes and propping his head as he hurled up spaghetti and pre-workout blend.

"Where does it hurt?"

"My arm. Right shoulder. Fuck."

The rain swelled heavier, avalanching, and someone yelled over it, "Your captain is down! Git on your knees!"

"*I'm fine,*" Brooks said firmly. "*I'm gon' be fine.*"

"Aw hell, you're trashed."

Brooks snapped from the trance to see Duke standing in the doorway. He forced his shirt down angrily. "I was out late," he spat, like it were his dark eye circles in question.

An extensive moment passed while Duke waited for explanation, already knowing he wasn't getting one. He eyed the open bottle of sports cream on the table. "I won't tell him, but you gotta know that stuff ain't gonna work no miracles."

"Oh yea dipshit? Well I don't have a choice now, do I?" Opening the cabinet, Brooks snatched the closest pain reliever and grappled with the childlock before popping four pills. "Don't be late. I'll kick your ass if I'm doin' pushups cause of you. And stop playin' with your banjo when I'm tryin' to sleep. It's annoying."

"It's a guitar."

"Whatever. Just don't let dad find you with it. Maybe find yourself a girl to keep your fingers busy instead. Holdens don't do music—"

"Holdens play football."

Sadie carried the last of her boxes into her new upstairs bedroom, hurling them on the floor—*shattering*. She opened the top box to see a polaroid of her and her friends back home with a handwritten message on the frame: *We'll miss you Sadie baby!* No obnoxious kissy faces or middle fingers were spared, except for her, doing her trusty demure smile and peace sign that screamed: *Sorry I'm here! I don't belong!* The glass was broken. Ironically, directly across her front teeth to give the illusion of a wide gap, as if the universe agreed—she hadn't belonged—and this was her official cancelation.

Sadie missed them already.

There'd been four of them. Tenley was the cool girl who'd rocked a Rick and Morty hoodie and bucket hat to spring formal and still got invited to all the parties after. Emma was the funny one, which paired with the side boob from her cut-out tanks she wore in gym and the fact that her family started IHOP, made her the second hottest hit at Calabasas High. The first hottest, undoubtedly, was Becks: a femme fatale in fishnets who'd successfully snuck into Cabo Cantina thanks to the bouncer mistaking her for the new Maxim Girl. Lastly, there was Sadie. Likeable, reserved, soft-spoken, medium across the board. 'Nice' was the exciting adjective she got most, typically a placeholder when her friends asked if they could bring her to a party, and the host had clearly never given her a second thought. "Sure. Why not? She's nice."

Sadie placed the frame on an empty shelf warily, kicking off her sandals hard in objection, then let her bare feet slide across the dusty floor, eyes roaming the antiquated room which, with a cheerier perspective, might've reminded her of a dollhouse. One floor-length bronze, oval mirror with little sunflower accents on the corners, a French walnut sleigh bed, and an ivory desk vanity with three of the five drawers missing. She remembered grandma Ida referring to it as 'Henri's room', though besides the fading G.I. Joe stickers on the door, you'd never tell. Most pleasant was the scent of butter pecan ice cream that enveloped the whole house, though that might've been a memory playing tricks.

Character, heart, tribute to new and old beginnings; no house in LA, even the one she'd grown up in with a two-story foyer and Italianate garden, had come close to providing any of those things. Nor had they smelled like ice cream.

Suddenly, Sadie's attention diverted to the tiny parallel ridges etched in the door frame, and as she zoomed closer, it became clear they'd been used to mark the height of a small child. Imagining her father two feet tall, she smiled to herself. Seeing him through the window now—pacing around the orange grove pond, fingers interlocked behind his head, stressed—her smile fell, and she stomached the lame and true fact that playing the angsty teen was causing her more grief than the thing she was supposed to be angsty about.

In the oval mirror, Sadie inhaled and fixed her posture, an ongoing struggle and likely self-esteem related, then tried to pry open her mind to it all. She considered a plus: this place had no memory of her. No prefixed plaster cast for her to jump into and be what it told her. It's easy to stay someone when there's an identity track record keeping you there. Sadie felt attracted to the wiggle room. Like opening the first page of a freshly printed book, *her* book. Then she asked herself: what kind of protagonist did she want to be?

Slim Jim. Under Armour. Abs. She shivered a little, slipping into an entirely different thought; one she'd saved in a mental filing cabinet to later indulge over a quality ballpoint pen, crisp cotton paper, listening to The Paper Kites, lights low, nighttime emotions high. Sadie loved the nighttime, because that's when she felt it more. Everything. Only this time, there would be no saving for later. The brown eyes reappeared. Embracing her new identity, Sadie decided to go look for them.

After freshening up, Sadie bounced down the stairs to the kitchen where her mom was sweating over bubble wrap. She'd traded her leggings and oversized Free People tee for a lacy white dress, golden locks curled in loose simple spirals, pulled back by a cream colored headband, and natural makeup on her face.

"Don't you look lovely!" Margot practically danced in place in seeing her daughter smiling again, and they hugged an 'I'm sorry for earlier' hug that didn't need words. "What's got this spring back in your step? Not that I'm complaining of course."

"Well mother, if you must know," smoothing her hem, "I've decided to take the high road. Appreciate the great outdoors. Rub some dirt in it, as they say."

"Yes, yes. They do say," Margot agreed with a puzzled nod. "Well, that's wonderful to hear. Do you need any help upstairs? I was thinking we would work on getting your room set up first."

"I'll finish it later. Um, I was actually heading out for a walk, maybe to find some coffee. Florida does have coffee shops, right?" Not a total lie; her eyelids were begging for a caffeine pick-me-up.

Henri used his shoehorn to peel off his steel toe boots at the door. "Only the best darn jitter juice this country's ever seen!" He joined them. "You'll have the best luck downtown I'll bet, buncha townee-owned food joints and a java shop by the name of Betty's Biscuits. Used to be at least. I'm sure they've turned it into somethin' else by now. Just look for the brick courthouse and the gazebo off Main, can't miss 'em."

"Perfect." Sadie remembered just the spot.

"Honey, can you help me get this atop the fridge?" Margot said, unwrapping a Williams Sonoma juicer. "I'd really like to have at least the necessities unpacked before nightfall. Then, I need to see that shed. We can get to cleaning and remodeling tomorrow. Henri's Auto Shop will be open in no time!"

Henri grinned wide before snorting at a head-scratcher. "Tha's right. For some reason I'll never understand, this town still loves it's Fords. Now Chevy might not have the same fancy computers and technical junk, but it sure all hell is reliable. You see that spoiled wagon out back?" (A vintage replica of the truck they'd drove here in, but with rust).

Sadie nodded.

"Been sittin' there about twenty years now. Bet it still drives brand new. But hey, that's fine, that's a'right. More Fords, more business. This town is lucky I'm back—"

"Yeah, yeah dad. Love it, trucks and tires and all that. Can I go now? I'll have my phone if you need me."

"As opposed to all the other times you left the house *without* your phone?" He chuckled in a warm, fatherly color. "You just wait until you meet a *boy* with a truck. Just trust me on that one."

She crinkled her nose and stuffed her blue journal in a leather saddlebag. "Don't forget your celery juice." She winked at her dad, because her mom was adamant about it, and he hated those green stalks almost more than small talk.

With a wave, Sadie glided out the door in a skip.

After the satisfying click, Henri pounced across the kitchen, lifting Margot at the waist and dipping her back until the ends of her hair grazed the stone tile. They slow danced amongst the empty wooden cupboards, every step in harmony like a routine they'd rehearsed. "I thought she'd never leave." He grumbled with hungry affection into her neck.

"Henri!" She reprimanded, but her avid laughter undermined any note of scold. It was eternally youthful, an alternative medicine; even more so than that coconut oil she put on everything.

"Can you blame me? Have you *seen* these legs?" His equally gentle, equally man, fingertips tickled at her hipbone before launching into another spin, savoring the familiar scent of her pomegranate shampoo, spinning and spinning, taking it all in more desperately than ever... just in case.

Once their speed fizzled, Margot did too, and with a sudden unease in her stance at the sound of a coyote shriek coming from the groves. "This is going to be good for us," she decreed decisively without preamble, "yes, this will be good." She massaged the earthy curls that caressed her husband's ears before repeating the mantra once more. "Good." Then, Margot left to pick up more boxes from the car.

Instantly, Henri's face fell solemn and honest, and he sauntered through the living room where he so clearly remembered being a scraped up boy: rambunctious and out of hand but guiltless from any real sin. With extreme tire, he opened the sliding glass doors to the immense porch out back, because the porch is a therapeutic place. The damp air filled his lungs and yet there was a bristly sensation of suffocating. He just couldn't believe it, being back where it all happened. The eternal aroma of citrus trees hadn't changed one bit, and he wondered now: had anything? Or would it all begin... right where it left off?

One key at a time, Henri's thumb typed a text, then scrolled for a drawn out while through his contacts. He stopped at the name 'Brant Holden'. *Back in town. Buck's still servin' beer?* Finally, he sent off the message to his pastlife best friend, who'd more than likely want to put a bullet in his everlastingly red neck.

Here, Henri's acid reflux sent dragons up his closing throat, churned caverns in his tightening chest. The harder he breathed, the more he felt every crevice of the black hole living inside him: the guilt, the shame, the bygones that never got gone. But now, there was no choice but to surrender, to face what he'd done. What they'd *both* done.

Henri Bexley, a good southern man, walked back inside to drink his waiting glass of celery as to not disappoint his wife. And because admittedly, if it all disappeared, even that he would miss.

It was early afternoon and the August Florida sun had reached it's brutal peak; powerful enough to sunburn within minutes. Sadie's vulnerable cheeks were a deep raspberry hue by the time she reached Main Street. She wiped the beads from her upper lip while checking her phone for the nearest Starbucks— one hour and thirteen minutes, by car. "Betty's Biscuits it is," she sighed.

Through the over-activated sun, Sadie squinted as she passed a few second-hand boutiques, fishing tackle shop, hole-in-the-wall hardware store, and a moderately presentable restaurant called 'Buck's BBQ' with a line of people out the door. Sadie pretended to take it in, but really she searched for... him. He didn't have a name yet, but she bet it was something bold, like Calum or Jax or Ryder.

Sadie was now standing at the exact coordinate where they'd exchanged glances, and she expectantly peered around for an athletic body, but clearly that was an oddity and he very well could have been it. "Help?" She looked up, not entirely sold on the big mighty man in the sky, but at least angels were definitely real. She'd read books on them. Her mother had told her stories, too. She conversed with hers, occasionally.

Sadie dottily realized: even if he *had* been there, would she have talked to him? No, definitely not. But having a crush from a distance, a real-life person to have not-real-life thoughts about, would make her time there much more bearable. That's all she wished for, really. A focal point for her mental narratives when watching cows chew grass got dull. A muse for her daydreams, would be enough.

How wholesome, she heard her friends snickering as they lovingly ruffled her hair, then adding a *It's for the best, he's not your type, we don't want you to get hurt.* Odd, how the guys that weren't her type, always ended up being theirs.

Quickly, finding air conditioning became mandatory and

Sadie stumbled into a preppy woman's clothing store with a chalkboard sign out front. In chunky pink letters: *The Lipstick Tree.* The shelves and mannequins were neatly dressed in flashy kittenish pastels. 'Sunday Best' dresses, tights, skirts, heels, but not very many pants or sneakers or anything that allowed for much moving around. A rather provocative, slinky fuchsia dress caught Sadie's eye—mostly because it was something she'd never wear— so today she skipped straight to it.

Under a signed Faith Hill poster, Mallory Jordan was slouching behind the register in a sparkly tube top and Miss Me jeans, an extra layer of waist trainer beneath. Her glossy rouge pout and heavily sprayed platinum pony were paired with a permanent eye roll, cavalierly clicking her manicured gels against the table. She was pretty in that unfair every-guy's-type way, and the word that was typically used for that type was 'sexy'.

Some girls so effortlessly gowned that appeal when they hit a certain age, the most imperceptible shift, yet powerful. When the same curve of their jeans, collarbone, and dimples on their body suddenly have luxurious purpose. But it isn't as gradual and sure for everyone. For example, Sadie had lots of dimples; on her lower back, cheeks when she smiled, a crescent moon on the right side of her butt; but hers were just cute. Not sexy—*cute.*

"Sit up, darlin'! And what did I tell you about that shirt? God did *not* give you halter top shoulders. Now your legs sweetie, *that's* what you should be showin' off. Wear this skirt and every boy in town is goin' to be beggin' you to be their homecomin' date!" Delilah Jordan dashed from behind a curtain, drinking her breakfast of lemon water and flailing a tight pink mini-skirt. Her tan skin showed signs of botox and miscellaneous filler, voluminous hair just as platinum as her daughter's pony, and double-D's loud and proud and often a magnet for men coming into the store 'shopping for their wives'.

"Mom, I already told you. It pinched my waist. It's too small," Mallory replied with shifty eyes.

"What do you mean *too small?* I saw you in it last month!" Delilah paused to digest, horribly shaken up. "Well that's okay, nothin' we can't fix. Do you want me to call Dale? I can set up a trainin' session for you first thing tomorrow mornin'. I know it's last minute but I'm sure he wouldn't mind." She flapped a wrist to further demonstrate the no biggie.

"Sure." Mallory forced a meager smile. "Thanks mom."

"Excuse me," Sadie squeaked eagerly at the counter; first day of kindergarten, light up Skechers, brand-spankin'-new crayon box kind of eager. "Do you happen to have this in a size small? It's really quite beautiful." Carefully extending the fuchsia cotton-spandex down her arm like an intricate piece of treasure.

Both Jordan women, poised scorpions, blinked in a flutter and appeared wildly offended. Sadie wondered if it was something she'd said.

"Oh sweetheart, I reckon that's the last one." Delilah lied in an upset fuss, before clapping with such sleek impact, Sadie jumped. "But I *do* have somethin' over here you'll like even better!" She guided her shopper to a dismal clearance rack stuffed in the back of the store, and excitedly waved a beige and entirely boxy piece of fabric. "My gosh, what a *dime* piece! Don't you think?" Delilah held the hanger under Sadie's chin and gasped. "Yes. Absolutely. I just knew it. I have a knack for these kinds of things, you know."

"It's... stunning." Sadie made note of the hideously stitched sleeves.

"The other one would've been far too showy for your skin tone. But *this* will highlight every one of those modest features just perfect! You never want the clothes to upstage you," she explained in zippy language with a built-in black art to them; so rapid and bouncy and zealous, she could call someone a fat cow and have them flattered by it. She'd done so. "I have a whole theory on this, dressin' for your beauty type. It's all science based, actually."

Sadie stared at her own toes scrunching nervously in her sandals. "I... I think I've heard that somewhere."

"Would you like a fitting room?"

"No, um, thank you." Her stutters were hiccup-like and squeaky. "I was—I was just looking." She felt any other answer would've earned a slap.

"Oh, of course you were." Delilah agreed and puckered, as if she'd just downed an entire grapefruit and was supposedly tickled pink by the taste. "I would say come see us again, but I assume you're just passin' through." Her eyes narrowed. "We don't get very many visitors so young and... goldfish, as you are."

"Oh... no." Sadie gulped. "I just moved here. Maybe... maybe you know my dad. He grew up in town. Henri Bexley?" She immediately felt silly for suggesting it, but maybe she shouldn't have, because the complexly accessorized woman suddenly found it imperative to review her head to toe, three... four times.

"The name rings a bell," Delilah hissed even happier, on the brink of peeling from every polished edge.

"Really? Did you two go to high school—"

"Well it was sure splendid to meet you, but if you'll excuse me, I believe I hear the phone. Buh bye now!" Delilah's compact smile twitched as a hand that smelled of Hawaiian Tropic sunscreen waved in Sadie's face, and very disoriented, she politely fixed a lopsided stack of monogrammed beach hats in apology.

Then Sadie curtsied; she did that a lot. With the backs of her knees clammy and wobbly, she fled for the door.

Once their uninvited guest was gone, an icy Delilah leaned over the counter. "You're much prettier than her," she cooed as she soothed her daughter's crown, mated to an inner estate of self-doubt that might not be there if it weren't for comments such as these. "My pretty girl, you're *much* more special."

Mallory's gels clicked against the table; it started a countdown. "I know." And from then on, their secret garden, a complicated tinderbox town, would slowly blossom and burn to the ground, until it's residents learned to listen to the flowers.

Tracking the scent of frosting and fresh brew, Sadie landed at a pastry café a few doors down, directly across from a red brick courthouse and *the* white gazebo. The window, in an elegant font, read *Elaine's Coffee*, and Sadie wondered where Betty and her biscuits were now.

It was outdated, with busy wallpaper splintering from the tops and couches patched up with tape, but with a certain sentimental quality that made you want to stay and play Sudoku under the glowy amber pendant lights. There were rustic, generic stock images hung up as artwork, but also local newspaper cut-outs of the football team winning the state championship, a feature on little Benjamin's battle with Leukemia with a tin watering can for donations, and a black and white photo of the Sinclairs (a couple in their nineties who'd loyally devoted Wednesday mornings to a box of powdered donut holes and a game of checkers at the window booth). It lacked any aesthetic, but all the mismatching personal knickknacks made it homey and alive; a universal grandma's house.

Every face in the room seemed to know one another, and Sadie found that inclusion aspect comforting. Even if she technically wasn't accepted yet, it didn't seem like a hard club to join. A life so temperate and free from vanity seemed welcoming to everyone. Really, *free from vanity* was more *struggling to make ends meet*, and Sadie was simply out of touch.

Elaine Dunn, wheat flour on her chin and utter decency in her aura, popped up merrily from behind the display of sugared pastries. Despite the apron and messy up-do, there was an angelic appearance about her. A classic Marilyn effect: so kind and resplendent inside and out, people flocked to her to soak that right up. But she was also a mother of three: perpetually tired, haphazard mascara on both eyes when she remembered to do both, and skin not as fastened and snug as she'd like. At least, those are the things she saw when she caught her reflection in the baking tray.

It was jubilant seeing a fresh face in her shop, and Elaine whipped out her notepad as so. "Mornin' sweetheart! What can I get ya?"

Sadie hummed a few seconds, then said, "Can I get a cappuccino to go please?" Becks had always insisted that girl bosses drink them, which before made Sadie shy away from ever trying one. If she had, her friends might've snickered at that too.

Elaine didn't seem to find her an imposter for ordering one. "Sure thing! Will that be all for you today?" Her words flowed finely tuned and rhythmic, Sadie admired, like delicately dripping honey melting pleasantly into the next.

"Yes, thank you." Bland and flat in comparison.

Elaine twirled to hand the order slip to an outdoorsy-looking girl around Sadie's age. It was Shelby Dunn, in her usual black Nike Pro shorts and baggy soccer tee, strawberry hair tied in a frizzy topknot with a stretchy headband taming the runaway twists, clumps of toasted coconut freckles on her nose and shoulders, hazel eyes with lashes and brows so light they almost weren't there. Shelby's arms suddenly stopped moving around the silver espresso nobs. Instead, they covered her mouth to stop from sneering at the heinously amusing sight: the living breathing cliché who'd just pranced into her family's cafe, wearing prairie frills. *Seriously, was the town putting on a skit?*

Sadie didn't notice her stare, only admired a tip-jar sticker reading *I love you a latte.* She giggled.

"Forgive my prying, but I don't recognize you." Elaine studied the curiously unfamiliar girl courteously, until her navy eyes suddenly widened to two glistening orbs. "Goodness gracious! You wouldn't... you wouldn't happen to be Henri's daughter, would you?"

"Yes, I... I would. How did you know?" Sadie wondered in shock.

"Oh, how marvelous! So it's true!" Clapping and gasping, eyes just as big and breathtaking. "I've been hearin' rumors that Henri was spotted in little ol' Weston Hills, and you have his smile."

She'd heard that before, but this time it filled her with rich limber warmth like hot chocolate as a kid. "So you knew him well?"

"Oh, very well. There was a whole gang of us back in the day, and your father, well he was the glue. We used to sit at that very booth." Elaine pointed, laughing all sultry like Michelle Pfeiffer in her early films. "Every morning we'd sit—the place was run by a delightful woman named Betty back then—and every Friday she'd bring Henri this heapin' plate of buttermilk biscuits. Told 'em if he could finish 'em, he'd have free biscuits for life. He tried and tried, but it was a big plate you see. Ten. Maybe twelve. Then mornin' of graduation… he finally did it."

"Really?" Sadie was enraptured by the story.

"Sure enough! Oh, it was amazin'! Just scarfed 'em all down like it was nothin'!" She laughed again, but dwindled somewhere forlorn. "Though, he never had the chance to take advantage of the offer."

"Why not?"

"He left, very next day." Her eyes glazed over, and she nodded painstakingly to some inner dialogue in her head. "Yes, yes. But it's good he left," she settled. "No one ever does." A knick of longing crossed her, but only for a moment. Then half-nervously she asked, "Can you tell him to stop by sometime?"

"I'm sure he'd really like that. You're… the owner? Elaine?"

"Yes, sorry. Elaine Dunn. I know it's been twenty years, but he should remember, I think…"

"I'm sure he does. He seems fond of this place." Sadie tried to hide her confusion over it. "I don't think he could ever forget."

"Right. Yes." She shifted uncomfortably. "Weston Hills does have a funny way of followin' people." Pulled towards a darker reverie, Elaine rubbed her arms as if a cold wind had crossed her, and before Sadie could consult on what she'd meant, the ginger-haired teenage barista was thrusting the drink in her hands, carelessly enough to cause searing foam to slosh on her exposed toes.

Sadie fought crying out as to not make her feel bad about the accident, but then the girl yanked the drink back again, thrust it out again, and though accidents *do* happen, they rarely happen… twice in a row.

"Oh! This is my daughter Shelby." Elaine pinched and turned a pearl earring. "You girls are goin' to be seein' each other at school. Might be nice to have a familiar face on your first day. Shelby, this is…"

"Sadie." She half-curtsied, of course.

"Ah, Sadie!" A timer dinged in the kitchen. "And that's the cobbler! Excuse me girls." Elaine waltzed away with one last wave.

"Hey," Shelby snapped, only because she'd been forced into it.

"Hi!" Sadie rocked gladly on her toes. "So, you work here? That's so cool. My friend Tenley worked at a Starbucks and she got like so much free coffee, and cake pops—"

"We don't have those."

"Oh, that's 'kay. I can't eat them anyway. I'm gluten free."

"Of course you are."

"People usually assume it's some diet thing, but I got tested when I was ten, and turns out the Eggos I was eating every morning *were* the thing giving me stomachaches."

"Fascinating."

"It was pretty hard at first, but then they came out with *gluten free*—"

"Cool story."

"Oh—well, it was nice to meet you." Sadie reached out her palm, but Shelby rejected it. For some reason, she kind of mean-mugged it.

"Ditto."

Letting her arm fall awkwardly limp, Sadie was again left wondering if it was something she'd said. A handbook, that's what this place needed. She'd put it in the suggestion box. On her way out, the door chime sang sweetly as she passed two boys with similar toasted freckles as Shelby, and whose jaws visibly dropped at the sight of their newcomer.

Colton Dunn; the contemplative middle kid of the family with buzzed hair and a more angular face than his other two siblings; plopped a sugar cube on his tongue, by the big oven where Shelby was organizing quiche cups. "So, *that's* her, huh?"

Shelby scowled. "That's *her*." Punctuated in her dislike, concealed with her reasons. She reluctantly picked up the coffee pot handle because Mr. Dawson was gesturing his empty mug at her through the pastry display glass.

Tanner Dunn; youngest, smartest and least contentious of the bunch; flicked the rim of his lucky cowboy hat. "Bout time things got interestin' 'round here. Hey, I wonder if she's a cheerleader. Mallory would just *love* that." Him and Colton shared a chuckle,

24

clearly both peckish for a little chaos. "Gotta love politics, right?"

"Don't get too excited, bud. If anyone's got first dibs, we already know it's gon' be Brooks." Colton casually licked an icing spoon left in a stirring bowl. "You think he'll take her to the dock?"

"The *dock*?" Tanner repeated salaciously.

"The *dock.*" Colton confirmed with equal raunch.

And with that, Shelby's hand squeezed tighter and deadlier around the handle of—

The brimming coffee pot dropped to the floor and split in two halves, as the best darn jitter juice this country's ever seen splattered the walls.

Indifferent to the mess, Shelby turned to her brothers with a look of revulsion. Under her breath, she hissed, "That… is not… his *type*."

But then again, she'd never been either.

CHAPTER TWO

The Orange Trees Remember

Taking the scenic route—the tiny pocket paths where trees laced overhead to form idyllic green tunnels—was a huge mistake. The arches of Sadie's feet were filthy and achy from the prehistoric trek down sidewalk deficit lands, and now the whole road had faded to puddly muck. Though, she had enjoyed sitting with a king size lizard on the way, picking it up to see if they still did the tail shedding trick. This one just bit her instead.

Hot and miserably lost, Sadie groaned upon arriving at a recreational middle-of-nowhere field with insects feasting on her ankles. Ogilbee Park: favored by locals for little league baseball and church wiffleball tournaments, with chain-link fenced soccer fields, a couple sandlots and a playground for little brothers and sisters. There were enough oak trees for shade, but not too many to prevent a breeze. Secluded and across the street from the high school, Ogilbee was a hotspot for lunch make out breaks, and riled boys who made appointments for getting into fistfights with other riled boys.

Sadie took a much needed pause on a bench to itch her bites, unstick the sweaty hair from her back, check the girls group chat that'd been weirdly silent ever since she'd left them her Sugarfish gift cards as a goodbye, and most importantly, journal about all of it. Sadie vented to a page with an upset wrist, accepting defeat and that she'd probably never see him again. *The boy with brown eyes.* She'd covered two whole pages in passionate chicken scratch before fully perceiving the unexpected aerie she'd wandered in to, as she should, because it was quite lovely after all.

The birds held a classically trained melody, her nose was treated by the scent of grass shavings that grew stronger with each inhale, and though the snack stands were closed, undertones of hotdogs and cheese fries still lingered. Sadie imagined both of those foods would taste exquisite paired with the minimalistic country-setting: metal bleachers, flourishing woodland, clean air, sporadic thunder and heat lightning that dramatized and textured the stripe of teal sky. Truly, the geography stood still but not stagnant, which Sadie sometimes felt when facing the ocean, but that was vast and daunting, where here it was all in soft focus; a hidden hideaway in a sense, the entire town.

"Yo! Pitch it!"

Startled, Sadie jolted on the bench, because she hadn't noticed them before: boys in red jerseys occupying a lot down the slope of grass that unfurled between two large live oaks. Her pen pushed a hole in her paper. They were looking directly at *her*.

"Well *day*-umn." Levi Tucker, one of the popular boys from the football crowd known primarily for that, and being Brooks' black friend, stood in the outfield tossing a baseball. "That chick up there—that's the new girl, right?"

Brooks stretched (and suffered) by third base. He glanced up to the willowing oak where the girl sat alone and unbothered by it. *Was that even allowed?* The ones he knew couldn't even go pee by themselves. "Looks like it. Aren't they sayin' she's from LA?"

"Oh Lord, please forgive me." Caleb Lindley, pastor's son and self-proclaimed heartthrob, smacked his friends on the ass before driving his palms in luscious prayer. "For I *may*... just have to sin." His mouth kinked to his trademark smirk, typically a prelude to enterprising intentions, like the cunning bedbug he was. "I heard... she's a Bexley."

Brooks' broken back turned rod-like. *Did he say...*

"Pretty boy forget he's savin' himself for marriage?" Levi threw his mitt hard at Caleb, who flashed those devilishly intense blue eyes in response (the same ones that'd copped him a collection of VS Pink panties from lonely girls with overly trusting parents).

"Hey now, what mama don't know won't hurt her." Cocking his head, Caleb bluntly observed the new girl some more, but just couldn't get past the flouncy G-rated outfit to maintain further interest. "She looks a lil' more Brooks' speed to me. You can have this one."

"What's that s'pose to mean?"

"Too horse girl for my taste. You know the type: user-friendly, perfectionist, no fun."

Duke pulled up in a blue truck and joined them in the outfield, practicing his swing. Eavesdropping.

Brooks jogged to home base and readied to bat, trying to see if he could pull it off with his damaged arm socket. "She's alright, I guess." Only, his attention kept begging to be pulled back to her. He silently worked out the probability of it: a Bexley girl, high school age, with gold-plated waves. *How many of those could there be?* "We should finish warmin' up b'fore coach gets here," he said.

"Oh com' on!" Caleb protested for a good time, always at the wrong time. "Go on and give her a little dose of that Holden charm, yea? New toy like that, small pond like this... she's gon' go fast." He gave his down south region a thrust and pat. "Alright listen, how about this? You can warm her up for me for when I —"

"How's 'bout you leave this one alone, Caleb?" Duke fumed from outside the circle, which was out of character for him, but he genuinely couldn't stand the repulsive way his brother and his friends often talked about girls, and today there was something transitional in the air. Knuckles hard and amateur, he stood there like he'd just committed treason.

Dazed, Caleb searched for the source of interruption, before his face lifted smuttily. "Aw, hey little man!" (Though they were both in their junior year). "How's 'bout baby Holden minds his own, yea? This is adult business. Ain't that right, B-Dawg?"

"How's 'bout you both shut up and pitch the damn ball?" Brooks' volume had raised, and for some reason, people tended to listen when it was. "Fastball. Send it."

Caleb inhaled an audible *I don't think so.* "It took you a whole hour to get up off the ground last night. Either you were bein' a crybaby then, or you're bluffin' about not hurtin' now. Look, don't push it if you don't have to——"

"I *do*," Brooks growled. "Get it? I said... *send it*."

Caleb hounded him with another long pause, because they'd been best friends since peewee and his alpha tactics didn't work on him. And shit—maybe he *gave* a shit. Eventually, he knew Brooks wouldn't budge, so he rolled up his sleeves and pitched the ball.

The bat spanked in a successful echo, ball soaring in an even arc, hurdling across twigs with a few deep thuds, and stopping right at the new girl's feet. "I got it," Brooks informed them with buttery satisfaction. Because yes, he'd meant to do that.

Sadie had been aiding a baby snail climb over a barrier of pebbles when the ball almost crushed it dead, and she yelped and stumbled on her side, which ironically crushed three more snails; and all of this would be relative. Before she could cry over it, because she surely would have, Sadie made out a jogging figure looming through the blinding white sun streaks: a boy. Shocked, she decided she should've started drinking cappuccinos a long time ago. The figure reached the top of the hill, decelerating at the trees where he became instantly recognizable, and the tender serendipity of all of this, would only wound them in the end.

If fate does exist, don't touch it. It doesn't need our help.

Sadie sprang up, hysterically flattening her humidity hair that had now expanded to a rotini perm. Her voice box pinched like clothespins had latched around it. She snapped a hand to her hip, put it down, hip, down, two hands—under *no* circumstance. Her ample cheeks turned to pillows of lead and made moving her lips a gummy exercise. Man this was stressful, *living* things out. Seriously, *what* was she supposed to do with her hands?

The boy with brown eyes coolly picked up the ball, caught his breath... and lost it again. It was true. This was the girl from the photograph.

From the sandlot, Brooks had appreciated her eventful legs, skimmed by floaty translucent fabric that layered like a slice of wedding cake. What floored him now though, was the way her gold hair shimmered in the sunlight, like it *was* the sunlight, giving the impression it should be garlanded to the ends with bellflowers. She reminded him of those oldtimey portraits of softly blended colors, with jade green eyes, sepia moles scattered in unique polka dots, full lips, porcelain skin with dry patches of concealer at the minor breakout on her chin. Bashfully, he admitted she looked too fancy for him, other-worldly against the limited world he knew, yet approachable. Definitely a girly-girl, but of finer quality than the ones at school who wore big hoop earrings and post duck-face selfies on the Internet.

Meanwhile, Sadie engrossed herself in the brown irises. There were many coats of them; lighter flakes scattered amongst a dark backdrop, like the bark of the Sycamore trees she'd once posed with in Big Sur. Then her gaze trickled down to his arms; an unexpected second stop considering she'd never been the kind of girl to fawn over a guy's biceps. But his were tight, defined, reckless in how they contracted, and ignited a swirling void somewhere below her bellybutton. He had dirt on his forehead. Actually, all over his face. The kind of guy who perpetually appears to have only just rolled out of bed—and makes you think of him in bed. Emphatically masculine, with that special soft something that hits a spot you didn't even know could be hit. Almost chemical. Inescapable.

An opening of silence nestled between them, but it wasn't catastrophic.

Believe it or not, Sadie went first. "I don't know much about baseball, but I'm pretty sure that's an out."

"A foul, actually. It was a foul ball."

"Right. Foul. I knew that."

"Did you?"

"No." She winced sheepishly as blood rushed to her cheeks, and she patted them like they'd caught fire, like this is a normal thing people do. "But now I'll know… for next time."

Brooks liked the sound of that. "You're new here, right?"

"Didn't do a good job of fitting in, did I?" She pushed her ringlets behind her ears. "I'm Sadie."

"Brooks," he answered with an implied smile. She talked

proper and formal, he noted, and suddenly was aware of how he did not. "And nah, it's not your fault. It's a small town, pretty much the same faces. It'd be hard to not notice a new one. I, um, I don't think anyone, anywhere, could forget yours." He hoped it would have a dedicated page in the blue diary she'd tried to hide from him; that felt like a prestigious place to be.

Sadie had no doubt her face had now flushed to the color of her mother's beets.

At the dugout gate, Brant and his clipboard scanned the team. Under his cap, he peppered. He was already peppered, because as of a few hours ago, someone who was dead to him had asked him for a beer, and if Brooks didn't get his do-whatever-I-want besmirched attitude back on that plate, he would lose it. "PLAYERS ON THE FIELD! NOW!"

Sadie peered downhill, silently huffing at the mean man for interrupting. "Does your coach always yell like that?"

"Only at me, because he's my dad." Brooks grimaced. "To give you a better picture, baseball doesn't start 'til spring, but we've been practicin' every Sunday all summer, which basically sums up my life."

"That sounds... busy."

"Oh, yea. I guess I just haven't come across anythin' else worth makin' time for."

"And if you did?"

"I'd skip sleeping." He shrugged like that was a no-brainer, and lingered on her for a few seconds more. "Ah, probably should head down. I'll see you at school though, right?"

"Definitely!" Sadie chirped in a fluting note she'd replay a thousand times later. "You, um, have any pointers for the new girl?"

It was meant to be silly, cutely facetious, just an excuse for two more seconds with the brown. Nonetheless, he mulled it over and Sadie watched him fall overcome with ultimatum. He'd measurably darkened. "Don't underestimate this place. If you like how somethin' looks, don't look too close. If you hear somethin' you don't like, don't repeat it. And remember, the orange trees pick up on things. They remember. I guess just... get ready."

"Ready?" Panting, because his stoic voice made her short-winded and faint. "What should I be ready for?"

This time, the smile was more than implied. It showed up completely, for her. "To be famous, Sadie Bexley."

A kaleidoscope of butterflies unleashed in her chest as she realized: she'd never given her last name. And now she was losing her moony mind, because this is what Sadie called a *sign*: ethereal hints the angels drop to point you in the right direction. Consciously or not, Sadie lived by them. She admired the divine scarves of moss swinging above, and said, "Okay."

His heels pivoted away, then back again, because he could also use two more seconds. "Oh, and if you get Mrs. Wilson for math, I'd sit in the back. She smells like she's got a lot of cats."

A full throttle belly laugh bubbled from her before the brakes kicked in again. Brooks decided he'd one day crack the code on deactivating them altogether. "See ya 'round, Bexley." He cantered off in slow motion as the impractical girl swooned at the fit of his pants, all the while writing a light fiction romance of them in her head.

Seconds later, Brooks was back at the dugout. He hopped the chain link rail with phony efficiency, metal cleats knocking the dusty home plate. With the swift ease of it, no one would've ever guessed a critically torn tendon was crying for rest, and thanks to the triple-strength Tylenol, he could play ignorant too.

"Well?" Caleb and Levi turned expectantly for the verdict.

Brooks manipulated his bat in a few tricks to show off. "Nice rack," he then announced loudly to the whole team, and it triggered a concurring chuckle, rowdy high-fives and whistles as the more viperous names kicked field mix at Duke, who was again preparing his knuckles to stand up to his brother, until he too... caught sight of the shiny girl sitting under the oak tree. And this time, he decided to go a different route.

Sadie stopped to journal at the gazebo after Ogilbee's, and text her parents that she'd be a while. Seven pages later, she'd skipped the entire way home. Sure, the pointy acorns were unkind to her feet and the extreme temperature made her thighs swollen, but rest assured, she basked and hummed and danced, which more adults should do, and locked out the impending reminder her mother always gave not to 'build cloud castles', to see things how they really are. *Blah blah blah.*

Her way was much more fun, and what's the harm in a little daydreaming, anyway?

Brooks. She'd never met anyone with that name. It was edgy, memorable, not one you'd find on a rack of tacky key chains at Six Flags. He'd been interested in her, flirtatious maybe, but the hopeful romanticism had made the encounter snowy in her mind and at that point it was impossible to tell. She'd have to wait until they saw each other next to know for sure, which she prayed to the angels, would be soon.

Upon arriving at the clearing in the groves, Sadie found an extra car in the driveway: a silver Subaru with a stick family and 'He Is Risen' sticker on the back. Her parents hadn't mentioned expecting guests, so she peeked inside cautiously, half expecting them tied to a chair with duct tape on their mouths. Metaphorically speaking, she'd had it on the nose.

"Hey honey! Come say hi to our guests!" Her mom's pitch was shrill and strained, how it gets when she feels inadequately prepared. Sadie followed it to the vast dining nook where the wall of sliding glass was gaped ajar and overlooking the halcyon pond of duckweed water lentils, heart-shaped leaves of submerged spatterdock, a softshell turtle craning it's snorkel-like nose. Even so, the oxygen in the room was stale. Her parents sat at an ellipse milky-wood table, across from a family she didn't recognize but wouldn't soon forget: The Lindleys.

"Oh my goodness gracious! Look how darn tootin' gorgeous you are! Henri Bexley with a daughter, oh I *never* thought I'd see the day!" A plump woman in a loose damask textile dress that masked her curves hugged and jerked Sadie like a ragdoll, while the dad and two kids watched with synthetically bobbing necks.

"Hi," Sadie started slow, unsure if she'd missed this briefing in the car during her two-hour difficult teen phase. "And you must be…"

"I'm Stacy and this is my husband David, the town *pastor*."
She gestured to the bearded, rosy-cheeked man in a cable knit
sweater vest; a little timid for someone who came with a title.
"I'm sure we'll be gettin' real familiar with each other once you
start attendin' the town's youth groups. Lucky for *you*, we're
startin' this Wednesday!"

Sadie ooh'd and ahh'd and forced a limp smile.

"Grace and Caleb will make sure you get acquainted with
our church so you feel right at home. Get over here kids and
introduce yourselves!"

Grace—itsy bitsy, lemon balm scented, and who by
appearance belonged pinned up in the retail window of an
American Girl Doll store—hopped from the table with the same
nutty exuberance. She was in a plaid skirt and yellow cardigan
buttoned all the way to her dainty cross necklace. Her small
mouth was so air-tight and jellied in smile, Sadie wondered if it'd
been engraved on.

"So lovely to meet you! My name's Grace, as in the healing
offered through the mercy and love of Jesus Christ. I have a
feelin' we're goin' to make great friends!" Like a wind-up trinket,
or one of the unsettling *It's a Small World* dolls at Disney, she
looked mechanical.

Sadie just blinked. "Uhhuh."

The boy was more nonchalant in style, but straitlaced and
formal in a mildly sarcastic way. Sadie recognized him from Main
Street and Ogilbee's, though it'd been from a distance. He was
definitely handsome by prototypic standards—tufts of fleecy
blonde hair, straight sparkly teeth, symmetrical face, agile lines in
his jaw, strong calves and broad shoulders that advertised he'd
score in the 99th percentile for physical fitness in any given
scenario—but also resembled the dudes that get paid to stand
outside of an Abercrombie and Fitch. The kind of guy who
lifeguards in the summer for a reason to publicly oil his abs.

"I'm Caleb." He gave a suggestive nod followed with a
decadent climbing gaze, a *real* rampant eyeful, and suddenly
Sadie was tugging down her lace hem. Slowly, he mumbled, "So,
you're the one that's got this town all strung up in knots, huh?"

He sucked on those words like a cooling mint candy.

The comment made Sadie unwell. She leaned down to make herself smaller. "Wh—what do you mean?"

Caleb let her soak in it a while longer, before finally answering, "You'll see." And smirked like he'd been waiting to give it.

"Brother, don't scare the girl!" Grace cried out in a panache belonging on Broadway. "We're super duper excited to have a new face, is all. Oh! I can't wait to recruit you to our girl squad! We have our own bible study every Friday—girls only, but of course. It's really the *most* fun!"

"Just look at that!" Stacy clapped in a way that made no sound. "Isn't it amazin' how God always has a plan?"

"It sure is." Margot agreed, as Sadie feared the subscription to Southern Living Magazine had already been made.

They sat down around the table, along with gifts of tea and a regale of pastries. A sword of setting apricot sun cast down from the skylight and exposed the powdered dust levitating above. It made the room of old objects look alive and temperamental, reacting to their breath and motions as if energy visible to the naked eye.

"So, um, what's the occasion? I mean… what are you all doing here?" Sadie asked innocently, and with a lingering dry mouth.

"Well, your father is an old *friend* of ours back in our own Weston Hills High days." Stacy's words seemed to fall out of her mouth all at once. "You remember those, don't you, Henri?" Her jolly pupils dilated, and bore into him.

David cleared some mucus, tugged at his itchy vest neckline. "We just wanted to come show some southern hospitality and say welcome. That's our way, newcomers or returning folks. We'd do the same for anyone."

"Aha, sure. Oh boy, is it nice to see my old pals," Henri uttered, but simultaneously threw back a pile of key lime so it muffled his words, meaning he could've said *excuse me while I stab myself with this fork*, and they'd have never known. "I don't mind the tea, but I reckon a cold beer would do me good right 'bout now. Anyone else? Before I head to the kitchen?" David appeared uncomfortable but Stacy enlisted with a firm hand. "Be right back." Henri turned stiffly, then under his breath, "Shiet."

The adults continued their absorbed chatter lip service, somehow about nothing, while the youngins sat separately at the table's end.

Modest and ducky in all but her *true* nature, Grace sneakily slipped her phone from her clutch purse. Concealing the screen beneath the tablecloth, she scrolled through a fresh batch of skimpy bathroom selfies from when she'd been bored rigid at the morning sermon. One of her bending, black string thong arched high over her hipbones, slimmed her waist so she sent it to her boyfriend Sterling. He was probably just waking up, and she enjoyed imagining his face when he'd open it: groggily admiring her body... hurriedly stumbling into the shower... clutching the screen with his one free hand. It made her feel alive, for a little bit.

Meanwhile, Caleb was spending long stretches of time appraising the adorable, tip-top little damsel with pouty lips and flushed skin. Watching, as she anxiously downed three slices of pie. Observing, how the harder he stared the more flushed she became. Loving it, for many reasons.

Caleb pushed her a glass of water; she needed it.

Confrontation and controversy were Sadie's two phobias. Basically, anything that could make her unpalatable gave her hives. *What kind of music do you like,* was her absolute worst enemy, because people tend to use it to make snap decisions on whether they'd like you or not, be friends with you or not. She couldn't be too mainstream and predictable, nor too weird and obscure, nor could she disclose her sad-girl coffee shop acoustic playlist that Tenley once said 'made her want to stab chopsticks in her earholes and swirl them around'. So, she'd gotten good at reading people—it was always obvious if you knew what to look for—and her answers zigzagged from Avril to Aerosmith to heavy metal band Killswitch Engage, to Garth Brooks *probably* in the near future. Always safe and agreeing, with no risk of being 'too much' of anything.

A 'diplomatic chameleon' Emma had called it. Or weak character, as she'd heard Becks smear behind her back.

Only, Caleb didn't ask about her taste in music; he did worse. Sat, stared, shoveling back pie, licking his lips, *still* staring. His hyper-lustful smirk was nailed on, and upon meeting it, coiled around her neck like a strap of hot steam. Most nettlesome though, was his barbarously smug demeanor, a constant mock, reveling at her timorous condition and knowing *just* how to rob her the refuge of catering to his liking.

Not knowing what else to do, Sadie kept her eyes on the softshell turtle outside to defy him, hoping he'd give up. She'd come across guys like him before, the ones always playing at some game. Except, they'd easily fallen tired once she'd established herself a negligent playmate, a non-participant, and moved on to someone more daring, like her three best friends who crashed parties like they crashed bed sheets.

Maybe she was giving him mixed signals. After all, she'd swapped her usual blend of *Young At Heart* blush for a saucy *Frankly Scarlet*, and she was drinking cappuccinos, so maybe it was a misunderstanding. She'd clear it up, in a minute. She'd inform him of her lack of spontaneity and thrill, just as soon as—

A tingling stroke met the untouched skin of her inner thigh, steely fingers running up towards...

Sadie jerked up in the seat and her knees thudded hard against the table. Floral teacups and plates clanked in place, as a jar of blueberry jam toppled and spoiled the clean cloth. She reddened. "Sorry! Muscle cramp!" *Did he just...*

Just as soon, Caleb gloated with a widely stretched grin, smoking of arrogance. This round he'd won; she was finally looking at him.

What the heck kind of church did these kids go to?

Too full of panic to inform Stacy and David their saintly son had reached for the wrong cake, Sadie did nothing. Then, in a soft fairylike voice she asked him, "What kind of music do you like?" And he, far too comfily, countered, "You *first.*"

"Henri has always been so vague about his time in Weston Hills," Margot regretted, passing out her contribution of non-

GMO cacao truffles. "He hates talking about himself. Do you two have any stories of what he was like in high school?"

"Oh, I don't know about that," Stacy crooned, but shuffled her chair closer. "I always thought Henri was the best at tellin' stories. Always so… thorough."

Suddenly, Henri's beer had slid down the wrong pipe, and Stacy jumped from her seat with the flourish of a preemptive hanky.

"See what I mean?" Margot kissed her husband's cheek. "Turns white even at the thought of being a conversation topic! Never would I think to be frustrated at the sheer modesty of a man."

Sadie noted how the floating air particles had stiffened, even when she blew on them to attempt a stir—deathly still.

"What *did* bring you back into town, Henri?" David asked chummily.

"You know, David, I s'pose I just missed the peace and quiet." The irony was clearly lost on them.

The pastor seemed unsatisfied. "That must've been a big sacrifice for you, Margot. Movin' across the country like that. That's a lot to ask for."

"Perhaps for some, but I knew I married a country boy from the start. It was only a matter of time until we ended up here. It'll be good for Sadie too, growing up away from the city."

In the safety of camo hats and rummaging pubertal boy hands?

"Isn't that sweet?" Stacy squealed, like one does when entertaining the nonsense of a toddler. "And what is it that you do, dear?"

"I'm an actress. Henri and I met on set of a small indie movie he was assisting on. Coffee at craft services lead to a rendezvous at Big Sur's secluded coves. We fell in love, I was quickly pregnant, and he helped me prioritize my career all the while. I'm more than happy to embark on a new adventure. I've actually been hired as the new art teacher at the high school!"

"How amazing!" Stacy praised, as if the toddler had just solved an arduous math problem. "The church is very involved with the school, so I'm sure we'll be seein' a great deal of each other!"

Henri knew more than well the nuanced ping pong game of hurrah women here liked to play; hardly fair when only one kept score. "Sadie darlin', why don't you run to the kitchen and bring out the next round of dessert?"

David so thoughtfully added, "Grace and Caleb can help too!"

Rhubarb custard waited in the fridge, ready to be cut. Sadie placed it on the kitchen counter and pillaged her mind for suitable conversation. "I really love your—"

"Well that was *fun*," Grace snarled from the Bexley liquor cabinet, sifting expertly through the collection and unscrewing the cap of her chosen poison: Jack Daniels. She poured the velvety brown liquid on her tongue.

"—Cardigan." Sadie struggled to not choke on her own saliva. "It's pretty."

"It's hideous actually. Probably from the same store as that sex-repelling prairie smock you've got on. Parents freakin' suck, don't they?"

"Oh—yeah. Totally. Suck."

Grace took another shot, swirled and burped. "Where's your pisser?"

"I'm—I'm sorry?"

"Are you deaf? Bathroom," Grace griped and made a face.

"Oh! That way. First door on your right!" Extra cheery and with an emergency curtsy, because this was *not* going well.

As soon as she'd disappeared around the corner, Caleb, notorious opportunist, swooped in to 'assist' with the portioning of tangy-sweet filling. A cloud of Big Red gum wafted from his mouth and contaminated Sadie's safety envelope. His piercing sapphire peruse marinaded her over and over, and *over*, hands steady and pronounced on the granite counter to show them off.

"What are you staring at?" Sadie finally demanded after almost a minute of stewing, noting how everything was just so gosh darn funny to him.

"What? You don't like bein' looked at?"

Hunching, "No."

"I don't believe that." Caleb stepped closer—even if all her social cues were begging him not to, he did—then surveyed deep into her vaulted eyes of pure basil green as though she were a long-awaited museum exhibit, and he'd come to verify authenticity. Without asking, he touched her hair. He smiled at it.

Sadie grabbed the knife, cutting the crust too shakily to keep it from crumbling, and when she was done, noted how her company was now snooping around the entrance of the house, far too instinctively to be normal. "What are you doing *now?*"

"It's not there anymore." Caleb exhaled his disappointment.

"*What* isn't there?"

"Nevermind." He shifted quickly. "So, your boyfriend must've been heartbroken about you movin' away."

"I don't have a boyfriend," Sadie corrected like the joke was on him, and he cackled in delicious leisure, sticking his finger into the pie and scooping the liquid filling.

"Mhm, yea, didn't think you did. But why not, huh? No one good enough for little miss… *princess?*"

Princesses were cool in her book, in fact, in all her books she kept precisely stacked on her nightstand. But the way he'd said it made her hate the word. "You're not."

"I'm no prince, no." He chuckled with a twang, and maybe it was self-deprecating, or maybe it was simple fact, or maybe Caleb Lindley had never had an impractical girl ever expect anything more from him than be the guy who stands outside an Abercrombie. "Just a thought, but you might have more fun with the frogs if ya give it a chance. We ain't afraid to get our *hands dirty.*"

"Charming."

"If you want me to be, princess."

"Look, I'm sorry," Sadie took a professional approach, "but I don't like you, and I don't want to date you."

Caleb had to stop himself from bursting. Who said anything about *dating?* "You might change your mind."

"I won't," she insisted.

"You will," he assured.

"*You* will!" she snapped, completely beside herself at the

plumb confidence and that he hadn't yet called it quits. "I'm not what you're looking for. Honestly, I don't know what gave you the impression I might be." She almost laughed then, thinking of Grace's 'prairie smock' remark. "I mean... *look* at me."

Caleb did as he was told, for once. "Don't mind if I do. Although, it's a bit of a challenge with all those clothes you got on..."

"You've got the *wrong girl!*" Sadie pushed away his nearing body, regardful that it was exceptionally tall and complete for a boy of high school age.

Caleb shook his head, humored once again by confidential information. "I really, *really* don't."

Sadie scowled. "I can't believe people actually fall for *you* being some paragon of virtue."

"Oh, I'm very lovable," he said absolutely. "And besides, everyone's got a mask, in some form or another. Stick around and you'll see. I'd really like to be there when you take off yours."

"And what about yours?" she countered, astounded by her own bravery.

"Eye for an eye." He drifted somewhere abstractly pensive, but came back just as rudely sensual when he whispered it again, "Eye for an eye, princess." His thick brow and solicitous sky-blue eyes dipped fluidly, right below where her heart was thumping. "I thought girls from LA didn't wear bras."

Officially fed up, Sadie put a shushing finger atop her *Frankly Scarlet* lips, let her gaze flutter and tilt above, and here, she did something radical. "Shh, *he's* watching." A joke.

"Amen," Caleb growled with a buzz.

"Your bathroom smells like Tinker Bell's farts." Grace reappeared under the high-ceilinged archway. "Oh, and sweet bidet, you lucky bitch. That adjustable nozzle does wonders." She added a spicy wink, which Sadie didn't understand. "Err, so... what's with the knife?"

Sadie jumped back, because as it happens, it was tightly wrung and erect in her fist. As she frightfully stared at her boding reflection in the blade, Caleb privately recalled the many hours he'd spent sitting in that very kitchen, several years ago.

* * *

Brooks had planted himself in the middle of the football field, nursing a beer. It was late, he didn't know how late, but late enough for his dad to have called nine times. His phone flashed with another voicemail, a couple empty beer cans astray nearby. He chugged, tossed, and cracked open another.

The Weston Hills High football stadium was substantially larger than any other in the county: sky scraping concrete stands striped red and black, a mural of a wolf baring it's teeth, and a state-of-the-art sound system that overplayed Baha Men's *Who Let The Dogs Out*. It was a beacon to the pride and history of a small town with big dreams. The list of current D1 college players that'd scored their first touchdowns on the revered soil was extensive; the list of current supermarket employees who'd screwed up that chance…

Brooks had always felt a connection there, like sitting with a childhood friend, someone that wasn't Caleb and whose advice didn't end with *I dunno dude, just hit that* and something about chafed balls. Maybe he could hear God better out in the open, when the rest had prayed and gone to bed, and he had more attention to give. Brooks hoped the line worked both ways, because that man was in for an ear full.

At that moment, Duke emerged from the shadows, his signature army-green henley and rubber boat shoes giving him away. Their father had asked him to go out and look for his brother. This was his first stop. "Ain't you a little too proud to be drinkin' alone?"

Brooks belched loudly, before drinking some more.

"The great Brooks Holden in all his glory, the unstoppable Weston Hills warrior, best high school QB in the state!" Duke exaggerated each syllable, like that one lisping Bay News 9 reporter in a newsboy hat who never shut up. "Golden Holden goes *all the way*! Ha, yep. Here he is, folks." He kicked a can at the pathetic drunk mass on the ground. "Sad."

"Yeah, I am. Now if you don't mind…" Brooks raised his can.

"It's your own damn fault, you know. The dogfight is a stupid tradition. If you hadn't gone and—"

"You don't think I know that?!" Brooks punched the warm earth with his fine arm and left a crater in it, before hunting in his bag for more Tylenol. "Don't pretend like you ain't enjoyin' this."

"Why would I be enjoyin' this?"

Brooks sneered a *oh, you know why* but went ahead and recapped anyway. "Because you follow me 'round with that smart ass chip on your shoulder, judgin' and pissin' out your say-so's like I asked for *another* person to breathe down my neck and nag on my shit! Sometimes, I swear, you're just rootin' for me to fail."

"IT AIN'T ALWAYS ABOUT YOU!" Duke shouted with enough momentum to knock him into the middle of next week.

And after recovering from that, Brooks charged at him with brittle tears in his voice. "Well not anymore, that's for fuckin' sure! Congratulations!" He rammed his brother's chest, and Duke stood there and took it. "Teams all *yours*!" He shoved again, and again Duke took it.

They stood here, heaving, frozen in fuming stillness, the sound of crunching gravel prefacing headlights coming and going behind the stands, until it was black and silent again.

Brooks knew he wasn't being fair, but none of it was, and Duke should know better than to try to reason when he's like this. His little brother was always there when he shouldn't be, and maybe that made him an idiot, but it also meant he couldn't hit him again. Eventually, Brooks calmed enough to sit back down.

"You know…" Duke joined him, pretending to be lost in thought but really he'd had the monologue barred in his gums for years, "if it were me who was hurt, dad would be relieved. Entire town would be I bet, because at least it wasn't the *Golden Holden*. I could lose my whole damn arm and they'd thank God for takin' the lesser brother. You act like bein' the center of this town is some kind of punishment. Imagine bein' the replacement."

The words grounded Brooks from his boozy state, the pricking pains of his injury escalating like a shark was gnawing on the muscle. He knew his tense status would be interpreted as doting, or at least caring, so he wore it and tried his best to listen.

"You remember when we were 'round ten doin' that summer camp in Boca?" Duke continued. "Dad picked us up on the last day, turned to us in the backseat with this fat dopey grin and said *My boy! My boy is goin' to be in the NFL one day!* Well, it didn't take long after for me to guess which boy he was talkin' 'bout. So yea, maybe part of me was waitin' for you to fail, and I gotta say— damn it took a long ass time."

Brooks chuckled in spite of himself. Any evidence of alcohol had now dissipated from his veins, replaced with annoyance, but also respect. "I remember. But you know, you can't be pissed at me for bein' better at football."

"I'm not. Cause you're not. As I recall, it just as easily could've been me who dad picked. We were at that age where he had to choose which one to prioritize. You had the opportunity to show him, is all."

Brooks considered it. He didn't need to consider it, to know Duke was right.

The coach hadn't allowed parents to come watch until the last day of camp. Brooks had impatiently woken from his sleeping bag, munched a half-eaten apple and ran through the warm ups three times while the others woke lazily and messed around on Game Boys. He'd worked harder than any of them all summer, which would've been baldly apparent had the coach not been writing up grades of 'smart mouthing' and 'foul conduct' on his haughty clipboard like a chump. And because of those grades, minutes before the game, he'd traded Brooks out for Duke. Gutted, Brooks watched from the bench as his mother readied her camera, their father's singular dose of approval swung over their heads, and he did what he had to do.

Kelly had packed them pre-game baggies of trail-mix in their lunchboxes: regular for Brooks, peanut-free for Duke because he'd recently been diagnosed with a moderate allergy. By 'moderate', it meant it likely wouldn't kill him, and for a ten-year-old with a still hollow sense of consequence, it'd felt like an innocent prank. It could've easily been an accident, the switching of the bags.

Brooks had replayed that ride home after their win a

thousand times. They'd gone for Dairy Queen blizzards to celebrate. Brant had rambled on for hours about Brooks' future athletic career, while Kelly lathered Duke's splotchy limbs in pink calamine lotion. Looking back, maybe it all really did fall back on that one day, when it was only a day.

"That's shitty," Brooks eventually murmured, giving him a wry face. "You know I'm the one who gave you those peanuts, right?"

"No."

"Oh." Not knowing what else there was, Brooks walked over to where his backpack lied damply, unveiling a beer and tossing it to Duke. They sulked together with their arms resting at their knees.

"You think Circle K is hirin'?" Brooks asked. "Now that Cameron Dickson flushed my plan A down the shitbox, can't think of a nobler plan B than sellin' Swisher Sweets and Snickers to the future kiddos of Weston Hills High."

"Shut up. You're gon' play."

"How do you know that?"

"Because you're my big brother." Duke chugged the beer to whitewash the emotion of what he'd said. "And you're stubborn."

Brooks heard this more than anything in a long time. "When did you get to bein' the better man?"

"Always have been."

"You shouldn't be if you ever wanna get laid. The ladies don't like that."

"The right one will."

Brooks' lips parted in laugh, trying to figure out when he'd stopped caring for his brother's company. "Looks like we have different tastes. That's good. Girls I know haven't been much concerned with waitin' for Mr. Right."

"Mhm."

The stars turned on in brighter gold, as both brothers— suddenly lost in thought—pictured who that reminded them of.

A few minutes later, Caleb and Levi pulled up aggressively in a black Ford Raptor, doing a few donuts to leave their marks before hopping from the windows, charging across the green belt of field with arms outstretched like two rebel birds of prey, free eagles in flight, until they crashed in the grass with hearts hammering in drumfire how teenage boys hunger for. These are the moments they'd long for.

"What uhh… what you valentines talkin' 'bout out here?" Caleb's chin withdrew waggishly, making a point to judge their intimate pow-wow.

Duke shrugged. "You know. Gettin' laid."

"Duke Robert Holden! You watch your mouth!" Caleb smacked him across the back of the head. "Now, pass me a beer."

Boyish laughter, revolutionary and familiar and time-freezing, echoed over the sound of chirping crickets and the silence of a deadbeat town. They did this often, each time blending uneventfully into the next, but tonight held a punch that would bring them back. At least it would, when it all changed.

"You think they got beer in heaven?" Levi inquired as he fell back on the grass, sprawling his legs and arms as wide as he could.

"If they don't I'll opt for hell." Caleb gawped numbly at the astral writings in the sky. The glowy dots were significantly glossier that night, perhaps something to do with the full moon, or some other intervention that lent a hand to all things light. Lying there now, Caleb recalled a time when he'd spent hours on his trampoline, stargazing, connecting the dots, conversing with God. He didn't do that anymore.

Suddenly, Caleb seesawed on his back, using the kinetic motion to kip up to standing. He flicked his beer with his truck key. "A toast!" he bellowed, waiting for his friends to catch up, turning reflective and solemn when they did. "To another year of runnin' this shit. To football, to brotherhood, to livin' everyday like it's the last, to gettin' the hell out of this town and never lookin' back."

The full moon climaxed opalescent against the black heavens above, as the sound of bottles clinking filled the stadium.

CHAPTER THREE

Detours

"You've got to be kidding," Sadie expressed disapproval at the sight of her new school from the protection of her mother's Cadillac, cheeks pouted (so pretty much the same).

It was a tan curdled concrete building with accents of spoiled red, a flagpole the height of Everest out front and a flapping American Flag with which all founding fathers could've scrubbed their periwigs at once. The need for pressure washing was at a crisis. The halls were outdoor and muggy. The campus and people in it: grungy and mean-looking and way too patriotic. Granted, the gardening efforts drew some charm, the shutter style windows were slightly endearing, and it wasn't blanketed with the smog and whirrs of an aggressive freeway.

Just as soon as she'd decided it wasn't a *total* catastrophe, Sadie remembered Jeepers Creepers. It'd been on TV last night. Her dad, by no means a movie-buff, had so literately informed, "Oh, hey! This movie was filmed just fifty miles north of here! Supposed to be based on a true story—did you know?" *Awesome. Thanks pops.*

But really, there was nothing around. Just miles and miles of various species of pine surrounding the lonesome reedy main road, and one single gas station. Sadie's neck craned towards the obnoxious honking coming from the dreary and crammed Circle K, just a short walk down Stadium Drive. No one was pumping gas, just loitering on tailgates with Dunkin' iced coffees and Polar Pop cups, bullying a senior citizen by stealing his cane—poor softie, Mr. Dawson—who'd only left the house to buy lotto tickets for his wife. Sadie decided the Circle K must be a 'spot', but whether it was the cool crowd one, their socks and flips flops didn't say.

Like a cold-blooded murderer, she smacked a mosquito that'd managed to munch red train tracks from her wrist to her elbow, and wriggled, because now she felt them all over her.

Margot picked up the slack on her buoyancy. "You just... *we* just... have to be open to the experience. Give it a chance to grow on us."

"I'd rather not let anything I find in a swamp *grow on me*. Becks said if a toad touches me, I'll get warts."

Margot sighed. "That's certainly a myth. Besides, you used to love playing with all sorts of creatures and bugs when you'd visit over summers. In fact, as I recall, you specifically had a very handsome toad friend named Chives."

Sadie threw her head back, vexed with frustration. "Mom, that's different. I was a child."

"You were you, then. You are you, now. I don't see the disagreement between the two."

"I meant that was before I realized those things are *gross*." Sadie pulled out a compact mirror and blotted her T-zone with tissues, hearing Becks chant her only religious belief: *Never let them see you oily*. Then, a small smile partially surfaced, because she'd almost forgotten about Chives. Those days, she'd named every inch of flora and fauna within exploring distance of the back porch—had sincere conversations with, confided her dreams in— because they'd understood her, and at that age with a silly frame of mind, it just made sense to love everything.

Her mother went on, "This is one of the best schools in this part of Florida, actually. It's all over the news all the time."

"For sports."

"Well, yes."

Sadie and her saddlebag got out of the car. "You're just lucky I'm not one of those rebellious teenagers, because I... I could be. I could run away, catch a train back to California, get a huge tattoo right on my back, or date a guy in one those screaming song bands—"

"No, honey. You could not." Margot suppressed a laugh, standing in front of her now. "I know my daughter. You're… what's the word…"

"Advanced? Precocious? Born in the wrong time?"

"Good."

Sadie frowned, because that may as well be the brown noser sister word to 'nice'. "Great, spread the word. The new girl at school plays with toads and is a *good* girl. She sounds enthralling."

Margot had so much she wanted to tell her daughter. Like for starters, these exact qualities *were* priceless. But for now, she'd let her roam. "You should get going so you're not late. Did you get Caleb and Grace's numbers? They were pleasant kids. I got a really positive read on them."

Woefully, Sadie's lips pursed. "Just peachy." Then she started across the lot and began searching for him, itching for some romantic potential to sink her heart into.

The ground below her ballet slippers rattled from a RAM's subs blaring Florida rap, though to Sadie it was just startling noise. She recognized one of the girls chatting against the front tire: Shelby. The soccer tee, death stare, strawberry-freckled girl who'd spilled foam espresso on her toes. Her face was just as rumpled and crabby now, so the good news is she might have a condition.

A few cars down, a clique of hoppy girls convened in a tight circle with matching Lilly Pulitzer drink tumblers in hand. They for one, looked somewhat from this generation: straight-A types with color-coded folders and an aptitude for manifesting the perfect pair of leggings. With a teaspoon of courage, Sadie headed their way, until the circle fastened tighter—how Becks, Emma and Tenley would do when their *allergies to cheap* were triggered by someone in H&M. Sadie got the message, though she had one for them if only they'd have listened: *Don't worry. I'm a background person. You'll barely know I'm here.*

Just once more she'd put it out there: a handbook. A few basic survival instructions wouldn't hurt.

As she continued shuffling forward, Sadie swore she heard

her name being whispered, but quickly dismissed it to the paranoia sprouts all tangled in her mind. Because that was impossible—she'd been there a day.

She reached the end of the lot, a safe zone she'd thought, until she caught glimpse of a lanky but surprisingly dense figure pummeling towards her. With a whiff of B.O., Sadie was battered to the asphalt, much like a bowling ball to a bobby pin, and someone nearby yelled: *Strike!* The graceless fall left road burn on her elbows; her knees had ugly gray scrapes and pebbly stickers stoppering the blood. Oh yeah, and they were *definitely* saying her name.

Sadie got up, commanded the searing bucket of tears to not tip, and scanned the area. The bowling ball, Sterling Ray, was obliviously passing a beat-up pigskin, shouting obscene slander across the flat maze of trucks. He was in his usual dirty wife beater and torn Wranglers, dragging his scuffed boots with staples and hardened mud on the soles. Sterling paused, but only to hock a loogie and aim it at a Jeep with the license plate *Off Road Princess*, to which one of the Lilly Pulitzer girls cursed and hurled a Twizzler.

Sadie decided not to wait for an apology, and with her open skin stinging, she noted something strange: how the scrapes and cuts and dirt residue should've made her feel out-of-sorts, broken down, but instead invigorated her like a resetting muscle memory to back then, an untaught and wild little thing. A child in the backyard. Whole.

The stairs to the school quad were a marathon to conquer, and by the end Sadie's armpits had cocktailed to a deodorant shea butter paste. Yellow flowers she couldn't name greeted her at the top, alive with tiny matching butterflies camouflaged in the petals. Also, patches of supremely green grass for students to lounge, kiss, and copy each other's homework.

The unwritten hierarchal order placed the town's acclaimed sweethearts at the center with an invisible ring of protection; picnic tables were exclusively reserved for pretty looking athletes with recognizable last names, and of course whoever they were sleeping with. It typically looked like a busy meshwork of letterman jackets and pom poms.

Sadie took it all in, just as—

"Hiya! You're Sadie, right? Of *course* you are. I'm Mallory Jordan. Cheer captain and oh so lucky for you, head of the welcoming committee!" A cat-eyed, creamy-skinned girl asserted her Juicy Couture perfumed presence, offering a sharp talon hand and sympathy moue in her cupid's bow, like her mere greeting was a queenly act of charity.

Sadie took it politely, distracted by prying faces tossing fertilizer on her paranoia.

"Oh, don't worry," Mallory solaced, and something about her voice did the trick; warm sap that quenches anxiety like sugar soda (it doesn't). "People will eventually get bored of candling your face like you're Kacey Musgraves on ice skates, probably by fifth"—looking her up and down—"fourth period."

"Thank you," Sadie said, unsure of every word yet flattered by them. "You're the girl from that store downtown, right?"

Her thick gloss tweaked to a contrived smile. "Yes. *Mallory Jordan,*" enunciating it slow and savvy like it were French. "Don't worry, you won't forget." In all but three seconds, Mallory did a profile on her. The feather barrettes and middle part said it all: understated but expectant, and a *whatever you're in the mood to eat* kind of girl. So inoffensive and slight, she might just blow away like one of her goddamn hideous barrettes. "A bit eager to impress, aren't we?" Girls like her were the easiest to prune.

Sure enough, Sadie went purple inside, suddenly hating the outfit she'd taken two hours to pick out. "I... I wanted to make a good impression, I guess. Am I not in dress code?"

"A little advice girl to girl—it just comes off a little desperate," Mallory cupped her hand to her skinny chin and squeezed her face, like she really didn't want to be the one to have to tell her.

This girl, Mallory, was new to Sadie, yet peculiarly familiar. For a moment, she found herself picturing Becks with a country accent and glitter lasso, until she was interrupted by a hard yank in her harm, stumbling to keep up as she was dragged away full speed...

"You'll thank me later." A witchy-esque girl who was two-thirds thick black mermaid hair blinked back at her. "I'm Maia."

Whiplashed, "Sadie. But let me guess, you already knew that."

"I see you're catching on quickly."

"Are you on the welcoming committee too?"

Maia laughed like a wind bell in a funnel storm. "Never. Not even if this school had one."

Maia was a natural beauty, with a personality on par to a singable alternative song that changes your life, and a refreshing bohemian attitude that's colorful to be near. Her unbrushed hair poured in jet scrawls down to her tailbone, body voluptuously shaped, skin tone a radiant honey caramel, while her sinfully long lashes framed the depth in her eyes like gatekeepers. She spoke with a fiery Latina dialect that could've been intimidating, if she weren't also inherently kind. Her mismatched outfit of corduroy flares, a thrifted Red Hot Chili Peppers tee and green striped sweater made the point she had nothing to prove, besides that she had nothing to prove.

On paper, Maia and Sadie were antithetical: moon and sun, fire and water, dark and light. Sometimes, that's just it.

They settled on the quad grass, sunlight bouncing off their youthful complexions, as Maia braided stalks of grass and Sadie numbered her campus map to her corresponding class schedule.

"Okay, as a girl who has extensive firsthand experience with the treacheries of this school, I am hereby appointing myself as your official guide and mentor!" Maia grinned and snatched the papers. "Let muah handle this."

Sadie sighed. "Just warning you, I'm a pretty hopeless case. Everyone looks so… angry with me."

Maia only chuckled at the concern. "Unless you grow some buckteeth overnight or got some gnarly bunions hiding in those flats, not gonna change."

How any of that was related flew straight over Sadie's head, so she moved on to Q&A. "What's the deal with the Mallory girl? Is she, you know, dangerous?"

Maia plunged a finger in her throat, and gagged. "Mal thinks she runs this place—granted, a lot of the time she does." Their heads turned to the taut-bodied cheerleader, adjusting an epic hair bow, leopard bra peeking from her halter-top and captivating two freshman boys spying nearby. "If she feels challenged, like say, if a new girl with shiny hair moves to town," exhibit A'ing at Sadie, "she'll make sure you're besties so she can cut your hair off in your sleep, or whatever, whatever. Basically, eliminate the competition. It's basic only-so-many-cute-guys-in-town physics. You can't let the good ones off the market, or *mini-mall* rather."

Sadie's thin brows knitted. "But, I don't want to compete."

"Uh huh. Tell that to *them.*" Maia pointed to Sadie's own group of peepers, four of them (two more than Mallory). "I guess it helps that her rich stepdad owns most of Weston Hills land, has a whole ranch off Paddock Road: Thompson Farms."

"And her mom?" Sadie turned anxious in remembering the monogrammed beach hats.

"Ah, Delilah Jordan. The town's crème de la crème. Drives a new Porsche every other week, owns The Lipstick Tree on Main. Apparently, she gets her hair blown out every day at the Bows and Ribbons salon by Publix. Other than that, I don't really know her story. Usually people have this giant family tree around town you can thread together, for rounds of generations, but I don't know who she's related to. I don't think anyone does."

"I met her, kind of. She ran off when I told her who my dad was."

"Oh no, *Delilah* doesn't run," Maia joked, popping open a bag of ranch sunflower seeds with one hand. "I'm not surprised though. Everyone's been talking about your dad. Guess he was some hometown hero in the olden days. My papá practically fell out of his chair when he heard he was back, told me a story about your dad and him shooting pool. I know, doesn't sound like much, but it was to him for some reason. Huh…" Maia paused, souring. "Maybe your dad and Delilah have some kind of *history.*"

"There's no way," Sadie stated firmly, only until now, she'd never given much thought to the archives her parents had lived before meeting each other. If anything, she'd imagined her dad a goggled woodshop nerd, not the class clown or Casanova heartbreaker that, so far, was what the data proposed.

"You're probably right, but the Jordan women *do* have some heinous voodoo hold over the male class. Don't understand it. Mal bats her lashes and they'd gladly lick the nail polish remover off her toes." Maia mischievously side-eyed Sadie. "Maybe, until they see you."

"Ha ha," Sadie coughed laboriously. "You're funny."

"Correct, and serious. Com' on, you had to have like a hundred guys pining for you at your old school."

"Wh—what?" Sadie's shoulders attempted to close like cabinet doors.

Maia squinted suspiciously. "Okay, be real, are you one of those girls that pretends not to know because you don't want to come off conceited, or are you actually just blind?"

Sadie answered by toggling her scabs.

"Jesus, okay. Well you're hot—congratulations! How did you not know this?"

The golden ringlet covered girl finally mustered the ability to look at her. "I have good cheeks."

"Cheeks?" Maia repeated.

"Yeah, as in facial structure." Sadie poked around at the high arched bone emphasized below her eyes. "At least, that's what my friends always told me. I have good cheeks."

Maia barely knew how to speak to such bendability, because she for one, didn't want to bend it any which way. She put a hand dramatically on Sadie's ankle, about to disclose life-changing news. "Girl, maybe at your old school you had good cheeks, but here… you could get any guy you wanted. You're like, a new Chipotle in the mini mall."

The small-town linguistic barrier made Sadie a little pixilated. Antsily, she rearranged her kneecap left and right with her chin. *That couldn't be true. Could it?* "Anyone," she breathed.

"Literally, any one. Him, him, even him—a teacher intern but he has a baby face— him in a heartbeat, him if you don't mind barbecue sauce breath…"

Sadie sat up straighter. "What about a guy named Brooks?"

Maia stilled in illegible thought, sinking back into the weight of her arms. She chuckled a little satirically. "Brooks Holden." Ambivalently testing it in her mind. "Maybe… even him." She checked the time, suddenly throwing back the schedule and scurrying for her things. "If you want to know all about Brooks, meet me at the top of the stadium after 7th period. I'll tell you everything I know." With one last sassy air kiss, she was gone.

Puzzled, Sadie watched her pinball through the crowd; she hadn't heard a bell.

For Maia Rosales, the walk was habitual, numbing, always too short. She passed the science building, burgundy math portables, Hot Topic couple who used each other's spit to wash each other's tongue rings, not to mention mist anyone in their wake. Maia picked up the pace. With each step, the hallway narrowed to a cold cell and the air pressure solidified like a birdcage lid over her head. But as depressing as life was, today was different; she'd made a friend. A frilly, la-di-da, sun-beamy girl who embodied better days, with buggy green manga eyes— and let's not forget—*good cheeks*.

The moon needs the sun to keep going, to wax and wane and gather some light, to occasionally be full again. And the sun, void of it's own moons, thinks itself deserted, floating all by one's self, until one moon chooses to reflect the light back to it. The moon and sun help each other, and under this team of friendship, flowers grow.

Maia's worn checkered Vans finally stalled at a door where a placard read 'Principal Jay Dunn'. Her young face slowly desensitized, eyes determining and changing, like preparing to take the stage in a live theater performance, one that her life depended on. Out of necessity, Maia Rosales, seventeen-years-old, had always been advanced for her age, held a mature presence compared to her peers. But maturity never came without consequence, scars, like alternating light and dark rings in a tree. Or only dark… hers were only dark.

"You wanted to see me, Mr. Dunn." She stepped inside the

office and turned the lock behind her.

Jay Dunn—a qualified-looking, all bases covered, on stand-by kind of guy—sat at a large maple desk in the center of the room. He was inviting, loudly virile, and aggressively charismatic. The town's beloved mayor and substitute school principal, though the second job was more for show. Ceaselessly well-dressed in a crisp suit and tie, much like a Hugo Boss ad. He smelled of cedar and tobacco and licorice. Jay used a little too much gel in his dark hair, skin always nectarous and confusingly wet, and some mornings, like today, he skipped shaving. But even with that spotty 5 o'clock shadow, Mayor Dunn was a certifiably desired man.

There was a wholesome photo on his desk: his wife Elaine and their three kids. Several more photos covered the beige walls, unnoticeably so, with the grand display of humanitarian efforts jenga'd across. Donation certificates to endangered manatees, a thank you letter from Planned Parenthood, newspaper articles about his efforts rebuilding homes for the thousands devastated by Hurricane Charlie, and the largest square, extravagantly framed, of the day their football stadium—*Dunn* Stadium—was born. Jay was a man of generosity, influence, money, and other things far too complex to be draped with poster putty; the beating heart of the town. How common again, was heart disease?

His moist scruff and fine lines crinkled upwards at the sight of his prized pupil. A large hand pet the leaves of an unusual potted plant on the desk: Deadly Nightshade. Matter-of-factly he said, "You're late."

Maia's sweater slipped from her shoulders to the floor. Jay exhaled and leaned back in his chair. Then it all unfolded, exactly as he'd told her it would.

Sadie scoped the sea of students crawling around her, but mostly she played *he loves me, he loves me not* with the bushes of yellow petals, shapes of circular fringed macaroons embracing like keepers around her. She wondered what might they be called.

Being an introvert went hand in hand with being a people watcher. Sadie did that now. It was easy to spot the blooming crushes, yesterday's ex's, seasonal besties; an inevitably close-knit history that stems from growing up in adjacent neighborhoods, family churches, same YMCA swim classes. All of them playing part in each other's imperfect upbringing, just like their parents, grandparents, and the greats before that. Sadie was the only outsider in this tribe. Meaning, there was no grapevine to snoop down for a good ol' southern Wikipedia lowdown. They really hated that.

She got up and took refuge against a wall of 'Clearwater Beach Clean-up Posters', leaning stiltedly amongst the happening but not *in* it. It reminded her of all the hours she'd spent stashed in corners at the upper class Malibu shindies Tenley used to lug her to. Tenley would disappear twenty minutes in, right after introducing Sadie to the C-level YouTuber she was planning on seducing. Later, Sadie would find Tenley on a sticky couch, half-unconscious with her Brandy Melville miniskirt ridden up and wet chunks of tequila, sweat and goat cheese bruschetta in her hair. Tenley would mutter, "Nothing happened, alright?" as if preparing to get out of a grounding. They'd gather their things, and soon order a ride to the Bexley house off winding Mulholland Drive with MGMT's Electric Feel as soundtrack. They'd run upstairs, draw a bath, and Sadie would feed them both gluten free Pita Chips while Tenley called Becks and Emma to excitedly tell them all about the guy who'd left her on the couch, and Sadie got to hear too… because she happened to be nearby.

There'd been similar cases where it was Becks or Emma in the tub, Sadie feeding the chips; their go-to plus one because *you don't have to worry about a girl like Sadie accidentally stealing your man.* Right now, Sadie remembered these nights differently, more clearly. And still, she hoped someone would be there waiting in the corner to take Tenley home from the couch.

That's when she heard him. Brooks… *Holden* apparently.

It was like returning to a really wonderful dream, under the oak at Ogilbee's when he'd looked at her like something radiant.

Cloud castles sprang overhead, embodying every expectation she'd ever had. Do you remember still, what yours looked like?

The dark hickory brown eyes waited atop a picnic table. Brooks had his elbows propped on his knees, turning a strange scaly brown object that sort of resembled a—oh, *football.* Sadie had only sometimes seen them on TV. To her dismay, big bulky bodies enclosed around him and made him untouchable, and then it hit her—the way they were angled, speaking to the masses but seeking opinion from one—*he* was their leader.

Her breathing weakened, because she'd just nominated the most sought-after boy in school as her main dish of what-ifs, and daydreaming is only fun if there's at least a one-percent chance of it coming true. She replayed Maia's response: *him, him, him,* just not *him.*

She needed to re-assess.

She didn't want to, though.

From her secret inquisitive vantage point, Sadie microscoped closer, because not doing so would make her unfed and needy. It felt sneaky and empowering to watch him act candidly and unaware of her gaze. Maybe if he'd known, he'd sit straighter, flex something; she enjoyed him inactive, as is. Fighting to stay composed, she discreetly stowed her burning hands in front of her burning legs, to hide the invisible flurry building between them. Sadie sunk to a crouch, back sliding smoothly down the steep wall, adjusting her hips in dips and bevels because the pressure and rub of the backs of her ankles on her underwear… helped.

Without mental dress rehearsal, Sadie's legs were stepping— sashaying—forward with a sudden urgency, defying the social barrier, crossing into restricted territory. Divergence is effortless, when no one's told you the rules. Ignorance is sparing, or as they say—bliss?

A string of necks careened her direction, and Mallory's did a kicky double-take.

"Hey look—your new girlfriend." Levi nodded at the incoming babydoll dress. "Aw, she dressed up for you man!"

"I don't have girlfriends," Brooks said plainly.

Caleb stole the football. "That's right. They all end up in my bed anyway, so what's the point?" He hurled the ball back so it jammed in the quarterback's gut, and turned, because she'd whirled to their feet like a quick whisk of gold pollen, and he wasn't about to miss this show. "Lookie, lookie." Caleb's smirk enhanced with electricity. "Miss Ella Enchanted."

Sadie mindfully tended her shoulders back. "Hi." It was meant for Brooks, and his bulky friends opened up like gates to present a path, all but Caleb who stayed put and snacked on a fruit roll-up.

It took the brown eyes seconds to look up. "Hey baby."

Muffled laughter traveled amongst the spectators, which had multiplied.

"Um—hi," Sadie greeted again, smaller. "So… you play football as well?" Pointing at the obvious in his hands.

Levi snickered. "Oh look! She's smart!"

"Yes ma'am," Brooks retorted with his gaze so polluted with indifference, she questioned if she'd mistaken him for someone else. Someone cruel. "Anythin' else?"

The natural rosette drained from her lips. Her castle, the whole kingdom, dying. "Oh, well I thought perhaps, possibly… we could compare schedules. Maybe we have some classes together?"

"You're a junior, right? I'm a senior. Unlikely."

"Right," she turned pale as snow, yet so on fire she couldn't think. "Well… do you wanna show me around? Maybe you have some more helpful tips? Like the one about the cats."

Caleb cackled, donning his amusement, before arching a brow at Brooks. "Com' on, don't leave the lady hangin'! You heard her. She wants a private *tour*."

When Brooks returned to her, his eyes softened with condolence, then they went disinterested again, and he'd been right: *If you like how something looks, don't look too close.* "I'd love to. Better yet, how about we start in the backseat of my truck? I can make it very educational."

Don't the cool guys know about the glass hearts they're playing with? Couldn't any one of them see it?

This time, the laughter spread like flame through paper. Sadie's fragile bucket of tears tipped, but she clenched every muscle in her face to hold them back. "I—I'm sorry?"

"You should be for wasting his time," Levi barked. "Do you even know who you're talking to? I'm bored. Let's go."

With that final incision, the team rose from the table, except Caleb who lingered to brush a finger against Sadie's like an arsonist tossing in a final lit match. She didn't notice. She was paralyzed. Her heartbeat manic in her skull, voices so hysterical and extreme she hardly recognized them as her own: *Didn't you know they'd see right through you? Who do you think you are? You're not her. You're not one of them. You're not her, so stop trying.* But they were screaming, splitting, piercing. And at the end of the day, this is what will shatter the glass, every time.

There was no stopping it. Her basil eyes swelled like the bucket had been a dam, and leaked furiously down her cheeks, painting ugly orange zebra strands of makeup and ruining her only winning asset.

As Brooks neared the end of the quad, he glanced back at her... *Lance's granddaughter... the golden-haired girl...* who would never, should never, be his. But, in his act of sabotage, he'd sensed how she'd overestimated him with simply a look, as if the estimations were likely to come to life at any second, and for that second, he'd wanted them to. He regretted pushing this one away. It was too late now. Wasn't it? Regretfully, Brooks jogged after his friends while reliving a precious memory: the first time he'd seen the sun up close, almost five years ago.

Sadie didn't know where to go to escape the horrible voices. She trudged on down the hall like wading against river rapids, with the air so heavy and viscous, her spirit fatigued and confused. It didn't make sense. One thing would lead to another, and soon nothing would. When you say you can't wait to grow up, don't worry. It'll go quick.

It won't hurt a bit.

Still fighting tears, Sadie stumbled from her blurry vision and slammed straight into a wall—warm, breathing, spearmint-scented, and also known as Duke Holden. "Sorry! I'm so sorry!

I'm so… stupid." She kept going.

Rattled, Duke witnessed the new girl catapult away, before he peered around the quad in the direction where she'd come. Shocker: he spotted Brooks and company, aloof and arrogant and high on life (some of them high on other things). From the coarse language and entitled halo emanating from the group, it wasn't hard to guess what had happened.

Duke decided to stay close.

The bell rang. The first day of school had only just begun.

Time began to trip over itself as Sadie stepped into first period English, headphones blaring Taylor Swift because maybe she'd been through this too. Her barrettes had been useful in improvising curtain bangs, and here she would hide, until further notice.

There was one seat left in the back of the room, beside a handsome shelf of Fitzgerald and Steinbeck. The desks were arranged in adjoining pairs of two. As she walked, Sadie skimmed the welcome pitch on the board, rejuvenating a tiny bit at the grammar pun: *The past, present and future walked into a bar. It was tense.* Setting down her stuff, she studied her new desk mate, who was also smiling at the corny play on words.

It was time to admit: Florida boys were *cute*. Honestly, Sadie hadn't expected to come across so many.

This one had an Ivy League haircut in a fluid shade of walnut, a minuscule gap between his front teeth, and intriguing deep-set hunter eyes. His back muscles were visible from under his shirt collar. His body language was accommodating of others. He had on a leather bracelet with a round bead of Tiger's Eye; the one he'd paid seven dollars for one randomly champion summer day in Daytona; and as he nervously messed with it, his fingertips revealed heavily calloused bumps, but positioned differently than typical workout ones. He was outwardly real and down-to-earth, qualities featured in his attractive *brown eyes*—

Sadie suddenly came down with a headache of déjà vu, but shook it off. "Is it okay if I sit here?" she asked.

Duke hid his reaction, not believing his stroke of luck, and attempted to flirt by answering "What would you do if I said no?"

After the morning she'd had, it could've set her over the edge, but instead brought her down from it. Sadie shrugged. "I'd sit on the floor."

"You would?"

"Well, yeah. That's not to say I wouldn't be mildly offended, but still, I'd respect your answer."

After a charmed beat, Duke pulled out the chair and patted. "All yours."

"I'd thank you if you hadn't beckoned me like a dog. Now I don't know if I want it." Sadie's nose tipped upwards in playful protest.

"So," he harked and leaned back triumphantly, "in order to combat that, you'd rather sit on the floor?"

Instantly, she covered her mouth, giggling. "I should've seen that coming."

"Ah, it's alright. You're a rookie."

"How do you know?" Sadie ignited in defense. "You don't even know my name."

"Does it rhyme with *Lady Hexley*?"

"Right... the weird small town telephone thing. Forgot."

Duke's grin split wide and fantastically riotous. "Well there's *that*, and there's you having it written on every one of your alphabetized binders, pre-instructed with *If Lost, Return to*." He knocked a catchy knuckle at the pristine stack, and this time, they both relaxed into the lighthearted moment... before they were farther and fewer between. In a cozy southern drawl, he gave himself away. "I'm Duke by the way. Duke Holden."

Sadie's breath was swiped from her lungs. Just barely she mouthed, "Holden?"

"Oh. Yeah. I saw you met my brother—"

"Yeah." Not déjà vu. De—genetics. "It's nice to meet you."

But he could see that it wasn't, and he had Brooks to thank for that.

Mr. Edwards appeared at the front of the classroom. He had a scruffy beard that ran down all three chins, bushy eyebrows, comb over, and a faded pink salmon shirt with tiny whales on it. Sadie decided he had George Clooney vibes, if George Clooney had a beer belly and Quiznos loyalty card hooked to his belt loop.

"'If love be rough with you, be rough with love. Prick love for pricking and you beat love down': a quote! From the first piece of work we'll be dissecting. And what might that be? Anyone?" He waited.

Sadie slinked a timid hand to shoulder-height. "Romeo and Juliet."

Mr. Edwards praised her an embarrassing amount before asking her to stand—the excruciating 'give us a fun fact about YOU'—like every sixteen-year-old was zealously updating their elevator pitch on blackhead breakouts and identity crisis.

Sadie contemplated before beaming with, "I'm a pisces," left dangling amid blank faces and one boy who yawned loudly from the back. "As in astrology."

"That's nice." Mr. Edwards nodded stiffly, clearly just as uncomfortable. "Now, let's talk syllabus!"

As Sadie melted back into her seat, Duke paid attention to the red motes orbiting her eyes and brainstormed how to cheer her up. He attempted an origami dove, but he wasn't great at it so it just looked like he was giving her trash. Then he took out his personal copy of Moby Dick to show he reads, and it wasn't until he stroked the binding to bring notice to it that he realized— coupled with the title—might've been misconstrued. He was about to start telling knock-knock jokes, until thank God, he had a better idea. Duke leaned and whispered, "What's the secretive blue book for? Do you write poetry, or somethin'?"

Sadie clutched the velvet journal tighter, like he might steal it. "No."

Respectfully, he yielded both hands up. "Don't worry. I don't have sticky fingers."

Now she just looked alarmed, and he finally heard it how she must have, and *damn* he was bad at this.

Duke cut his losses with his forehead dismal and a quiver in his calloused fingers, and this little tell, set everything straight.

63

"It's not for poetry, exactly," Sadie began. "I write down things I want to remember. How photographers take pictures to capture a momentary thing, my pages are that for me. My own interpretations of what that picture looked like." Rose-pink heat cracked and pounded in her temples. "I'm sorry. I've bored you. I... I use too many words to explain things sometimes"—Emma would tell her.

"I like words," Duke replied to counteract whatever subconscious thought had distressed her. "Besides, writers are usually the best people."

"They are?"

"Aren't they? Typically, how I see it, they're on a completely different wavelength than the ones just speedin' through it. Pickin' up on details other people miss, showin' us an account of ourselves, keepin' life from fadin' away."

The grainy, southern, dragging of vowels wasn't roughneck on him, but fond. A fanciful music box opened up inside her, and began to turn. "So, you know a lot of writers?"

"Just one." Duke smiled, kind eyes hanging back to make sure that'd landed right. "You should write about this place sometime. I've always thought someone should."

"Yeah, maybe."

"I'd do it myself if I had the talent."

"Maybe you should pay more attention in English," Sadie pointed out in a sly voice, but hoped desperately he wouldn't take the advice. He laughed and she lit up over it. Their ankles bumped on accident, if she believed in those. "So you're not a writer, you're a... jock?"

"Is that how I come off?" He sounded as worried as he was.

She pointed to the wolf badge on his jacket. "It's the same one... the other ones were wearing."

"Oh—yeah. I play a few sports."

"What's your favorite?"

"Soccer."

"I like soccer too—but watching, not playing. I got kicked in the shin by Tabitha Hastings in second grade." She visited that day with a shake of her curtain bangs, undoing them. "Still not over it."

Duke never noticed himself drifting closer to her side of the table. "Good at holding grudges, huh?"

"No," she answered with soft transparence, "just really bad at not getting hurt."

He figured she'd meant physically injured, but wasn't entirely sure. "Did you get a snazzy band-aid at least?"

"Baby blue with polka dots and llamas in yellow rain hats," Sadie boasted with a reminiscent dance of her shoulders. "Thank you for asking."

"Of course." Duke turned slightly away to feel like he had at least some jurisdiction in how smitten he'd fallen; the three-second timeout was excruciating. There was a fabled watercolor quality about this girl, like at any given moment, she might start dissipating to thin air. She was still novel like an unchipped seashell, because she'd never lost her way. Duke wanted to warn her about the bottle that gets passed around at bonfires, that inside these lines you become blind to what's out of 'em, the dogs in yards are trained to bite, most high school sweethearts divorce by forty, it's pedal to the metal because they're not quite old enough for real drugs yet, the creepy crawlers in the bushes are lethal, natural selection *is* their political system, that you can't trust any of it. But as much as he wanted to tell her to run, Duke needed her to stay.

Sadie had come to the conclusion *these* brown eyes were *vastly* different; lighter than a Sycamore, more river birch or red maple; and so maybe everything else was different, too. She appraised the tiny pointed scar under his ear, which was identical to the one she had from nights of passing out with her pencil on her pillow. "Hey, where did you get that—"

"Don't hang out with Brooks, please."

"Wh—what?"

"If you know what's good for you." Duke feared she didn't.

Before Sadie could round up any form of response, the Quiznos card shook—

"Mr. Duke Holden!" Mr. Edwards wore a reprimanding frown, before easing to a rollicking persona with a Popeye voice.

"How's this season lookin'?! You think we can take back that 'W' from Orville this year?"

Sadie had fallen from the metaphoric saddle, again. Orv— *what?*

"Those coonhounds don't know what they've got comin', sir. I'd say it's in the bag," Duke answered automatically.

"Now that's what I like to hear! Hope Brooks has been keepin' that arm of his in shape!"

"Oh, he's definitely grinding it out, sir." *Like a sack of trampled meat*, Duke thought.

"Brant ain't goin' easy on him, I'm sure. I heard some scouts from Auburn got their eyes on him. Good for him. He deserves it. We're all real proud."

Duke's mouth pinched. "Yes sir."

Meanwhile, Sadie strung together context clues and wondered how qualified an English teacher who uses the word *ain't* could be.

The intercom screeched above the door, summoning Duke to the gymnasium.

Mr. Edwards waved a flappy wrist. "You know what—don't worry about the assignment. First week back is gon' be chapped with practices, and that's where your head should be. God forbid Brooks gets hurt or somethin', we might really need you out there."

"God forbid."

"Well, you tell your dad I'm prayin'."

"I sure will."

Sadie felt astonished and unnerved that the pimply, out-of-shape boy in a Jurassic Park jacket would've never been given the same pass. Faith and football; she picked up the rules. As she dreamily watched her understudy muse get up, she said to him, "You don't think I know what's good for me?"

Duke responded with a small melancholy smile. "The good ones usually don't." Then he walked out the door, leaving Sadie in desperate need of a tall glass of water.

Hearing it again, she frowned. *Good one*, he'd deemed her.

In her sultry stupor—a fixed state of being that day—she

almost didn't notice it: a red spiral notebook abandoned under Duke's chair. It was bent with horribly crimped edges. It must've been years old; slept on, stepped on, spilled on by what she could only hope was sour cream. She picked it up carefully and turned to a page where the ink smelled fresh. In typical chaotic boy handwriting, but formatted sprucely like a sonnet, was a front and back chockful of untold thoughts. She didn't need to read it to understand the bleeding vulnerability in which it'd been jotted. It was obvious.

Duke Holden *was* a writer.

He'd lied to her.

Why?

Sadie felt like she was helplessly watching her glass heart get juggled back and forth by athletic hands; only the boys didn't know how to juggle, just hurl it full speed; and they were just practicing with her. Eventually she'd learn: she could practice with them, too.

In her own journal, Sadie wrote down something cutthroat: *Grow up*.

CHAPTER FOUR
Pinky Promise

The cafeteria was a madhouse; hundreds of students linked to the arms of their friends, quarreling for the tables farthest from the teachers' lounge. Of course, the top-tier outside ones were pre-saved for the varsity sweethearts.

Sadie inched her way through the lunch line intolerably slow. After a few annoyed breaths from a girl with purple braces, and the lunch lady, she finally put a boxed salad and bag of Lays chips on her tray. The disapproving stares drilled holes in her back as she thread between the crammed rows, almost tripping twice on a stray Jansport strap. After two laps, she panicked. Everywhere was full.

A pint-sized girl whizzed past. Sadie recognized the fatal feline disguised as a gazelle, and on a helpless whim, "Grace! Hi!"

"Yes?" Grace groaned with whiskey-iced-tea breath, not quite stopping.

"I was just wondering…" Sadie toddled in her pink ballets, heels clicking and fighting the urge to scream *there's no place like home.* "Do you want to sit together?"

"Daw! Ain't that ca-ute!" The sneering coming out of her small body was emphatic; unsettling like the high frequency shrieking of two cotton balls rubbing together. She snatched the bag of Lays. "You actually thought our little play date made us besties? Listen, you seem like a *nice girl*"—Sadie's raised cheeks fell tart—"so I'll give you some advice. Ready?" She drum rolled on her gapped thighs. "No one cares! Literally… no one. I felt like you really needed to hear that. Anywho, you're welcome. And next time, I'd prefer pretzels." Grace winked and pirouetted off, whipping her hips like the screws had flown off.

Comebacks Sadie wouldn't dare say aloud poured over her like that one time she was a raging out-of-control mess, *almost* cursing at the ending of *500 Days of Summer*. At least the movie had a disclaimer. This town didn't even have a 'Slippery When Wet, Which Is Always' sign.

Once she'd come back from the film trauma, Sadie noticed a vacant table through the window, by the yellow flowers in the shade of the veranda. As she went to grab it, she found it odd no one else had done so. Once sitting, she thanked the angels with her fingertips delicately teepee'd and peeled open her caesar dressing. There was only enough to splash three sad leaves of romaine, the rest tasting wilted and dry, so she pushed it aside and opened to the dolphin charm bookmark in her vintage Louisa May Alcott novel, mindless to the voices coming through the flowers…

"The rents are leaving at 7:30 so no booze until then," Shelby said to the notorious three—Brooks, Caleb, Levi—repeating twice to make sure they'd heard it. "Ali and I will run to RJ's for beer, but otherwise bring your own shit. Oh, and Caleb, if you bring another Orville slut to my house I swear—"

"Fine, *fine*. You're right. I apologize." Caleb bowed his head, stole her freckled hand to kiss it all better. "I'll bring extra sheets this time."

"Gah! You know what? Try me, angel boy." Shelby wiped off the spit in his thicket of lovelocks, then flicked his neck so it left a mark. "I'm sure pastor David would *love* to hear all about his son deflowering half the volleyball team in the upstairs church closet. Wouldn't cha think?"

"Well played, Shelbs. Well played." Caleb whistled a sarcastic tune through crunches of Funyuns, before sputtering out crumbs. Something had tickled his left nostril hairs, a profound floral stench, like he'd rolled up bills of rose petals for nose plugs.

The group hadn't yet noticed their accidental infiltrator: an unsuspecting girl and her *Little Women*.

"Don't get none of that nasty Fireball, a'right? Tell RJ we want the good shit!" Sterling guffawed, sitting his bare chalk-white back end—the end where his jean pockets would've been had he opted for the right size—atop the table. "Get me some Keystone, will ya? I'll pay you back later."

He wouldn't, but Shelby added it to the list anyway.

RJ's was the drive-through beverage chest on the outskirts of town. Arguably, the rougher parts. It was worth the drive for something stronger than a Dr. Pepper, since RJ wasn't a stickler for IDs (as long as the security cam caught you showing something flat and plastic, and you tossed in a couple extra bucks for his Marlboro Reds).

"Says the guy who gets drunk off his ass on half a Four Loko. We'll ask RJ for a happy meal for you." Levi picked at the chain hanging low on Sterling's neck. "Boy, you dirty. Your mama never buy you no clothes?"

Sterling chuckled, keeping up the levity as he was entrusted to do. "Shit, you know I got plenty'a clothes. I got a Louis and just 'bout every Vuitton."

"Alright. You're just wearin' that same rag everyday, wanted to make sure you had options." Levi threw a grape at the signature wife beater.

Some days, Sterling truly got the sense he was part of the group. But other times he was the funny-looking insect to poke their sticks at, *to see what it does this time.* "Yea? How do you know I don't have ten of these rags hangin' in my humongous walk-in closet, huh? I got options."

Levi ate a nugget, and with ketchup teeth added, "Not from where I'm standin'."

Sterling quickly mumbled, "Then maybe your vision's gettin' blurry bein' so dang far up Brooks' and Caleb's ass all day long, huh? What's that like?"

"Penis game! Go!" Caleb jumped up, and though they didn't bite, the moment had passed and the ego escalators returned to cruising altitude. "Guess I win. That was easy."

Under his breath Sterling breathed, "All comes down to who's got a damn number strapped to their back." And it was true. On the team, it's fostering brotherhood. Off it, it just sucks.

Shelby waited the appropriate five Mississippis before refocusing the discussion. "Alrighty then! Brooks, do you have any special requests? Err, liquor I mean," she added quickly.

"What?" He'd checked out a long time ago; 7:59 that morning to be exact.

"Beer? Tequila? Capri Sun?"

"Yeah, sure." Finally, he saw her. He was already moving his feet. "Hey, I'll be right back."

Caleb checked out the young lady Brooks had set his compass on; caressing a book and sitting there alone like a pretty heirloom. Like a memory. "Why bother?" Caleb called after him.

"Weren't you the one that said 'you can have this one'?"

"Yea, til' I realized there's nothin' to have. I recently came into some new insight. Trust me bud, you don't want nothin' to do with that. That girl right there is an *Eiffel Tower.*" Caleb didn't actually know where he was going with this, but winging it was his thing anyway.

"No, that is Sadie Bexley." Brooks wasn't in the mood to entertain his bulldust right now. "Eat your applesauce, Lindley."

"Oh young grass-humper, you have much to learn!" Caleb boomed, and stepped in his way. "You see, there's two types of girls in this world: the fun ones, and the Eiffel Towers. The latter you'll never touch. They're bags of tears with boobs just waitin' to explode when you forget to post a 'women crush Wednesday' every Wednesday, or don't prom-posal under the Eiffel Tower with a fuckin' flash mob and a pony. Do you really wanna spend your senior year practicin' the Dirty Dancin' lift for a candlelit toe-dip into second base, *maybe*? Ain't no point chasin' a tease, B. You know I'm just lookin' out for you."

Brooks studied him silently through the smoke and mirrors. "You seem to have put some thought into it, into her."

"Didn't have to. It's pretty damn clear."

"Then maybe I need contacts." Brooks clicked his tongue like a suave 'move' cue for a horse, and then this cowboy kept on walking.

"Who're we talkin' about?" Shelby returned from shoo'ing away two social climbing freshman girls, just as soon sniffing out a *much* bigger problem. "Too stuck up for any of us, huh? Seriously, is the new girl really hoggin' a whole table to herself? Who wants to be the bad cop on this one? I'm happy to volunteer!"

"Shelbs—it's her first day. She doesn't know anyone yet," Caleb defended Sadie, and surprised them both.

"Whatever. Why would he want to talk to *her*, anyway?"

With a suggestive tongue motion, Caleb coaxed around a toothpick unpredictably up and down, raised his shifty eyes at her... and she got the gist.

Nauseated, Shelby's stomach dropped. Her nose burned like a whole chlorine pool had filled it. Her head ached like when she'd taken a soccer ball to the spongy hollow by her eyebrow and needed stitches. She fantasized kicking one at her, reshaping that tiny even snoot free of charge. She'd known girls like Sadie her whole life: mimsy ones who spend hours swatching their wrists in Sephora with pink tick marks, with spoiled complaining voices, calling themselves mermaids or butterflies or sports fans—because that's just as believable as mermaid—and just *can't even*. Brooks hated high maintenance. The Brooks who was her best friend, did.

"Hey," was Brooks' first choice pick-up line. A hard bargain to fight, that one grand syllable. So grand, he said it again but put a spin on it. "Hey... you."

Sadie fixated on a stubborn crouton that kept escaping her fork—swirling, stabbing—and he took it as an invite to sit.

"You should've got the pizza. It's pretty greasy and the crust is always burnt, but it's definitely better than the salad."

"Did you come over here to advise me on my choice of lunch?" She acted mad, but don't be fooled; she'd thawed in advance.

"Ah, no. Actually I... I came over to invite you to a bonfire."

"No thanks." *Swirl, swirl, swirl.*

"It's tonight." He bit his lip, and in her defense, this was the very era of blog shrines dedicated to that phenomenon: the hot guy lip bite. "Maybe... you wanna think on it?"

"No thanks." *Stab, stab, stab.*

Brooks had gained an angry itch at the stem of his neck; an anxious tick he got before games, but never before with a girl. He leaned to check if his friends were in earshot, and when they weren't—"I'm not a bad guy."

His serious tone made her feet scamper in place, the hairs on her arms sticking up like a spooked porcupine. "You're not?"

"I don't know why I said those things. It was stupid. *I* was stupid. But I'm not a bad guy, Sadie."

"Okay."

"That's it? You're not going to give me another chance?"

"Why would I?"

"Because you're... you."

His decisiveness was staggering, because what did that even mean? Of course she knew, but how would he? Without pretense, she wondered aloud, "What do you suppose these yellow flowers are called?" And gestured to the leafy padding around them. It was an ingenious move on her part, because now it was in the universe's hands. *Right answer*: I go. *Wrong answer*: I'll ask again later.

"The—the flowers?" Brooks stammered.

"I'll tell you what," Sadie perked, admittedly auspicious, "if you can tell me what kind of flowers these are, I'll go to the bonfire with you."

Brooks gave her an incredulous look, before percolating with intense fascination. He mindfully plucked an ebbing posy from the bushes, as to not cheat any of the budding ones of a full life, and stepped closer. Nestling the short green stem behind her ear, he surrendered from himself. "Marigold." Brooks took her in. "Definitely Marigold."

Sadie ogled up at him in expensive sensitivity. She felt with her whole face. "Is that your final answer?"

"It is," he owned confidently.

"Very well." She awkwardly came to terms with one flaw in her method. "Since, um, I don't *technically* know the right answer... let's say you're right."

His stance sort of rebounded up and down in a jailed laugh. Mostly, because it made his shoulder hurt like hell. "I'll take it. So you forgive me? For earlier?"

"I said I'd go to the bonfire, but I said nothing about forgiving you."

"Okay, alright." He put his palms together. Sadie eyed them. "Is there anything… I can do to make it up to you? Is there anything… you want?"

Plenty, she thought. But for a girl who dressed like a dollhouse ornament, her truest desires were simple. "You said the orange groves pick up on things… that they remember, right?"

He nodded, "I did."

With her misty sea-green gaze, she begged him not to go easy on her. "Then I'd like to give them something worth remembering."

And just like that, that nowhere town became an everything place. Every kid with a sunburnt heart setting off on an adventure of a lifetime, because growing up is the greatest one of all. There's always a tomorrow, but yesterday won't come back. The good news: those wide-eyed dewy bygones never fully leave, as long as you remember there's someone to reminisce with, waiting down the street.

Brooks leaned down towards her gold head of hair, and with his height, it was kind of this sensual encasing trapping her under him. Sadie's reaction: *What do I do with my hands?* She'd no longer have to worry about that, because he took them in his, looping a girthy outer finger in her dainty one so they tangled sweetly, and whispered softly, "Pinky promise, to give 'em somethin' worth rememberin'."

"Mhm," was the only weak reply she could manage. There was an avant garde push in her hips. She checked the time to document their first touch, and this led her to ponder how they'd evolve and mature as they went on, let's say, on the thirty-seventh touch. How would that go? And if she may—*where?*

They were standing still, yet Brooks' pounding chest was only gaining momentum. A push. A charge. A *rush*. He wanted to do right by her, and by some unfathomable turn of events, Brooks believed he could. "I'll see you tonight."

"Tonight," Sadie exhaled.

"I'll pick you up at 7." He started backing away.

"Wait," Sadie called. "I didn't tell you where I live."

For some reason, he appeared amused. "Don't worry. I'll find you."

And if she'd been too easy on him, she didn't care, on the off-chance this was all meant to be. On the off-chance, *nothing* was off-chance.

"Did you need advice on where to get lip injections?" Shelby scoffed readily once he'd returned from ditz-topia.

"Hold on. *That's* that glamour puss from LA everyone's talkin' about?" Ali leaned to see, and with one eyeroll at the ringlets, "I've always wanted to see hair extensions in real life." Flipping her own jet-black bob, the one that made her look more Asian than she acted.

Ali was Shelby's only female friend, decidedly so when their mother's simultaneously went into labor in a JCPenny. Her dad was a lawyer, her mother an orthopedic surgeon, and Ali had just hit her Guitar Hero 500-note streak to The Police's 'Message In A Bottle', while high.

"Did you hear her mom is the new art teacher?" Shelby continued. "She showed up in a blazer and *heels*. Like hello, what planet are we on? A washed up wanna-be Nicole Kidman teaching high schoolers how to draw a circle—how rich!"

Levi tossed back another nugget. "I heard her first gig was an extra on *American Pie*. You think Mr. Bexley ever takes long, weekend business trips?"

"Too late. I've already been over for *dessert,*" Caleb bragged with a wide grin. He enjoyed dropping all kinds of antagonistic bombs. People tend to be distracted by them.

"Hold on—what?" Brooks turned to stone. "You've been to her house?" Of course, it might've been more accurate to say '*back* to her house'.

"Sure. It's no big deal though. Ate some pie, some chocolates. Damn, they were scrumptious—sweet crunch on the outside, gooey in the middle. Though, poor new girl got so nervous 'round me she practically scarfed 'em all down herself." Then, in an immature inflexion typically saved for locker room exposés, "We *did* have a friendly chat, I'll admit. Gotta say, real feisty for a gal who wears nude pantyhose under her skirts."

"You're lying," Brooks snapped, jaw in contortions.

"On God," Caleb wised back. "And you *know* I don't kid with God."

"Then you're exaggerating."

"Eh, you could be right. Guess I forgot to mention Gracie and my parents were there too."

"You're not funny."

Caleb negated that by busting over his lunch tray. "You should've seen your face! Why's it matter so much to you, anyway?"

"I just didn't know. That's disrespectful. You've been fuckin' disrespectful lately."

"*Disrespectful?*" Caleb sounded it out with a scathing smart-mouth, because *com' on*. "Golden Holden afraid of a little competition, yea? Is that it? Why don't you tell us how you really feel?"

"Forget it."

"You like her?"

"This is ridiculous!" Shelby cried out, and it cracked feebly at the end. "Are you boys all on your periods or somethin'? We've wasted enough time. So Brooks, you're still comin' over early to set up tonight, right?"

"Can't. Have somewhere to be." Brooks didn't even look at her when he bailed. He didn't even look at her.

Shelby drank from her soggy carton of chocolate milk to try to wash down the lump he'd so easily lodged. The lump was spiked like a silk floss tree. It was made up of the trick soccer move she'd wanted to show him, and other old times, when matching silly bands were a binding friendship agreement, and spending the day climbing backyard elms was everlasting. Chugging Arnold Palmers until their stomachs stretched and bulged, wrestling on the couch, competing in lemony burps, watching ESPN on mute and improvising their own commentary.

Sure, there weren't photo booths or heartfelt notes or any *actual* kissing, but there had been a few spitball fights, and that wasn't far off. Did you know silk floss trees are smooth when young? The spikes come with age.

"Fine. Whatever. Don't forget, BYOB." Shelby picked up her things and started down the hall, casting her condolences to the trendy flowerpot every guy's untrained stem had set as target; how *tragic* that was for her. Then, she grappled with a buried memory: Bethany Hart's fifth grade mermaid-themed sleepover, when her desk had been the only desk without a pretty pink invitation.

Time stood still as Sadie waited for the clock's hands to signal the end of 7th period biology. Naturally, she solaced herself with hypothetical scenarios of what the evening had in store, nostalgic for a sequel before she'd seen the foreword. It was a similar charge of feelings as the ones she'd given herself on drives down gloomy Malibu Canyon, before the sun had melted the gray somber marine layer. Theatrical sighs to the window, imagining up depressing music videos to the Pride and Prejudice soundtrack, mustering emotional pennies of heartbreak just to see what it's like. But however close her simulations came to the real thing, ended with each song. *If only, right?*

What was your sad song? You had one, didn't you?

Sadie piloted across campus in a skip and avoided stepping on cracks. When she emerged from under the giant concrete stands, her blithe presence distracted some of the football players.

A disgruntled Coach Holden squinted at her too—lollipop curls, contagious smile, goddamn garish likability—a model Bexley munchkin. Brant slowly put the pieces together... *Henri's daughter.*

"Hey Sadie!" Duke jogged to her from the bench, and instantly she went wobbly. His practice jersey was far more revealing than the varsity jacket and pale blue Hollister button up from English. When his arm reached up to smear the sweat from his brow, the jersey lifted and fully displayed the strip of navel body hair trailing downstairs into his tightly hugging black elastic…

Sadie lost her balance, again. "I—I think they need you on the field. I heard your name called."

Duke chuckled in spite of himself. "Doubtful." A wave of insecurity made him temporarily inoperable. "So, um, what's up? What are you doin' here?"

"I'm looking for someone." She ballerina twirled and went around him.

He followed. "Who is it? Maybe I can help."

"You don't know her."

Duke tilted his head back exhaustingly. "And now your 'new in town' is showing. Just try me. If you're right, I'll spend the rest of practice without my cleats. You can hold 'em to make sure I don't cheat."

Sadie stopped in her tracks, but only to point out the lunacy of what he'd proposed. "So if *I* win, *I* get to hang out with your dirty, smelly, athlete's footy shoes?"

"That's right." The grin grew, and spread wholly to his maple brown eyes. "Better hurry up and spill it. The offer expires."

Clearly Duke was nuts, and his jokes were weird, but something in her chest squeezed every time he didn't back down. Standing there—one boy in front of her, one yards away by a Gatorade dispenser—Sadie picked up juggling. "Alright, fine. I'm looking for a Maia."

"Maia. Maia Rosales," Duke named without thinking. "The girl who in second grade dried her booger on my shirt then gave me a Snoopy 'sorry' card and puka shell necklace to make amends. Yea, we go way back." Pleased with himself, he pointed to the top of the stands where a mountain of raven hair glistened. "Hey listen," he shifted a little nervously, "we ain't got much to do around here, but there is a bowling alley, and I thought maybe we could—"

"You left this," Sadie blurted with sudden urgency, "under your seat in class. It looked important, so… here." She handed him the frayed red notebook from her bag.

Duke blanched, all of him ashen and restless, and for some reason this made the brotherly resemblance much more salient.

"Did you read it?"

Sadie shook her head. "I wouldn't want anyone to read mine, so no."

"Thank you." Though, Duke wondered if she'd have looked less indignant, had her integrity granted more leeway. He wished she'd read it. "You're wonderin' why I lied, aren't you?"

"I was," Sadie said, ostensibly content. "But not anymore."

She started up the infinite ascent of stairs, the flimsy soles of her footwear making small shuffling noises, gossamer cottage dress willowing from the rouse of a breeze. Honest, Duke hadn't meant to probe her, to see the finely-spun nude cotton underneath and imagine the curving arcs of her thighs triangling at a lucky peak. *It was hot out, okay?* He swallowed hard, and before *things* got too out of hand, turned to watch Caleb flicking his dandruff at the new JV graduates. Duke turned back to Sadie. What was it she'd said again? Not... *anymore?* He looked for his older brother, who surely by no coincidence, was probing her too.

Sadie and Maia observed the boy's practice from a bird's-eye view at the second to highest row of the stands.

Maia poured her ranch sunflower seeds in her mouth, occasionally spitting the chewed up fragments over the railing. "Where did we leave off? Oh, right. *Brooks.*"

"He invited me to a bonfire tonight. I told him I would go." Sadie tried her best to be chill, *casual,* not at all mentally writing her signature with his last name behind her first.

"Oh yeah, that's tonight," was all Maia said, bluntly turned off by the subject.

"So you know about it?"

"Shelby Dunn's back-to-school soiree, though Tanner and Colton technically live there too. Yeah, it's an annual thing."

"So you're going?"

"Nah, her dad's the principal. I don't know, that's weird. Getting drunk at the principal's house? Like sure, let's all chug some Smirnoff screwdrivers and ask Mr. Dunn about his budget plans for industrial laminators!"

"Really?" Sadie's flats did a swivel-slide toe dance back and forth on the cement. "I find that kind of riveting."

"I find… you should get out more." Maia grimaced lovingly as Sadie thought: *Is it that obvious?* "And 'riveting'? You read those pocket regency novels they sell at airports with the horny couples on the cover, don't you?" She ignored the cherry blotches budding across Sadie's arms and chest. "No one talks like that here. Tip number one: throw in a few 'aint's' and 'y'alls' here and there. It'll make you look less like you should be called Anastasia."

Secretly flattered, Sadie glowed a healthier violet. "Aint. Y'all. Got it." She folded her hands in her lap, chin up and attentive. "What's Shelby Dunn like? Tell me everything I need to know."

"Mmmm, Shelby makes your Anastasia look like Maleficent. She's crazy tough, which makes sense having two brothers. She's one of those girls who's super cut out for becoming a CEO, like intimidating, firing and yelling at people all day long, but doesn't know how to keep a relationship—god, that's bleak. But she's bossy, you know? Oh, and if she has a *problem* with you… she'll tell you."

Sadie flashed back to the cappuccino 'accident', but upheld her comfort pretend. "I don't really know her well yet, so I should be fine."

"Mmmm, not exactly. Because remember, you're the new Chipotle all the guys are in line for, and it's like the damn Hunger Games out here for football players, meaning every girl has a problem with you by default." Maia bopped her gently on the head. "Physics, remember?"

"I think I'm going to be sick." And here she'd been worried over people judging her *taste in music*.

"So, the Dunn brothers! Colton is the second youngest of the trio: junior, soccer prodigy with a full ride to any college of his choice, probably reading a Marvel comic. Tanner skipped a grade so he's also a junior: literal genius, dresses like a Republican dad, sobs during the morning pledge of allegiance, will for sure end up President one day. Both clean-cut, preppy, rich. But they're apart of Brooks' little 'group', so they get up to some sneaky shit too."

Sadie fanned her overheated cheeks. Whatever stuffing was in there was definitely insulated. "Sneaky... as in..."

"Mayor and school principal Jay Dunn is their dad, and former debutante baker Elaine is their mom. They live in Lake Josey, the gated community east of town." Sadie was surprised to learn they had those here. "They're the perfect family, the suburban keen-as-mustard ones with big smiles in Honey Maid commercials."

"You say that like it's a bad thing," Sadie pointed out as if it'd been a mistake.

It wasn't. "I just don't buy any family being that perfect." Maia turned away for a second to redraft her brave face. "There's always... something."

"You mean... like a leaky roof, or lying about sorting your biodegradables?"

The brave altered to sympathy, to envy. "Sure."

The girls sat in silence for a moment, maybe two, because time liquefies in those southern landscapes. You can actually watch it melt if you stare down a straight highway on a scorched day; it's all runny. The clouds were a spread of white woolly dryer sheet in the sky. The distant clashing smacks of shoulder pads had a hale and engraving effect. Across the street, telephone poles were overgrown in clinging invasive Skunkvine, and a preschool sign with a rainbow on it had been eaten for breakfast by some prolific Carolina Jasmine.

The roof of Sadie's mouth had gone cottony and dehydrated, but she felt finely moisturized in other random places, in watching Brooks play. The finesse with which his rugged contours forced her to feel every part of her own skin, made her slightly involuntary and buzzy like a hummingbird. For once, she wanted to skip the terms and conditions. Simply put, Sadie wanted to wrap herself around his body like some Skunkvine.

"Another example," Maia spoke again suddenly like no time had passed, "the Lindley twins have the entire town fooled. Ever since the 'Birth of Jesus' Christmas play in kindergarten—Caleb played Joseph, Grace played a lamb—it's like the costumes never came off. Even if Caleb sleeps with half the girls in Florida and

Grace's nudes get passed around like Tic Tacs, they can do no wrong."

Sadie's gaze unwillingly floated to the panna cotta hair on a surfer's body, shamelessly flirting with a group of cheerleaders; exactly seven who were 'bending and snapping' over their poms. Sadie caught herself wondering how many of them he'd undressed.

Maia pointed at the two bombshell cheer captains reprimanding the squad from the mat: one con-artist gazelle and a Miss American beauty. "Grace and Mallory." Maia kept on going down the scandal sheet. "They started this all-girls 'bible study' in middle school, which it probably was at the time. I mean, jeez, they were like 12, you know? Then around a year back, I started hearing rumors about them sneaking college guys into Mal's bedroom, getting drunk and hooking up I guess. Grace especially... she's been... I don't know. She used to be different. Kind of like... well..." Maia foraged for the right word. "*You.*"

This surprised Sadie, and instinctively she saddened. "I wonder what happened."

"I think she just... grew up."

Sadie eventually nodded, even if it still didn't make any sense.

"The worst part is, Grace has been dating Sterling Ray since freshman year. He's that grubby Joe Dirt one by the fence." Sadie recognized the dirty-wife-beater-boy who'd pummeled her in the parking lot that morning. "Poor guy has no idea. Sterling could definitely use a shower, maybe some ADHD meds, but still that boy has never *not* had the biggest grin on his face. The sweetest jackass you'll ever meet. He has a heart."

"Everyone *has* a heart," Sadie helpfully patched her error. "We can't live without one."

Maia wanted to borrow her secret, how she'd managed to convert her rose colored glasses to contacts so no one could ever break them. "Hmph." She chuckled forlornly. "I must have met a few zombies then."

Disheartened, Sadie sat with that melancholy note. Her mind spun like a gyroscopic top. The more she knew, the more dreary it all felt: the sullied houses too close to the ground, squishy streets that swallowed up tires after a light sprinkle, how at night it was so quiet you'd think you've gone deaf, the way everyone's eyes looked just barely distorted, dimmed, as if they'd been saran wrapped in a blurring translucent veil. Sadie couldn't explain it, but everyone had it. Mallory. Grace. Caleb. Even Maia.

Even *Brooks.*

"Tell me about the Holdens now. Or… maybe don't. I'm a little scared after the rest of it." Sadie pulled her knees up on the step and packed herself into a ball.

Maia paused before continuing, because she knew it wouldn't be what she hoped. "I'm not an expert. I know just as much as anyone. It's the cliché small town tale. Brant Holden, their dad, was the token player at W-Hills high, failed going pro, pretty much dropped off that premature peak his high school graduation day, and now coaches to live through his sons. Well— live through Brooks. No one really pays attention to Duke."

That was rude of her to say, and as if to make up for it, Sadie declared, "I did."

"Then go with him." Maia ran out of sunflower seeds. She burst open a second bag. "If you know what's good for you—"

"Got it." Sadie cut her off, because she didn't *want* to know. Hello? Didn't anybody get that? One person had seemed to. "That Caleb guy… he's like… a player. Not just a football player, but like a *player*. Right?" Sadie inhaled a hard, uneasy breath. "And he's friends with Brooks…"

"Yes."

"Does that mean… is Brooks also a…"

"Douchebag?"

Not what she was going to say, but exactly what she meant. "Yes. That."

"If I'm being honest, Brooks has a bit of a… reputation." Maia searched for language with the most cushion. "I've never seen him with a girlfriend. From what I've heard, he doesn't spend more than one night with a girl. I'm sorry."

Sadie processed as her lashes fluttered in stiff winks, like waking up from heavy dreaming and there's guck in them fighting to keep them glued shut. "Sorry? You don't have to be sorry. I'm fine. Totally cool! I was just wondering anyway." She watched the boy with brown eyes take off his helmet, shake off the surely fragrant perspiration. "But you know, maybe, it's possible, he just hasn't met the right person. I mean—that's possible, right? That happens? Like, sometimes that happens."

"Sometimes." Maia whispered, and allowed a moment of silence for the death of her ideation, but knowing she'd still extend it like a dried flower between a book. "Just please, don't bet on being the one to change him. You're way too nice for that."

Nice. You're the nice girl. Let them have their fun, but you *play nice.* "Funny. That's exactly what my friend Becks said to me after Max Kallis tried to kiss me in a Sequoia Park porta potty. Except, not that last part. Complimenting something other than a mirror doesn't come natural to her. Not in a bad way, just how she is. Unapologetically sure of herself.

Maia turned insulted at that, and it was about time someone did. "Okay, your old friends clearly sucked. So, did you do it? Kiss him?"

"No." Sadie brushed it off, shrinking. "It was for the best though. Becks had liked Max for years, so…" She shrugged again, and that was it.

In an instant, Maia felt like she'd learned so much more about her. "Right."

"Maybe I shouldn't go tonight?"

"No, go. Just be a little stingier with your wishful thinking, you know?"

"No." Sadie blinked blankly. "I don't."

Maia was sort of glad she didn't. "Then you better make him fall madly in love with you. It's one or the other, home skillet."

Sadie knew she thought that, but Maia didn't know about the lucky ace up her sleeve. That soul mates tended to run in her family, and she'd been sent a sign. That there were two sets of brown eyes so her chances were better—

Shh, don't repeat that. Please, don't tell anyone.

Sadie giggled in soft fits as Maia sprang up and used the side railing as her stripper pole, shaking her butt like Beyonce does in her music videos. But not to impress anyone, it was actually more ridiculous. Maia reminded Sadie of Bellatrix Lestrange—crazy sorceress hair, a naughty fierceness in her spirit, unfearful of anything and everything—which must make her Luna Lovegood in comparison. A bizarre duo indeed.

"Wait." Sadie froze that instant and squinted down at the long green turf. "Is that… my *dad*?"

Caleb rammed into Brooks on the field, tackling him to the ground.

"WHAT WAS THAT? SON, YOU PULL THAT IN THE GAME NEXT WEEK AND YOU'LL BE SAYIN' BYE TO AUBURN! TAKE A LAP!" Brant's uvula vibrated against his angry volume, the rest of him set in the same stone they built Rome with. He adjusted his cap with strict red stitching that read 'Head Coach'.

Another man's approaching frame—much more relaxed and leisured—crossed his arms beside Brant. He was also in a cap but with the Chevrolet logo. "I always saw you as a softy," Henri cracked his aside; his twenty-year term of silence. "Shiet was I wrong." He planted his boots at the fifty-yard line, like the hotshot he didn't miss being.

Brant recognized the smiley sarcasm like it was a long-lost part of him, but said nothing. Suddenly, skilled claustrophobia bested him as if it'd never left; as if it'd been gradually inhabiting his skin like cigarette smoke to furniture, sinking it's toxin with subtle permanence over time. Brant would've never realized, never recognized it in himself—he turned to face his old friend—had it not been staring back at him now.

Henri had less wrinkles than he'd have imagined—even in the peak of junior acne days, he'd never used more than a cheap bar soap for face wash, when he did wash—more beard and, apparently, just the same amount of annoying humor. The informal cobalt shirt looked like one of the classic three he'd rotated in high school, and knowing Henri, it just might be. Even if he'd had a fortune out in California, made something great of those back-pocket inventions, he'd never show it. Probably still drives that beat-up red pickup.

"Might I suggest runnin' the ball a time or two? Your quarterbacks lookin' a little stiff but his legs work just fine," Henri suggested, as Henri would.

Still, Brant didn't budge.

Henri kicked up the humorist another level. "Strange bein' back on this field, ain't it?" He smacked a hand to his mouth. "Damn, I'm sorry. I forgot. For you this is just another afternoon at home, isn't it?" In other words: *How's it feel bein' the sucker who stayed? How's it feel to never get out?* Except, if you knew the circumstances: *How's it feel bein' the better man, after all?*

Brant looked him straight in the eye. "Why'd you come here, Bexley?"

"You didn't give me much choice now, did you? You check your phone? I texted, waited, took my crossbow out in the groves this mornin' to try and scare out some of those coyotes. I was out there for hours. When I came back, still no answer. So I asked myself: where can I go, where I *know* I'll find you?" Henri scanned the stomping grounds that'd raised them. "So here I am."

"I meant," Brant grumbled, and in a strange note of desperation not akin to him, "why did you come back to *Weston Hills?*"

Henri seemed to have suddenly misplaced his funny bone, and there was a long pause before he knew what to say. "Oh... well I, I came to tie up some loose ends."

"Those ends would've tied themselves up by now, I'd say."

"I'd say the same," Henri put forth more critically, "and we'd both be wrong."

Brant was now spewing with frustration. His eyes checked around in deep-rooted paranoid habit, as if they were being watched. "Whatever you're here for, whatever you need, I want no part of it."

"You already *are* a part of it." Hushed now, as if he could feel it too. The acid well of sins Henri was carrying inside eroded another layer. "You won't be able to endure this one away Brant, I assure you. It ain't goin' away on it's own."

The two hardy men maintained their poker faces until

someone called for the coach. Henri didn't linger, and Brant watched the back of his head as he walked away, taken back to the last time he'd done so, disappearing up the pitch-black driveway, in the heart of an orange tree maze... *on that one grave night in May.*

"Is this heat makin' me loony or did I just see you talkin' to Henri Bexley?!" Kelly darted towards the coach in her usual lanyard-clinking, firecracker form. "My heavens! I haven't seen him since—"

"Graduation," Brant finished.

Kelly shook her head, absolutely gobsmacked. "Well from what I remember, when you and I weren't *occupied* behind the bleachers, you two were pretty inseparable back then. You know what? Why don't we invite him over for dinner?"

"I don't think—"

"I'm sure that hardworkin', big-time-travelin' woodsman could use some mustard greens and fried okra. I'll whip up some buttermilk biscuits! You remember how he loved those, don't you?"

"Hun, I—"

"Oh, this is so dandy!" Perhaps a leg in the past would help to bring him back to her. "How about Wednesday? Thursday? Should we invite the whole family or do you wanna first—"

"I don't have time for dinners!" The coach barked much harsher than a husband should *ever* pitch to a wife. More publicly, too.

Kelly scrunched a doubtful lip, doing that *I'm not going to give you the answer but I will help you get there* bit she used on her students. "I think you can find the time for an old friend darlin', mhm?"

"You know what I think? I think I have a team gettin' ready for the most important season of their lives. Our SON gettin' ready for the rest of his life, in case *you forgot!*"

Kelly didn't waver, didn't glance around embarrassingly to see who'd heard. Women smell weakness like sharks smell blood, and—as everyone knows—it is the wife's fragility that is blessing to a husband's mistress. Kelly hadn't yet given up on their marriage. Not yet.

"Forget?" she said, calm and forgiving. "You really think I could forget? With the practices, games, dinners, booster meetings, fundraisers and rallies servin' as reminder? No, dear. I am your wife, in case *you* forgot." Kelly searched up at him longingly. "Dinner will be ready at six."

Swiveling in her Skechers, Kelly busied herself wrapping ice packs for the boys, busy handing out waters, busy picking up dirty towels, busy being busy. Lord only knows what would happen, the day she stopped being busy.

All the while Sadie had watched it unfold, like watching a game of chess. She'd never understood chess.

CHAPTER FIVE

Moss, Moxie, and Minor Scrapes

Tangerine light glazed every inch of Sadie's bedroom as the sun dipped behind the radial gardens of citrus trees. Orange had always been her least favorite color, but here, overlooking her window, she'd never witnessed a more breathtaking palette.

After checking all her angles in the oval mirror, staring down her armpit fat for five minutes, Sadie pressed on her guava lip balm where she'd like to be kissed—*crap*—the tiny can of salve dropped and drizzled between her legs. She wiped it off with a tissue, hoping the wet mark would dry quickly from her shorts.

She'd opted out her usual ruffled dress for some Levi's denim cut-offs and a silk camisole. *The* silk cami: ivory and spaghetti-strapped and one Becks had worn to movie premiere after parties, swearing it was the lucky juju in her reign of seduction. It still smelled like champagne, which she'd once spilled to make it see-through. Becks had given it to Sadie as a going away present, and a *getting-it-on* present, right before she'd made a whispery joke about Sadie being a virgin until thirty.

Her phone buzzed punctually on her dresser. *'Pulling up'*.

"Angelic, you are!" Her mother sang from the living room where she was waving kindled palo santo over an oceanic abalone bowl, then returned to the stove in the kitchen that was overflowing with aroma-rich spices. Indeed, Margot was cooking her renowned soup of root vegetables no ones ever heard of—sunchokes and rutabaga—while Henri supervised over a beer.

"Angels are kind of like nuns, right? With the temperance,

and such." Henri flinched at his daughter's exposed legs, and it triggered his sciatica. He opened his arms out. "Our little angel!"

Sadie curtsied with an airy *ha-ha*, and slid into her shoes. "So what's my curfew?"

Her parents exchanged a confused look.

"Curfew?" Margot asked with a laugh. "You've never had a curfew."

"Okay yeah, but I probably *should* have one now that I'm getting to that age. Don't you think? To keep me in line and stuff."

"In *line?*" Margot had a wild time with that as she stirred the steaming broth, and it irked Sadie how they weren't taking it seriously. "Okay, if it's that important to you, let's say 11. That will be your curfew." She wagged a finger of warning. "And not a second later, young lady!"

"Angels don't kiss, right? They're huggers. Everyone knows they're huggers." Henri was still stuck on that. "What's this boy's name again?"

"Brooks," Sadie replied after a pause.

"Brooks what?" Henri asked with apprehension.

"Brooks… Holden." She observed the strange wilting it did to his expression. It was a very odd reaction. "You know who he is, don't you? You must somewhat, because I saw you talking to his dad today."

"That's… right." Henri nodded slowly. *Did his flower child just corner him?* Impressive. "The Holdens are a highly respected family in town. I'm sure if Brooks is anything like his father," he gulped with misery, "you'll have yourself an exciting night. Full of *hugs*, but not long ones." He grinned despite the loss of feeling in his legs. "Two second limit on the hugs."

"Of course." Sadie smiled like a winner.

"Can you… do me just one favor? To give your daddy some peace of mind?"

"Sure."

"Mention your dads got a gun." He patted her shoulder to make it a done deal. "Doesn't have to be a long conversation, just slip it in somewhere. Will you?"

Sadie smiled again, then winged straight into his warm fireplace chest, because he had that watery look in his eye and usually this is the part where he bolts speedily from the room. *Not this time*, she thought, and imprisoned him there. "Hey dad," Sadie looked up, arms still wound and smelling his shirt.

Henri's glassy eyes took silent photographs, which he did more often than anyone knew. "Yeah darlin'?"

Her father's calming country accent had always been a 'him' thing, because she'd never heard it on anyone else. And now, here she was in a scary foreign wilderness that coddled her with *darlin's*, and that very thing made it feel most like home. "You know I'll always be me, right?"

Henri laughed that off, but not really. "Well, of course."

"Like, I'll always be the same girl with pigtails, doing headstands in the living room."

He seemed to visit a specific memory out of the millions, and somehow she knew just the one. "I haven't seen those pigtails in years."

"Yeah, but you know. In theory." Sadie was overcome by a lovely tumble of sentiment. "You know?"

Henri was trouble-free, steady as the surface of a millpond, but not really. Not at all. "I know."

"Okay. Good." She inhaled once more. "Well, I better go."

He didn't answer right away, but a few silent photographs later, "You go run off now."

Sadie adjusted her mature-woman camisole and slipped out the door, just as a white F-150 pulled up the driveway.

Henri lingered by the window curtain, watching her scramble up the passenger side, knowing too well what the endorphin-hungry boy was thinking as she did. "You think it's safe to let her go out with some kid we don't know?"

"You just said you knew his parents." Margot aired the mashed potatoes, paying him little mind. "Come sit down and eat your soup." The fridge door swung open. "Did you skip your celery this morning?"

"A highly respected family 'round town, is what I said," Henri mumbled back. "You know who else is highly respected?" He frowned. "Politicians."

"Don't make me sage *you*," Margot cautioned. "Oh honey, don't you remember bein' her age? They're just havin' a little fun."

Henri straightened like he'd been shocked with a taser. "Darlin', I love the hell out of you, but your words really ain't helpin. Jesus Christ——" Sciatica pricking, he fumbled through a drawer of miscellaneous. "Where's that arnica cream you like to carry around? My back is killin' me. You know, my sciatica never acted up like this when she still had those pigtails. Not once."

Margot smiled sympathetically, passing him the spatula for licking, then the homeopathic lotion from her purse. "Our daughter is a smart girl. She was raised by you, wasn't she? Here, take some magnesium."

"For my back?"

"That, and the *nerves*," she half teased before returning to stirring, humming, blissfully uninformed on the *go big or go homes* that 'kids' get caught up in, when the moss looks like security bumpers, and the dramas become the joyrides in a bored town, with bored nights.

They make their own fun, Henri knew. But sometimes, some of them don't make it. "We raised a good girl." He salved just a little, until he caught the cagey taillights hanging on by a thread. "Huh," he grunted in disapproval.

"What *now*?"

Henri sulked. "The boy drives a Ford."

The F-150 cruised steadily down Paddock Road, over HeLeup Hill, gaining speed from then on.

Once Sadie had put on her seat belt, Brooks opened with a compliment, "You look nice."

That stupid, mediocre word *again*. Sadie despised it; she had an overwhelming need to break free of it. After a disappointed, "Thanks," she pulled her shirt lower and said, "you too," although he was dressed rather casual for the special occasion: cotton lounge shorts and a black hoodie without a brand label to let her know if it was GAP or Gucci. In searching for a logo, Sadie realized it was something her friends would've asked her after the date, but that she in fact, couldn't care less.

The Mr. Zog's 'Sex Wax' scented car fell quiet and Sadie's hands sweaty as she stared at the absurd air freshener dangling from the mirror, racking her brain for an epic thing to say… nada. All she could do was sit there like a petrified gargoyle. It was infuriating; she came up with romantic car-scenes packed with chemistry in her head all the time, but she didn't know how to *do* it. She needed to learn how to do it.

Did they even have anything in common, besides awkward age and a continual current of springtime hormones? Did they need to? Sadie was positive Brooks had never fawned over soliloquies, and she couldn't name a single NFL guy besides Tom Grady (so none).

"I have a spot I want to show you after the bonfire. Do you have a curfew?" Brooks finally asked, and she was oh so grateful.

"Yes, 11 o'clock," Sadie bragged proudly, then in an unfitting kittenish manner that gave away she was a novice at this, "but we can totally break that."

He also didn't take it seriously. He chuckled with a sexy hum at the end. "We'll see."

"How *did* you find where I live, by the way?" Falling acorns tapped the roof as they talked.

"Everyone knows the Bexley house," Brooks answered scarcely, then snorted into a smile that turned on a fan and depressurized the small space. "Mrs. Ida and Mr. Lance were recognized people, a lot of stature but discreet about it. They made donations to the football team every year, but they never came to any games. I think it was their way of keepin' the peanut gallery at bay. They were private, which is highly discouraged in these parts, and no one could complain if they had their money." He slapped his knee like it was a glorious running joke that tickled his ribs every time. "Genius."

It was the longest duration she'd ever heard him speak, doubly notable, because it was about her grandparents. The energy behind his words honored them with beautiful regard.

Sadie wiped her eye and waited for more, because they were gone and this was all she had left, but also it made the cavity intimate.

Brooks obliged, resting on the wheel and tapping mindlessly to the John Mayer he'd put on for her. "Back when I was a knuckle-headed middle schooler, I agreed to a house-eggin' spree with Caleb and Levi. It was Halloween night and we were bored," he justified sheepishly. "Your house was our gran' finale, because Lance had three gun safes in his garage and part of the thrill was in takin' a bullet. Like I said, knuckle-headed. So there we were, rollin' up on our bikes, but in the middle of the ambush Ida comes out and starts hurlin' some back. Except they were rotten, like *bad*, and after the counterattack we smelled like sewer water and pet store fish food on a hot day." He laughed painlessly, and the specialness of that night lingered in it. "Definitely woulda preferred a bullet. My hair stunk for weeks."

Little chokes of gasp escaped from Sadie's parted lips. He had *memories* of them, *experiences* with them. What are the chances of that? "That sounds like grandma, at least I think," she said. "I only had one week with them in the summers, when my parents would ship me off with a bag of Luna Bars and bugspray."

"Yea, I know. I remember you."

"You—*wait*—huh?"

He'd already said too much. "Well… I saw you once. You were with Mr. Lance up at the produce stand on Eiland, the day they had Key West shrimp by the bags. You had on pink heart sunglasses and you wanted kiwi." She was looking at him now how she'd probably looked at Zac Efron back then. "I wasn't stalkin' you, I promise, just behind you in line." Brooks glanced once more at her adoring disbelief, because it felt rehabilitating and he really needed it. "Told you we ain't forget a face. Least, I don't."

"That was five years ago." Her eyes sparkled damp while she recollected the memory, that before now, had been entirely uninteresting. It'd been July 3rd, which she remembered distinctly because she'd missed Tenley's America-themed sleepover and projected it the whole trip. "We were preparing for a pontoon boat day in Homosassa. Grandpa wanted mangos, I wanted kiwis, and yet we ended up with ice cream cones." Brooks felt her smile without having to look. "It was the last summer… before…" Her voice dropped rashly like from a cloud's ledge. "The cancer came quick, and after grandma was gone, grandpa only stuck around a week later."

"That's real sad. I'm so sorry."

"Her passing was yes, but grandpa's I felt coming. Can you imagine loving someone so much that their departure literally makes your heart stop beating? That was them. It was like he decided—*alrighty, guess that means I'm headin' out too*—and just went to her, as if their souls couldn't exist in a world without the other." Sadie yearned all aswoon at a Texaco Food Mart. "You know what I mean?"

"Like the old couple in The Notebook?"

It wasn't that impressive, really. Every guy has been forced to sit through it at least once.

"Exactly!" She perched up in the seat, defying the belt that was supposed to prevent that. "Just like them."

Brooks changed the music to something overplayed and Drake. "Too bad those cases are pretty rare. Like, the whole soul mate thing. It's better not to expect it, right?"

Completely absorbed, Sadie obliviously hummed back, "Mhmmm," which was the sound of her double dipping a big fat spoon into that pool of expectation. She could see it so clearly. *That* was the problem.

The quarterback and the romantic sat quietly for the rest of Paddock; the chief artery back road; lined with untrimmed palms, level pastures, and rectangle homes with lime green algae thriving on all sides.

A few minutes later, the F-150 arrived smoothly to grandiose gates with a fancy wrought-iron *LJ* in the middle. Lake Josey: where every home had a cleaning lady, doorbells came with a symphony of wind chimes, Kate Spade mimosa-a-day mothers power walked *all* the way to the clubhouse bar, and dads in clean Lacoste visors golfed the lush course and debated the one thing they all had in common (taxes). The houses were all three-story with salt water pools, steam showers, and four-car-garages, organized around a nature-strewn lake.

Brooks rolled down his window to give the security guard a salute.

"Ah! Good evening Mr. Holden! Nice to see ya!" An older, round-faced gentleman in a bolo tie roared. "Where to?"

"The Dunn house, sir."

"Sure, sure!" He handed a prewritten pass. "I shoulda guessed! Seems like jus' yesterday you and Shelby were catchin' earth worms and ridin' around on those dicey Ripstiks! Man oh man, it was a real treat to watch y'all kids. Well anywho, you're good to go now. Just right up on the dash there, you know the drill."

"Thank you, Joe. You have a good night now."

"You bet. The wife and I are lookin' forward to seein' you on that field!"

"Thank you sir, I appreciate that. Tell Mrs. Pam I said hello, and that I'm lookin' forward to some more of that homemade taffy."

"Oh, I'll tell her! You betcha!" The man beamed and it was obvious; he'd be telling people about this for weeks.

The iron gates split open down the middle as Sadie thought, *what's a Ripstik,* and other jealous things she didn't want to admit. But it wasn't traditional jealousy; she was envious of all the phases of life Shelby'd had with him. From capture-the-flag flirting, to prank *67 calls, to seeing their bodies grow and change, making gawky faces at each other when the science teacher goes over what that means in Human Growth and Development class. Brooks and Shelby got to bloom side by side, and that was really cool.

Sadie distracted herself by admiring the beach-house-style mini mansions and their cute matching mailboxes, the view gradually migrating as if from a slow carousel. She archived the sensation of Brooks' hand softly landing on her bare thigh, miles from her knee and nearing the opposite cusp, above where her cut-offs cut *off.*

He has a reputation, Maia's words intruded, but Sadie's

optimism gifts kicked into overdrive and she'd entirely forgotten by the time they reached the house.

Once they'd parked at the cluster of trucks in the yard, Brooks went around front to open the door for her.

Their third touch, mind you. Sadie blundered down because she'd forgotten to heed the surplus of room between the seat and ground; the enormous rubber tires and huge molten rims with way more girth than the tiny Prius cars Becks would get picked up in for her dates. But that wasn't important. Or actually, it was.

Brooks caught her on the way down, and swear to *God*, his entire broken arm almost ripped off. Through the ricks and vertigo, he muffled curse words into her golden hair to antidote them, as Sadie happily blushed with the thought: *Aw, he kissed my head.*

Up the roundabout driveway they went.

The couplet reached a fire pit surrounded by premium patio couches and a foldable table of Mountain Dew, Sour Patch Kids, and PG board games in a Target shopping bag. Dragonflies and other native insects hovered over solar charged lanterns, accompanied by smiling garden gnomes and a sign by the brightly red painted door: *Love Lives Here.* An old basketball net, Wilson Ultra tennis rackets and speckled soccer balls were amongst the items peeking from the garage, but no skeletons, to which Sadie would be sure to let Maia know so that next time she would come. She still didn't understand why she hadn't come.

The party turned surly and whispery at their arrival. *Her* arrival.

Shelby's fist crumpled a s'more, and she couldn't help it—she charged at them. "Um, hello? Invitation *only.*"

Brooks let go of Sadie's hand, because his pockets apparently needed them more. He rocked in his Nikes. "Yo, Shelby, this is —"

"We've met." Shelby glared at the trespassing girl, instead of the unaware boy who was technically at fault.

Sadie curtsied, and Shelby stepped back three feet like she was afraid of contracting the mechanism. "H—hi! I, um, like your outfit."

Shelby was in an oversized Tampa Bay Lightning hockey tee with nacho cheese stains, gray tube over-the-calf-socks, and Crocs. "Mhm, I'm sure." She took a look-see at the lingerie tissue Sadie had apparently fashioned as a top. "You wanna trade shirts then? If you like it so much?"

"Oh… no thank you."

"Didn't think so." *What did she say she was allergic to again? Gluten?* Shelby eyed a box of Chips Ahoy. "You know what? I'd *love* for you to stay! Are you hungry? Do you want a snack?" She shoved the box at her, blowing crumbs in her direction in case that was enough to do her in. "Have some cookies!"

"Remember, I——"

"*Cookies!*"

Sadie accepted it with a frightened smile and ate three, and tomorrow she'd curl up on the floor with a wrenching stomachache. Shelby would too, for different reasons.

The fire began to blizzard in skittish crackling embers, as Brooks led Sadie to their seat amongst the other handful of attractive teens in town.

Jay Dunn—in an immaculately tailored suit and designer dress shoes—and lady Elaine—matching white pinstripe blazer and skirt—emerged in a power-couple catwalk. Catch phrases and eager hellos erupted from the band of high schoolers, each waiting their turn to be acknowledged.

"Hey Mr. Jay!" Brooks hollered, and cut past the ordinary rest.

"Woah!" The tree-trunk of a man ripped into a mimed football maneuver, hurling a pretend pass. "Look at Mr. Quarterback roastin' mallows on our turf! I thought that was you, Golden Holden!" Clamping a hand on his shoulder—*shit*—and using the other for a chummy noogie. "How's that billion dollar arm doin', champ?"

"Like brand new, sir!" Brooks screamed inside.

"Atta boy!" With a high five, Jay turned to the rest of the disciples. "Alright kids, the Mrs. and I are goin' out on the town for the night. Apparently I'm bein' honored at some fancy schmancy banquet up at city hall. Told 'em I don't need nothin' like it, reckon it ain't gon' be nothin' compared to a basket of Buck's wings but I figured… hey, I'll make an appearance to keep 'em happy." He threw up his arm before patting it funkily on his wife's lace glove. "Next time I'm stayin' home and partyin' it up with you youngsters! Now y'all be good, you hear me? And don't forget it's a school night."

"You got it, Mr. Jay!" Caleb plunged an enthusiastic thumbs up, Christian-boy-mode in full effect. "Thank you for havin' us over. And the lemonade—you've really out done yourself, Mrs. Elaine! I taste lavender. Did you use lavender?"

The Marilyn-esque woman smiled splendidly but partially in response, as if the smile itself was keeping a weather eye on things. Perhaps it had to do with how her arms swaddled herself like the Spanx she didn't need, the sidewards tilt away from the man at her hip, the minimal but noticeable flinches, that made Elaine appear unrested. She wore the same wary face as Sadie's mother right before an ugly movie scene, where bad guys do bad things, and she fast forwards with a *we can skip this part, it won't make us feel good* but makes it impossible to understand the rest of the movie.

"Caleb, I'm puttin' you in charge. You keep these kids in line, alright?" Jay said with a wink.

"You can count on me, sir!" The cunning boy smirked as the eerie blue stars turned on as wildly above, as they did in his eyes. "I'll keep 'em real tamed."

Elaine raised an effete hand, suggesting her speaking would otherwise be out of turn. "There's extra snacks in the kitchen if anyone gets hungry, and more sodas in the pantry, and ice in the freezer—"

"Thanks mom!" Shelby adjourned with a lift of a game box from the Target bag. "Who wants to play a game of Risk? I call red!"

It seemed to satisfy the parental unit, and Jay led them down the bonny landscaping to a luxury Mercedes.

The party fell silent as the tires rolled away, until the very last of the silver exterior had blended into the Grandfather Oaks…

Caleb stomped high and cocky on the table. He shepherded

his friends like sheep. "You heard the man. I'm in charge. Now, where's the booze?"

Levi and Colton had already taken up arms with setting up the beer pong table. Mallory fished a shoplifted handle of Bacardi from a Michael Kors tote and began pouring shots in bosomy Betty Boop glasses. Shelby tore open a case of Coors and went to work distributing. Ali helped her distribute, right after she'd lit a tight twig of rolling paper and fastened it at her lips. Grace straddled Sterling's tinged Wrangler jeans and started posting the way she'd learned riding English horseback.

The aggressive music, purposeful dancing, public display of clothed S-E-X...

In a matter of seconds, Sadie's date had been hijacked. She'd really gotten her hopes up about Risk.

"I'll go make us some drinks," Brooks whispered, before giving Sadie's shaky fingers a squeeze and leaving her unattended.

She preoccupied herself with warming her hands over the fire, though it was 82 degrees even after sunset, and her under boob sweat was threatening to streak.

"You'll have to excuse my sister. She's not too big on the whole bein' nice thing, though you seem to really tick her off. What's your secret, Sadie?" Tanner introduced himself in a senator's getup and gargantuan cowboy hat.

Sadie turned ruby hued at his comment, though it hadn't felt patronizing. "Tanner, yes. I've heard about you."

"Likewise." He smiled without an ounce of sly subtext; it was just a regular smile. "I'll be applying to Berkeley's political science program in a few months, you'll have to tell me more about California sometime! The west coaster life. Ya know, hang ten and all that." He attempted the shaka hand move but did Spiderman instead.

"Hmm, let me think. You ever heard of tempeh?"

Tanner's brow dipped quizzically. "Does it have something to do with weed?"

"No. Wait—yeah, no.

"Then no."

"I'd look into it. It's a good conversation starter."

"Cool! Thanks!" Tanner grinned with a dorky overbite—kind of a skinny Chunk from The Goonies— and Sadie realized he reminded her of a boy from her old school: Jeremiah. A Lord Of The Rings addict, grilled cheese advocate, stockier boy who'd grown up on the other side of Mulholland, and who every March brought Sadie homemade birthday brownies, up until last year, when Becks had slammed the door in his face. The door was closed, but it wasn't soundproof, so he'd heard Becks when she'd said, "The only way that loser is getting a piece of you, is if he ends up some grotesquely loaded tech inventor in Silicone Valley. We'll check back in ten years." Sadie didn't sleep for days after; it was horrible. She found out later Jeremiah's mom had been having an affair with Becks' dad.

"So what's the deal with Orville this year? They still got Cash wide receivin'?" Sterling kicked back on a cooler, girlfriend still suckling his square earring stud. He packed some chewing tobacco in his lower gums and slurped on the juices.

Levi shook a spurred 'no' and racked red plastic cups into a diamond shape over the table. "Heard he transferred to Tampa. You already know those coaches probably recruitin' on the low again."

To say the least, this was… *very* big news. The teenagers hooted and chugged in celebration.

"Aw hell! Ain't no way they're winnin' this war now!" Sterling guffawed.

"War?" Sadie piped in politely, because that sounded intense. Frankly, a little alarming. The entire circle chastised with looks that could beat the living daylights out of someone, as if she'd mentioned 'Tom Grady'.

"The eight-mile *war* is a football game." Tanner came to her rescue, not as easily petulant as the rest of them. "Alright, so, Weston Hills and Orville have been rival high schools since our grandparents were playin'. The schools are exactly eight miles apart, thus… eight-mile war," he repeated almost holily, and with a thicker hillbilly accent as if required for such a telling.

Sterling revved over his favorite topic. "That's right!" He

marched up and spit smelly charcoal froth in a cup, some dripping in Grace's pony. "Most important event that happens in this town! No—the *world*!"

"Football?" Sadie made sure she was still on the same page. "Like, with the brown ball with the pointed ends and the yellow pole thingies…" She got the sense she should stop there.

Now, Sterling turned Rottweiler-provoked, but then chillaxed from the drippy tobacco. "I understand you're not from around here, so I can't blame you foreigners for questionin' our American sports."

"Oh no, I'm from Cal—"

A slow moist breath slithered up Sadie's ear, and jarred a startled hiccup in her throat. "Hey there, princess." Caleb had been inches behind her the whole time, and the discovery made her squirm like he'd used one of those head ticklers from Bed Bath and Beyond on her whole body. He sat down and carried on with visually making a meal out of her, while Tanner gave bonus facts.

"Can't forget that whoever wins the eight-mile game gets the woods behind Ogilbee Park for a whole year. It's a pretty darn sweet spot; just easy enough to find, deep enough for no cops to want to follow. You'll see." His lucky ten-gallon cap dipped. "This year is *our* year."

Finally, Sadie's soul mate candidate returned with their beverages. He was even sexier in the firelight. "Sorry, Ali was hogging the vodka. Vodka is okay, right?" Brooks asked.

"Totally! I love vodka! It's my go-to, actually." But as Sadie gulped down the liquid like a parched child with apple juice, her violent coughing said otherwise.

"Too strong?" Brooks teased and handed her a napkin. "Do you want me to get you a… *different* go-to?"

"No, no. I'm fine. It's just… been a while." Sadie took another large gulp and turned into a pufferfish from holding it in her cheeks; there was room.

"Yeah." Brooks couldn't help but laugh in an endeared way. "I can tell." Then he affectionately slid a muscly arm around her, and kept on grinning like it might never leave his once-moody face, and his close friends noticed like gravity had flipped inside out, because in all the years of knowing Brooks Holden, they'd never seen him like this.

An hour later, the nightfall had sharply amplified, and that darkness can be hard for some people who have dark things already living inside them. It could help to talk about it, but drinking looks cooler—doesn't it?

A hunched over Grace wobbled to the table of alcohol, hazier and hazier, feeling better. Mallory was there too, her best friend in the rhinestone Miss Me jeans. "Hey Mal, can I talk to you about somethin'?" Grace asked with a heavy chest.

"Anything, babe." Mallory didn't glance up; she was scrolling Poshmark on her phone.

"Do you... remember that party we went to with Avery Owens?" Grace kept stumbling, losing her balance. "Like a while back? Chris Corwin and some of those guys might've been there. Do you... do you remember?" She stubbed her toe hard so it bled profusely on her Jack Rogers sandals. "Oh... I didn't mean to—"

Mallory sighed dramatically, because she was tired of being the drunk girl's babysitter. It was the same thing every time. Kamikaze Gracie, from schoolgirl to sloppy before anyone else has even finished their first drink, headed straight towards topless waitressing some ashtray on the Ybor Strip. I mean, what more could you expect from her parents shoving God down her throat like it was Activia yogurt, but still. "Babe, go chug some Dasani, then we'll talk. Kay?" Mallory unscrewed a clear ominous bottle of moonshine, the only bottle still untouched. "In the meantime, I'm goin' to go spike Sadie's drink with *this*, so she makes a complete fool of herself in front of Brooks and life can go back to normal." She blew a snappy bubble with her gum.

"But—"

The upper lip Mallory's mother had over lined for her tightened. "Water." She pointed. "Now."

Grace tripped some more on slippery air. "Talk later? Promise?"

"Call me tomorrow, yeah? When you're hungover out of your

mind and thinking of trying that gross pickle juice thing again."
Mallory giggled freely, lavish and playful, like someone who's still
gullible. "Pedis and Panera on me!"

"Pedis and Panera," Grace repeated—alone once again—
recognizing how disgustingly pointless those two things, like most
things in life, were. She faded in and out, hugging her most loyal
listener tightly to her chest: goes by Jack, last name Daniels. You
know him? She took a relieving swig, then another. The strong
substances dependably caused the world to turn slower, and
tonight she wondered how many it would take... for it to stop
altogether. Grace Lindley, blessed pastor's daughter and role
model starlet, poured another.

Sadie, heavily distracted by the hot rough fingers stroking her
wrist, was oblivious as Mallory topped off her red cup, mixed
with a cocktail umbrella, and stashed the outlaw bottle behind a
lawn gnome. Zeroing in, Mallory watched her pick it up and...
hold it? For twenty freaking minutes? Com' on virgin Mary. Drink!

"I'd like to propose a toast!" Mallory announced once she
was sure Sadie was planning on running to the bathroom and
pouring it down the drain. "To our latest addition, who I for one,
think is just as cute as a bug in a rug! Cheers to officially
welcomin' a new friend: Sadie Brentley!"

"Bexley," Sadie corrected under her breath, knowing it didn't
matter how much dowdy country jargon or bad grammar or
weird bug similes she used, that girl language was girl language—
a rosy contact popped out—and this girl was a bitch.

There was a long pause of dubious inactivity, before the rest
lifted their cups towards the nettings of soft moss swinging above;
their special security blankets handmade by God who must've
known they would need them.

"Friendship! Yay! Drink UP everybody!" Mallory suddenly
paid mind to the invisible corset erecting her waist, and thought
maybe her mother got phone alerts every time she slouched, and
would make her take daily barre classes again until her spine
stood tall enough. "Chug! Chug! Chu—"

A hushed gritty voice rustled from the bushes by the pool
screen, as one single bullet of orange paint exploded on Grace's

ass, and the rest… was some bred-in-the-bone history. The unidentified company declared themselves with howls; *coonhound* howls. Then, they attacked.

"Coonhound Nation!" a husky voice clamored as the party crashers emerged from the surrounding golf course, piled on stolen clubhouse carts, with a few more on foot. A dingy truck that didn't belong screeched in front of the house, and one boy planted an orange and black flag on the lawn with as much glory for the taking as Neil Armstrong. Acts of war began flailing left and right.

"Call Of Duty: Central Florida Suburbia," Shelby groaned with annoyance, before casually taking out a black expandable baton from under her seat. In a total badass way, she singsonged, "Lights out, boys."

Meanwhile, Sadie just watched in horror as the figures in hoods took over like animals in the wild, beating their chests, shooting yellow 'liquid' (Gatorade, but how would she know) with plastic water guns, and throwing water balloons of the same stuff.

They were on all sides now. Rounds and rounds of paintballs terminated gnomes. The Orville guys keyed cars while Weston Hills ones slashed tires. Grace hurled on herself, Sterling took a leak on some garden roses, Levi and Caleb stormed out of the garage swinging baseball bats—just a regular school night, really.

It didn't take long for Caleb to put a name to the leader of the ambush, the very toerag who'd recently bumped himself to first place on his hitlist: Cameron Dickson. He couldn't believe it. First, the clown smashes up Brooks' arm—which maybe if Cameron didn't consist of a sack of hush puppies would've left some real damage—then shows his face *here*? The guy had nerve, but Caleb had more. He went for the kneecaps. Have you ever seen someone play football without kneecaps?

"It's not worth it!" Brooks called after him, knowing just how blind groomed hatred could be. That there was a fine line between payback and a felony. That Caleb wouldn't care.

"I got him!" Levi beat him there with a doggedness atypical to him, strangling the head of blonde with more effort than needed. He shoved Caleb on his back so it dazed him. Truth be told, Levi was protecting for two. "*Leave it*, Caleb!"

The so-called saintly boy got so pissed that he spit. "What the —WHOSE SIDE ARE YOU ON?!"

Amid the few safe seconds of struggle, Cameron Dickson nodded at Levi Tucker; Levi Tucker nodded back at Cameron Dickson. Tonight, that was it.

Sadie still hadn't unfrozen when Brooks shielded her under a scratchy fleece blanket—the circumstances wouldn't erase the facts, Sadie counted touch *six*—rushing them both around the house, down the drive, and ducking behind a bird-of-paradise's big banana-shaped leaves.

"You okay? You alright? You sprain anything?" Brooks checked her for paint, for injury, then studied her expression to see if he'd messed up for good. "I'm so, *so* sorry."

"No... I'm fine." She could barely catch her breath. "I'm more than fine. I'm great. I'm... *wow*! That was exciting!" A new side of her effloresced and burst forth, like a true night-blooming Phlox flower, only glowing after hours. "Does that happen a lot?"

Brooks exhaled in relief. "Sometimes, once or twice."

"A year?"

"Week."

Sadie shivered with delight. "Where to next?"

They snuck around back, hopping from one heroic oak to the next, so they wouldn't be seen sneaking away. Soon, the two escapees had scampered to a soft knobby path with an abundance of tropical foliage and some toads snoring under the shrubbery. Sadie's legs pushed double time down the detour to keep up.

Brooks had clearly taken the secret passageway a hundred times; the impressions in the dirt matched his Nike soles perfectly; but there was a second set of footprints, too. Daintier, wedgier, girlier.

Like magic, a silhouette appeared between two trunks, resembling a mirror image to Brooks but one that made Sadie a ghost. Then she noticed the brown eyes were kinder and deeper set, and the figure wore boat shoes. Duke Holden—*alone in the thorny thickets?*

Brooks turned on his phone flashlight. "Who invited *you*?"

"Hmm, let's see," Duke stalled them. "Colton. Tanner. Shelby." He shrugged a little smugly. "Oh, and Mrs. Elaine tagged me in a flyer on Facebook. She said there'd be Risk."

Sadie half-smiled but pretended to sneeze to cover it up. "You're funny, and unfortunately late. Party's over, dude."

"Bless you," Duke said to Sadie, and then to Brooks, "Bummer."

It was pitch jet outside, the only source of light coming from the fire pit in the distance, but Sadie had no doubt Duke's eyes were checking hers for some kind of cue.

"From the looks of it, the party's just begun." He peered past them. "Where y'all goin'?" Of course, he already knew the answer. "You really passin' up the opportunity to shank a few of Orville's best show dogs?" His gaze narrowed strategically. "What would the team think?"

"Maybe all three of us should just go back?" Sadie suggested, teetering.

"Nah, it's fine. Duke can handle 'em. That's what he's here for, ain't it?" Brooks fixated on his brother with an air of warning. "For *backup*, right?" He pulled closer his decorative moonflower. "I've had enough of those idiots for one night. Just go and make sure no one burns down Jay and Elaine's house, alright?"

Duke was still for seconds. "Yeah. Sure."

They left him there alone in the thickets.

In their flee, Sadie suddenly longed for her journal, sensing the sharp unexpressed words, a sophisticated unease clogged like searing alphabet soup at the tip of her throat. She pictured the velvet cover: smooth then coarse as her fingers grazed across, depending on which direction she went. There were ten pages inside addressed to Brooks, and only one, but *at least* one, for Duke.

CHAPTER SIX

The Dock, and Everything That Came After

The moon unveiled and reflected an orb over the still Lake Josey basin, acting as lighthouse for Brooks and Sadie as they finessed a path through anthills, mole holes and prickly tick-trefoil plants that attached green stickers on their clothes. After about five minutes, they'd made it down to the base where the grass was wet and marshy. The silence amplified in the peaceful place where there were no distractions to rely on, the pressure for it to feel effortless. But since nothing did at that age, the natural separation of one heart too gaping, another too closed, kept them as displaced as engine oil and rosewater. Or just a boy, and just a girl, taught to be so.

Let's face it: Sadie didn't know even a fraction of what was waiting behind those brown eyes—though, some blanks had been filled with placeholders she remained optimistic would be true—just that she was too fascinated and affected and entirely electric to settle for a muse, a writing prompt. She didn't want to *watch* him. She didn't want to *think* about him. She didn't want to *write* about him. She wanted him.

Sadie spun elegantly towards the water, profile to his eye line, hoping solid cheek structure was enough to be a turn on, and blowing discreet puffs of air down her camisole to help dry the sweltry layer of sweat. Her lips drew ravishingly apart, long neck lifted, back arched, shoulders high, until it didn't feel so outlandish to take up space like the other girls do.

Her senses tingled at the scent of fresh cypress; evocative of air that's clean and healthy and a little balsamic; but Brooks' cologne beat all that. She guessed Givenchy. She'd spent hours with Emma parading the Macy's men's fragrance section and using up stacks of tester strips. They'd say things like *Hmm, oh yes, I sense bergamot and gooseberry, perhaps a hint of apricot* while swirling and sniffing the way wine connoisseurs do, and making wishlists for their future husband's bathroom cabinet. Sadie's top pick was Bleu De Chanel, but Givenchy a close fourth.

Brooks helped her up on a retired wooden dock, questionably sturdy and showing signs of abandonment. Still, it must've been somewhat functional, as there was a paddleboat tied to the left edge with that week's paper and a banana peel that hadn't yet browned. The holes and missing nails in the boards made it a challenge to get across, so Brooks offered to wade in the shallow water and provide shoulder (the good one) for support. He eyed her slender frame swaying for balance, resembling a semiplume feather in the wind. The lunar light accentuated her arcs and he traced them twice, from her heart-shaped mouth to the contouring sash of collarbone to the fullness of her breasts... *Oh.*

Contrary to what he'd said to his friends at Ogilbee's, Brooks hadn't spent much time roaming the vicinity because—well, his momma had raised him right—and her face was just *that* pretty. But now that he'd ventured, the few beers stirred and pumped fresh blood to places he'd thankfully already tucked in the elastic of his briefs. The best part: she seemed truly unknowing of what she was doing to him, and if he'd informed her, she'd have probably blurt, "Oh, I'm sorry," and tried to amend to something dimmer. Selfishly, Brooks decided not to inform Sadie how sexy she looked.

"Careful." His wrist went to her hip. "This parts not too sturdy. See that gap right there? It's from when I fell right through it."

Sadie giggled before covering her mouth. "No, I shouldn't have laughed. That's not funny at all." But another stronger wave bubbled and she couldn't help it. Weird, Sadie was the girl who could always help it.

"Hey now, I could've been eaten by a gator. Can't believe

you're laughin' about this." He flashed ironic eyes that wore bewilderingly at her pelvis. "You should feel real bad."

"I do!" she pressed as they reached the end, with him swinging up to join her. "But... there aren't really alligators out here, are there? I'm cool with snakes, crawly things like spiders— I used to actually name the ones I found living in the orange trees —but alligators..."

"You ain't in California anymore." He chuckled in a mischievous son-of-the-soil flavor, how tornadoes howl through trees, to go with this very point. "Don't worry, I'll fight 'em off if they come at you."

"Ha, thanks. That makes me feel so much better." Without fail, it really did.

"So names, huh? Are we talkin' Aragog or Cuddles?"

"Mmm, more so Frederick and Augusta." Sadie added an obvious, "They were fancy."

"Sounds like you were a very open-minded child."

"It's too bad you didn't talk to me at that fruit stand. You could've come over and played with me and my spiders."

"I hate spiders."

"Your loss." She flipped some of those majestic gold locks that appeared alive and visibly growing, curling at the ends like string beans, before ogling into the vacant lagoon of black water in front of them.

"So, what do you think?" Brooks asked, and gestured into the endless horizon. "Does it have that je ne sais quoi you Eiffel Towers—I mean girls—I mean you—like?" He winced.

Sadie blinked up at him, amused. "Come again?"

He shrugged. "I took a year of French, just don't quiz me."

Amicably, she turned back to appreciate the motionless habitation like it were a folklore, because the quieter it got, the more she intuited burps of trapped air breaking the water's surface, flies buzzing, cottontail rabbits scampering on twigs, leaves' steady breathing of oxygen. It all came to life as one complete picture. Intricately designed yet uncomplicated; dirt every which way but nothing to be cleaned; segments growing slovenly out of order and heartily in it's place. Perspective restores without the disruptive fluffs of life, the hurry, the excess. Where you can't run from it, so you learn to run with it.

It would take some time, but eventually even Sadie would come to prefer the ground over the clouds. The ground has flowers.

Startled, Sadie gripped Brooks' arm tight as a sunfish flapped in the water, before excitedly clapping at it's backflips. "It's nice," she said, and immediately felt like apologizing for using such an inadequate word. "No, it's *more* than nice."

Brooks agreed. "I like comin' here before games. Helps me clear my head. Used to belong to old man Yates behind those trees there." He pointed at a white-paneled home with black trim and almost entirely consumed by ivy. "He moved up north but never sold, so now it's nobody's and everybody's." He brooded a few seconds (at least that's what Sadie called it when that stoic expression took him away). "It's always quiet out here. Well, except for..." He cupped a hand to his ear and motioned for her to listen.

"Crickets?"

"Yeah." He creased up over the steady chirping. "Those little guys never shut up."

They took a seat synchronously together at the far edge, legs dangling back and forth a foot above the water and lily pads.

"It's like music," Sadie noted, "the crickets," as she closed her eyes and let them transport her adrift.

"Really? Is that the kind of music they listen to in California?" Brooks chuckled. "Man, I bet you've been to some crazy concerts out there."

"Mmm, nope. Not really." Her double-jointed elbows locked, palms digging under the fleshy cushion of her sit bones. "I'm just not a big concert person I guess. The crowded room, blasting volume, tossing bodies all blind and... yeah. I usually hide in the bathroom until it's over." Sadie shuddered at a life-flashing-before-her-eyes memory: Tenley's post breakup celebration at The Fonda when she'd been slurped inside a mosh pit vortex and went home with a sprained ankle and phobia of studded belts.

Brooks studied her with a slight skepticism, because she

wasn't at all the worldly-wise city girl he'd expected. Attractive people aren't born yesterday; they're born more entitled, far ahead, with an upper hand that enjoys using it, moving around people like a monopoly board. They're more experienced, usually. "What kind of person are you then?"

"Oh... I mean... I do other fun stuff, like parties. My friends and I would go to after parties and release parties and... and other kinds of parties."

"ABC parties?" That stood for anything-but-clothes.

Sadie wasn't aware. "Oh, um, definitely. Those kinds... they were our go-to."

A ruche trickled in the corners of his lips, because her purity was too bumbling and unfiltered to be an act. That made him feel like he could trust her. "Did you ever find any cool *books* at those parties?"

"Actually, yes!" Sadie clicked on like a light. "One time, there was this whole dusty box of Jane Austen first editions in the hallway that drunk people kept spilling on..." She realized he was kidding as hot embarrassment submerged her buoy cheeks. "Seriously, is it something about me?" she respired, folding droopily in half so she was blubbering into the squished skin of her thighs. "I really thought I was selling it."

"Well, you *do* kind of talk like you're givin' a book report at all times of the day. Just very... put together."

Then might he be interested in helping take her apart? "Ain't! Y'all!" Sadie impulsively shouted at the lake. "Dope?"

"There we go." Desiring physical contact, Brooks' sturdy arm slid more local to her back, allowing her to lean and loosen up against it. "Though I gotta say, as much as I do love hearin' you speak my language, I brought you here to get to know you. And by you... I do mean... *you*."

Sadie's green gaze delved deeper into the striated brown of his, because she felt she'd been invited to. Did you know people don't often say what they mean? It sounds different when they do. "My favorite book is Perks of Being a Wallflower. I've read it seven times."

Brooks bragged, "I know that one."

"Everyone does now that it's a movie," Sadie shot down, but not without a perpetual lovelorn look to show gratitude for the small incidences too. She asked him, "What's yours?"

"Playbook."

"What's that about?"

He worked out how to synopsize it, taking his time as if it were a hard one to nutshell. "It's a description of football strategies, with pictures and everything."

Her pillowy smile split wide in an accusing laugh. "Sir, I don't think that counts!"

"Oh, it counts," Brooks rumbled back. "It's either that or Green Eggs and Ham. That's all I got." He was laughing now too, the ready arm slipping enchantingly around her waist and making everything extraordinarily serious again.

"Ten," Sadie whispered under bated breath.

"What?"

"Nothing."

"Huh."

She steered the attention back to him. "So, what do you do for fun around here?"

"Tha's easy. I go muddin,"

"Mudding? As in a verb?"

"Yes ma'am."

Her belly kinked in pleasure at the southerly endearment. "And, um, what does 'mudding' look like?"

"There's a place up Highway 301. We used to take our four-wheelers there, ride down the trails after it rained real hard, get stuck and spend hours shovelin' 'em back out. I'd come home all muddy, momma would yell at me for trackin' dirt in the house, then I'd give her a *biiig* hug."

Sadie scooted closer and draped a thin leg over his leaden thigh; they watched each other precisely as if silently sharing the heat of that step. "You don't go anymore?" He'd spoken in a sad reminiscence, as if describing a past life instead of a thing he did on weekends.

"No." Brooks took a flat rock from a stack he'd left last Thursday, and chucked it like a Frisbee. It skipped pleasantly three times before submerging in the slimy waterweeds. "Now I play football."

"For fun?"

He snorted but didn't answer, or maybe that was it.

It began to rain very suddenly so they shuffled under a hanging tin roof for safety, the tin making it echo more violently as if they were under an immense waterfall at the center of a racetrack. It fluctuated in agile mood swings, soft shower to heavy downpour, an up and down rhythm and highly immersive in how it encouraged a responsive want to do the same.

Sadie was bundled snugly between his legs now, powerful ropy thigh muscles that could easily crush her if they squeezed too hard. As it happens, he'd had the same thought: she was so tiny right there in that teasing vicinity, perfectly portable and light and easy to lift...

Up and down, the rain shuddered.

They could sense each other's temperatures rising, but they didn't need to talk about it. They wouldn't know how to, anyway. It's a wonderful age, when even the taboo is tinctured with innocence. That'll change soon—next year, or next week, or tomorrow. It never lasts long. It never comes back.

Little by little, step by step, these two beginners were well on their way before they'd ever known it. That's how the first time goes. Short and sweet and quick. Remember when I said it wouldn't hurt a bit?

I lied.

Brooks, sweating in his patience to do so, kissed the back of Sadie's neck in gentle airy pecks, and the cadenced glees that it brought her made her almost vibrate in place. Her fingers ran in fountain tickles down his knee, and he also quivered. Their inhales were heavier as if they weren't in a restful position, but luckily the wind rustling over the lake drowned it out, so they didn't have to be embarrassed about unraveling so vulnerably, exploring the feelings that came up.

It hit her then that this was all real, so palpably actual it sent a sudden shock up her spine. That her, *Sadie*, and him, *Brooks*, were cocooned up against a damp post, bodies knotted like a

roller derby bracelet with her ear resting on his chest, close
enough to hear every beat. The beat was so strong it seemed to
be happening in multiple locations on his body, the second
bumping lower behind her second denim belt loop, near where
her lip balm wet spot had somehow reappeared. Sadie knew
exactly then, she'd never be satisfied with only a muse ever again.
Daydreaming is a low impact sport, you see. There's no physical.
No touch. *His touch...*

' The night was wonderfully young so they discussed in detail
the funny polarities in their childhood: her a not-so-pop-cultured
valley girl, him a boondocks pillar of society with a future
preprescribed (which he hadn't outright said but she'd gathered).
But always agreeing on the important stuff: the Magic Tree
House books were epic, cilantro tastes like soap, and that big dogs
are way better than small dogs. Sadie attempted revisiting
football, but every time they got anywhere close he turned absent
and tense. The third time, he threw another rock. This one didn't
skip. It just sank.

"I don't think your friends like me very much," Sadie
admitted in a moment of dead air, because it'd been weighing on
her mind. Surely Brooks Holden had *plenty* other options; girls
with Soffe short butts he's french kissed at pool parties.

He brushed that off. "I wouldn't take it personal. No one likes
anyone around here."

"They like *you*."

"That's just 'cause I can throw a stupid ball across a field."

"Well crap, then I guess I'm screwed."

Brooks had to permission the grin; it was the least gracious
thing he'd ever heard her say. "You're a wild card, you see. No
one knows what hospital you were born in, what you're better or
worse at, if you've gotten mono and who from, how many people
you've dated..." He stopped there, passing the baton.

The answer was two, but also maybe none. Both Dean and
Maverick had initiated and terminated the relationships over text,
forgotten to get her flowers on Valentine's Day, and dates were
exclusively opening night action movies and Shake Shack.
They'd both asked Becks out first, but everyone asked Becks out

first.

Sadie revealed her cards. "Cedars-Sinai Hospital, better at group karaoke, worse at singing anything that's expected to sound good, never had mono but I get strep once a year, and two wannabe crossfit guys who wear beanies to the beach... kind of."

"Oh... uhh, good to know. Really good." Inspecting her tone, Brooks wondered if that was still her type. "But you could be lying."

"I'm not."

"I know. But they don't. And that makes you a threat."

"A *threat?*" Sadie reiterated in case he wanted to take it back. "Yeah, right. I'd sooner argue myself a phenomenal public speaker. The Internet has proof I'm not if you know where to look."

"Fantastic. Googlin' you as soon as I get home."

"Nice try. Didn't you know?" Sadie rotated so their mouths were inches away. "Everyone in LA has a stage name," she taunted straight at the sliver of warm tongue flapping around his teeth as he talked.

"Hmmm." He nibbled on that information, and once again, on her neckline extra susceptible to goosebumps. "You do have secrets, huh?" His voice subdued but the effects of it heightened. "I'll get 'em out of you eventually." Then he captured her in tickles from behind, the strapping thighs locking her in so she was entirely helpless and desperate. Sadie shimmied, handcuffed. She was riveted by her own liberated squeals. As they let go together, they became part of the complete picture, as natural as photosynthesis, or first love.

Finally, Sadie got away and crawled to the opposite edge of the wooden dock, and as the rain continued to drip and border around them, both gasping and engaged and at risk, Brooks and Sadie involuntarily signed a waiver refusing them the right to ever erase it. Even if one day they tried, it wouldn't work. You know that double-edged spell too, don't you? Isn't it fascinating how our brain decides which memories of trillions get slipped into that special chest of forevermore? It just knows.

For minutes, they challenged one another with come-hither

eyes, more intense from the low-lit scene and the fact that their clothes were slightly wet and see-through. Brooks, built like a real wolf, managed to pull her back on *top* of his lap, where the strike of attraction lulled, lured, compelled them less young.

Inevitably, Sadie ruined things again with deep and dumb words, just barely audible in her whisper, picking at the green stickies on her shorts. "What if… what if I'm not that mysterious?"

"What do you mean?" He asked as their eyes rested into each other.

"What if I don't have secrets? That what you see is what you get? That there won't be any big surprises down the line, new things to keep people impressed, to keep…" *Him.*

Brooks rose to his feet automatically, tugging her gently up too. "Do you trust me?"

"Wh—what? I don't know. No," she lied, and he could tell.

He leapt into the deserted paddleboat; it rocked harshly so the cool waves lipped at her toes.

"What are you doing?! Whose boat is that?"

"I dunno. Get in." Brooks yanked the rope so the vessel lied comfily against the dock, easy and accessible even for a feather. He reached out both hands, ready to catch her, and wore a hardly-tough boyish enjoyment she somehow knew was a private occasion. "Get in," he begged again. "I promised you a fun time, remember? The orange groves, they're not too easily dazzled. We have to get their attention."

The silly logic menaced her just a little. "But, isn't that stealing?"

"I wasn't gon' take it *home*," Brooks droned mockingly with his foot tapping and mouth quirked. "I'm waiting. Ah, no. Let me try this again." He canceled that previous attempt and courted her properly, bending over and picking her a slice of Maiden Cane grass. "Your carriage awaits, madam."

Sadie crossed her arms. "What about the alligators?"

"Hmm, well, I'm a lot meatier than you, probably better tastin' too, so they'll definitely go after me first." Brooks winked. "Com' on! You'll have plenty of time to swim away." He paused, unsure on how to phrase his next question. "You... *can* swim, can't you?"

"Of course I can *swim!*" she whined back, completely insulted but mostly frustrated with her caution and fear and lack of worthwhile it'd caused her. "It's just—I can't—I'm not—"

There did exist one word in the English language Sadie despised more than 'nice'. The first time she'd been called it, was the day her friends had voted to skip Sunday brunch for cliff jumping. Sadie had lectured them on the teen death rate of the recreation all the way from Calabasas to Laguna, looking up morbid articles in the backseat, suggesting snorkeling in the shallow end instead. Tenley had pulled over her matte black BMW in a Jack In The Box parking lot, launched a half-empty boba cup at Sadie's meek face and screamed, "Fine! We won't do it, MOM! Jeez, pick one Sadie. Are there guardian angels cupping our asses or are we all going trip to our deaths on a freaking banana peel?" Lukewarm matcha dripped from the gold ringlets. "Next time, bring your big girl blouse. Okay, *mom*?" The anti-fun label caught on fairly overnight, and at the Grier's New Year's party they'd made her wear a name tag and tasked her with passing out Emergen-C dosed water bottles. But it was okay because they'd also pampered her with *Isn't Sadie just the sweetest little butterfly? Where would we be without her? You should totally hang with her too; her bathroom lighting is bomb.* Tenley had put a flashy silver necklace around her neck that said 'bad girl', and Becks immediately demanded she take it off. "Sadie could never. She's a good girl. She's the best of us." It incapacitated. Those cashmere compliments from vocal girls who know what they're talking about. Did that make any sense? Here in this quiet scene of perspective, it was starting to.

They were on the other side of the country and yet it didn't matter; they'd written her book for her. They'd written her character secondary to theirs. She'd believed them.

Seemingly frozen in time on that dock, Brooks simply observed the overly sentient girl, blown away by the amount of thought she was giving it. Honestly, he wasn't used to people having a conscience, or refinement, or much mindfulness at all, and here stood a girl hoarding enough for the whole county. Living like you'll die tomorrow was one thing, but living like you'll live forever seemed just as much a loss. "My turn to speak your language, okay?"

Sadie gave a small nod, uncertain what he meant by it.

Brooks knew what came next would become one of his greatest achievements before he even achieved it. He didn't, however, consider the responsibility. "Sometimes, people use thought to not participate in life."

"What does that…" Her fuzziness went still as his words echoed again. She sensed a familiarity like she'd heard them before. Like she'd read them. "That's from Perks of Being a Wallflower, isn't it?" If he'd said *We accept the love we think we deserve,* she might've argued it a lackluster line. But this was too specific. Too right. Say it with her, all together now: It's a sign.

The rain clouds cleared to a sweeping film of stars smiling down at them as they paddled to the center of the lake, him splashing when she wasn't looking. They did this back and forth for some time.

"No fair! You have two arms!" Brooks cried out accidentally.

"What? Did a gator take one of yours already?" Sadie poked back, and the game continued.

Once they were drenched and spent, he hugged her close like they'd done this a thousand times, brushing his fingers through gold silk tangles, reminiscing on the first time he'd seen the sun almost five years ago. The first time he'd seen Sadie almost five years ago.

A round of nerves went rogue in Brooks' chest, which made him wonder how someone so soft-spoken had made him the terrified one. He leaned down and whispered something not even the crickets could hear, "I don't care what you say, you're one hell of a mystery to me."

They weren't alone on the lake that night.

At the top of the hill sat a white Jeep braked in the road, and through the gaps of branches Shelby had watched Brooks laugh with his whole face. It was the one she'd called his SpongeBob laugh in the second grade, after Mallory's blonde mop of hair had caught in the Elmer's glue bookmarks they were drying on pencil boxes. That was *her* laugh. This was *their* lake. And he'd given both away... like it was nothing.

Shelby didn't have many friends, not real ones who asked about her day and would drive to CVS to get Midol if she needed it; only Ali who stuck around because her house smelled like bakery churros and Betty Crocker icing, her favorite munchies. Brooks had been there, not for the Midol necessarily, but for the Taco Bell Baja Blasts and Crunchwrap Supremes after.

A single drop fell from her eye, connecting to each strawberry freckle, before descending from her chin. Two more leaked from the corners and soon there were too many to stop. Shelby started driving around the block, circling some number of times until Little Big Town's 'Girl Crush' had ended on the radio, and she'd sung every word.

Brooks helped Sadie dry off with a musty towel he'd found in his backseat, and asked if she was hungry. She replied with an unspecific shrug, which he took as *feed me fries now.* He knew just the place.

"Wait—you aren't a vegetarian, are you?" Brooks winced as his truck parked in a busy lot off Main, by the gazebo that'd become a landmark.

"Would that be a deal breaker?" she asked him.

"Honestly... I just don't know where you'd eat around here."

"Then it's a good thing I'm not. My mom tells me the first time I tried steak, I refused to eat anything else and threw tantrums over it for two weeks. Apparently, filet mignon was my Velveeta."

His grin stretched so far wide, it might've hit state lines. It was incredible. "This ain't exactly a Ruth's Chris, but you're in for a real treat."

Sadie recognized the mom-and-pop restaurant from her first day scavenger hunt: Buck's BBQ. It had the same chronic line out the door as it did that first morning, casual with women in tube tops and pajama pants, men in jorts and construction worker vests. Everyone let them pass.

They sat down in an exposed middle booth, far enough from the Sports Center commentary on seven flat screens, yet with as much romantic ambiance as a Beef O' Brady's with an obnoxious neon jukebox.

An elderly gentleman with a cane—sprightly Mr. Dawson in stretchy waist trousers, the one who'd been harassed on his Circle K lottery run that morning—introduced himself to Sadie as her father's old history teacher. He illustratively shared a beloved memory of teenage Henri dressing up as Thomas Jefferson for spirit week. "Still got the photo up on my refrigerator, see it every mornin' when I heat up my eggs and sausage!" By the end, Mr. Dawson's pearlescent eyes had gone red and misty, and he limped to retrieve his wife's to-go order after announcing how disappointed she'd be if her gumbo arrived cold.

"Chivalry is alive and well," Sadie decreed in a soft inspired purr, and looked forward to growing old. Realizing, she asked, "What's gumbo?"

Brooks had gone enigmatically tentative, and browsed past it. "Did you... know our dads were friends? There's a picture of 'em in the locker rooms from winnin' state. And I think he came by practice today."

"I saw," Sadie admitted to spying. "Is that bad? That they know each other?"

"No, it's kind of cool actually, just weird that my dad never mentioned him throughout the years."

"I didn't even know my dad had played football."

The doubt in his eyes intensified threefold. "Are you serious?"

"Yeah." She tested the big deal. "Why?"

"Well, people that win state, usually talk about winnin' state. Like a lot." His head shook in undefined emotions. "Really, I don't understand how you could spend your summers here and not get bombarded with questions from a hundred Mr. Dawsons."

"I never left the house unless it was farther out of town," she explained. "Maybe once or twice we'd stop at 7-Eleven for slurpees, or the fruit stand on Eiland." She blushed multitudes of pink. "I never saw anything wrong with it, not like there's that much to see. But I did hear my dad on the phone one time, angry at grandpa for taking me inside the SunTrust bank with him." She paused, remembering. "Grandpa didn't get it either."

"Sounds like he didn't want people knowin' about you."

"You've said how nosy people here are. He's just a private guy, like grandpa was."

"Okay sure, but about his *daughter?*" Brooks wore a cynicism that didn't sit well with her.

"I don't know, okay? Can we just leave it at that?" Fevered over any insinuation her father could be deceptive, Sadie hid behind her menu. But he did have a point, didn't he? Why, if her dad missed Weston Hills so much, had he not joined her on her visits? Why had she played with spiders and toads in weed-grown orchards, instead of making real human friends at a park like the other kids?

Sadie scanned the menu options: straight or curly fries, or a rainbow basket of both, or turn it into a 'Million Bucks' and get a collectibles bucket.

Brooks kindly ordered for the table, "We'll have a double Buck's Special, two rainbows and a mudslide to share. Oh, and sweet tea. Buck's 12-points, please." He didn't glance at the menu once; he hadn't since he was nine.

Karigan—a curvy girl in a Charlotte Russe striped tank, seahorse anklet, blue streak in her heavily flat-ironed hair—jotted it all down. "Be ri' ba' with yu' teas swee'hart!" She danced gutsily around the room, calling all the hungry sitters by first name, throwing insults and affections like it were a rowdy family living room floor, until the fuss ended with a working class pop crowing, "How's that younger sister of yours in Charleston doin'? She still got that boyfriend? He was a Panthers fan, wasn't he? Y'all come over next Thanksgivin'. I'll talk to him."

Brooks turned back to his terrified date. "You had the same look on your face as the one I get doin' chemistry homework. Hope you don't mind."

"Not at all. Thank you. I'm uhh, not very good with decisions," Sadie confessed.

He didn't exactly know what that meant. He would, though.
"Noted."

Karigan dropped off their individual pitchers and bendy
straws, and she might've gotten something spicy in her eye just
then, because her lashes started fluttering like they'd lost control
of the mechanism. Then, she popped her round butt in the air,
her elbow slammed on the table, and her big boobs spilled from
their assigned cups onto their now unusable napkins. "I've got a
few cousins playin' for Chapel, but even they don't think they've
got a shot against *you*, sweet pea," she meowed.

Sadie, submissive little lily, quietly examined the Delta Karma
Chihuahua, or *whatever*, sorority pendant around the plump flirty
girl's neck. A *college* girl. She hadn't realized the extent of Brooks'
fan club.

Peering around the room, the other girlish hearts already
fallen from their graces cheered Sadie on to fall from hers, too.
Go ahead, *jump*, they coaxed from the other side. It hurts less
when you know it's coming, and no one gets to keep their lovely
petals forever. We're already so clever if we just know the song
Ring around the rosie, pocket full of posies, ashes, ashes…

Two waitresses at the host both—Britney and Whitney—
made guesses on how quickly she'd run through half the football
team. Shelby and Ali were at a nearby table making fun of her
attention-seeking shirt. Through the window, the clique of Lilly
Pulitzer girls from school were putting on a play of curtseying
prim and proper, one with a dark spot of Sharpie above her brow
(the mole on Sadie's forehead her mother called a 'beauty mark',
which she'd been dressing with apple cider vinegar since age six
in attempts to burn it off). You may think they were being mean
and conniving, but in truth, they were simply entertaining
themselves. For when photogenic girls aren't tee-heeing in fruity
gales of laughter, they're often quite depressed.

And so, a ring of flowering girls *all falls down*, at the hands of
their own scandalizing mouths, and usually… a boy.

Sadie rose from the booth, knocking over a cup of ranch.
"Ladies room. Be right back." She was beginning to feel like
everyone around her was wearing a mask. She wished someone

had warned her.

While Brooks waited her return, a group of noisy country chaps reeking of illegal activities cut the line and made a few devilish passes at Britney and Whitney. Brooks ducked from their sight, but not soon enough...

"Aye B-Dawg! We been lookin' for ya!" Levi's eye drops poked up from his V-neck pocket, which paired with his layers of gold chains, made him look like the town Sound Cloud rapper who also watches Glee.

Caleb and Sterling were with him. All three of them slid into the booth.

"Well, well! Look at you, without a damn scratch on ya! You're a real champ, ditchin' and leavin' us to take care of your dirty laundry." Caleb locked his fists hard on the table, but in a familiar exact form, so onlockers would surely take it for some passionate praying.

"What'd you do to Cameron?" Brooks demanded in a growl. "I told you—"

"Relax, dude. I didn't do nuthin. Not a damn thing, all thanks to this peace activist over here." Caleb smacked the back of Levi's shiny head. "So, where's the lady? You obviously didn't come here alone." He flicked the evidentiary guava-tinted straw, and began sucking on it. "Where's *Sadie?*"

"Bathroom. She'll be right back. You guys should probably go—"

"She better be one hell of a time to abandon your teammates for in the middle of an ambush. Tell me you at least got *some* action, and not just some blue ballin' over the pants crap." Caleb Lindley was a first class button-pusher; he knew all the right buttons to make people squirm.

Brooks hesitated, which was how it always started.

"Hold up." Boozy Sterling shot up a dirty fingernail, nose scrunch crazed and oozing with rude connotations. "Did you... take her to the *dock?*"

Levi chortled with his tongue out and thrashing. "Oh shiet!"

Sterling high-fived the tabletop and thrusted his Wranglers all over the poor family-friendly seat. "You did, didn't you?! You took the new girl to the dock!"

"Fuckin' legend dude!" Levi used fries to 'make it rain', and make a mess, dripping of ketchup as he helped himself to more handfuls of their food. "Easier than she looks, I'll admit. I hear those California females are like that though. Damn Caleb, you were way off about this one. Eiffel Tower who? Sadie Bexley is the Vegas *strip*!"

Brooks couldn't get a word in, and after a few minutes of trying, it was harder to want to.

Leaning in the shadows, Caleb smoldered with a tight jaw, trying to decipher the source of guilt on his best friend's face. Was he lying to them, or lying with her? *Which one is it, Holden?* Caleb looked for the next button. "Tell us… how was she?"

"Huh?" Brooks deadpanned as if he'd missed the question.

"How was Sadie?" Caleb repeated with exaggerated curiosity. "She clearly fooled me. Now I'm intrigued."

"Y'all know I don't kiss and tell. Never have, never will." The front would've been fine and foolproof, just believable enough, had he not simultaneously reached to the nape of his neck and itched that pesky little scratch: his nervous *tick*.

Caleb smirked at the new insight, reading him for filth like a best friend could. Not knowing he wasn't already, Caleb relaxed. "Got it. Loud and clear, soldier."

Levi and Sterling started babbling about offensive formations, kissing the ground Brooks walked on basically, but Caleb didn't feel like sitting still just then. He got up, passed out a few energetic hellos to friends of his parents, and suavely blocked Sadie at the corner by the jukebox playing 'Honky Tonk Man'. He serenaded a few lines for her, but stopped when he realized she'd been crying.

Her pursy cheeks were a marble tie-dye magenta, temples yanked tight, bottom lip swollen like it'd been injected with whale blubber, and her array of lashes had stuck together in exactly three spiky clumps. She walked like a normal person too, lacking that springy hop at the end of each step. Caleb followed her troubled eye line to the window, spotting the Lilly Pulitzer cult now skipping and twirling on their toes, mimicking Sadie. Caleb asked plainly, "You want me to go tell 'em off?"

Sadie's weakly cold shoulder rejected the offer. "Please, move out of my way."

He pointed at the one with the Sharpie dot on her forehead. "Here's the funny thing: one time McKenna shaved her whole eyebrow off and had to marker it back on for two months. Then last week Brianna, whose got a webbed toe by the way, at Ali's house peed in her cat's litter box after one too many Mike's Hard Lemonades. Pickle was at the vet, so that kind of gave it away. And Mercedes, well she projectile vomited chunks during the SAT—"

Sadie scoffed at what was surely another ruse. "I said... *please move.*"

Caleb's eyes sparked in recoil as he countered with, "Don't say 'please' and maybe I would. Go on, get mad. It's more effective if you *mean* it."

"I do mean it, I just have manners."

"Aha, the most prized skill of the jungle." He leaned closer, so she could actually count the micro blue corkscrews of his potent blue irises. "Manners."

"Why are you here?"

Caleb shrugged. "I don't know."

"Well, just... don't be."

A gruff acidic sneer came from deep inside him, and it made her lurch against the wall. "Don't what, Sadie? What did I do wrong this time, princess?"

"Don't talk to me." She stood taller than ever, without deciding to do so.

"I'm tryin' to help you out here."

"Well, I'm not falling for it."

"Clearly." He smirked and snickered, that talented sharp-witted tongue coursing back and forth across the supple inner lining of his lips. "Just answer me one question." Tactfully, his hands swathed hers like they were devotedly talking to Jesus back there. "Did you like the dock?"

Sadie's heartbeat arrested mid-float. "Yes."

"Uhhuh." He nodded. "Did he tell you about muddin'? Did

you listen to the crickets? Did you go out on the boat?" Man oh man, did he get high off some sabotage. But truthfully, this was far more than that. "I bet you loved it, didn't you? I bet he'll call you tomorrow. I bet you'll do it all over again." The sharp tongue arranged a quick play date with her undefiled earlobe, and corrupted it in one breath, "I'll even bet, Brooks is the *one*."

Sadie felt despicably seen, like he'd extracted her unique florid nature in a vial, and made it look like water. "I have to go." She rushed past him with her ringlets slightly straighter, clutching to the shavings of her ultimate cosmic sign Caleb had just shoved through a metaphorical pencil sharpener. She looked back to scowl at him, and to just look. "Who *are* you?" she whispered, before climbing back into the booth with her quarterback.

By the lit up jukebox, Caleb stood idly a moment longer. But his mind was elsewhere: recalling the stiffness of his hands that'd for hours gripped a tatty hammer, the dizzying effects of midsummer days in the sun, the countless blending hours it takes to put up plywood roof sheathing on a shed, the residual scents of orange blossoms littered in small winds, the legendary stories of a soft girl with an affinity for unusual friends, how very long it'd been since he'd paid a visit to the Gardens of Weston Cemetery. Brooks wasn't the only one who remembered the photograph. Caleb might even argue, there was someone else who remembered it best.

Caleb spritzed a few hints of Bleu De Chanel on his forearm and made his way to the host stand, where Britney and Whitney were expectantly waiting for their evening consultation.

"Are you alright? You haven't spoken since we left Buck's." Brooks switched off the headlights of the F-150 that he'd parked smartly behind the sunken Bexley shed, out of sight from any kitchen windows where her parents might be waiting up. "Did you hate the food? I'm sorry the guys showed up. They didn't... say anything? Right?"

"I'm not very competitive," Sadie said abstractly, but with her own crystal clear reasons.

"Okay..."

"So I won't be very proficient in fighting other girls off, if that's what you want me to do."

"Other girls?"

"I'm just letting you know, I don't do that. I don't compete, because I don't know how. And it's not that I don't want to, because I think about doing it, but I can't go through with it. Like, if I'm in line for the last muffin, but I know the person behind me also wants that muffin, I'll buy it for them instead of keeping it for myself."

"Why would you do that?"

"Because I think I'll be rewarded later on, as if I'm racking up points to cash out later, and the universe will give it to me, because I've done everything right."

"You really think it works that way?"

"I'd prefer to believe so."

"And why are you telling me this?"

"Because I'm scared I'm wrong," she admitted. "And that it won't matter how many doors I've opened for people or how many muffins I've sacrificed, that you'll still throw me away in the morning like the other girls you've taken to the dock, who maybe didn't hold any doors at all, and you won't just be ruining this perfect night for me... you'll ruin everything." There was a long pause. "And I don't think I'm ready for that."

Brooks stared hard at his steering wheel. "I don't know where you got that idea from."

"See, the grand thing I wanted to cash out on, was *this*." Sadie's finger tilted slowly from herself, to him. "So when people warned me you don't 'do' second dates, I thought: That's okay, because I've earned this." Sadie had never understood *too good to be true*, but now everything she'd ever known was.

Brooks sighed, defeated and irritated at the curveball in conversation; he felt like he'd lost an advantage, or that he'd never had one to begin with, or that maybe that's beside the point. "You have some pretty gnarly expectations."

"Yes," she agreed. "I've been told, now and then. But that's how I am. That's how I've always been. And maybe you think I have my head in the clouds, but I've seen it, so I know what I want exists."

"People see what they want to see, sometimes."

"Just as much as they don't see, what they don't want to see."

"I think we just wrote a poem."

"Welcome to my life." Sadie didn't smile or make it cute; she was firm and grave.

Brooks shifted uncomfortably. "You shouldn't believe everything you hear, you know." It was lazy and coward, but all he had. "Listen, I like you. Okay? And no, I haven't been the guy who sits at a nail salon waitin' for their girlfriend to be done gettin' a hibiscus painted on their big toe, because I haven't had time, like I told you when we met. But... I don't know... who knows?" There was a choking sensation he didn't know how to fend off. "Can we just... like... not think about that right now?"

Sadie responded to the one thing she'd heard from his speech. "I like you, too." Then, amid a streak of emphatic and unskillful eye contact, Sadie uttered, "I almost forgot to tell you, my dad has a gun."

"Great," Brooks answered with confidence, and leaned in. "Tell him we should go shootin' sometime."

Sadie gingerly wondered if what came next was truly the forbidding effect her father had counted on with that line. *No*, it definitely was not.

Brooks unbuckled both of their seatbelts in swift unison, scooting closer to cradle the curve of her chin. Her basil eyes were startling, but only for the reason there was genuinely nothing startling about them at all. Brooks felt her gentle hand go to his chest, where he'd been punched and battered a fortune of times, but never just touched, and her face deformed from it's reassured shape like she knew; like she was soothing every jab and welt to disappearance, to make space.

Their foreheads met and noses brushed, and the meager distance left was nearly agonizing to resist.

"You're so beautiful," Brooks breathed, accidentally thinking aloud, before inclining further—glancing up towards heaven as if for permission—and kissing Sadie on the lips.

The first kiss was a tormentingly brief four-second occasion, before Brooks retreated as a respectful young man. Only Sadie, in a sudden distress, pushed back for more, and he matched her there without remorse, more rapaciously this time around. The sultry truck climate was soon nuanced with watermelon Jolly Rancher wrappers, the raw scent of rubbing skin, an essence of rosewater, and of course the Mr. Zog's air freshener. Windows, minds, inhibitions fogged all blurry and damp, and like a ribbon, they pulled each other's ends. That memory chest of forevermore gained a slip, for sure.

Brooks had never kissed anyone like this; with feeling. In little compels and presses, his mouth baited hers wider unlatched, staying here a moment, before graduating to fleeting dulcet slips of tongue, experimenting to tender tugs with his teeth. This rocked her a quiver, which activated him further. He sensed a hungry churning knot expanding against the deck of his abdomen; entirely frustrating and wonderful. And she was just wonderful. Brooks lifted her over the console, and he'd been right —she *was* light.

As they embraced and kissed, Sadie felt as though she were a freshly binded book falling open for the first time. The book was blank and she was ready now, to write it herself. Her sleepy eyelids succumbed opened and closed, and the image was the same now: in her head, and out of it. She was doing it. *Life.* And so the blossoming of Sadie Bexley began, in the front seat of a F-150, in the yard where she'd played forest fairy, in the orange groves that would document it all.

Heart thumping in a wildfire, she had a reddening thought: *Is it normal to be this sensitive, all over?* She'd always hated being sensitive, but perhaps it was a balancing redemption. Because *this* kind, she'd never mind. A perk in the rub—oh, what a perk it was.

As he sprinkled her neck with more sweet kisses, her nipples puckered under the excellent silk, and she pulled him in tighter, grabbed his shoulder—

Brooks jolted away and slammed Sadie against the wheel.

"I—I'm sorry," Sadie gasped, a trembling mound in her throat. "Did I do something wrong?"

"No!" He fought embracing her again—demolished shoulder throbbing—and instead reached for her hand. "I'm more sore than I realized, um, from practice. That was my fault. I didn't mean to scare you."

The following moments were spent sedating their untrained urges; Brooks his broken arm; pulling down clothing and trying to conceal the wiping of an arm across their wet mouths.

"I hope that was okay," Brooks whispered with bated breath, to her and whoever else might be listening above.

Sadie barely nodded, and in a faint worried voice she said, "I hope... we do this again."

They nestled close with a safe handhold, as Brooks dealt with the excruciating aches. In the back of his mind, he could hear Lance Bexley's disapproval. He could hear his fuck-ups to come. He could hear him breaking her, like she'd already told him he would.

Meanwhile, Sadie was emanating a feminine sense of power, and maybe it was foolish and young that it'd taken a stamp of approval from a big-name high school boy to get her there, but at least it was a start. A running start. Sadie pondered writing Becks a thank you note for the lucky camisole. Perhaps the note would read: *Hey babe! How was your date with the Prius guy? Miss ya!* That's it. She'd get the message. She invented the goddamn language.

They said their goodbyes with one final kiss and hooking of pinkies, before Sadie hopped down from the lifted truck so dexterously she awarded herself a mental gold star.

The Ford F-150 curved and faded at the end of the dirt road.

Sadie caught herself wondering where Duke had spent the rest of his evening.

Brooks arrived home later than expected, avoiding glancing at the obnoxious novelty Texas Hold 'Em wall clock his father had hung up freshman year to annoy them into being on time. It'd been a failure the first day, and now it just hung there, dominantly ticking and giving the whole house the quality of a busy Sunday at the driving range.

He'd assumed the house would be crashed out by now, and

was surprised to see the flat screen flashing green in the living room, Duke's legs sprawled on the couch.

"You're up late." Brooks sauntered in mid-yawn.

"So are you," Duke replied flatly with crumbs of Pringles scattered across his shirtless chest.

"I was out." Brooks plopped luxuriously on the leather. "What are you watchin'?"

"Dad asked me to go over some game tape from last season, again."

"This against Crystal River?" Brooks asked. "That was a great night. As I recall, dad actually smiled."

"Yeah," Duke confirmed. "He did."

"He said we got lucky that game, but I don't think so." Brooks leaned over and patted his brother's back, and not ironically. "That one was all you."

Severely freaked out, Duke didn't know what to do with the mushy gesture and goober grin slopped on his older brother's face. Brooks was one note. This wasn't that note. "Team work makes the dream work, I guess."

"Nah, man." He said it again, so it couldn't be an error. "All you."

The clock ticked until seven minutes had gone by. Both boys —one still slaphappy and the other unsettled—squinted at the screen.

Duke eventually asked, "You were with the new girl, right?" As if her name wasn't as virally discussed as the rising gas prices. "Sadie?"

"Yeah. So?"

"Do you like her?"

"Huh?" Brooks turned. "Do I *like* her? She's hot, sure. Whatever. I'm tryin' to watch this—"

"Are you gon' do somethin' about it?"

"We hung out once."

"Are you gon' tell her the truth?"

"Does it look like I've got a goddamn promise ring burnin' a hole in my back pocket? You wanna check? Shit. What do you want from me, huh? She's just a *girl*—"

"A girl?" Brant restated resolutely from the porch door, and waited there with his usual strict presence. With visceral tension constricting the walls, he walked to the kitchen to place his mug in the sink. The porcelain clanked so it hurt their ears. "Girl?" Brant asked again.

"Yes sir," Brooks answered with his head low. "It's not a big deal though. She... isn't."

Brant checked the wall clock. "I'd say so, if that's what kept you out this late. Either she's important or you're careless, and I sure hope it ain't both."

Brooks flinched. "Yes sir."

"What's her name?" Brant chuckled unnaturally, collecting the milk carton from the fridge and squinting at the expiration date.

"Sadie Bexley."

The carton dropped in the trash just as the little color left in Brant's face drained away. "Pretty name." No one moved for nine loud seconds. "Well uhh, you boys got an early mornin'. Time for bed now. Go on."

Brooks and Duke sauntered down the hall and into their bedrooms without another word.

After showering and icing his arm, Brooks eased under the sheets with a small smile living on his dejection. He pulled out his laptop and in the browser typed *Perks of Being a...* lost on the rest but thankfully that sufficed. Truth was, Brooks hadn't read the book or seen the movie. The only reason he'd

known the quote he'd so gallantly excerpted at the dock, was from Cindy Britton's horridly long 6th grade Tropicana Speech. The book had been her chosen topic, and her first place title at districts led the school to play it for weeks on the morning news, which Brooks and Caleb had drowned out with Teen Wolf on their iPods until Mrs. Rowe confiscated it to her pointy bosom. Turns out, he'd still remembered some of it. *Thank you Cindy*, Brooks thought, and pressed play.

The Holden household went under around midnight, all but Brant who lied wide awake, taunted with each tick of the gruesome clock that, for some reason, he'd paid twenty bucks for at the Oldsmar Flea Market. He fantasized running it over with a mower while counting every notch and groove of the popcorn ceiling they'd recently installed. Kelly loved the texture, but to him it just looked like lumpy oatmeal. Brant scarfed down two more melatonin tablets. Then two more after that. The Sandman must've been lazy and skipped him that night. And every night, for the *last twenty years…*

Brant gave up on waiting for slumber and the notion it could provide any relief, instead tiptoeing past the dull hums of the dishwasher, the sputtering of the ancient A/C, all the way to the sliding doors out back. He sat down lifelessly on a cold step, though the step had been warm before he'd sat. A lone russet moth fluttered about, causing the sensor light to flicker annoyingly, before landing on Brant's pocket: the phone he'd turned off. It'd been going off every hour, on the hour. Suddenly, Brant was hit with the chilling fear of what it could mean if it stopped altogether.

He powered it back on and typed: *Meet me at the gymnasium in ten.*

Henri waited up in his father's antique rocking chair, reading some of Lance's equally old books where he'd left smart-mouthing footnotes. Henri humorously replied his own comments below those, imagining Lance standing behind him with a puckered brow, enormous bifocals falling off the bridge of his nose.

Sadie had of course broken the 'curfew' she demanded she have (by exactly five minutes), and Henri reprimanded her for it on her way through the door. But after, it was him who appeared discomposed, from seeing his baby girl all growing up in her own way. Brant's son with the Ford must be a real talented hugger, because her cheeks were all types of flushed and red, but a complicated sort. Somehow, Sadie looked as happy as she did dispirited; both fulfilled and conflicted. Henri only hoped he could be there, if things ever went awry. "Did you tell him?" he asked, and she knew what he meant.

"I told him, dad," Sadie answered, and it was then, with her incisive bitter tone, that Henri realized the confliction in her eyes was directed towards *him*.

He wondered about that. He wondered about a lot, these days.

After lights out, Henri rested in bed atop the smothering linen covers. His phone screen glowed on the nightstand, sooner than he'd expected. Margot had indulged in an extra cup of chamomile tea before bed, and that always made her a heavy sleeper: all rolled on her right side, one leg curled up, rump in the air. She wouldn't wake, he knew.

Henri slipped outside unnoticed, except by the groves, and induced his Chevy to a hollow moan. The drive was surreal in the dead of nighttime, when being the only one out felt wrong and punishable. The headlights encountered dense fog along Paddock Road, and made him doubt he'd made the right turn. Soon enough, the fairgrounds seeped into view, then the beaten Circle K, the stadium stands—suppose some things were harder to forget.

The gym was dimly lit, just a couple flickering white lights, and Brant standing in the middle of the court. Henri didn't care much for dramatic effect, but Brant had always had a knack for it. He held a stale-smelling basketball, when he asked, "You tell anyone you were meetin' me?"

"No."

"Good. I see no reason for speakin' about it. Don't want to give folks no reason to ask questions."

Henri wanted to tell him to cut it out, the managerial façade. "I'm sure any normal-minded neighbor would assume us catchin' up. We were friends, after all. You do remember that, us bein' friends?"

Brant didn't give any indication he did. "What about the folks who ain't so normal?"

"I suppose this towns got a few of those too."

"Yea. A few." Brant chuckled. "But then again, how would you know?"

The exchange was civil for the kind of friends they'd once been, considering the drunk shitty nights comparing blisters from the hay work at Thompson Farms, jabbering on about which junkyard clunker they'd one day buy with the cash, how Henri later lost his virginity in the backseat of his to an entire chorus of 'Strawberry Wine', Brant on a white-sand beach with an Eliza from Raleigh who'd swimsuit modeled for Billabong. Those types of things can't be unlived. That's what Manny would have told them, if he had lived.

"When's the last time you touched one of these?" Brant tossed the ball.

Henri caught it, eyes closing burdensomely shut, as the rubbery fibers transported him in time. A cobwebbed cassette shelved in his darkest depths writhed reluctantly to life…

Rewind, rewind… re—play.

A young Henri dribbled the ball, passing to a young Brant, passing to young Emmanuel who'd always gone by Manny.

They were on an outside court at night with yellow streetlights in the distance, on a cobblestone road with rows of picket fence houses, a red brick church with a cross on top.

They had a cockiness in the way they moved, talked, as if God had chosen them for greater things, easily interpreted as cunning disrespect deserving of two black eyes. The men there with them, had come to give just that.

The opposing team's blurry bodies moved around them, taller and stronger, weathered by sordid lives and some months spent in prison.

Henri continued dribbling, dribbling, dribbling.

Manny waved, "Yo! Over here!"

Pause.

"That night. That's the last time," Henri whispered from a place of unspeakable pain, leading both men to cower in their anguish that no amount of distance or will or even morphine if they had it, could annul.

"I should've listened to you." Brant's confession came out staggered, each syllable more defective than the last. "We should've told someone."

"What's done is done." Henri's entire person went crippled

and irregular, like he'd been shot.

"No." Brant shook; he detoxed. "I'm not done."

Henri agreed to listen.

"I hated you, Henri. Hell, I wish it had *been* you. I woke up that next mornin' thinkin', 'well shit, at least we ain't alone'. That maybe havin' someone to share the burden made it more livable. But you were long gone by then, weren't you?" The heavy betrayal in his bones let up as he spit out the words. "You weren't comin' back. No, you never came back." His nose dripped in yellow and gray, and he wiped it on his sleeve. "I ought to applaud you, cause I never could have done it, something so *selfish*. You left me to fester, to rot, like some damn road kill. You left me here to take the fall, didn't you?"

"I—" Henri swallowed, but millions of shards had clogged like hair in a pipe. "I was young. I was scared. I never meant—"

"Then why didn't you stay *away?*" Brant growled, nostrils flaring and with a twitch in his hand that so longed to dislocate that angular Bexley jawline cougar mom's used to salivate over, before eighteen and liability, before sleeping with someone you shouldn't or manslaughter could haunt you forever. Before one of those things had. "Tell me WHY!"

"WE'RE BEIN' BLACKMAILED! THAT'S WHY!" Henri hurled the ball across the empty room. "They have a video… someone has a video. I didn't come back to piss out sorries, or reminisce on tarpon fishin, or cry over our shit luck in the Walmart parkin' lot, alright? I came back for a reason. I'm here to fix it, for both of us!"

Brant's thoughts fluctuated behind his stony lens, and somehow through the wreckage, it was nostalgia that made it through. "Parkin' lot? No, that's all wrong. The view was much better from the roof."

Henri understood the reference immediately. *"What's football and women got on a sunrise like that?* That's what you said morning after we won state. Set up camp above the broken 'W'. Just us, that blue cooler, a couple of lawn chairs, and a half missing pack of UNO cards."

"Yea, I know. It was overcast too, you r'member? Couldn't

even see the damn sun." Brant momentarily ached for things to be so god-awfully simple. "Just a couple of pig-ignorant kids, weren't we?"

"Yea," Henri agreed. "Just a few Florida kids."

Brant sighed, before forcing up his chest. "You got it with you now? The video? I wanna see it for myself."

Henri pulled out his phone, pressed the appropriate buttons and turned away for the duration of the film. Meanwhile, Brant bit back unusual curse words, then hurled them out so fast and loaded they'd blended into one long run-on.

It warmed Henri's torn up heart, for one time, their most memorable teacher, a kind one named Mr. Dawson, made them come up with replacement swear words in front of the whole class, and they'd chanted 'fart knocker' and 'gee willickers' back and forth for a half a period, until the young boys almost passed out from laughing so hard. Until the lesson had stuck. And well, whad'ya know, it really had.

Brant offered an arm. "Alright then Bexley, how about we get to work trackin' down this doggonit bull-twinkie son-of-a biscuit-eater, huh? What do you say?"

He didn't. He just hugged him.

Sadie was ready for sleep to come swiftly, more than scintillated by the idea of an encore in her dreamworld. Her daisy pillows were fluffed, herbal lozenge dissolved on her tongue, and earplugs readied to quell the coyotes. The chandelier bulbs of her room needed replacing, so there was just a warm cantaloupe glow from the Himalayan salt lamp her mom had set up for her, next to a glass of almond milk.

Only, just as she'd hit that blurring weightless threshold, right before you're out and under, a frightening thought pulled her back. *What if she couldn't remember it all? What if, next week, or next year, it began to fade?* The kayaking place he wanted to take her to, how his Adam's apple wriggled all adorable when he sang with the crickets, the tweak in her massaged heart every time he said her name in that slow, hoarse southern accent, the tan boat shoes all muddy from the—no, wait. *Wrong person.*

Her hands had already grabbed for her journal, wrist cramping, writing so fast she wouldn't know what she wrote until she read it back. But she didn't read it back, just quickly closed it when she was done and sat there quietly in a strange intoxication, toes wringing up bunches of her quilt. She wished her room had a fan, because somehow, it'd become a sauna.

Just then, her phone notified her of a text. It was from Maia. *'You bad girl'*.

'What?' She typed and sent with hesitant scurry, forehead crimped to a shagged rug. She sent it again, in caps.

A few restless seconds later, her phone flashed again. *'I heard you and Brooks did the deed'*. Then another. *'I need details'*.

Sadie rubbed the sleep from her eyes with vengeance, but the little black letters didn't budge. A deed? What deed? Like a good deed? Or... as in...

Her pulse fell into a dreadful defibrillating shock, until anxiety swooped in to take the evening shift. She typed with inept thumbs. *"Heard from who?"* But what she really sent was *"herd ffrm who?"* Then waited for what felt like hours, hovering over the green call button and deciding she'd press it in three, two, one...

It was the middle of the night. She didn't want to bother Maia. Maybe, possibly, she'd run to the bathroom, or gone for a glass of water, and if she just patiently waited another three, two, one...

The sauna was now the center of the sun, and Sadie begged the tiny device for a reply. She paced, chugged the almond milk, spilled half of it on her lacy nightie, did some jumping jacks and four sit-ups. She counted three, two, one and a half, one and one quarter...

The phone vibrated against her stack of princess books. *'Everyone'*.

CHAPTER SEVEN

Camo Crocs and Dangerous Allegations

The sun was perpetually setting over the groves of citrus from then on, it seemed, slipping just beyond reach over the fluffy green heads of trees; more dark than light; in what they call this Sunshine State. An ephemeral sense of innocence making it's grand exit, like a spring once overflowing, now drying up.

Brooks didn't text Sadie after their date, which was okay. He didn't text her the next morning either, which was also pretty fine. When she saw him walking up the quad steps and their eyes locked, he didn't stop. That was less alright. Sadie was in her summeriest, lilac, off-the-shoulder blouse; the most attention-grabbing item in her closet; and he still didn't stop. Why didn't he stop?

Who was Sadie Bexley to Brooks Holden, they would ask. Just another girl in his truck, they would say. That's right. *Just another girl.*

Today marked eleven days since their date at the dock. An oath had been broken; Brooks had technically never made one, but Sadie had been accustomed to believing the universe had.

The little green town was more richly saturated in the early blush of September morning, especially the football field, reflecting millions of water droplet prisms, the blades of grass brighter and whiter like they'd been dipped in paint. Some of them, had.

The school was ambitiously vibrant. Zingy girls in uniformed skirts that they'd purposely shrunk in the dryer traipsed the halls with dumdum lollipops pushed high in their pinched cheeks. Elite football players hovered at the quad tables with philosophical expressions, wearing dress shirts and ties they'd given the same amount of elbow grease as the time it took them to finish a McDonalds hash brown. The rest of the students, naturally, stayed out of their way.

Today was a big day. Game day. *Brooks* day. Not everyone was in the holiday spirit.

"*I say it's true. She looks like a slut if I've ever seen one.*" A pale and bruised Sadie, buried in a hardback, accidentally tuned in to two girls walking by. "*So what, Sarah? It's not like you wouldn't do it too. I've been waiting for Brooks to ask me to the dock for like, ever. She's so lucky.*" A third girl hopped in. "*I saw them together at Buck's durin' my shift. Poor girl looked wrecked, like she'd been dragged through a lake or somethun'. Saw her talkin' to Caleb in a corner right under his nose too. I swear, I'll beat her ass if she tries somethun.*" Whitney from the Buck's host stand; sweet girl.

Sadie's knees felt untrustworthy as she found her safe place against the wall, but even out of the way, bemused intrusive faces slowed down before lighting up as they passed, elbowing their friends to say 'that's her, that's who I was just talking about'. Sadie wondered if she might smile and wave, give them a jolly spin, stand on one leg and balance a red rubber ball on her nose.

"Hey hey." Maia knocked on the cover of her latest sad-girl read: *The Fault In Our Stars*. "Still nothing, huh?"

"No." Sadie slapped it closed and hugged it like a life raft. "Not even a 'hi' or 'how are you' or 'I'm sorry for making the whole school think you're a slut'."

"Oh com' on, no one thinks that," Maia bluffed. "Okay, the *whole* school doesn't think that. I don't. See?"

"Nothing happened," Sadie whined and stomped a foot, probably to further demonstrate how grown woman she was. "We just kissed."

Maia fought a sympathy laugh at the tizzy. "I know."

"But everyone else doesn't."

"And you have absolutely zero obligation to give two shits what they think. It might help to remember: they're *jealous*. You have no idea how many girls want to be Brooks' secret-dock-girl, even if it is for one night. Maybe you're going about this all wrong."

"So, you're saying I should be happy about this? That I should be basking in the publicity and the fact that one of the quad poles reads 'reserved for Sadie Bexley'?"

Maia's beautiful raven curls shook. "I'm saying it wouldn't change anything." She sighed, striving to come from pure compassion, even if Sadie's degree of *my life is over* problems were measured on a more privileged scale than her own. "Let me tell you how this school works, okay? Listening? Something vaguely scandalous happens—could be a hook up or that Caleb's peepee burns or that a cheerleader ate nine oatmeal cream pies for breakfast—that somehow every loser in camo crocs knows about, and guess what? In a week, no one cares! It's a vicious, full-proof cycle."

"Don't *you* own a pair of camo crocs?"

"Yes—ugh. My darling Anastasia, that is so not the point."

"Well clearly I've broken the system because it's been almost two weeks."

Maia popped a sassy hip and implored her to grasp some nonexistent flip side. "So you broke the system, and you *don't* see how that makes you kind of more awesome?"

Reflecting, Sadie visited last June, when there'd been a rumor circulating: that Tenley and Sadie had gone to an All Time Low after-party at the Roosevelt Hotel penthouse, posing in their underwear for the band photographer. Two days later, Sadie's name was subtracted from the headline, but Tenley's notoriety didn't fade until August, and of course she'd figured *phew*, but also couldn't help amounting the removal of her name to the fact that her involvement didn't make the scandal any more or less gossip worthy. Tenley *was* the story; she was an expendable detail that hadn't made the cut in the retelling.

Sadie wiped her nose on a hankie. She'd been having weird nosebleeds twice a day, like something inside really had ruptured. "Maybe, I guess." She winced. "But where did it come from? Do you think... do you think Brooks started it? Would he do that, do you think?"

Maia wished she had more answers, but in her experience, the more questions you ask, the further you get from them. "Could be, yeah. But the Weston Hills rumor factory has more say-so than even the Golden Holden himself, so also could not be. How many times did you text him again?"

"Please don't make me say it out loud." Sadie sunk lower into the wall of Dali Museum field trip flyers. "They... keep... staring. *Look.*"

Maia scanned the perimeter, squinting at two sophomore boys with exactly three fragile chin hairs, peeping through the yellow marigolds via hunting binoculars. "HEY YOU!" She pegged her mom's homemade horchata at their baby beards, middle finger up, spewing an angry cyclone of Spanish words.

"Ah!" Sadie thought she was dying. "Maia! No! I can't believe —"

They melted in uncontrollable teenage belly laughs, ebbing and flowing and fast-growing all over the grass. They hugged each other up, and toppled again. They couldn't stop laughing. For a moment, Sadie thought if she focused hard enough, some of Maia's headstrong splendor could flow contagiously onto her, and oppositely, Maia crossed her fingers for her to spill that endless cup of sugar and soft spice.

The bell rang and the hallways busied.

"Either you stand up for yourself, or I'm gonna do it for you." Maia's face had tenderized, and Sadie swore it made her look even fiercer. "Your choice."

"Thank you." She'd never meant it more.

"So pep rally—second trashcan next to the boys smelly gym bathrooms? Yes? Meet ya there! Oh and Sadie, don't forget: don't let boys be mean to you." She blew away in an artistic flight.

Sadie couldn't help but think: duh. But it's never that simple, is it? Maybe it could be. Maybe avoiding heartbreak could be as easy as swatting a fly. Yes, exactly. Now let me ask you this: how many flies have *you* successfully slayed by swatting?

Below the main campus, on a sidewalk path leading from the boy's locker rooms, Brooks, Caleb and Levi were freshly worked out and showered, eating Rice Krispies Treats for breakfast as they walked.

"I swear that's what happened!" Caleb was in the middle of recapping the New Tampa kegger he'd undoubtedly 'scored' at. "These two girls jumped me, buck naked."

"Shut up," Levi groaned, eyes rolling to the back of his skull, quickly running out of the energy he typically allots for Caleb's morning puffery. "You know you're lyin'."

Caleb ignored that. "One of them was unhooking the other chicks bra with her *teeth*."

Levi's brow raised. "Thought they were buck naked?"

"Well, you know, pretty much."

"And why would some random girls at some random party do that to a guy they don't know?" Brooks was also losing interest. "Hm? Mr. Farfetched?"

"No, they knew me." Caleb shrugged. "They planned the whole thing."

"Planned it?" Brooks repeated.

"Apparently, there's this whole group of church girls over there who have a thing for pastor's sons. They think I'm godly." He did a little dance move on his toes. "They're not wrong."

"Sure, makes sense." Brooks patted his ego. "These upstanding girls, with their bibles and heist maps, attacked you buck naked, *but in bras*, to get closer to God and shed their sins. Who *wouldn't* believe it?" He sent Levi a repressed glance, and then they both ripped into spasmodic jeers that dug stitches in their sides.

Caleb was now fuming under his tufts of beach blonde. "I told you! It happened!" He shoved Brooks, somewhat hard, but hadn't expected it to knock him headfirst into the ground. "Shit, Holden. Hope your arms workin' better than your legs, or we're all screwed tonight."

Eyes red-rimmed and determined, Brooks shot back, "I'm fine." He walked faster. "I'm goin' to class. I'd rather listen to Mrs. Wilson drill us on PEMDAS for the billionth time than listen to any more of your fake fantasies."

"Don't trip," Caleb spat back, much more irked than he

should be. It could've been pregame jitters, those turbulent spikes in testosterone his mother so loved to moralize about, but that would be episodic, up and down, where the desire to flash bunt the weak fold of his best friend's knees had become a round-the-clock impulse, for almost two weeks now. On that note, Caleb spotted a bashful girl in lilac-colored clothing, alone and afoot towards them. "Hey man, been meaning to ask, whatever happened with Sadie?"

A quake rippled on Brooks' expression, like tectonics plates down a fault line. "Nothing happened. Took her to the dock, and that was it."

"You two don't talk anymore? At all?"

"No."

"Interesting."

"Why is that interesting?" Brooks felt baited, but didn't know what for.

"Oh, you *know*. It's not like there's an endless pool of pretty pickin' in this town. Didn't we already talk about this that day by the dugout? We decided it: you warm her up for me, and then I —"

"Stop." Brooks could just crack up from imagining it; it'd be like the Little Mermaid with the Big Bad Wolf. A beauty and a beast. Frickin' ridiculous.

"What did I do now?" Caleb asked blandly.

"Nothing."

"Okay, well since you don't like her like that, you don't mind if I go for it, right?"

"No, I don't mind." *He'd never touch her anyway*, Brooks thought.

"So you don't care?"

"No, I don't care."

"So you, Brooks Holden, don't care or have feelings for Sadie Bexley?"

"NO! I, BROOKS HOLDEN, DON'T CARE OR HAVE FEELINGS FOR SADIE BEXLEY!"

The lilac shirt was standing a mere two yards in front of them now, sea green eyes so sickened with disgust, Brooks actually thought she might hit him. He half-hoped she would. Of course, she never did.

"Sadie—I." *Didn't mean it, I'm sorry, I don't know how to do this.* "How are you?"

Caleb boasted with a haughty smirk at their star-crossed romance crumbling to soot, behooving for them both. But then he saw her face, and it no longer felt good.

Sadie couldn't recall ever witnessing a six-foot fly swatter, or where to buy one if she had. She anticipated tears like the prolonged building before a sneeze; the longer the build, the more potent you know the expulsion of air will be; but she never cried or sneezed or threw up, even if any of those things would've made her feel slightly better. Instead, she graciously stepped forward and opened their classroom door for them, without saying a word.

Dumbstruck, the football boys ushered inside.

Once that was done, Sadie sashayed ferociously down the hallway, pulled a damp metal door handle, stepped into first period English, and happily took her seat next to the boy with the brown eyes. You know, the *other* one.

On the other side of campus, Maia was on her way to the computer lab for a printing job Mrs. Torres had requested, rubbing balled fists in her eye sockets to wring them to life. She flipped through mental biology flash cards about fungi, mumbled the wrong lyrics to *The Smashing Pumpkins*, came up with her own photo album of celebrities with handlebar mustaches, hounding her brain with continuous shapes and colors to keep it from—

"Wooooah there!" Principal Jay Dunn's booming voice raised every baby hair on her body, mouth earnestly drawn to a smile that should be showing teeth, but wasn't.

Aka, *some backwards manifestation shit.* Maia put on her best face. "Good morning, Mr. Dunn!" she replied, but already knew it lacked the pizzazz that sprinkled happy dust on his twisted sense of authority.

"What a lovely... surprise," bellowed the almighty man, who appeared to be holding a fresh copy of her class schedule. His meaty palm met her back. "How are you, dear?"

"I'm fine, thank you. I—I didn't meant to run into you. I can be clumsy sometimes," she explained in a pretty etiquette; one that felt like a party of mutinous horseflies on pogo-sticks were blasting behind her sealed mouth.

"Oh, not a worry. But you really should be more careful. We wouldn't want you to get hurt now, would we?" Oily tips of a forefinger and thumb trickled up her shoulder, squeezing. The memo: *Do better than that, sweetheart.*

"No, we wouldn't!" Maia refurbished, perking her shoulders to where her chest stood high and plainly in sight. He gobbled them with his eyes.

Jay Dunn and Maia Rosales were alone, but in a wide open hallway with two thousand students and teachers close enough to hear her shouts, if she managed them. Still, Maia wondered what risk he wouldn't take.

"How about you come stop my office during lunch? I have some tips on hallway safety I think I'd like to share with you."

She couldn't breathe, yet still said, "Yes sir. I'll be there."

"Fantastic." The chunk of his thumb swabbed her neck once more, before the handsome principal, the talisman mayor who had an entire town fooled, continued along the spring-themed garden of bird feeders, caterpillars and an under-appreciated pond of orange koi fish. The image of him against the undisturbed garden reminded Maia of the metaphoric poster of the iceberg in home ec class: humble tip peeking above the water, a malignant ship-sinking portion lurking beneath.

She sprinted down the hall to a vacant girl's bathroom, slamming a stall door and weakening on the gross tile. Clutching her tossing stomach, she rested her elbows on the toilet bowl, which once upon a time, she wouldn't even let touch the backs of her thighs. *Once upon a time…*

A different breed of evil suddenly struck her lower abdomen, twisting and stabbing and curling her into a ball. Maia reached for a tampon from her bag. The standard-issue ritual of that—cramps—was a day in paradise compared to the rest they'd never taught in Teen Vogue. The body aches, blemishes, cravings for all the chocolate in Willy Wonka's Factory; those things Maia had come to cherish. Anything that made her feel like a normal teenager, she cherished.

After she'd smothered the worst of the panic, Maia slapped her face to increase blood flow, overturn her sickly gray sheen, and checked herself in the dirty mirror. Her brown-black hair was vast and straggly, impossible to manage, but still she'd never cut it. Maybe if she was paid to do it, but probably not even then. It was the only part of her, unwavering and true, that hadn't changed. Not ever. Maia flipped through her memory bank— yeah, *never*.

Like here: She'd been at Orville Woods park with her mamá on the day mamá had less houses to tidy, feeding ducks, chasing squirrels, hitting a new record on the monkey bars. The caroling ice cream truck made it's second round by the underfunded tennis courts, the boppy music making her mouth yearn for something freezing and rich with sugar. "Go on, you can do it," mamá encouraged, passing her a crinkly five dollar bill, and Maia took off with such speed, she tripped on the red mulch and by the time she'd asked for a LifeSavers Push Pop, the blood had seeped and stained inside her Hello Kitty toe socks. "Look mamá! I paid! I paid!" she'd yelled, remembering the funny look on the other mamá's faces, with whiter skin and whiter shoes, whispering something about Mexicans and the ongoing shoplifting investigation at Kmart.

Mamá then swooped her up in her arms, and in the reflection of her stylish cat-eye sunglasses that made her look so business-woman, Maia saw herself. Both front teeth missing, a sticky ring of rainbow sherbet on her tiny lips, and impossibly immense unruly dark hair that made her head hurt if she ever wore it up. Since then, she never did—no ponytails, messy top-knots, or even space buns when Miley made them cool—Maia had never put her hair up.

But Jay Dunn, *had*.

Mr. Edwards stepped out to retrieve a wheelbarrow of Charles Dickens from the library, and in the meantime, Mallory put on a nonprofit presentation of standing splits for the class.

"Hi hoe," she jingled to Sadie, who'd gotten up to sharpen her pencil.

"Hi, Mallory."

The head cheerleader bent over with her legs in an upside down 'V', spandex bloomers so formfitting and wedged, they graphically contoured all her areas. "Do you like your new nickname?"

Sadie thought about it. "Better than my old ones, actually."

"I tried to help you out, but you didn't want to listen."

Sadie uncovered a crisp paper pouch from her saddlebag. "Muffin?"

Mallory laughed. "Killing with kindness? Or just really that pathetic?

"Yeah. Maybe," Sadie sighed, then considered telling her all the forced woe-is-you frowns were doing nothing for her jowls, and that maybe she should consider preventative botox. That's what Becks had used on Emma, pre-Whole-Foods-check-out-guy fiasco, before they'd become besties over their mutual hatred for dairy. Somehow, Sadie knew it wouldn't make her feel any better. "It's weird. You remind me of my friend Becks."

"Except, we *aren't* friends," Mallory sang in a high pitch.

In spite of herself, Sadie smiled. "Exactly."

Students leaned over their desks of pencil graffiti, waiting for a catfight to break out, because apparently that happened a lot.

"Did he at least lay his hoodie down for you?" Mallory pretzeled her arms in front of her, flaunting a wicked flexibility and squinching up her cleavage. "Or did you just go and bone on the pine needles? No! The *truck*—you did it in the truck, didn't you? Real roomy, don't you find?" She recited as if from a dignified script, as if only doing her job.

Duke stood abruptly, chair slugging on the floor. "Forget to take your bitch pills this morning, Mal?"

"Aw! Look everybody!" Mallory bounced up and down. "The Holden brothers know how to share their *toys*." Her glossy lips designed a thick bubble of Juicy Fruit gum, which everyone knows is no easy feat, then she just ate it.

Sadie gasped, because didn't she know how dangerous that

was?

"Aw! Look everybody! An insecure cheerleader with a comeback." Duke imitated her bouncing, before showing off his impressionist skills with a snarky Aussie enthusiasm. "Here we see a real hungry animal, the territorial beast in it's native humble abode, *deep* in the Florida wetlands. But don't get too close, mate! Crikey! This one's hungry!" He mimed tug-of-warring with a tiger or croc, then being eaten alive.

Sadie reminisced on wildlife clips that would play on the Discovery Kids channel, deciding Duke had watched them too, maybe in an Indiana Jones costume. Some brave students chuckled, the others probably too familiar with the 'Bring It On' movies to piss off a self-destructing cheerleader.

Mallory's head turned all the way like a possessed doll's. "I would say good luck tonight, but everyone already knows we only need one Holden on our field, *especially* the coach." Blooming side by side, Achilles heels become hard to hide. "Have fun on the bench, plan B!" Then to Sadie, "Stay out of my way, okay?"

Sadie wanted to scream at her: *Can't you see I'm trying?*

Mr. Edwards returned and began passing out large books with the Penguin Random House symbol that Sadie had long ago named Skippy.

"Thanks for the backup," Sadie whispered to her sincerely charming desk-mate, and slid him a cacao coconut truffle. She giggled as he stared hard at the alien candy, equally doubtful as he was diligent to not hurt her feelings. "Try it. It's yummy. My mom's special recipe."

Duke swallowed it whole, still fixated on the bendy cheerleader and the painful arrow she'd put in him. "I wish she wasn't a girl, so I could punch her."

Sadie wasn't proud to admit, "Me too."

"So," Duke transitioned, "Is bitter chocolate your idea of a peace offering?"

"I hadn't realized we were at war. Does that mean you don't like it?"

"Oh no, that stuffs better than banana puddin', and I *love* banana puddin'." He licked his fingers for scraps.

"She has more in her classroom fridge." Sadie radiated. "Room 303 in the art building. We could stop by after class if you want?" Then, she heard it the same way he must have; like that would be a *huge* deal. "I mean, I didn't..." If they were spotted, there'd surely be a poll on which Holden was the father of her unborn child by lunch. "Nevermind."

"Weren't you mad at me?" Duke asked, and privately wondered if she knew about the four-leaf clovers living in her eyes. They were so green, it was difficult to look away. "Because of what you saw in my notebook?"

"Oh, right." Sadie summoned back the dismay she'd felt, but it was gone. It was hardly a punishable offence, as Holden offences go. "I guess I was a little mad that you lied to me. Is that why you switched seats last week?"

"Kind of," he confessed, and she was relieved.

"Why'd you switch back?"

"Did you not want me to switch back?"

"Kind of," she confessed, and he too, was much more comfortable.

Shy smiles of potentiality and prohibited heart waves connected them briefly. They read from their separate books for a moment, before ridding one of them, and sharing.

"You know, you could've just told me about your poems." Sadie's cheek swept his bicep, before she snuck another truffle. Mr. Edwards was struggling with his open fly in front of the projector, so she plopped one in Duke's asking mouth too.

In a hushed voice that generated an intense field of heat, "I don't write poems."

"But Duke, I saw—"

"I write *lyrics*," he clarified with a straight face, and Sadie's balls of clovers bugged a little too obviously, which painted on him a triumphant grin that would always be more irresistible than infuriating. He changed the subject, picking at his calloused hands. "You comin' to the game tonight?"

"Isn't everyone?"

"Yes. But I didn't ask about everyone, did I?" He crossed his arms, leaned all the way back in his chair so only two meager legs were in contact with the floor. He teetered here treacherously.

"It's not true," Sadie stressed very suddenly. "What everyone is saying... about me... and Brooks. We didn't..."

"I know."

"You know?"

"I mean—I don't *know*. But I figured."

"How did you figure?"

Because I heard Brooks playing Arctic Monkeys in his room after your date, and the lotion and tissues were missing from the bathroom. "Just a feelin'."

"So you don't think badly of me?" she asked.

"Think badly of *you*?" That was both amusing and sad to him. "Nah," he breathed, more honed and intent, before asking a question in the form of a statement. "But maybe now... you'll know what's good for you."

Certainly this boy, who made fond concrete efforts to be caring, and was in touch with enough to want to author it on a page, would be the practical choice. Certainly, I could tell you the story ends here. But just as you're thinking *how boring would that be,* so was she.

The bad-boy complex is one scientists and astrologists and wizards should study, because it's a perplexing phenomenon; how worth of an emotion rises, as the chances of it's success drops, and relationships are only meaningful and fun if they beat all odds. Because then it becomes more—special, magical, utterly meant to be—it could only happen with *you*. That's my theory. What's yours?

Troubled and hyperaware of her lack of life-smarts, Sadie dwelled on why she couldn't let go of that night at the dock. Seriously, was there a bug in her brain wiring it all wrong? Was there a designated WebMD page she should know about? Perhaps a cautionary vitamin she should be taking? Because Duke was absolutely perfect, but his attention wasn't shocking or larger than life, and honestly, she was afraid a guy like him would never break her.

What scared her more than everything being ruined? Never giving it the chance to be.

And besides, there'd been no signs for Duke. Had there? Had there ever?

Sadie's phone buzzed on the table, earning her a stern look from Mr. Edwards. She opened the message under her binder. No vitamin would save her. It was from Brooks: *'Hey'*.

CHAPTER EIGHT
Recollections

A few periods later, Sadie sat down between the *Got Milk* poster of Lebron and the line of blue trashcans, which were putridly wafting of Uncrustables and spoiled creamed corn. The grand hall of cafeteria kept the acoustics at a steady head-splitting volume, static loud noise that only once allowed Sadie's ears to pick up on a specific.

'Okay, sleeping with one guy doesn't make you a slut. She's probably a nice girl.' I am! I am! Sadie wanted to scream in an unexpected turn of events. *'Whatever, I still hate her.'* She unboxed her homemade lunch of caprese salad and an organic fruit roll-up, feeling glum.

Maia had been approved to switch her lunch period to match hers, but sometimes got booked for tutoring Spanish to a small group in the library. On days such as these these, Sadie sat alone.

"Hey honey!"

Sadie choked on a mozzarella ball. "*Mom?*"

"What?" Margot laughed warmly. "You're surprised to see me?" She was in a modern black-and-white pantsuit and pumps, like a scholastic Super Woman; starkly unfair to the rest of the female administration with cankles or spider veins or jealous husbands who lied and said Old Navy was hot.

"Aren't you supposed to stay in the teacher's lounge?"

"Ah, you're right. The guards will be very angry with me." Margot's superb facial features scrunched into a 'don't be silly' raisin. "Oh honey, why are you sitting by yourself? There's plenty of room at the other tables. Look, right there by the window! Do you see any of your classmates?"

Sadie's neck spasmed in frantic shakes. "Really, I prefer—"

"There's Grace! Grace! Over here!" Her arms were already waving in airplane propeller movements, as the tiny girl with a squeaky clean disguise, pranced angelically towards them.

"Hiya! How *are* you, Mrs. Bexley?" Grace effortlessly spun cobweb silks from her lips.

"I'm doing wonderful, thank you for asking. I was actually just on my way out, but I wondered if maybe Sadie could join you and your friends at your table? I noticed an empty seat."

Sadie's hearing had suddenly impaired, selective and shielding just as her other senses, like a turtle reeling into it's shell. *La la la la la,* she played in her head.

"Abso-posi-tutely!" Grace tap-danced. "The cheer girls are just buzzing for the pep rally. You can help us decide: braids or ponies! We're fifty-fifty right now and it's always such a hassle. Please, *come* and take us from our misery!"

Like every other parent in town, Margot was smitten. "Oh, that sounds fun! Now I wish I could stay too, but unfortunately I have collages to grade. You girls enjoy your lunch!"

Sadie wriggled in place, as she typically does in situations where others would cuss. "Thanks so much mom."

Margot waved, and then her long henna locks dashed from the door.

"Hi, hoe." Grace reverted back to herself.

Sadie had expected nothing less. "Hi, Grace."

Grace swiveled to check in with Mallory, whose strictly shaped brows were all the way up in question, then turned back with some give in her scripture-sculpted decorum. "It's bullshit, isn't it?" she said bluntly.

Sadie was almost knocked over by the haunted look in her eyes. "What?"

"Politics. Most sequels. That right now, little girls are bein' taught to be on their 'best behavior' as little boys are given boxin' gloves to get out their aggression. Bullshit. All of it. Life in general." She echoed once more, "Bullshit."

"Um. Okay."

Grace studied Sadie like a memory, then said, "Nothing happened with Brooks, did it?"

"No! Wait… you actually believe me?"

"What would you believe? If everyone at school was callin' me a slut, with some story to back it, would you think I did it?" She was stock-still. "Think about it."

Sadie wasn't sure if she should tell her: they did, they *had*. After a moment, she decided no, because through the dejected saran-wrap cover over her eyes, Sadie could see she already knew that. "I would probably believe it, yeah." After all, she'd never questioned Maia's status report on Grace cheating on Sterling, just how Maia never questioned her sources, and so on and so on, and long live the gossip mill, for what else is there to do?

"Exactly." Grace wasn't mad, just used to it. "So when I hear things, I never believe it." She half smiled. "You know, I'm not as scary as you think."

"I'm not so sure about that."

"You will be." Grace's lips loured into a confusing ridge of grief, before pointing at Sadie's puffy sleeves. "I have that same shirt by the way. I don't wear it anymore, though."

Sadie asked, "Why not?" And noticed the question had taken Grace's round blue eyes by surprise, or perhaps the gesture of it had.

"Mmm, well, do you ever associate outfits with memories? Like, if something really fantastic or really horrible happens, you remember exactly what you wore, and think of it every time you see it hanging in your closet?"

RIP to the lucky silk cami long gone to a poshmarking New Jersey girl's doorstep. "Sometimes."

"Something happened that I don't want to remember. Plus, it's ripped." Grace did another check in behind her; Mallory was throwing a fit. "You didn't really wanna sit with us, did you?"

Sadie inhaled an uneasy funnel of air, eyeing the girls rubbing anti-cellulite cream on their thigh-gapped legs. The kind of girls that on Wednesdays wore pink… camo. "Not really."

"Good choice." They shared an awkward real laugh, a fluent

similarity to the sound of it. "Your mom is really nice by the way. You seem close." And that was all she gave before floating back to her squad of look-alikes, appearing much more human than she did before the interaction.

See, Grace Lindley was simply trying her best, and maybe that trying looked different than another girl's trying, but it was the same. Maybe they—maybe we—were all the same.

For the rest of lunch, Grace pondered what constituted a true friend, and if sharing Chinese wonton soup take-out with Mallory over a Facebook trash-talking rant, or the fact that they'd both started shaving their legs before anyone else, held any primacy over someone who *listened*.

Enjoying the walk along the campus butterfly garden, Margot felt like an accomplished mother. It was a beautiful thing, watching her daughter blossom, and even if she required the occasional tender nudge to do so, she'd never run out of nudges. *Nudging*, is what mothers were made for.

A spurt of remindful joy overtook her, back to the days of shy Sadie clinging to her calves when she dropped her off at daycare. The teacher, Melanie, would have to manually peel her from her pant leg, hold the bawling child in her lap for morning recess and most of the day, until it was time for puzzles. Thankfully, Sadie loved those.

At precisely 4p.m., Margot would find her daughter meandering the perimeter of the playground fence, eyes wandering in a dream-like state, unresponsive to the games and squeals of the other kids piled in the sandbox. Melanie would express her concerns daily, suggesting a childhood development professional to assist with Sadie's social indifference. "Indifference?" Margot would laugh. "Clearly, you haven't been paying attention."

When in the car, Sadie's zoo of deep-felt imaginings would continue where they left off, until they were parked in the driveway and she'd excitedly announce, "I finished it! I finished my story!"

"What was it about today, sweetheart?"

"There was a barn," she'd explain with dynamic eyes and lively hand movements to make sure she got the full picture, "and horses, and goats, and a mystery to be solved."

"A mystery? What kind of mystery?"

She'd put a puny finger up for *dot dot dot*... "There were turkey feathers in the barn, but no turkey!"

"Wow! Now you have me hooked! Where did the feathers come from, then? There must be a turkey somewhere close by."

A whole teensy hand for *dot dot dot*, then the most elated panoramic grin she'd ever seen since yesterday. "A TURKEY FEATHERED COW!" Tumbling back in the seat, tired and accomplished, Sadie would hug her knees, before explaining how the other children just ran around in circles all day long, and that it looked so boring to do. "They're always yelling," she'd say, "but I don't think they should."

"Why not?" Margot would ask with gentle curiosity.

"They can't hear anything."

"You mean the teachers?"

"No." Young Sadie had paused. "Everything else. The leaves. The flowers."

Come evening, Henri would wrap her in a Blues Clues blanket and she'd tell the same story, eyelids flopping midway through, to-be-continued over a heaping plate of waffles in the morning, but by then she'd often moved onto her next adventure.

Little chemists of light, children are. We should listen to them more.

Margot realized then, perhaps she shouldn't have interfered by inviting Grace over to the table. Because while most young ones are lonely when they are alone, Sadie has always been perfectly abundant.

To parallel this thought, Stacy Lindley—Grace and Caleb's overly kinetic mother—waved to her from the front office. Their paths crossed at the end of the koi bridge. Stacy described how the church was having an Autumn Bible Brain tournament, that she'd come to drop of a sign-up sheet. Margot thusly asked questions out of courtesy, which dispensed unpredictably lengthy answers. But despite the time it took from her day, Margot found it a lovely exchange. People in town had proved kind, most commodious in character, and thoroughly interested. Stacy especially, seemed interested.

"Oh, one more thing before you go, now that I have you..."

Margot checked her watch, before nodding.

"Um, well you see, I wanted to express some pretty pressin' concerns I have. There's been a few, shall I say, explicit and worrisome details shared amongst the parents about your daughter's extracurricular activities. Some of the other PTA moms and I got together for beignets at the gazebo downtown, and Delilah Jordan had some interestin' insight. Our daughters are best friends, have been for *years*. Anyway, apparently there'd been some... *behavior* at the Dunn bonfire just a little over a week ago. Do you recall? I don't know the specifics, but they did say somethin' about a boy, a bad-news dock in the woods where the troublemakers go. Do you know anythin' about that? Well anyway, everyones talkin' about it, and I'm sure you can understand how a negative influence like that can just ruin the whole bunch, don't you? Talkin' to Sadie might do some good, and I can give you some brochures on some helpful church programs we partner with in Georgia. Bless her heart; some of the more malleable young girls just get lost along the way. Oh, I'm sure you have it all under control. You're her mom after all, not me. Please, tell Henri I said hello. It's so sweet to have him back. Alrighty. Buh-bye now!"

Indeed, *nudging* is what mothers were made for.

The bitch slaps were just for fun.

"SADIE BEXLEY TO THE GUIDANCE OFFICE"— the intercom rasped, as if she needed *another* zip tie to fasten her ruined reputation, currently being advanced by boys forced to wear them in place of belts because 'swaggy sagging' wasn't dress code.

For the record, when she'd said she wanted to stray from being known as the 'nice girl', this isn't exactly what she'd meant.

Sadie gave out more muffins as she walked, past the blazes of lunchroom whispers, and out the ugly cafeteria doors. But hey, look at the bright side. At least now she was within a ten-feet distance of Brooks' lunch table in case he wanted to ignore her some more, and at least Caleb and Shelby were there to watch, and at least *angels were real*, Sadie almost hooted in song and dance. She checked her phone; it was 11:11. Did she still make a wish? Yes, she did.

"Maybe she got expelled." Shelby beamed with a conspiratorial grin, fingers crossed under her AE jeans that bunched in the crotch yet were baggy at the waist. It'd always irritated her how girls' clothes were designed around the body type of a hanger.

"Don't be ridiculous." Tanner's rebuttal came out muffled as he chewed a smiley fry. "What could *she* have done to get expelled that the *rest* of this school hasn't?"

"I heard from Hatcher Kent she was caught offering 'special services' in the old home ec room. Apparently she uses this system of Snapple caps. Slip one in her pocket, and she'll be waiting patiently in the craft corner before you even have time to get it up, probably enjoying the Real Facts and warming up her ja—"

"SHUT UP!" Brooks growled with a wolf voice, yet nothing beast-like about him. The flat surface of his nose tipped down, breathing small sips of air. "You don't know what you're talkin' about."

"Mmmmm," Shelby extended her words, "where there's smoke there's fire…"

"YOU DON'T KNOW WHAT YOU'RE TALKIN' ABOUT!"

The whole table freeze framed mid-chew, and there was a heavily drawn out moment of recovery. Brooks outbursts were next to none in frequency, so no one knew what to do when they happened. Especially, him.

"You didn't have to yell," Shelby finally mumbled. "I'm just tellin' you what I heard."

"Sounds like you're startin' a dumb rumor to me," Brooks snarled.

Yeah, *from your damn gateway rumor*, Caleb scuffed the toe of his

Dillard's loafers over and over and over.

"I don't wanna hear another damn thing about Sadie Bexley," Brooks said to all of them. "Who—and not that it matters—has about the same amount of Coyote Ugly in her as Cindy Britton."

"The school *your versus you're* girl with the sunflower shoes?" Sterling slurred with his mouth ejecting crumbs of Cool Ranch Doritos. "She's real smart! I copied off her in Spanish and got a better grade than Paola Diáz."

"But the dock…" Caleb's baby blues narrowed.

"Is none of yours, theirs, or anyone else's damn business for that matter." Brooks' pained face reacted like a rubber band had released at it. "Y'all don't know a *thing* about her." He brooded into the bushes of marigolds. "Not a damn thing."

Shelby saw it intimately from that front-row seat: his feelings for her caulk the brown strands of his eyes, like they'd only just now been recessed to make space. "And you do?"

Again, Brooks didn't even look at Shelby, like she wasn't even there anymore. "Yeah, I think I do." In his far too dashing game-day attire, Brooks jogged down the runway of naked hall, oxfords untying, like if he ran fast enough, maybe he'd make it all the way back to that day at Ogilbee Park. So he could tell those girl-next-world features it was a foul ball, and just leave.

So he could save them both from whatever *this* was.

"Sadie! Wait up!" The quarterback called after her.

Her golden waves were freer today, heavyweight and wild, how they probably look after she's gone for a plunge in the ocean, and the wind and salt have tossed it dry. She wore a genie-in-a-bottle outfit; one that made her appear raspberry-scented with hips straight out of a half-time show; the same lilac flowy top as the day after their date, when he hadn't stopped. But there were no feather barrettes, her mood ring was the color of a bruised avocado, and her smile wasn't jumping from the page.

"Hey," Brooks stammered. "Erm, I mean… *hey*." The second one identical to the first.

"Hey," she replied.

"You… you didn't answer my text, from earlier."

"So you came to deliver it in person?" Sadie waited, but he hadn't thought this far ahead, and it's not like he could play one of those dumb boys who just didn't know any better. She'd already told him *exactly* what not to do. "Maybe I would've answered, if you'd answered any of mine. Did you not get them? There were fourteen."

"I—I did." He scratched his neck until it bled. "I've just been so busy. With practices and work outs—"

"And signing autographs with Caleb? Taking more girls out on your mysterious boat? Remember, I don't know how to compete, Brooks."

"You don't *need* to compete, I swear it's not that!" His pulse was itchy now too, amplifying every sliced fiber of his arm. It'd started to puss. "Can we jus' talk about it? Please? I'm sorry I screwed up the whole high hopes thing—"

"You didn't," she assured, and glanced back through the cafeteria window at a handsome ivy-league haircut of walnut. The brown-eyed body double was watching her back.

"I didn't? But you said I was the—"

"I have to go," she whispered, gaze snapping from Duke back to Brooks, and stepped away, slowly slipping from grasp but still with a lovelorn look that disoriented him seven levels more.

"Sadie, please," he begged.

"Good luck tonight. From what I hear, you're going to be great." Sadie handed the quarterback her very last muffin, as he got the sinking feeling she'd found something else to save up for.

The honeycomb tresses disappeared around the corner, but Brooks Holden didn't run after Sadie Bexley again; not anymore. And he'd try his very hardest to keep this promise, against the lifetime of others he never could.

As knuckleheaded as they'd been at that middle school age, Brooks, Caleb and Levi hadn't gone looking for bullets in their black cassocks and white Scream masks, on their egging-spree Halloween night; the one he'd narrated for Sadie in his truck on the way to Lake Josey. The plan was to get close enough to the reclusive shut-in called Mr. Lance Bexley, to see if the legends were true: that he had a fire-spitting dragon tale, or a deadly lava-lamp glass eye, or a pretty granddaughter their age that every once in a while visited.

Brooks had purposely left out that part, and others. For example, that after Ida's stink-bomb counterattack, Lance had dragged all three of their scared sorry asses to the kitchen table, handing them cokes and towels and in his solemn rumbly voice said, "Sit down, boys. I'm gon' teach you a thing or two about life."

Lance was well into his seventies at the time, with corked dark pores and sagging skin; durable yet shapeable like the texture of rawhide; chunky glasses, burly suspenders, and weathered hands entirely scarred of perseverance and workmanship. The alleged town Scrooge, who'd spent the next hour of his Friday evening nurturing the curiosities of three trespassing misfit boys that'd only just busted his best window.

Lance Bexley had been an orphan before he could walk, living scraps of a life until purpose met him on the battlefields of the Vietnam War. A veteran of the U.S. Marine Corps, with two artificial knees and some third degree burns for memento. Or Memento Mori, Latin for 'remember death', tattooed on his inner arm. In his more peaceful years, he'd been wrangling and rescuing Burmese Pythons in the Everglades, eventually settling in Weston Hills and building a house for him and his wife. Secluded at the center of an orange grove sun, surrounded by rays of evergreen, and the precious comforts of silence and routine.

After the experienced man had run through their list of appetent questions, twice, he agreed to show them his 'Dirty Harry' .44 Magnum, in a secured gun safe in the garage. Last, Lance brought them back to the kitchen for his most important lesson.

"Now these hardy things might interest you now, but boys, I'm about to tell you what the real rush in life is." His crinkled face leaned in close to whisper something top-secret. "You see that hot mama over there?" He pointed excitably, like a kid in a school yard, at Ida on the couch who was engrossed over her needle and patchwork.

The three misfits slowly nodded with weirded out faces.

"True love, that's the rush that never dies, kids. Without love, we may as well be dead. But with it, we'll never be. One day you'll understand. You'll find that rush, too." Then he'd gone and planted a yucky smooch right on her old-lady lips, as if that were allowed. It was the kind of kiss that breaks into a laugh, and Brooks made the safe guess they'd been laughing their whole lives.

After they'd finished their cokes, Mr. Lance offered them a ride home in a red Chevy with their bikes in the back, only they'd told their parents they'd gone trick-or-treating, and the Bexley place was the farthest thing from door-to-door. He changed the offer to driving them a block away from home, to which they agreed.

On their way out, the boys passed a framed photograph of a girl their age who looked like Goldilocks.

"Who's that?" Caleb had asked nosily.

"That's my granddaughter," Mr. Lance had answered proudly.

"Is she a princess?" In hindsight, it'd been a fairly foolish question. But in his defense, she had on a tiara and easily looked the part.

"A princess?" Lance smiled up at the girlish rosy cheeks and green eyes, misting behind his thick fish tank glasses. "She certainly is, isn't she? If you ever meet her, make sure to tell her for me." He winked.

For some reason, Caleb reached out to touch the photo. Then he said, "Okay. I'll tell her."

Brooks, Caleb and Levi each spent the rest of the night on a beanbag, scarfing down Butterfingers and playing World At War on the Xbox, watching the avatars die and bleed, like Mr. Lance had watched his best friend Claude. Pressing the off button, they'd climbed into bed earlier than usual.

The next summer was when Brooks saw them together at the fruit stand on Eiland; Mr. Lance and the golden-haired Bexley girl from the photograph. She'd wanted kiwis. A few months later, Mrs. Ida's passing was printed in the paper, and a few weeks after that, Mr. Lance's followed. There'd been talk of the son, Henri, returning for a joint ceremony, but he never did. Or if he had, no one knew.

Brooks recalled a difficult sort of sadness from the news; it was the first of it's kind at his sheltered age, and an unexplained amount for a man he'd barely known. Or maybe just the right amount, for a man he'd barely known, and yet taught him more about life and what it is to be a man, than his own father had ever bothered trying.

Brant Holden was a coach, fractions of a father, and on the days he felt like it, moving through the motions of the husband. This is what Holden men were made of. This is what Holden men become.

Sadie Bexley deserved a lifetime of rush, to feel rush, to be rush.

Brooks Holden had only been taught to avoid *the* rush.

Sadie knocked on the door marked 'Guidance', instantly welcomed in by a small-statured pixie-like woman with the tempo and traits of Reese Witherspoon. She seemed the type to collect highlighters and sticky notes and big hair curlers, and never use any of them. The teenage therapy room was standard and crammed: dying pots of lucky bamboo, hectic bulletin board of scribbles and magnets, about five dirty mugs with lipstick rings and a stockpile of mini flavored creamer packets sugar plastered on the desk.

Sadie sat down in a cushioned chair and crossed her legs nervously.

The counselor's hands clapped. "Well, isn't this just finer than a frog hair split four ways?"

"I—I'm sorry?"

"I was just happy as a clam hearin' about Henri bein' back, but I never imagined we'd be gettin' two sweet new Bexley women with him! What a gift, I'll say. Welcome Sadie. Oh honey, don't look so alarmed. I only invited you here to say welcome."

"Oh!" She unclenched her anxious hands. "Invited."

"My name's Kelly, the school counselor for all intents and

purposes, but you can consider me a friend. I'm *very* involved with my kids—my office, my phone, even the front door of my house—always open! And if it's not, you can just go on ahead and break down the pool screen. Our neighbors, Jenny and Mike, they patch it up in a jiff and with no extra charge, so no harm done if you do." Mouth moving a mile a minute, she finished the spiel in all but one breath.

Sadie concurred with whiplash. "I'll, um, keep that in mind."

"Terrific! So, is there anythin' you'd like to touch on today?"

"No. I'm—all good."

"So you like the school?"

"It's great."

"And the students?"

"Even better!"

Kelly's finely penciled brow arched in acute disbelief. "You really think so? Because, between us girls... I find them aggravatin' as a rock. The boys are too big fer their britches, gals never been taught to mind their P's and Q's, and I'm the one tapin' 'em back together, lord willin' and the creek don't rise! Ya know what I mean?" She grinned so wide her bright teeth bared like a blacklight was on them.

"No." Sadie's face fish-hooked to one giant question mark. "I mean yes. Honestly, I'm unsure. Is this a test?"

"Heavens no!" Laughing airily, Kelly pretended to flick away the concern from her jeans. "But I do hope you feel comfortable comin' to me if somethin' comes up. Like I said, this town ain't cake."

Is that what she said? "Well... I guess... there is this one thing."

"Uhhuh."

"It's a rumor."

"Nasty thangs."

"And it's about me." Sadie sniffled and stared at the pot of sad bamboo.

Kelly frowned simply, the most simple response that'd ever left this woman, then swiveled in her chair to jot something down on a mint gingham clipboard, while Sadie debated whether her new country Elle Woods counselor was bat-shit crazy, or just passionate.

The answer of course, like most of Weston Hills, was both.

Sadie's slightly prickly legs swung beneath her as she enjoyed the industrial-strength creamsicle scent, a still-life painting of a bowl of apples and oranges, a mega bag of candy corn that'd been there for three years, family photos in silver frames—

Sadie's shoulders tucked shut. Lungs halted. Mind a white blank. Right there, smack dab on the middle of the desk, a Marshalls trifold frame touted a serious husband and two brunette sons. Next to that, a name placard in capitalized text: KELLY HOLDEN.

"Now what's this rumor weighin' heavy on your heart, dear? Tell me all about it."

"Oh… um… it's not… I can't…" Short-circuited, Sadie zoned out on a decorative hanging with fancy font and verses somehow familiar to her. It read: *A bushel and a peck and a hug around the neck.* She couldn't figure out how she knew it. "Huh?"

"The rumor?" Kelly reminded.

"Oh, no. There's no rumor." Sadie's mouth forced to a frumpy crescent shape. "I'm fine!"

"But you just said—"

"Football!" Sadie erupted in instinct, since it usually sidetracked people around here. "There's a game tonight, right? Go… um… wolves!" It took a second to recall the right mascot.

"Huh." Kelly tightened her scrunchie, chatted some more with her clipboard. "Are you *sure* you're alright? This is a safe space love, I guarantee it."

Or her money back? Sadie thought she might throw up. *Or all her pathetic muffins, back?* "Hunky dory!" She finally yeehawed with an exaggerated arm swing, one short of having a deep fried dessert named after her. She jumped up. "Thank you… Mrs. Holden. I'll see you later."

Kelly gave in on pushing her, and instead hauled her into a hug. "Very soon, I hope." It was an extraordinary kind of hug, and suddenly Sadie's heart was stinging with a happy warmth again, because she really felt like Brooks' and Duke's mom liked her, and it was kind of a two-birds-with-one-stone accomplishment. Efficient, you know. Just in case.

The room was still spinning as she stumbled past the clinic, principal's office, and tardy pass counter with a stoned senior giggling at South Park on his phone; perhaps a Holden second cousin or a life-long family friend who they'd played Sharks and Minnows with since birth.

One thing was absolutely clear: everyone knew *everyone*. An entire little green town, with three main roads and three hundred back ones, configured the same as an airplane route map, countless invisible dotted red lines criss-crossed and tangled. Sadie could run from Buck's to Ogilbee Park to the Talkie-Land drive-in theater on the outskirts of town, a total seven-mile distance, and she'd never escape it. *Get ready*, he'd said, *to be famous Sadie Bexley*, and he'd known exactly who she was before she'd had the chance to tell him. Everyone had.

She'd never been more perceptive to the strong ground beneath her feet, replaying the curious words from the chalkboard: *A bushel and a peck and a hug around the neck, a hug around the neck and a barrel and a heap.* "Ow!" Sadie yelped from an elbow to her eardrum, and dropped all her books in a clattering racket. "I'm so sorry—"

"I knew it was just a matter of time before you were throwin' yourself at me, just try not to hurt yourself next time." Caleb Lindley in his actorly stud-suit and tie, that air of residential pomposity, flashed her a decadent grin.

Sadie groaned just as decadently, scowling. "I don't have time for this."

"What's the rush, *rush?*"

"You're not making sense," she critiqued. "I told you to please not talk to me."

"And I told you to stop sayin' please so much."

Sadie crouched over on the white splotchy tile, he followed her on the way down, and here at the bottom, their breaths mingled over the tattered pages.

"Let me help you," he offered, but his offers somehow never failed to sound deceitfully unethical, like he'd instead said *let me help me.*

"I don't want your help." Those doofus buttercream curls always egged her to run refreshingly unfiltered. "I said I don't want it!"

But by then, he'd already collected the mess in a neat tip-top stack. The ripe hands passed them over as they both rose to standing with unbudging stares.

"You know," Sadie took one step closer, tipping her head all the way back because he was a steep foot taller, "if you're such a fully booked ladies man, shouldn't you be plenty busy plaguing some other girl's life instead of stalking mine?"

He laughed in a mocking amusement. "Stalking? You really think you're so special, princess?"

Her foot stomped. "Stop... calling... me... *that!*"

He trimmed the distance between their eyes to paper-thin, cocked his head just slightly, and made his own promise, without a pinky needed, "Not a chance."

As he went away, probably to pull up the skirts of JV tennis girls, Sadie's pupils dilated, the skin of her inner thighs sweated, and her whole body was on the brink of furious convulsions, as if somewhere in their trade, the big bad wolf had slipped her a large quantity of honeysuckle berries. She could actually taste hatred on her saliva.

Before continuing on, Sadie wiped her arms and legs like wiping off bugs, and again the music began to play. It was much louder now: *I love you, a bushel and a peck, a bushel and a peck and a hug...*

An impossibly sustained memory tugged at her heartstrings: Grandpa Lance and grandma Ida spinning and spinning all across the living room dance floor. A record, *this* record, played on the turntable they enjoyed every Sunday. A day of dancing, kissing, laughing. Ida's sewing project left unfinished on the sofa, a scattered puzzle on the rug, dewy-eyed Sadie wiggling and cheering them on as a little girl. "Com' on up here, princess!" her grandfather had shouted in his southern jubilance, bifocals falling, suspenders hanging, before lifting her over his shoulders so she was on top of the whole world. "Show us those moves, princess!"

She'd completely forgotten. How had she forgotten? Princess; that's what he'd nicknamed her their last summer together in the orange tree maze. Or someone else, several months before on a Halloween night, already had.

The warm ethereal whirlpool splashed their reflexive waves inside her, but all Sadie could think was *what a weird... coincidence.*

CHAPTER NINE
The Pep Rally

It had officially come time for the pep rally. Students thronged into the gymnasium like an ant pile stepped on, engaging in a battle royale of *who's sitting with who*. The bottoms of shoes squeaked against the slick floors, snuffed by the claps and yaps of cheerleaders on mats, plus some smooth easy listening—'*WHO LET THE DOGS OUT?*'

Mallory pirouetted front and center, hips pumping an invisible hula-hoop, best foot forward with an attractive smile even if she didn't feel like it. Even if the hyperextension ligament tears were swelling and her hipbones protruding from her diet of edamame and Water-X capsules, she sucked in and danced pretty.

Co-captain Grace did a few herkies behind her, before fleeing to the bathrooms. Ever since lunch—after her moment with Sadie and the familiar shirt she'd been wearing—Grace had been having palpitations, and the lunch ladies in hairnets didn't serve any whiskey, so she wasn't doing well. The pastor's daughter was ordered to be an everlasting godsend, despite what God *did* send, so in his name, she hid.

Lastly, Britney and Whitney simply bopped in their bows; shallow and apathetic and the most beautiful little fools; the happiest in the room.

Sadie ogled at the massive red and black balloon archway, a sculpture of a grizzly wolf sinking it's teeth in a golden football, and the seashore of dashing students with the tide coming in. She expected to be pushed around, like always in crowds, but today everyone heeded her bubble. They waited for her to go first and moved respectfully around her. Though, she *did* have to dodge a mascot doing physical stand-up to the cha-cha slide.

"The town's best kept secret." Maia nodded at the wolf suit going low. "No one knows who it is."

"Really?" Sadie took one look. "Mr. Edwards, for sure."

"What?! No way! How do you know?"

"Are you kidding? He smells like banana peppers and mayo, and there's a Quiznos sub wrapper stuck to his paw."

Maia's mouth dropped in amazement. "Oh my god, you're right! Way to show us up, Velma."

Sadie laughed but wished she'd said Daphne instead.

As they climbed up the jammed bleachers, Maia flapped her arms to scare away the guys in baggy Ecko shirts speaking exclusively in Wiz Khalifa lyrics. "Honestly, I don't understand the point of these things. I've had enough perky bitches yell 'defense' in my face to last a lifetime. Besides, how is school spirit going to help the team win a game?"

Sadie shrugged. "Maybe it'll boost their egos?"

"Dear God, their poor heads are going to explode!" Maia groaned, then pointed. "Calling it! That spots ours!"

Finally, the joyous hall settled into a semi-restful state.

Jay Dunn, with hints of licorice masking the bitter odor of Deadly Nightshade, in his Italian suit and slicked back hair, approached the center podium. Charisma engaging, he tapped the mic with a 'is this thing on' joke, before admiring each of their impressionable heads, and proceeding with a speech. "My my, would you just *look* at you kids. Now, I thought I told y'all to stop growin' up on me. The older you get, the older I get, and trust me when I say, y'all don't wanna see Mr. Jay with that salt and pepper hair, alright?" The gym fractured in bright laughter, and Jay milked every second of it. "Alright now, off topic, movin' right along… I hear there's some football comin' our way." He induced devotion by the thousands. "Well, I for one don't know if we're ready for all that. Do *you* think… we're ready?" Frenzied roars mauled the tall walls of championship banners. "Hmm, I see."

The applause went over a minute, and Jay always let praises take their sweet time. The craze was spectacular—from the students, to the teachers, to the custodian waving a mop from the corner closet—it was like they'd do anything for him.

When it was time, Jay's Tony the Tiger mannerisms went serious. "Tonight, our players are gon' give it their all. Our team is gon' play for us, and we… we'll be up in those stands cheerin' and prayin' for their safety, as a family." A meaty fist clutched his chest dramatically, two tears squeezed from his eyes, and his arms outstretched for a group hug towards the crowd. He chanted, "The wolves are back!"

An invigorating soundtrack of football reborn filled the room; each individual vibration nagged at Brooks' shoulder. He eyed a nerdy group of Pokémon traders in the back of the stands enviously.

"*Golden Holden! Golden Holden!*" The student body yelled.

Brooks couldn't help but think, *you mean broken Holden.*

Amongst the bleachers, Sadie stumbled from the collective shouting and gust of bad breath. "This is insane! Help me!" She giggled and fell back into Maia, who had gone stiff. "Maia? Hello? *Earth* to Maia." Sadie had never used that phrase, but if only she had a penny for every time it'd been used on her.

Her friend was there, yet hopelessly missing. Thick lashes open but eyes startlingly blank, flickering violently—and for some reason—pointed directly at the podium at the center of the room. It must be claustrophobia, or an allergy attack? Had she mentioned any? "Maia!" Sadie tried again, not knowing it was pointless. That it would be received muted and distant as if shouted from the bottom of a pool. As Maia went from hyperventilating breaths to a still vacuum in her lungs, Sadie resorted to desperate measures and jabbed her side. "MAIA!"

Maia turned to her with a frown, as if nothing terrifying had happened at all. "Stop that." She didn't appear herself somehow. "That hurt."

Sadie blinked in a few exclamation points, quietly asking, "Are you okay?"

"Yeah, I'm chill."

"But you… you looked really ill…"

"Must be the cabin pressure of all the egos." Her hand did a few aloof waves. But Sadie wasn't dropping it, and Maia had picked up on enough by now, to know just how to *make* her. "Jeez, take a chill pill, alright mom?"

A fun fact about the early wounds in life, is that they're highly recyclable. No reason to add more, when you can reuse.

Sadie hid her hurt face and dabbed at her new nosebleed. Today was officially her least favorite holiday.

Their principal had moved on to diagramming that 'one touchdown that put 'em on the map'; the very same locals still analyze and get heated over in the checkout line of the Ace Hardware store. "Let's bring out the man himself, Mr. Coach, Brant Holden!"

Brant led the football army from the side oaken doors, and the young men lined up in front of the stage. Some of them were cropped and heavyset, others thinner and built for speed, but all cream-filled with a vainglory sovereignty they'd need to survive the evening.

The cheerleaders arranged into a country burlesque tunnel, high-powered poms and silken legs flaunting and flailing.

Mallory, with a very seductive mic in hand, announced the player's names one by one. "Number 3… Duke Holden! Number 26… Levi Tucker! Number 45… Caleb Lindley! Number 2… Brooks Holden!" And the crowd went wild, wilder, the wildest they'd ever seen.

The quarterback carried himself with an ounce of humility, unlike Caleb who was blowing kisses to a girl in the crowd— *several* girls—though all of them oblivious to his all-inclusive fine print.

To distract herself from looking at Brooks, Sadie gave out mental compliments to every head in the room, sort of spewing them like sunny bullets—*cute shoes, awesome hairline, you rock those unattached earlobes, did those boots come with grass stains or did you do that yourself*—perhaps in a last-ditch effort to collect enough points, to cash her tickets on something amazing. She'll have one grand gesture, *please*.

Then she asked again, without saying please.

Elaine Dunn, big barrel curls bouncing, glided through the entrance behind the bleachers. A last minute order of carrot cake for the Ferrel family had kept her late at the cafe, but still she'd been hopeful about making it in time for Jay's speech. Mealy bleach enameled her complexion upon realizing she hadn't. But that's okay, it was the same speech every year. Surely, he could look past it. *No one can read your thoughts, Elaine. You imprudent woman, be honest with yourself for once.* She smoothed her carnation-pink shift dress, wiping the dollops of butter and flour. A stain. In public. *Strike two.*

Sure enough, her husband's beady eyes seconded that from the opposite wall, before coming over to give her a hug, and subtly gripping her ribcage until it felt it might snap.

"This right here is special." Brant squinted into the disorganized mob, his peripheral highly conscious of the fickle fluorescent bulb that just last week, him and Henri had confessed under. "I've never known a greater joy than the joy football has brought into my life. Sharing it with all of you, it's a blessing I'll never take for granted." He rubbed his jaw, as the lightbulb above cackled *I know what you did.* On, off, on, off—it flickered.

"Most of you know, maybe some of you don't, but—I—I used to play. Football, that is. On that same field. I'd train, I'd sweat, I'd bleed..." *Manny bleeding, your fault.* On, off, on, off.

"I gave it my all, but in the end, uh, in the end... God had a different plan for me. This whole time I've been preparin' to be here today, as your coach, and... to help these men make history! I see myself in every one of you"—*a killer*—"a product of hard work." On, off, on, off.

Fighting a sickly nausea, Brant turned to his eldest son. Maybe one day, he'd apologize for hinging his life of dishonor and sin on the notion his rightful one could repair it. Maybe one day, he could tell him everything. "I know... we know... you won't let us down..." *Because I already have.* On, off, on...

By now his voice sounded like he'd swallowed a jar of cinder dust, and Kelly raced in with a Dixie cup of water, lanyard clinking like copper cowbells. While the coach sipped, he gestured for Brooks to come up and give a few words of sentiment, as he was expected to do at these types of things.

Usually, he'd at least thought up a stylish opener. Usually, he wouldn't spend three periods tripped up on what a pretty girl thought of him. Usually, had lost it's luster.

Brooks, that absolute heartthrob from those sticks, loafed to the podium as girl's necks careened like string cheese. "Hey guys," he said, and half the audience keeled over. "I just wanted to give y'all a thank you for all the support." In the upper right, a beautiful girl finger-combed her honeylike waves. But the girl wasn't looking at him. In fact, she was looking at everyone *but* him. "Um, yeah. It's been a wild ride through the years. And tonight, win or lose—"

People scoffed roughly and with scathing expressions, like that was outrageous.

"Um, right. Ha ha." He paused. "Okay, no—look." His arms slacked. "I ain't perfect. Y'all ain't perfect. Even *God* ain't perfect, right? I still remember my first game." Brooks licked his dry lips and chuckled to himself. "Man, it was bad. I was so nervous and green, and all I could think about was how many people I might be lettin' down. But then I realized somethin'. That those people had shown up to watch us play a sport we loved, and that's all there was to it. A game, like when you're a kid, and it all became so simple. I guess my point is, I'm goin' out there to have a good time, and I hope y'all have a good time, too. Cause ain't that the point of these things? To have fun?"

Starved disapproving scrutiny waited for him to cue some facetious laugh track. The students whispered amongst themselves as if the next person over held all the answers, the next person after that swore he really did, and the next person after that offered up a 'Holden Answer Key', selling copies for five dollars.

Brooks felt like screaming at the cheerleaders to *shut up*, telling them all it was over, exposing the marred muscle bruising stained on his back. Instead, he fist-pumped. "Go wolves!" And everyone was happy again, except for the one person whose opinion he cared about. She'd wanted kiwis.

As Brooks stepped back towards the stage, he froze, because Caleb was holding a coke, and suddenly he could hear Lance's starchy Rambo voice say *Didn't I teach you a thing or two about life?*

Brooks lurched back at the mic. "Just one more thing," the quarterback breathed easier, lighter, and burst into an impulsive smile. "While we're all here, I wanted to welcome a new student this year. Her name is Sadie Bexley. I'm sure you've heard her name by now, probably from that rumor about her rejectin' me. Well, it's true. I struck out with a really great girl. Maybe one day I'll get a second chance."

From 'slut' to 'girl the quarterback can't get'—what all great small town it-girls are made of.

Maia prepared a trust fall basket. Duke rashed up like he'd eaten a bag of peanuts. Mallory steamed as if she'd snapped all ten ombre acrylics. Caleb stayed neutral and fine, the most chilling of all. Teenage girls' hearts collaterally shattered on the shiny floor, meanwhile the student with the answer key crumpled and tossed it in the wreckage, and all Brooks could think was: *what a rush.*

An up-beat Lady Gaga song sounded from a boom, the squad of high ponies engineering a diamond pyramid followed by a routine of body rolls and high kicks, which they'd rehearsed over a rigorous six-week summer boot camp. Howbeit, that on the final eight count, the girl banished to the back row corner who looked far too much like Violet Beauregarde in blueberry form—Harley? Darley? Mallory called her thunder thighs—kicked with the wrong leg, slamming into Grace, who slammed into Britney, who twisted her ankle and snagged the rope at the bottom of the balloon archway fixture.

The metal wireframe toppled and ignited cavernous pops of red and black rubber latex confetti. The spooky light bulb finally exploded and rained in sparks. The rest of the lights went out too. The bell rang. It was time to go home.

As students ran like wild geese in the chaos, two silver-bobbed advanced-in-years teachers opted out of the havoc behind the stage curtain.

"Anna Mae, you hear Henri Bexley has a daughter at the school now?" The first one said, nibbling on a zip-locked brownie.

"Sure did, Loretta," the second one answered, shaking her head and tut-tutting about how this same thing happened twenty years ago, and that she wouldn't be surprised if the town burns to the ground by playoffs. "The end of oyster spawnin' season at best."

"I reckon you're right. Henri did cause trouble 'round here, in his days."

"No, my dear." She shook her head. "The trouble's here all on it's own. He just has a talent for rattlin' the grillwork 'til the whole town's cryin' shames are all splattered on the highway 301 billboard like a can of Pam."

"And you think his daughter's just as talented?"

"Look around. Orange doesn't fall far from the tree, now does it? You go clean out those gutters, Anna Mae. We would all do well with cleanin' out our gutters."

"Oh… my… GOD!" Maia vented through squeal, stopping and going on the brakes, until she whipped the steering wheel like a racecar prowess, her yellow Volkswagen bug reversed from the gates, and they surged down Stadium Drive with nowhere to be, fast. "I haven't seen Mal gal that red since Mr. Hanson told her leggings weren't pants!" She checked on the sore losers with lift kits in her rearview, then on Sadie. "Girl, *what* are you doing?"

She was up on sturdy knees, in a much too willful crouch for the chiffon fabrics she habitually wore, dangling half her feather-frame out the window. And here, with enough momentum, capful spools of steady wind in her hair, a heavenly high like no damn other, Sadie screamed with as much might and main as her out-of-practice voice box allowed. She had arrived. She was ready. She wasn't stopping for anyone.

"What the hell?!" Maia slapped her on the rump bone. "Are you crazy?"

Sadie smiled, pesticide-free. "Yes, I am. Aren't you?"

Maia grinned and shook her head, but couldn't be more on

board. "Hell yeah, I am!"

Without further ado, the two girls were taking turns shrieking and singing, preposterous giggles in between. Everything about it was cleansing; shouting at the century-old oaks by Big Lots, the sand hill cranes that rendezvous on the median strip of 14th, the toffee-nosed moms in pleated skirts tattling outside The Lipstick Tree (might as well give 'em something to talk about), and finally, a lonely man in a threadbare WH Wolves hoodie lounging in the shade of the gazebo. Sadie asked Maia about him.

"Otis?" she said, like Sadie could confirm. "Yeah, that's our Otis."

"Who?"

"He's homeless, a wanderer you could say, though he never goes far. He 'resides' in this makeshift tree house behind Home Depot, but mostly he's here in town. People like him a lot, they'll sit and chat, invite him in for some wings at Buck's when they have the extra cash to spare. He doesn't need much, and half the freebies I've seen people hand him, he feeds to the ducks. Oh, except for beer. He'd drink the Backdoor Brewery dry if they let 'em. He's tried." Maia smiled proudly at their lovable roamer. "You don't have to be afraid of Otis."

Sadie watched him some more as he straightened to a sit, opened a Sports Illustrated comfortably with his feet up, like this patch of downtown grass was his living room, and it was odd how cars kept driving through it.

"You'll see him tonight," Maia added.

"At the game?"

"Definitely. Otis *loves* football. He's our lucky rabbit's foot." Maia chuckled in a touching hum. "Every game he comes to, we win. A few years back, the coaches started inviting him on the bus for the away games."

Sadie, vibrantly moved, saw no resemblance to the knocked-down vagabonds who'd mug and steal to survive in LA, because here, Otis was taken care of, and by an entire community. There was something really beautiful about that. "Maybe this place isn't too shabby after all." Sadie leaned into the window and watched the blue sky explode, like beauty itself, could implode.

"Yeah, maybe." Maia felt it best to leave it at that.

Minutes later, they were in the quaint upstairs of the Bexley house, knee-deep in cream eye shadows, charcoal liners and half-used drug store mascaras. As they prepared, the giddy ladies carried with them a youthful gaiety, as if tonight, this *one* night, anything was possible.

Sadie sifted through pastel clothing, before pulling a sweet yellow sundress over her head. Maia tickled her pits traitorously while her arms were up and face covered.

"Oh man!" She teased. "Look at those *shoulders!* I don't know how on earth Brooks is going to keep his eyes on the ball with those babies exposed."

"This is like, the shortest dress I own."

"You look like a gumdrop—cute—but a gumdrop."

Sadie plopped down on her bed, falling onto her back with a bested grunt.

"Do da doo da doo." Maia took on a stylist role. "Here, put these on." She tossed over a pair of light-wash jeans of Emma's that Sadie had accidentally packed; the super stretchy kind you could do acrobatics in if you wanted. Emma always wore them to the mall for easy undressing in fitting rooms, and parties.

Sadie shimmied in to them with a few squats and leg shakes, before turning to face the mirror. "Um, I don't think… I can wear these."

Maia grabbed her by the shoulders and forced her to stay. "Are you kidding? You look sexy!"

Sade squirmed. "But I'm not… that." Her hand reached out, grabby and anxious for the *cute* yellow. "I'm more of a dress person, anyway. You can wear them if you want. They'll look great on you."

"I know," Maia replied flatly. "But what does them looking great on me, have to do with you not wearing them?"

In her head: *um, everything?* "Do you want to borrow something else, then?"

"Sadie, shut up. We're not talking about me."

Her green eyes felt heavy and swelling. "Okay."

"Look, I could be a fake friend and tell you to take them off so you don't look better than me, if you want. I could also tell you a bob-cut would look amazing with your face shape, and that yes, you should keep plucking your eyebrows. But honestly, if it were *my* choice, I'd rather both of us look hot out there. That's what real friends do, you know?"

Sadie thought about that. "No. I didn't know."

"Well, now you do."

The gold head spun a few times to get a better view, and she shifted her weight from left leg to right, to watch how the denim supported and lifted. Her body hadn't changed from thirty seconds ago, but it had. She sparkled with a rather sly grin chockful of breakthroughs and said, "I've got good cheeks."

"Hell yeah you do, mamacita!" Maia salsa danced in place and fanned her mouth like she'd slurped a jar of jalapeños. "That'll spark that boy's imagination, for sure. Whole game he'll be thinkin' about where he wants to *put it.*"

"Put what?" Sadie chimed. "Oh, right." She distracted from her blushing by packing her things in her saddlebag: guava lip balm, travel concealer, rose quartz, crinkled twenty.

Maia had her inklings, and normally she wouldn't think twice about asking, but she could see Sadie was affected by these topics, uplifted or disturbed, depending on how the context was presented. "Can I... ask you something?"

"Sure."

"Have you ever... I mean are you..."

"Is it that obvious?"

"Yeah, but in a good way."

Sadie sighed. A *good* way. "I've dated a few guys, sort of. I've just never met someone who it felt right with. I'm not expecting some life changing thing to happen, but I don't want to do it, just for the sake of doing it, you know?" She had a feeling Maia knew she was downplaying, so she finally just came out with it. "Or maybe I'm just waiting to meet my soul mate."

They laughed together in a grounded way, and knew they'd reached a new level of friendship.

"I think that's cool," Maia supported. "I wish I'd waited."

"How did... yours happen?"

"Wilder Copeland, a senior, asked me to homecoming last year, I think because he liked Latina girls and I was the only one who hadn't been asked yet. He bought me sea lavender, like the already dried-up flowers, and those hazelnut chocolates with the gold wrapping that you think are fancy but you can get from CVS. We took pictures by Pretty Pond, danced with all his friends, and we talked about going to Busch Gardens for the Christmas lights, and the Gasparilla Festival, which were both months away so it felt like a long term thing. Like, we'd date, have inside jokes, stupid pictures in our camera rolls of us doing nothing but that'd still mean something. So, that night at his brother's lake house, we did. It was good—I mean not *that* good because it was my first time—but I was good, like alright. I knew that even if we broke up down the line, there'd be this special thing connecting us. That even if the pictures on the camera roll were deleted, we'd keep just one."

Immersed in the flashback, Sadie put her ballets on the wrong feet. "When did you two break up?"

"We didn't, because we never dated. He hasn't acknowledged me since."

"That's horrible!" The ballets kicked off in different directions, one knocking over the salt lamp. "What does that— how could he—where was the—no." Sadie whined and melted on the floor. "*No.*"

Maia consoled her with a light backrub. "I felt that way too, for a while." She made sure to follow with, "But I'm sure it's different for everyone. For you."

"Mhm." Emptiness assaulted a romantic's stomach where butterflies usually lived year-round.

"Wilder Copeland never professed his adoration for me in front of the whole school."

"That's true," Sadie agreed, but she wasn't thinking about herself anymore. "Was there anyone else? Like a second guy?"

Maia's throat tightened. "Yes."

A rare ferocity struck Sadie's features as she stared into the dispersal of sunset over the groves. "I hope he was better towards you. I hope he was respectful and kind. I hope he did better than dumb Wilder Copeland."

Now Maia's eyes were blurring, and she just nodded, saying nothing.

CHAPTER TEN

The Serious Business of Tailgating

Henri's red Chevrolet braked into a vacant spot, right outside the Weston Hills High stadium entrance.

It was around 7:15, golden hour. Blends of fluid sherbet, like sidewalk chalk art after it rains, radiated over the field. The strength of the night could be heard for miles: marching band drums, Dollar Tree clackers, Ned the announcer, cheerleaders, echoes of fans under the stands. The breath of a town once dormant returned to life. As much a game as an integral social event, people stopped to greet their friends, friends' friends, neighbors, bank tellers, pool guys, the zumba instructor their husbands cheated with in high school. A melting pot of kith and kin, the town's nearest and dearest, and buttery back-handed flattery only they could understand.

Sadie and Maia jumped down from the backseat, said their brisk goodbyes, and ran ahead to hand Mr. Edwards their admit-one tickets.

"Hmph. Are we embarrassing?" Henri opened the car door for his wife with an amorous diligence, and with this marchy trooper walk that made it also silly.

"No. I think we're pretty hot," Margot answered, an effortless long and lean head-turner in a divine vintage slip and sweater, very Anthropology and royal. She looped her arm of crystal bangles in his. "We're the hottest."

"Speak for yourself." He nuzzled lips against her neck as they began a slow walk, not even looking forward to make sure they didn't trip on a wheel stop. As they moved, the environment moved with them. Married couples in love are on a different planet than the ones passively aggressively discussing the dishwasher. "You know what I wonder? I wonder how I got so goddamn lucky with you." Henri's earthy curls shook back and forth. "I reckon God favors me."

"Aha, so that's why you brought me here. You want to show me off to all your old friends."

"Right on the nose! They'll probably reckon God favors me too. Hell, they'll be weak in the knees and green in the face after one look at you." His fingers found her waist that made him stoked and rapt at the touch, lowering some, restraining at the sensual incurve of her back. The perfect pair shared a carnal look secret to them only, and Delilah Jordan who'd been watching from her Porsche.

The intense floodlight beams seemed to concentrate on Sadie and Maia as they emerged for all to see; sun and moon elementally unstoppable as one. Sadie waved to Brooks in his bulky yet tight uniform, who didn't outwardly give anything back, but his chin did dip a flyspeck amount, so she knew he was happy to see her.

"LOCKER ROOMS! NOW!" Brant roared to the team, and cut the connection.

A lively tailgating section was astir and boisterous to the right of the field, frisky trucks bumper to bumper to bumper, etc. The countriest of country music was the tail that wagged the dog, and drinking.

Maia wasn't super close with Brooks' group of cool, but she was one of those people that everyone liked, so it wasn't weird when she went up to them and said, "What's up, you Budlight bums?"

"Hey," Colton replied, basically an official invite, with his butt-chin slopped of yellow suds and foam.

"Howdy ladies." Tanner tilted his jumbo cowboy hat. "What can we do for yer?"

"We came to join the party." Maia sat, patting the black hard surface for Sadie to do the same, which she did hesitantly and hyperaware of Shelby's disapproving freckles.

"By all means!" Tanner shouted, as if for everyone. "Now it's a real fiesta. I heard you chucked some horchata at some sophomores today."

Maia established validity, before casually swinging her feisty eyes to Shelby with a message. "They were being mean to my friend, so they had it coming."

Meanwhile, Sadie was busy studying the weedy hangout venue. "Is this the VIP section?" She shrunk at their amused chuckles.

"Aw, com' on. Don't tell me this is your first football game." Tanner's face went from beer and skittles to utter devastation. "Shit, is it *really?*"

Sadie was afraid of offending them again, so she just shrugged.

"What in *tarnation,* you really never—this calls for some celebration! Here, try this." He handed her a cup marked with Circle K branding.

She obeyed and went for it, perhaps with too high of aspirations, and suddenly she was coughing and choking as mousse burned and went up her nose. "That's awful!" She laughed in good spirit. "And my mom makes me drink celery juice every morning, so I'm pretty used to gross."

"Let's test that theory." Sterling tapped her shoulder excitedly from behind like they were total homies now. He was in an almost-clean maroon shirt, the first time she, and a lot of others, had seen him in anything other than the grody wife beater. "Give this one a go."

Sadie did, and terminated half her taste buds in the process. "Agh!" It took her half a minute to get it down. "I taste… Shirley Temple, some sort of lemon lime, and a very slimy touch of cough syrup. I'm sorry, was this supposed to be *better* than the first one?"

Sterling doubled over from the fun, eyes half-closed and dopey. "Nope. But it'll get ya shit-faced real quick."

"Sterling hun, don't poison the *poor* girl," Shelby so helpfully mothered, and it only leant more fuel to his spitfire of cackles.

"I think she can handle herself. She's a big girl. Right, Sadie?"

Sadie's head turned back and forth, and eventually she just decided, "Right." She took another sip of Sterling's concoction, and this time, it was just the thirst quencher she'd been needing.

"Tanner, your stupid hats blocking the view," Colton complained in a deep gravelly voice, much like the Turner or McCreery coming from the speakers.

"Hey! Don't hate on the hat! This thing is a lucky charm and you're gonna hurt its feelings!" He patted it to say *don't listen to them.* "Besides, the bigger the hat, the closer to God."

"Off." Ali demanded in a cool skater girl outfit from Tilly's, hurling a boiled peanut like the ten-gallon top was a basket game.

Sterling snagged it and put it on himself. "Damn thing don't even fit me! My head really that big, or is yours just small?"

Ali threw another peanut: score! "Maybe you're too close to God already."

"True," he mumbled in sleazy mischief. "You already know I'm *hiiiiigh.*"

A broken trumpet peal hailed out of Shelby. "I'm sure Pastor David would love to hear you say that, might just marry you and Grace right on the spot."

Sterling's expression fell red and fervent like several wasps had stung it, and suddenly he recalled that one time in second grade when she'd likened him to one of those hairy screaming armadillos when he got worked up. Like right now. "Grace and I have a complicated relationship, but you're welcome to stay out of it, thank you very much."

"You mean… a *secret* relationship."

"Yeah? And what about you, Shelbs? Make out with any softball players lately, cause lesbi-honest, ain't no guy in their right mind ever puttin' up with your bitch attitude."

The Achilles heels might as well be tagged on their necks; they knew where it would hurt the most. A gashing tension cut through the group of best friends, who would always have plenty of material to recycle. No one laughed. But no one spoke up either.

"Guys." Colton stood up sharply, as his facial bones kneaded with rage. "What's Orville doin' on our turf?"

A pimped out pick-up with blackened windows, spiked metal rims, and a subwoofer you feel in your gut, put on a vulgar matinee of mud slinging across the tailgaters. Two boys in orange and black waved to them from the windows, flapping that flag with 'OHS', spitting at the ones with 'WH'.

"Let the games begin." Tanner adjusted his hat.

"The war," Sterling corrected with narrow, delirious, bloodthirsty eyes. "Let the war begin."

Inside the locker rooms, adrenaline was rising, drugging the players with blind power and concentrated skill. Each of them went about their private rituals to lock in, and by that, I mean using whatever they had stored in the depths of their minds to get *real* angry.

Levi sat on a bench and meditated with his eyes closed. Caleb slammed his forehead into a locker until the freezing metal numbed his skull. Duke kneeled on the floor and tied his cleats over and over, because he just couldn't get it right. Brooks isolated in the corner and did push-ups until his tortured arm socket made life a living hell, but he kept thinking of Sadie, and that made him feel better—*dammit.*

Interrupting their rituals, Brooks' phone buzzed on the bench, then Duke's buzzed on the floor. It was impossible to tell whose came *first.*

"She happy about that little stunt you pulled at the pep rally?" Caleb snarled, watching. "Hope she's worth pissin' off coach."

"I was just bein' nice." Brooks fought a smile over the text.

Caleb couldn't help it; he felt extra antagonistic tonight. "I almost believe you, but you never were a good liar."

"What's that supposed to mean?"

"What I just said," Caleb spat, and caught Duke fighting an awfully similar face. "Damn, both Holden brothers got goofy ass grins tonight. Who's *your* girl, Duke?"

"What?" He stiffened.

Caleb snatched the device and read the message aloud, making sure to impersonate an airy fairylike voice so they knew *exactly* whom it was from. "Good luck tonight! Can't wait to watch you play!" He sneered lucidly. "Well, would you look at that?" He tossed the phone back. "Seems our new girl has a type."

There was a split, peaceful, olive branch moment when it hadn't yet hit Brooks. This was his baby brother, for Christ's sake. His punch-able, complaisant, do-good little brother who writes music in his bedroom, uses terms like 'coolio' and 'going steady', and thinks being friends with a girl is just as important as the rest of it. The olive branch turned to poison ivy, the moment was over, and he'd just described her *perfect match*. Brooks glared at him and remembered the last muffin. "You talk?"

With time running out, Brant took a stand in front of the team and waited for them to kneel. "I know you men don't need another speech remindin' you to leave it all on that field tonight, so I'll leave you with this: every decision you make right now, will determine the man you'll stay the rest of your life. So tell me, do you want to be great? Or do you want to look back on that one moment of weakness that kept you from bein' great?" He spoke directly to his son, the more important one, whether he admitted he felt that way or not. "Greatness isn't earned, it's taken. Just as easily, taken from you."

Under their helmets, Caleb glared at Brooks, Brooks glared at Duke, Duke glared at his father, and everyone was angry...

And now it was time to play some football.

Hand-in-hand, Henri and Margot ascended up the stands. The return of the famous long-lost alum caused quite a ruckus as heads turned, pushy high-fives were passed, and 'good to see ya's!' were roared eagerly in his face. Henri considered turning around and fleeing home to be a loner with his much quieter toolbox. Oppositely, Margot's delicate slip dress received tight-lipped scowls from the mothers in their Old Navy; the well-trained fathers did their best to avoid glancing at all.

They found an open spot by Jay and Elaine, two rows below David and Stacy.

"Oh you made it! And just in swell time!" Elaine celebrated them, as she genuinely knew how, sitting as elegant and ladylike as ever in white linen pants and a Michaels DIY iron-on shirt. "You haven't attended one of these in a long while, have you Henri?"

"Sure haven't! Hey Jay, you care to remind me the rules of the game?"

The mayor jaunted up and down in a cartoon quality. "I ain't fallin' for that one, bud. Don't think anyone here has forgotten, just a few years back, it was you out on that field. You and Brant, the superstars of our days! Shucks, we ain't that old, are we?"

"Depends on whether or not y'all have added more stairs to this place, don't ever recall gettin' so winded climbin' the damn steps!" Though Henri was talented at the cushy chitchat, it truly was the bane of his existence. "So, y'all got a kid playin' tonight?"

"No," Jay answered before Elaine had the chance. "We got two soccer players and one with all the brains in the family, but no football stars for us. Say, it's a shame you didn't have a son, Henri. Just think: a Golden Holden and a Bexley 2.0, a whole second generation of state-winners! What a waste, huh? It's a real shame you didn't have a son."

Margot sensed an implied 'instead'—*it's a shame y'all didn't have a son, instead*—but decided he surely hadn't meant it that way. Still, her gut did a strange churn every time the mayor boomed.

"Nope, no son for me, but as I hear it... Brants got *two* of 'em."

"He does, doesn't he?" Jay nodded, a little more checked out. "I'll tell you what, that Brooks is gon' be our saving grace against —"

"Grace is the nimble one on the mat doin' all the flips!" Stacy careened forward. "And our Caleb is that brawny 45, startin' receiver since his freshman year!"

Of all the pesky chit chatters Henri had come across throughout the years, Stacy by far took grand prize. "Right. Yes.

We were just talkin' about that."

"I thought so," she cooed. "Oh Margot, I wanted to ask, did you have some time to chew over what we discussed? The camp sign-up deadlines are movin' fast. I actually have some brochures handy right here in my purse…" She rummaged.

Margot flicked her black tourmaline bracelet, to revive it into effect. "Look honey, there's Sadie." She gestured to the bottom of the steps, and perhaps for Stacy's benefit added a positive, "She's already made so many new friends."

"Hmmmmm." Stacy's short-bob-cut hair swept to the left, then to the right. "I would be careful with who you let your daughter associate with. Where God lives, the devil sure tries to keep up. That scraggly boy, the one in the maroon, he's a troubled young man."

Elaine courteously refuted that with a dense exhale. "His name is Sterling and he's a very sweet boy, actually. Helps me with the dishes at the café, just because."

"Well, that might be true. But he also has a history of destructive decision makin', will probably get himself locked up in juvie before graduation. *Bless* his heart." She paused to consider that some more. "You know Elaine, I'm surprised to see *your* young ones spendin' time with a tyke from that side of town. Surely you've heard about his parents. Dad in prison, the mother arrested just last year, as I recall… *drug possession*? These things are always such hearsay so I don't care to assume, but it sure is troublin' for civil people like us."

Margot simply noted, "He has a nice smile."

Stacy drove on like she was driving a bulldozer. "Of course, nothin' unusual for the folks comin' from Sunny Skies Trailer Park. Those poor kids growin' up in those circumstances, breaks my heart, it really does."

"I wouldn't lose too much sleep over it," Henri told her.

Him, she did hear. "Oh? Why's that?"

His rebel spirit was really something to believe in. "I always said: the scruffier the better! This town ain't nothin' without 'em."

Elaine merrily clapped her hands together. "There's the

Henri I remember!" Then she gave him a tap-tap on the back, just a little something to quietly say *you tell that bitch*, but only in good clean fun. It was always, *always* in good clean fun.

Well... mostly.

The coin was flipped and the fans went mute, anticipation of kick-off settling over the little green town.

Digging his cleats into the ground, Brooks shut his eyes. He squeezed them rigorously closed to shut it all out. Alone in the darkness, he was thirteen again, throwing a ball in the yard with his dad. Just throwing, catching, throwing, catching, then diving to the ground with such commitment, he swallowed a share of dirt. "You should take a break," his father had insisted, cupped both his hands under his baby ears, and pulled him close. "Never forget, it's only a game."

His eyes were open now, he was seventeen, it was more than a grass rash on his arm, and all he heard was: *So tell me, do you want to be great?*

Center snapped the ball, and the quarterback ducked in and out like he anticipated their every move. His arm drew back, arm fibers tearing with kinetic force peaking... until he launched it over the colossal range of field, right into Caleb's hands, who took it all the way down the sidelines.

Ten seconds in, the wolves were up by six.

The instilled anger Brooks used for fuel didn't last as long as usual, for some new reason, and by halftime the scoreboard was showing a tie. Still, Brooks felt more fulfilled than he'd been in years.

Sadie reapplied her guava lip balm in the bathroom mirror, then wiped away the black mascara marks from her lids; a side effect of profusely dewy Florida skin. It made her think of Amabella Hill, a geocache-loving girl who'd lived down her street, who'd also had dewy skin. 'Krispy Kreme' Becks called her in fifth grade, and in seventh when the hormones hit, 'Krispy Kreme with sprinkles'. Amabella moved away in ninth grade, but Sadie knew that didn't matter. It didn't matter that no one in her new hometown knew, because Amabella would remember and carry it with her. Just how Sadie carried 'mom', just how Shelby would carry what Sterling said to her at the trucks, just how every girl who's ever had a mean thing said to them would carry. Wearing it beneath their clothes where no other girls could see it; see that they're wearing the same thing.

Just then, Shelby exited a stall and turned on the water at the other sink. Both girls, a submissive lily and an outspoken violet, washed their hands in the dead of silence. It was uncomfortable, sure. But it was also separate from everything out there, and right *here*, they had no reason to not like each other.

"I like your nail polish," Sadie said indirectly through their mirror reflections.

Shelby evaluated her chipped black shade under the faucet. "Thanks." Out of obligation, "I… like yours too. I could never pull off pink."

"I think you could. You have that skin tone that looks great with everything."

"I do?"

Sadie nodded. "Mine is that weird inbetween color where no foundation is ever the right shade."

"I don't really wear makeup."

"You don't need it." Sadie dried her hands. "Anyways, I'll see you out there."

"Yeah," Shelby answered without any grasp on her grudges. "I'll see ya."

The door creaked closed behind the ballet flats, and Shelby just stared at it for almost a whole minute. Finally, she stormed out of the bathroom, terribly annoyed she'd been forced to conversate with a mermaid wannabe, but also feeling mildly more okay than before. *You have that skin tone that looks great with everything*, Shelby replayed, and this she would wear. It was her favorite thing she'd ever worn.

Henri waited alone in the concessions line, so consumed by his thoughts he almost stumbled when something woke him from them.

"Now *what* am I suppose to do with this?" A prima donna

belle, something of a southern Pam Anderson, waved a cup at the counter like it'd personally offended her. "I ordered a sweet tea. Do I look like the kind of woman who drinks root beer? I am missin' my daughter's halftime show for this. Do you *know* how much time goes into a cheerleading halftime show?"

Henri slipped the frightened freshman girl working the concessions a five dollar bill, then an extra ten for the trauma. "Thank you. We appreciate all the hard work back there." With an odd amount of emotion in his eyes, he turned to the one and only pistol in a miniskirt, 'dilly Delilah', as he'd once called her. "The root beer might actually be better for you, just sayin'."

She trembled at the sight. "Henri?" And smiled in a way that didn't care about causing wrinkles. "You're really back."

He examined her funny glitz and bit his bottom lip. "Ain't a thing in this town that's changed besides you."

"Oh yeah?" Despite the deficit in tea, her hard-to-please appeared fully gratified. "I'm goin' to take that as a compliment."

He nodded, weakened by the memories as it all caught up to him. "Tell me," he pressed with a sadness that he even had to ask, "how ya been?"

Margot and Elaine were getting to know each other by the chain link fence, a natural bond of friendship blooming. They were both evolved and thoughtful women, and those things paired with their unfair beauty, loathed for it. Not to mention their happy marriages, or one so-called, and this *is* indeed where their lives disagreed. They'd been in the middle of discussing Margot's chocolate truffle recipe when an exhausted coach's wife sauntered past.

"Kelly!" Elaine compelled her to join them with a flappy palm and toe-heel totter. "Your boys are just on fire tonight!" Though, one of them hadn't left the bench.

"Thank you dear, that's mighty sweet." Kelly sighed long and drawn, and with an obscure groan mixed in. "I have to say, it's a relief so far. Can't tell you how stressed Brant's been over this game. The man can't think of nothin' else these days, and win or lose, I'm the one goin' home with him. It's either cleanin' up mason jars of celebratory floats or sweepin' up the glass from the broken beers outside." She'd meant it as a light-hearted anecdote, but the words were rooted in too much truth to not sting as she heard them aloud. "Oh, heavens! I haven't got the sense God gave a goose! Please, excuse my manners." She whirled Margot into a hug. "Just a little riled from all the crazy. I saw you at lunch the other day, but I didn't get a chance to say hi."

Margot felt like she was often falling behind in conversation, with so many accents that took focus to hear right. "Ah, yes. You're the counselor?"

"It's one of my many hats, yes." She perked both hands on her hips. "I have got to tell you—that Sadie of yours is just a *doll*. And clearly, I'm not the *only* one who thinks so."

"Oh, you mean Brooks. You're Brooks' mom."

"Brooks and Duke, yes. Those two rowdy boys are all mine."

"Duke? I don't think Sadie has mentioned him."

"Well he sure has mentioned her. Didn't one of them take her out last week?"

"Yes, Brooks did. No—Duke. Which one has the brown eyes, again?"

That's when Kelly spotted Henri getting chummy with a root beer, and she beckoned him over with animate waves. Too animate, because Delilah came too. "Hey Bexley, you plannin' on runnin' off again anytime soon? Cause next time I'm gon' need a warnin', mister!"

"You tryin' to get rid of me already?"

"Absolutely not. Simply wanted to make sure you weren't gon' up and go without sayin' goodbye like last time. I never quite understood what happened there."

Disheveled, Margot glanced up at her usually noble man. "You never told your friends you were leaving?"

"Speakin' of back in the day," Henri changed the subject, "Elaine, didn't you get offered some fancy modelin' contract up in New York?"

"Oh, that was nothin' big," Elaine said quickly.

"No... no," Henri racked his brain. "Yes! I remember now, there was some famous agency that wanted to put you up in Manhattan after you got plucked in the mall for that Logan's

Seafood Shack billboard. I r'member you tellin' me, all giddy to start your new life after graduation. Even had yourself a Big Apple subway map ready to go. What happened to that?"

Elaine shifted, unsure of the right words. "Well, I… I guess I just…"

As if he'd been cued, Jay barged over from cultivating control in the masses, wrist deep in a wet bag of peanuts, free hand stroking Elaine's curls and settling securely around her side.

"I suppose I just found something more important," Elaine finished the thought with an unfelt smile, and something about it made the sentiment sound counterfeit.

"I think it's sweet," Delilah donated supportively. "I mean, where would this town *be* without Elaine servin' us all those delicious muffins and cups of coffee?"

"She meant being a *wife* and *mother*." Kelly's voice shot two octaves and swore without swearing. "Obviously."

"Yes, that's right! All three of your boys are just so darling." Delilah, with that catty poise she was known for, clasped a hand over her mouth. "I'm *so* sorry. Sometimes it's just hard to tell with all those baggy clothes Shelby wears. She really should stop by The Lipstick Tree sometime. I'm sure Mallory could help her find somethin' more… accentuatin' at the waist, girl appropriate, if I may—"

"Cut the crap, Delilah," Kelly finally released like a satisfying sneeze.

"Excuse me?"

"You've always been jealous of Elaine, since high school. *Everyone* knew it."

"Oh hun, do you need to sit down? Sounds like the pressures of bein' a coach's wife are gettin' to your head." Delilah pretended to brush away dandruff from Kelly's grown out roots. "Hm, it does make sense now. Brant *does* seem to have gained a wanderin' eye as of late…"

"Wanderin'?" Kelly threw her head back. "You mean when you're practically beggin' every john in town to take a magnifin' glass up those naked itty bitty toothpicks?"

"This is nice," Henri hummed and wrapped his arms around

them. "Just like old times."

Kelly snidely added, "Perhaps because *some* of us never left high school." And she kept spewing without solid rhyme or reason; purging sticky saps like it'd been a long time coming. "No one wanted you around, even back then. Whole group only agreed to tolerate you because Henri insisted we make you welcome, for what reason is far beyond me."

Delilah slapped the back of a moisturized hand to Kelly's crumpled forehead, checking for fever. "I really am concerned with the toll the pressures are takin' on you. You do know how to keep a man, don't you Kelly? Kids almost ready to fly the coop, and what might happen then, when there's nothin' left for you two? Hmm."

"At least my husband doesn't pay me a pretty penny to keep the bed sheets warm!" Kelly dashed through the silver gate and slammed it.

"Do you pay *him*?!" Delilah strutted off too.

Jay held out his soggy bag. "Peanut?"

Henri somehow felt horribly responsible for all the turmoil. "I'm gon' go make sure she's okay," he said to Margot, who was again flicking her crystals. She'd assumed he'd meant Kelly, so you can imagine her surprise as she watched her husband chase after the woman in tight burgundy spandex, and all the juicy commodities stuffed in it, as if there was something more to be explained.

There always is, isn't there?

By the time Stadium Drive had unclogged it's line of cars, Buck's BBQ had one stretching and honking around the building. Trucks were parking in the town square grass, in front of the courthouse, on sidewalks, friends' lawns who they knew wouldn't mind, everywhere except the corner where Otis had set up camp under an old shower curtain. Though, people stopped to gift him lotto scratchers and beers as a thank you, because tonight they'd won.

The Holden bunch sat in a pedestal booth, frequented by

friends and strangers congratulating the star player and his brilliant coach. Appetite lost, Duke chewed stingily on a cold fry, and after an old woman in a white shawl and dentures looked to him and said *you ever think of playin' ball like your brother,* he'd had enough. He got up for the arcade. Colton, Maia and Sadie were already there, bent over the four-way air hockey table.

"Just in time! We're in need of one more." Maia tossed him a striker. "Hey, I've never asked, but you still have that puka shell necklace I gave you in second grade?"

"No. Threw it at Brooks' hard-ass head after he put a condom full of mayo under my pillow the day mom washed the sheets. Shattered to pieces on impact. Sorry." He shrugged, and they all lost it.

The four of them started a fresh game.

After a few clanks, Maia swiped the plastic and sent it whirring in Colton's goal. "SCORE! You owe me a shake."

"What? Says who? That's just one goal!"

"Says the girl with a craving for a shake." She danced victoriously, and of course, Colton ordered her a double fudge mudslide with 'extra extra whipped cream'.

Three more times the puck swooshed, clanked, and slotted in Duke's goal. "Dude, you're pretty bad at this." Maia took no pity on him, but she did grin with rich sludge all over her teeth.

"Guess I'm just tired tonight," he replied with the neon jukebox glow putting shadows under his hunter eyes.

Colton swirled a witty finger at his temple, seemingly extracting some cryptic hindsight. "Hmm, you know, it's probably from all that playin' you did." As his best friend, he was the only one allowed to make that joke.

Any other night, Duke might've chuckled to keep things light and comfortable—God forbid, things got uncomfortable—but he wasn't interested in being the solver anymore. It hadn't done him any favors. "I'm tired," he repeated.

"You already said that," Maia reminded.

With an unnerving scarceness of feeling, he angled directly at Sadie. "Yeah, I just really meant it."

She absorbed his despondency like a parched sponge—an

empathetic sensation her mother would amount to her missing tourmaline—but Sadie couldn't help but find the link more phenomenal than that.

"We playing or what?" Sadie playfully nudged Duke's side, only her thumb caught his pocket and she accidentally saw his underwear when she pulled away. "I um—I think I want to bet on a shake too."

Duke was instantly in better health. "You're on."

They played on teams this time; boys versus girls; putting three pucks in at once and madly snapping their wrists until the competitive buzz had them screaming from all the excitement.

Karigan, the college waitress, was twirling a fibril of blue hair and bragging about her cherry-stem tying talents, when Brooks heard the confusing mishmash of signals. Peering through a beehive of bodies, he caught Sadie's long voguish legs in denim that should probably be illegal on a body like hers. Next to her, boat shoes. He got up, walked over, and waited for them to notice him. She didn't even notice him. "Hey."

Without hurry, they paused their game and gave him the attention they should've given four and a half seconds ago.

"What's up?" Maia slurped her shake with sonorous artistry, pinching Sadie's leg under the table so she was unexplainably squirrely.

"We're headin' to the woods behind Ogilbee's in a few. The crew just left for a RJ's run. Sterling is gettin' there early to make sure the coast is clear. You guys in?"

"Hold on," Colton horned in with skepticism. "You mean... *the* woods? Eight-mile war territory?"

Very recklessly he said, "That's the one."

Sadie looked to Duke to see if he had an opinion, then back to Brooks. She asked, "Who's to say Orville won't show up and start hounding us with paintballs again?"

The moody heartbreaker conceded, "No one is to say."

She couldn't answer fast enough. "I'm in."

"Great." He smiled in slow motion. "Meet me at my truck in ten. It's the white one with the—"

"I know," Sadie almost moaned it out, a warm trickle

traveling to her deepest depths, as she clenched muscles she's never clenched before. "I know exactly the one."

After the quarterback was gone, the back-up one put his hand on the air hockey table so the edge of his finger brushed Sadie's. "You still want that shake? Before you go?"

She blinked at him. "Huh?"

"It's full of sugar, all kinds of additives, fat topper of whipped cream. It's really bad for you. So I figured you'd want one." His eyes pleaded her to stay. "Isn't that your thing?"

Sadie felt like a wishbone being pulled by two very muscular arms; hot and cold like there was lava in her hair and snowflakes in her lashes; and she hoped neither of them got too close, to put out the other. Turns out, Sadie did enjoy some conflict, so long as it was in the shape of a triangle.

Outside Buck's, the parking lot had started to empty, leaving a litter of high-rise trucks and low-maintenance youth figuring out a plan. It was getting late, the sky entirely black with the new moon, without any moon at all. Sterling howled at it anyway.

Sadie, spry and tip-toeing like she'd just broken loose from captivity, stood against Maia's yellow beetle, which had a comical toy-like quality amid the rest of the machinery. "Are you sure you can't come tonight? I really need you there."

"Ah, yeah. I'm sorry. Just way too much homework to catch up on." Maia fixed her makeup in the mirror, which was unnecessary if she was going straight home.

"But, don't you have all weekend for that stuff? It can't be that bad, teachers aren't allowed to give out homework on home-game nights." Sadie boasted her new swampland fluencies, quite a bit of progress since her first day, and without a handbook!

Maia sighed like she was completely burnt-out from the soft insisting. "I tutor, remember? I don't have all weekend to flirt with football players and daydream of the perfect French kiss."

Sadie couldn't help but wince at the plural 's' in 'players', but decided it probably meant more in her own head. "I didn't think you did, I just meant—"

"Brooks is waiting for you."

"Okay, but—"

"You're a really good friend, Sadie." Rising from the car, Maia squeezed her and whispered, "I'm rooting for you." Then she ducked back into the tiny vehicle and drove away.

Sadie felt suddenly uneasy, even worse once she spotted a dark blue pick-up rounding the same exit. "Hey!" she called out loudly, hitting her highest record for volume, and hopped on the convenient step stool thingy some people call running boards. She hung on the open window, breathing hard. "You're not coming?"

Duke crushed a quick fist into the stereo to turn off the tender Thomas Rhett that'd started playing from Bluetooth. "Oh, um… I don't really drink."

"I don't either. Or, I guess I do now. But you don't *have* to drink if you come." The irony of those words coming from *her* mouth left a buzz on her tongue, much like the cadenced purrs of the engine rumbling against her chest. "Please come."

Instead of giving her an answer, Duke lightly put the flat stub of his thumb to the small sepia birthmark on her forehead. "Did you know they call that a beauty mark?"

Sadie fidgeted with the Tiger's Eye on his leather band bracelet. "Or flaw."

"People see what they want to see, sometimes."

"Just as much as they don't see, what they don't want to see."

"I think we just wrote—"

"No." It was too much. "Don't say it." How was this happening? How could there be two of them? *It didn't make sense.* More engines turned on behind her, and so she told him, "I have to go." But before her fingers could unfetter from the window, she needed to know one thing. "What do you see in *me*?"

It started to sprinkle then, as he lied, "I see a friend."

"A friend," Sadie seconded, in deep and total agreement, like they'd both said something far more poetic. Honking and yelling told her she had about five more seconds of allowing the water drops to ricochet and glide down her cheeks, jaw, neck, cleavage, legions of drizzles going down her insatiate belly.

Have you ever stopped being bothered by the rain, long enough to recall what it feels like to need it?

Duke cleared his throat, and with this pained expression whispered, "They're waitin' on you." Once she finally slipped away, he drawled under his breath, "And I will, too."

Goldilocks waves scurried in the back bed of the sexy F-150, where Caleb, Sterling and Grace were already sprawled with smelly cans in their hands.

Brooks poked his head out of the driver's window. "What are you doin'? I saved you a seat up here."

"No thanks." Sadie inhaled all that life had to offer, and let it in. "I want to feel the rain."

CHAPTER ELEVEN
Above All, Tradition

Buried in the slums of densely grown porous woodland, lovers, players and boozers doused their troubles and savored their freedoms, as tradition summoned them to do. The fire warmed the hands and hearts of those young, masterful at being young. It would all go down right here in plain sight, where no one could see them, hear them, help them; a hideaway place where high-speed blossoms meet their slow burn. A nowhere hometown.

Caleb shot gunned a beer with Sterling as witness, tossed the can where the rest decorated the tall grass, and complained that Britney and Whitney had bailed but that they 'weren't that pretty anyway'.

Tanner set up the foldable table for activities.

Colton played J. Cole from the aux, and the low rap, a haunting owl, slurring hums of flirtatious exchange, would be the score of the evening.

The night breezes were so fragrant they etched their lungs so it'd never leave them, whisking up the lawless split ends of the girls and making them look like beautiful runaways. Grace chugged a bottle of whiskey, Mallory wondered if she'd worn the right underwear, Shelby and Ali shined flashlights into trails of cone pits and taunted the ant lions with crumbs of Takis.

That leaves us with Brooks and Sadie. They were by the truck, his heavy arm draped protectively around her, which made her feel pleasantly petite. Her fingers wandered his valley and hills of back aimlessly. They hadn't talked about it, anything. She shoved her face into his admirably strong chest to keep it that way, breathing in the Givenchy cologne until her nostrils burned from intoxication, and the brotherly pros and cons list had vanished from her mind.

"I'm sorry, Sadie." There was a foreign insecurity coating his gaze. "I told you I'm not a bad guy, and I've done nothing right to prove that."

"That's not true." A current of blushes overtook her cheeks, and she strained to be closer to him, barely possible this clothed. "Today's been pretty right."

He smiled a true smile that'd first hatched that night at the dock. "It has been, hasn't it?"

Sadie requested, "Just no more surprise changes of heart, okay?"

"You think I had a change of heart after our date? Sadie, I'd made up my mind about you the first day we met." The delivery of his words held such substance, pledges of old fashion that suited her well.

"What did you decide?"

With a vulnerable look of dismay, "That I'm no good for you."

Sadie just beamed brighter at that, urged her hips harder into him. "Then we're on the same page."

He was going to ask, but instead the stacked muscles leaned in and kissed her, quick and soft and mind-numbingly affecting, triggering a subtle sense that her legs were drooling. No one saw the kiss, but it seemed he wouldn't have minded, even if they had.

"Just think," Brooks whispered, slow and cowboy on the edge of her ear, "if my mom hadn't spent my entire life obsessively planting marigolds around our house, if I hadn't passed your test, you might've been kissin' some other guy tonight." He tried to gauge her reaction, but again she'd shoved her face in his chest.

"Anyone bring cups?" Caleb shouted, on the distinct brink of drunk.

Tanner passed him a stack. "Got some right here."

"Sweet. What we playin'?" The Abercrombie boy rubbed his palms sensually together, and somehow Sadie knew the display was for her benefit.

The dysfunctional group hovered around the rectangular make-do table, all uneven and tilted from the turf.

"I call Brooks' team!" Sterling already had a cigarette dangling from his chapped mouth.

"Sure, if you like losin'." Caleb dealt the cups into familiar triangles.

"Hell naw, Holden ain't lose at nuthin'."

"Your momma teach you to kiss ass like that?"

"Nope." Sterling's signature wife beater was back. "Yours did."

Mallory groaned from the side, before putting herself at the center, making a demonstration of her body as she line-danced up in bling buckle boots. "This is *boring*." She cinched her hands at her waist to show how tiny she was. "Can I make a teensy suggestion?"

"Whatever it is, I'm in baby," Caleb mumbled, wobbling.

She rolled her almond-shaped eyes, before slipping her blouse over her head, lashing it like a whip, holding two ends and resourcefully adapting it as a noose. She seductively hung it around the blonde beau's neck, tugging, tugging, tugging him around, before mouthing on his breath of cinnamon and bravado. "Strip... beer pong."

Caleb was really having a blast now; her exposed ravine of chest was so near he could lick her glittery body if he so went for it. "Mal, if you wanted a peek, all you had to do was ask—"

"Girls only. Guys can watch."

There was a prickly moment of doubtful silence. A few of the football guys clapped in blessing. An elusive gray fox judged them from the shadows. Thunder struck a few miles west of the pines. Then, a thick wet clicking noise detached Grace and Sterling from their lip lock, before Grace volunteered to join.

"Sure. It's Friday. Why not?" Grace smiled.

"That's the spirit." Mallory's shiny lips pouted. "No more takers? Hmm, that's too bad. Hey Sadie, would you be a doll and hold our clothes so the ants don't get on them?" She looked around for her.

But to everyone's surprise, Sadie had already escorted herself around her knight in shining Nike, opened a drink, grabbed a ping pong ball, and was only waiting for the rest to catch up. "Sorry." The ball bounced on the table. "I don't think I'll have enough hands."

A sprained look tinkered with the Miss America's sparkly smile, because Mallory had been raised to be one hell of a woman, but to make sure she's the only one who's one hell of a woman. "Fantastic."

The first twenty minutes were a major disappointment, considering the only clothes discarded were Grace's Tory Burch sandals and her oversized church camp tee that'd been hacked to below the bra anyway. Both teams; Grace and Mallory; Sadie and Ali; took turns taking shots at the cups.

Caleb moped by the campfire, fist pushed in his jaw, observing with an abnormal trace of choler. "I'll be damned if the only naked girl I see tonight is my sister." He threw a Taki. "Grace, you're a slut."

"Why, thank you brother." Grace pertly curtsied, before winking at Sadie.

Sterling crossed his arms across his nipples showing through the cotton. "I don't like this game."

Brooks, muted and swirling some spit, also wasn't a fan of the risqué recreation. He breathed a little easier with each miss, and even if they didn't miss, Sadie wouldn't do it. Yeah, maybe a shoe, an earring—that counts, right? It would take an awful lot of cups, trajectory skill these girls didn't have, to get to somewhere to write home about. But even then, she wouldn't do it. She wouldn't embarrass herself. She wouldn't embarrass him.

Rotten juvenile boys picked her apart, getting a real mechanical kick out of the whole thing and covering their crotches with a beer. Brooks told them to get out.

A ball splashed in a cup, one Sadie threw.

"Friggin' finally." Mallory began stripping off her white under tank, introducing the ivory bra she'd been wearing that one night at the Strawberry Festival, when her and Weston Hills High alum Graham Ivey played the Nervous Game behind the Himalaya. He'd told her she *wasn't like the other girls* and that she *was mature for her age*; both of which she'd taken to heart. It was the first time a boy had touched her there, and somehow, he'd managed to climb his cold fingers through the tight leg of her denim shorts, so if anyone saw them, it'd appear they were harmlessly holding hands. The way his eyes rolled back in yearn when feeling her clench at his massage, the way he complimented her body when she stroked him too... it was the closest Mallory had ever gotten to love. Honestly, she didn't quite understand the difference. And so, naturally, she did what she had to, to get it. "Hey Brooks? Mind pourin' me a shot?"

"Oh... sure." Unscrewing a bottle, he walked it over and tipped it upon her ready mouth, but she stumbled so it strewed like sprinklers all over her shimmer-dusted chest. "Oops." One French-tipped middle finger wiped the waxy nectar, and then she licked it up with her eyes on him. "Tsk tsk Holden. Seems we need to work on your aim."

And for the record, he'd been focusing on the dried booger lodged in her nose, that her hair was a green tint from pool chlorine, how her peach fuzz sideburns came out in the firelight. That's perhaps the most infuriating part; the boys we're fighting over like the damn Hunger Games, don't even have a clue we're dying out here.

Sadie reverted her saddened eyes to the flames, debating how combustible the spilled alcohol had made the bathing Miss America, and what would happen if she were to tragically fall in. Except, when she imagined it, she saw Becks instead. "I need some water," she announced, and just like old times, no one heard her.

The clump of tears only swelled on her way to the cooler, where Caleb was rubbing knees with ground roots and digging elbow-deep in the ice. "Um... what are you..."

"I punched a tree."

"Because..."

"I don't know, Sadie." He grunted in barbed exasperation,

baby blue rings resenting around in a temper, like she was the thorn in *his* side. "It gave me a funny look, okay? That's why."

"Aha." Her lips pursed.

"And I just felt like punchin' somethin'."

"Sure, that happens."

"I know it doesn't to you. Cause you're a *good-goody*, a north star, a Cinderella that sings with birds and bunnies and shit." His pupils were so large now, black piercing marbles swallowed the beautiful blue. "You've never had a bad thought, an ill wish, a forbidden want." He slowed it down here. "Just sunshine and rainbows and free muffins for everyone. That's you, ain't it? That's *all* there is?"

Sadie was suddenly furious. "What's your point?"

"That shit ain't healthy. You've gotta give yourself some fuckin' breathing room. Look at you, all bottled up. I don't know how you do it."

"Do *what*?"

"Mallory just marked her territory all over your man, and you're over here talkin' to me. You're hiding."

"No, I came to get a water," she explained, and kicked a pinecone.

"Uhhuh. Right." He passed her one and smirked as she stayed put. "So, would you have done it? Stripped?"

"Maybe."

"Really? Takin' off the mask so soon? I would have figured it'd at least take until daylight savings, when the days get darker, and it's a whole lot easier to… disappear. Like a dried up dandelion flower, just a"—he puffed hot air in her face—"and you're gone." His arm circled around in the ice like stirring a pot, then he flicked water at Sadie's dispirit as if performing his own kind of ceremony on it. "You don't even know who you are yet, and at this pace, you never will. I'd give up on the shy-girl treaty you have with yourself, before you get stuck that way."

His sweet-talking never ceased to be half encrypted, but this time, it struck. "What is *wrong* with me?!" Sadie cried with her arms up and flailing. "Why am I so spineless and weak? They haven't called once, no texts either—not even in the group chat that they probably just took me out of! All this time, I was some punch-line to keep around to make them look like they're better people than they are, *and with bomb bathroom lighting.* They never even liked me. I never liked them either. I... I... I hated them!" Her big green eyes widened in shame, like admitting it was the worst thing she'd ever done. It wouldn't be, for long. "I shouldn't have said that. Why am I talking to *you* about this?"

"I'm all ears, princess." He smiled as if his secret ceremony had worked.

Sadie giggled, carefree. "You're all *something* and it definitely isn't ears."

Caleb did show agreement, before considering something distant. "You know, you kind of have a lisp when you talk all angry. It's sort of cute, princess."

"Shut up. I do not."

"You do. You really do. I r'member him tellin' me, and you do."

"Remember *who* telling you?"

He didn't answer her question, and before she could pester him further, three over-sized armored trucks forced through the trees and sped a few circles around the clearing, clubbing soppy soil and jagged pebbles, while one boy behind the headlights hung from the window and snapped photos of Mallory and Grace as they stumbled for their clothes.

Eventually, the tires finished their fury, and three pale spindly boys in orange and black varsity jackets, laced with the stench of damp animal fur, descended with cutting prejudices written on their twisted mouths. It was the Orville captains come to claim back their land: Dakota, Dustin, Cameron. Gaunt yet strong, and deeply roughened somehow.

Brooks intersected them, Caleb and Levi forging a unified front. The two sides, wolves and coonhounds, growled at each other in gridlock, guarding this one tradition above all, without understanding the depth of their own history. That's how hatred usually works; they're just tatty hand-me-downs.

"Didn't think y'all could be this stupid. But shit, whad'ya know." Cameron stepped forward. "What? You got a death wish or somethin', Holden? Thought I already knocked some sense into you."

Brooks' brown eyes narrowed, ignoring the revolving whispers behind him. He tried to calculate how on earth he could take him on with one arm. The conclusion: he couldn't. "Woods will be ours this year anyway, reckoned you wouldn't mind us movin' in a little early."

Dakota sneered. "Last three years ain't teach you nothin', Holden? We don't lose." His jaw milled noisily, bone on bone, crookedly like it'd been hit one too many times.

Brooks prayed it wouldn't escalate, not tonight. "Yeah, we'll see."

Sadie curiously watched the plot unfold, the bullish boys' eyes turn excited over the fight. She dare say, there was nothing they wouldn't do. This wasn't boredom, living la vida local to fill the eve of a moonless Friday. This was as real as any warfare, and Sadie just stood there as an outsider, apathetic to the cause, hard-pressed with the notion *football* wasn't their true cause at all. It was something bigger.

"This year will be different. You'll see." Caleb wore his signature amusement, but the smirk twitched. "Gotta take out the trash at some point. Shit stinks."

"Big talk for a pastor's son. Daddy teach you to use bad words?"

"Suck it, Cameron!" Grace waddled to those frontlines, swatting at Mallory and Sterling who made attempts to hold her back.

But it only appeased Cameron more. "Aw." He winked, eyeing her cropped church tee. "That's more *your* thing, ain't it sweetheart?"

Caleb swung but Levi's arm instinctively caught him at the last second. "LET—ME—GO."

Dustin cackled, and behind him, the gray fox was urinating on some practice clothes that'd fallen from his truck bed. "Close call. Names Levi, right?" He grinned with crooked teeth, one missing one. "You're quick. I can tell. I imagine your coach values that on the field." His yellow animal slit eyes flickered with fascination, cocking his tiny chin like leveling with a dimwit. "Interesting breed... aren't you?"

Caleb swung again, unleashed and carnivorous, as the blow to Dustin's nose sent gushes of red blood spattering across all three of the captains' faces. "You're dead, Dickson! You hear me?" He'd become a beastly machine of destruction. "*Dead!*"

Brooks tailed it with frenzied kicks to their ribcages, their stick-like bodies rolling and curling in the weeds, making vain efforts to defend their dangly bits.

Dakota managed back on his feet. He blindly launched at Colton, who had no choice but to smack the glass bottle in his hand across his skull. It broke, and Shelby screamed at the pool of lustrous ruby, like an instant bed of liquid roses seeping across the mulch.

Sterling, with a rebel yell pouring from his stretched tonsils, projected as a human torpedo from the truck, tackling both Dakota and Dustin in one hammered belly flop.

All the while, their friendly neighborhood owl was hooting smoothly along.

"Get in the truck! GET IN THE TRUCK!" Brooks was shouting at Sadie, frustrated and agitated that she hadn't already. Where were her instincts? Where was her head?

It was with the owl, just up there on the branch. *Can't you hear it? It's so beautiful.*

"SADIE! TRUCK!"

She stumbled back a few steps at the harsh sound of his voice, and then the more infected one echoed too... *what was it that Dustin had said?* Her senses had seemed to muffle it, but Levi's face had been so injured, not in a way she'd ever known someone to be injured. It was inhuman, minimizing to less than human. She tried, but she couldn't spin this one; it was too heavy. Growing up isn't ever a gentle acclimatizing path, like falling asleep; it's quite the rapid departure, because you're waking up now. *Just five more minutes...*

The palliative lullaby of the owl was gone, and all Sadie could hear was the warped hissing of burning brush.

Brooks' priority lied only in Sadie; the brawling had spread, the cops would be there soon, and he *needed* to get to Sadie. He charged through the mare's nest, and since she still hadn't responded to the all hell-breaking-loose motion picture in front of her, he sucked it up and tossed her over his shoulder, really testing that borrowed time. The searing pains knocked all wind from his lungs.

In that black fog, he'd somehow managed to pelt Sadie's squirmy legs in the passenger side and begged her to stay put. She nodded, might've wiped a tear, but he couldn't focus on that now. "LEVI! COM' ON!" He was just standing there. Why was he just standing there? "GET YOUR ASS IN THE TRUCK! I'M LEAVIN'!" He couldn't wait any longer. A tendon in his arm popped—maybe in, maybe out, maybe off. "LEVI! NOW!"

Of the list of horrible emotions a young boy might come across in that moment—loathe, fear, worthlessness—Levi felt only small elements of each, numbed by now, or perhaps thick-skinned and welded hard like the rest of his under-supported neighborhood brothers who, by age eleven, had their chests slammed against a cement wall by a Walmart security officer, on the grounds they'd walked by a Walmart security officer. As Cameron rose up from the dirt with bulbous wiry veins in his arms, exemplifying the narrative they'd been given, Levi felt one element the most: heartbreak.

"*Hit me!*" Cameron hissed privately, falsely holding back a loading punch. "*Do it now!*"

Levi observed the spots of soil and Takis on his face, a scrape on his temple that might need stitches, how that provoked an unaddressable pang under all the other elements he'd learned to live with—but not this. His neck swiveled back, barely forth, just enough to let him know: *I can't do it.*

So Caleb did it for him. Made a savory five-course meal out of him as Cameron folded atop a jagged pine-needle stratum like a tree that'd been axed, clutching his soft gut. But his eyes lifted to make sure Levi knew: *It's okay. I couldn't either.*

The wolves managed to jump in the backseat of Brooks' already-moving truck, just as red and blue flashing lights flickered through the striped shadows of the woods.

"Orville pricks! I 'bout broke my hand!" Caleb grumbled, overcome with a second wind and pounding the roof over and over, probably to finish the job.

"You threw the first punch, you idiot!" Brooks focused steady on the rearview mirror to make sure they weren't followed. He'd only had one beer, but his driving could've easily proven otherwise. The slippy terrain made any adjustment in the wheel a drastic one, and without a moon or road, the pitch darkness of sticks and leaves only emphasized as if driving down a dead-end tunnel.

"You think I had a choice? You heard what they were sayin' about Gracie! And that Dustin—oh I swear—the next time I see him, I'm gonna kill 'em! Racist scum is what he is!"

Levi scratched at the dried blood on his wrist. Cameron's blood. "You shouldn't have hit him. You really shouldn't have hit him."

"Woah." Caleb's neck snapped. "Are you serious right now?"

Realizing he'd said that out loud, "We could get kicked off the team, or worse! I'm just sayin' it wasn't smart!"

"Well you must be a damn genius standin' there catchin' flies in your mouth. What was up with that, huh? You had him right there!" Caleb's voice cracked with a snag, but probably not emotion because he didn't have many of those. "You had Cameron Dickson on his knees and you choked! And you of all people have reason to hate those guys!"

"He's not the one who said it! *He* never has!"

Caleb cupped the sides of his head like it might detonate. "You don't say, you really don't say. My apologies, I didn't realize the *leader* of those ill-bred imbeciles was such a saint. But yeah, you're right. Cameron wasn't trying to break Brooks' spine at the opening dogfight, HE WAS JUST GIVIN' HIM A HUG!"

"LOOK OUT!" Sadie belled in sheer terror as a toddler deer pranced onto the narrow off-road, and she squeezed her eyes to brace for shards of windshield glass, and her body picked up air, because for the first time in her life she'd forgotten her seatbelt, and she would've had her head crushed against the dash had Caleb's arms not wrapped around the seat and strapped her to it.

Brooks slammed the brakes so hard the car's backend velocity swung them in erratic circles; with cleft ditches and stakes of timber and marsh sinkholes ready to take the pains away; but the bumpers of moss said *not today.*

In their blurred daze, the teens watched as the young deer wagged it's little white tail, perhaps to say thank you, before clumsily flitting to a visibly anguished doe pacing nearby. The doe calmed once her baby had returned to her, nuzzling it with her neck, and then they pranced away side-by-side in natural elegant synchrony.

Sadie had never seen a deer up close, but she'd watched Bambi twelve times the summer she lost her first tooth. When she was still persuaded by unabridged trust, wrapped in an airtight fortress of goodness that'd hugged her to sleep every night. Dream catchers, angel figurines, fairies to come purchase the pearly whites she hid under her pillow. She'd never had the chance to say goodbye to all of that, too busy concocting escape plans out of naivety to say goodbye.

"Anyone got a huntin' rifle?" Caleb asked with a straight face.

Sadie hadn't remembered that part of the movie, until now.

Returning to the present, she looked down to see Caleb's large hands groping her chest. "Wh—what are you doing?" No one had ever done that to her before; touched her there. "Get off of me!" she wailed and squirmed around in the seat, daring him with angry eyes to try and defend his greedy self. "You... you..."

"I fell forward. I didn't meant to." He said it to Brooks, not her, which made her even more livid.

"How could you... why would you..."

Caleb grunted a mediocre, "Sorry." He waited for her to get it, and when she didn't, "Sadie, I wasn't grabbing you like that. You weren't wearing your—"

"No! Just... stop... *talking!*" Sadie was shaking, because she'd actually never been so alight with feeling in her whole life. Not when Tenley poured warm water in her hand at the Sequoia Park camping trip, and she peed her sleeping bag right next to Max Kallis. Not when Emma pointed out her razor bumps at the ninth-grade beach volleyball tournament. Not even when Becks told Liam Bassett Sadie had printed his profile pic, hung it on her wall, and practiced making out with it, when Becks was clearly the one with paper cuts all over her lips. Caleb Lindley outshined them all. Caleb Lindley drove her to abandon all thought. Caleb Lindley made her *fight back*.

They were passing the high school now, and Sadie's attention was stolen to yet another impossible conundrum. There, outside her window, a caramel-skinned, witchy-haired girl slipped through the front office doors and climbed into a yellow VW bug. Maia was bare-foot, hugging her arms, limping. And there'd been no signs for any of it.

Sadie felt an end, just as much as a beginning. No longer sleeping, but not quite awake.

It began to rain again as she wondered: *What else wasn't she seeing, when she was too busy looking?*

Exhausted and betrayed, an impractical romantic leaned her head back against the seat, allowed her eyes to fall closed, and for one of the last moments of her life, remembered what it felt like to simply pretend.

Henri and Margot spent the evening in the living room, existing presently together and yet lovingly apart; him with his news specials, her with her sketchbook. This is something they were skilled at, existing silently and effortlessly together without the pressure to preoccupy or hover. Henri was convinced it's what every failed marriage was missing. After all, his father and mother had been masters at it. His father and mother had been happy.

Eventually, Henri did sense some incoming withdrawals, and joined his wife on the loveseat, observing her with infatuated bedroom eyes. He rubbed her back as she hummed in approval. "I've got a real hankerin'," he whispered mischievously.

"Mhm," she scrunched her lips to one side, giving him a teasingly dubious squint. "Tell me, what for?"

"Somethin' real sweet," he persisted.

"And what did you have in mind?" She ascended his lap with a captivating excellence, and enjoyed the sandpaper scruff of his cheek on her freshly bathed skin. She kissed in constellations around his nose, jaw, neck. They both knew where this was going, and when the going got going, there was no going back...

"So, um, I was thinkin'—"

"Thinking, thinking, too much thinking." Margot initiated the untying of her bathrobe, pushing her goddess hair back and out of the way, how she typically did before an old-fashioned striptease. "We have the house to ourselves, what *ever* will we get up to?"

He captured her hands on the move. "Well, how about you wait for me right here, maybe put on that red silky thing I like..."

"Uhhuh."

"And I'll run to the market for some tea."

Margot frowned. "Tea?"

"Uh, yeah. But when I get *back*—"

"Tea?"

"Can't ever underestimate a country man and his Arnold Palmers. Ha ha." Henri had always been a horrible liar. Probably because he never did it. "But it'll just take a minute, I'll be back before you even have time to light one of those incest-stick-thingies."

She thawed slightly at his mix-up. "Incense," she corrected.

"Well, I would sure hope so." He sent over a quick smile and air kiss while searching for his keys, and slid efficiently into his work boots with a helpful shoehorn. It gave him a hoot—just so gosh darn nifty, those shoehorns. "You want anythin' while I'm out? Chips and salsa? Wine? Roses?"

"All of the above." Margot crossed her arms, half-naked on the loveseat that, indeed, would not be seeing any love making tonight. "You sure are something, Henri Thomas Bexley."

"Somethin' you love." He hoped.

"Hurry back and we'll see."

At the door, Henri delayed for a surpassingly long beat, to take her in, the same way his father had taken in his mother before he'd left to tend to the chickens. Only, Henri wasn't leaving to tend to the chickens.

In the Chevy, he lapsed into survival autopilot, reversing from under the carport and making the once-ordinary drive to the abandoned basketball court on Church Street. Brant was likely already there, debatable whether he'd ever *really* left. After all, that was the scene where it all happened. It was the first place they'd look for clues. Right now, it was all they had.

Under the warm roof of home, an anxious Margot corralled the latch to the attic, pulling on the little string that unbuckled the stairs. With a flashlight, she went up, sifting through dusty boxes until she bumped into the one stamped 'YEARBOOKS'. They were each black and white and heavy as history books in her arms, appropriately so. Picking a random one, she skipped to the autographs page in the back. Though it felt sneaky and prying, it wasn't as if she were snooping through his texts or email; this was basically public knowledge. She was sure she wouldn't find anything anyway...

Margot's glow suddenly lost it's healthy sheen. In the centerfold of pages, amid summer well-wishes, a pink gel pen in a curly font read: *Have a great summer! Ps. I'll never forget that night. I'll never forget you.* Squiggly heart. Squiggly heart. *Love, Delilah.*

Behind Lake Josey's wrought-iron gates, Elaine was tucked in bed with a stack of *Bake From Scratch* magazines. Although Jay always stressed it unnecessary, she'd vowed to stay up and wait until he arrived home, no matter the hour, because doing so helped her feel less useless. Slumbering away peacefully while her husband labored late nights in the office felt unjust, and the least she could do is welcome him into bed with a warm smile and kiss.

Somewhere around 2 a.m., the tree-trunk man, smelling of licorice and Nightshade, skulked upstairs to be rattled by the amber glow coming from the bedroom. "I told you to go to sleep," was his thank you.

"It's nice to see you too," Elaine's sleepy voice lulled from the pillows. "Extra late night tonight, huh?"

"Just part of the job, dear. They call, I'm there." He undid his tie in the mirror.

"No, I know. I know. I just wish you didn't have to leave in the middle of the night, that's all." She hugged her papery knees to her chest, playing with the sheets, before a cute smile crossed her. "You missed two holes in your belt, dear. Look at that." Elaine laughed and pointed. "You must've gotten dressed in the dark again, silly you."

"Silly me." Jay changed into plaid pajamas, making a mental note to take more care with these details, next time.

She gently inquired, "Will you be late again tomorrow?"

"What do you want from me? Do you want me to quit?" His head flung so swift, it almost snapped off.

"No, heavens no." Her heart beat faster. "I was simply curious. Let's forget I said anything. Come to bed so I can massage your shoulders." But it didn't matter how pleasantly she spoke, she could already see his unsettled gears turning, alter aura expanding like a pressure pump inside those small caged walls.

Her huge husband leaned down for a smooch, if only to assert his ownership, caressing her neck to get a buzz from the utter flimsiness. Her loose, easily accessible, nightgown was practically asking for a ravaging, and so he obliged. The other meaty hand captured her breast, which in combination with her utter pliancy, was almost *all* too much.

To this day, it astonished Elaine how unaware her husband was of his strength. Most impressive, evidently, was her own suppression in knowing he just *didn't care*.

His pores oozed with bourbon, sweat, and belladonna poison.

Elaine pulled away cautiously, holding her breath and finally relaxing as Jay returned to his bedtime routine in the connecting bathroom.

"Your speech was beautiful today," she said. "You're always so good with those kids. The pep rally, the game, oh it was just so upliftin' seein' the town alive again. Havin' Henri back really made it somethin' extra. I sure hope Margot isn't havin' a hard time. After all, I do know how difficult these other mother hens can be—"

"Where were you?" The booming voice returned with vengeance, and he glared at her from the doorway as tarry tension seeped up from the floorboards.

"Wh—what?" Elaine flinched like a baby bird.

"You were late to the pep rally. That's unacceptable."

"Honey, I... I was backed up at the shop. The Ferrels, they needed carrot cake for little Johnny's birthday party tomorrow. I thought I could make it, but I..." The trembling spread first in her wrists, as it always does. "I'm so sorry for missin' your speech."

His masculine dominance was overwhelming, even in silence —isn't that what her mother's marriage books had called it? Something about *all fertilities of a marriage stem from a man's power, the wife's willingness to give herself over.* Hadn't she done so?

"Don't lie to me." Jay didn't need to add an 'or else', for one to be implied.

"I'm not lying—" Elaine begged him to believe her.

"I don't want you around Henri. I got a feelin' he's bad news, just showin' up in Weston Hills. No story, no explanation. It doesn't add up."

"Jay... sweetie." Elaine was still as a vase. "I'm sure he's just missed his home, nothing bad news about that, now is there? I would miss it too if I'd..." Her throat went dry as a sand dune, just as Jay lunged forward.

He took her torso in one hand, lifting and pushing her back onto the bed so her fallen barrel curls slammed against the headboard. "You wish you did, don't you? You wish you went to New York instead of marrying me!"

"No! Of course I don't! I could never be happier anywhere else, than right here with you!" Elaine was very convincing in her tone, but it wasn't enough to stop him from striking her across the face. Crude pinks broached on her cheek like a rake had been dragged back and forth across it. "I didn't mean it! I— I never wanted that!" Elaine sniffled again. "Please." She shrunk to a fetal ball on the mattress.

But he wasn't even listening, only invested in the the rubescent buds of raised blood only he could bring out in her fair complexion. That overachieving strength latched to her shins, and with a dire yank, he dragged her to the base of his thighs. A rough-hewn grip twirled the light hair into a bun, until the fist had tangled into an unforgiving snare, and he pulled.

Elaine held in her sobs, wrists trembling, praying to God, before wondering if God had any say in those marriage books that had led her here.

His stranglehold kept coiling back until her spine was nearing to snap in two. An obstructed windpipe denied her any air. She thought about backfiring, replying as a person would in a dangerous situation, only Elaine wasn't a person, but a *lady*.

He let go and her graceful ghostly frame collapsed on the floor. Her deprived limbs filled once again with oxygen, as did the raw pink gardens on her skin. Jay's knuckles softly pet the back of her ear, nape of neck, gliding across the purple stamps that tomorrow would be blotted with tiers of professional-grade makeup.

Who knows what might be hiding in those small hometown environs, with robust plant life all growing and overlapping into one—have you checked yours, for those beguiling berries?

The mayor of a tinderbox town cradled his wife in his arms, hugging her close. "I love you so much, baby."

And she, never knowing of another way, answered with, "I love you too."

CHAPTER TWELVE
At First Sprout

"Go away," Sadie said to the sun, groaning into her daisy pillowcase, which had started to smell like mold, while the less than musical moos of cows patterned in the distance.

The scent of her mother's espresso machine wafted up the stairs, compelling enough to lever her dead-weight body to a sit, and give up on her feeble four hours of sleep.

As her eyes blinked groggily to the waking dimension, Sadie realized she hadn't dreamed. She couldn't remember the last time her mind's eye had seen such blank. Because even if there weren't solid pictures, there were at least colors, shapes, some form of vague notion she could sanctify in her journal. Today she opened the blue binding, wrote down the date, closed it, and set it atop a pile of Topshop denim on the second-to-highest, can-barely-reach shelf of her closet, where it would be forgotten for some time.

Sadie flipped through an Italian Vogue on her bed. Her mom had fancy friends in Sicily who often sent them with a block of Parmesan the same size as their Louis Vuitton Neverfull totes. Sadie studied the models' cool expressions, paper-thin hunched backs, long extortionist limbs that made them so magnificent and desirable. But as she stared longer, she noticed something she hadn't before: that aside from their immaculate beauty, they looked perfectly chicly miserable.

Sadie replayed last night. Brooks' breath lingered on her lips, thick and musty and transporting to anywhere but herself. After the chaos in Orville's rat's nest, they'd dropped off Levi and Caleb at the white picket-fenced Lindley house on Church Street, when Sadie had been so tired and tipsy, she'd hallucinated her father standing in the middle of a degenerate basketball court across the street. Then the tires rolled sneakily to their familiar out-of-sight spot, behind the Bexley shed and under the property's grandest oak. The yellow glowing 'M' from the McDonalds could be seen hovering over the groves, as well as the faintly flickering blaze of Tampa's nightlife in the far distance. Here, they talked and kissed, and most definitely broke Sadie's 'curfew'.

Being curled up into the smells of his clothes had made Sadie feel okay again; the small crusted pieces in her chest breaking away like sediment down a river. And wasn't that the very cardinal point she'd gathered in her years of preparative research? *That love conquers all*, or something just as flowery and ideal. Sadie would hold onto this as if her life depended on it, because it felt like it did.

After willing her legs to life and checking her undone appearance in the oval wall mirror—magenta giraffe pajamas she'd had since she was twelve, knee-high socks with a big-toe hole, last night's make-up, dried drool on her chin, loose braids—Sadie did something really stupid. She went downstairs.

Downstairs, where Brooks Holden was sitting on her grandparent's loveseat linen cushions discussing duck calls with her father. Downstairs, where her mother greeted her with a celery juice, a bowl of over-night oats and the fleet of vitamin supplements advertising 'colon health' and 'regularity' on the bottles. Downstairs, where her giraffe pajamas made their bold entrance, folded three times over and bunched in an atrocious wedgie-camel-toe wad.

"There she is!" Her father exclaimed like it was about time.

"H—Hi." Sadie squeaked with the helium of a Macy's Day balloon. "You're... here... in my living room... with my *parents*." She was astounded by his casually amused expression.

"I came to give you something," Brooks said.

A heart attack? "What is it?"

"You left it in my truck. I thought it might be important." Reaching into the pocket of Hollister khaki shorts, he withdrew a fist and dropped a thin and light-weight object in her palm.

"My hair tie?" Yes, one meaningless elastic black hair tie from her drawer of thousands that she'd inevitably misplace, but never miss. "Oh yes." Sadie nodded very seriously. "I've been looking everywhere for this."

"I thought so." Brooks smiled, and watched her slide it on her wrist.

"Well, it's nice to finally meet the boy bringin' out those dimples on your face." Henri placed a loving hand on his daughter's braid, eyes flashing in photograph again in case sweet mornings like these were running out. "And rentin' out a moonlight parkin' spot behind my work shed."

Both Brooks and Sadie, guilt on their faces, turned cherry-colored.

Henri chuckled informally, indicating he was okay with it, for some reason. "Remind me to tell you a few stories about your father one day. Think you'd really enjoy 'em."

"Yes—yes sir," Brooks stammered.

"So what've you kids got goin' on today?"

"Ahem. Well," Brooks cleared his throat, shifting in his socks and slides, "actually, I wanted to ask if Sadie could come trail ridin' with us. It's a small group, just a few friends from school. The Lindleys will be there too." As if this were the real seller.

"Muddin'? You talkin' about Bandit Bog up 301?"

"Yes sir."

"Aw, shoot! Now *that's* a spot you gotta see darlin'! Ain't no one seen the south 'til they got their drawers deep in God's green! At least that's what my father used to say. You ever meet Lance, when he was still around? Wore glass lenses the size of steak plates, Marine Veteran cap, probably airin' his grievances over some new bill about home vegetable garden restrictions bein' unconstitutional."

"Actually—"

"Ah, probably not. He was a real solitary individual, a 'misanthrope grump' they used to say, though I doubt they ever got past the mailbox to get a closer look. Hey, you want somethin' to drink? We got juice, cokes. Honey, can you grab us some cokes?"

"It's nine in the morning." Margot scolded, a discreet but activated suspicion stapled to every word.

"So? Never too early for men to share a few cold cokes when it's a boilin' hundred degrees outside, ain't that right?" Henri rocked Brooks' shoulder, the good one, and for a brief second Brooks imagined himself accepted into the family.

Margot walked into the kitchen, returning soon after with troublingly empty hands. "We're all out, somehow. We're out of cokes and the sweet tea you bought… just last night." The one he took an hour and a half to buy from the market a quarter of a mile down the road. "I didn't see it."

"I drank it," Henri fixed quickly.

"All of it?"

"That's right. Like I said, us crazy country folk and our Arnold Palmers. Ha ha. Right, Brooks?"

"Um." He didn't exactly know what was going on. "Right."

"Well, maybe next time you should buy *two* so I'll have something more exciting than metallic-tasting well water to offer our guests," Margot said.

Heeding nothing unusual about the dialogue, Sadie peered out the glass porch doors to check for storm clouds because she *had* sensed a strange fall in air-pressure, only the sky was an articulate teal and sunny. Maybe she was coming down with something; she suddenly felt feverish.

"Thank you, Mrs. Bexley, but we were plannin' on stoppin' by Elaine's on our way out anyway, for bagels and donut holes." Realizing, "Oh—err, I don't think they got much gluten free options, but I picked up some muffins from the health food store down the street."

"Down the street?" Margot asked. "Henri said the closest health food store is forty minutes away."

"Oh, um. It is."

Sadie watched her mother fall wholly overcome with approval, as she tilted her head to say *I like him.*

"I should get dressed." Sadie declared, though that much was painfully obvious. "Five minutes." She dashed upstairs.

She'd only had time to smooth her snored-in braids with hairspray, gargle toothpaste, and dab touches of concealer on the more starkly sleepy bits of her face. Without much prior instance of trail riding, or knowledge of what one wears to do the 'mudding', she went for an extempore pair of running shorts and Zara peach tank. Then, like the little comet of lust she was, returned to her back-country prince charming like she'd already decided this was the best day of her life.

Before they were off, Sadie hugged her father and whispered, "Thanks for not bringing out your guns."

"Next time." He winked, and took in her wonderfully fresh face, which had gained a certain grownup confidence he wasn't quite ready for. Henri made sure then to measure every freckle, catalogue every curl, behold all the wonderful details of her tender complexion. "You decided to bring back the pigtails."

"Dad, they're braids. Not the same thing."

"They are to me." He smiled and told her he loved her, which was always expressed but rarely said, as Sadie wondered what it was in his voice that sounded like a goodbye bigger than was needed.

Sadie was surprised to find Duke waiting in the backseat, who greeted her with a cold nod, before going back to scrolling his phone. It made her want to call him out, but on what exactly? She didn't know why sitting in a moving vehicle with them both made her overwhelmingly dizzy. Or maybe she felt dizzy, because she knew *exactly* why. It didn't help that Brooks was red-handedly drawing little hearts on the critical apex of her inseam, or that Duke was leaning against the streaky window residue of moist breath left over from the passionate kissing that'd occurred six hours prior. Sadie gulped the discomfort, before deriving a teensy bit of pleasure from it, and Lord have mercy... *was it about to get messy.*

The truck lazied along Paddock Road's green pastures of horses and cattle and one small donkey itching the flies off it's back against a splintery fence post. Brooks rolled the windows all the way down, and the everlasting summer-in-September breeze whisked damp yet brittle against their supple morning skin. These kinds of Saturday drives, average and easeful, they stick with you forever.

Soon they'd arrived in the lot behind Elaine's, where the rest were already waiting. Shelby, Colton and Tanner appeared with cream cheesed bagels and ice coffees.

Shelby bounced to where Sadie was waiting by the hood, nibbling on her chalky muffin. "Just in case you change your mind about your 'gluten diet'." She used her fingers for air quotes.

"It's an allergy, so—"

"Eh, potato poh-tah-toe." And then she bounced happily to hand Brooks his.

Sadie could've sworn she was wearing pink nail polish.

Three trucks started piling to the brims with tangled teenage bodies and an invincibility still unacquainted to life's great fumbles. With trailers hitched to their ball mounts, four-wheelers secured, each set of tires put on a show as they rolled out down highway 301, crossing the county line and just cruising.

Four Brad Paisley songs later, a torn hanging black tarp painted with white letters told them they'd reached Bandit Bog. In the middle of the open property, was something called a 'mud hole', which Sadie knew because there were big signs with arrows as if someone might miss it. Around the estate of mud, trails of soggy earth ran deep into the steady land, surrounded by small lagoons arranged in dynamic networks, soft-stem bulrush and cattails lining the marsh prairie, while cypress trees slumbered restfully in the water, breathing with their knees that protruded roughly vertically from the roots. Sadie found them sweetly amusing, like little cypress dwarf babies snuggling up to momma cypress, each their own family.

Though seemingly separated from society, it was also plentifully, intimately noisy. A constancy of overlapping crickets, puffy-throated croaks of toads searching for a mate, pig frogs and bullfrogs, soft movements of animals in the brush, and the harsher cranks coming from the engines.

Intimidated, Sadie took it in: women in skimpy bikinis bathing in clay, their boyfriends in Oakley sunglasses getting off on the tracks left by their 'various things on wheels', both speaking in a remote slang she had no hope of understanding. Not that she'd ever felt much sense of belonging, but she certainly had no hope of it here. She didn't even know how to take one step without being swallowed to the ankle. Luckily, Brooks intertwined his hand in hers, and suddenly this exact mud hole was the only place she'd ever imagined wanting to be.

Sterling was the first to mount an ATV, cold beer in hand, doing a few donuts before inviting Grace to hop on the back. They sped off.

Caleb showed off with some one-handed wheelies, shirtless.

With Brooks' help, Sadie mounted a bright lime Kawasaki and he took her over the basics. "Here," he pointed, "don't forget to go easy on the throttle. It can be jumpy, and you're light, so it can toss you around if you accelerate or brake too hard."

"Thanks, but I think I got it down now."

"I don't know… maybe we should go over it again."

One of her pinkies poked around at his kinked eyebrow. "Are you underestimating me?"

He chuckled at that before fixating hard on her, as if she were suddenly the most impossible person on the planet. "I think I'm estimatin' you just right, considerin' you've never been on one of these before." He came closer, slightly troubled. "What? You're scared to jump in a boat on our first date, and now you're a little hell-raisin' desperado?"

Sadie shrugged. "I just feel like goin' fast."

"Okay purty girl, but listen—"

With an unafraid twist of her wrist, the motor released a revving growl, the vibrations titillating up between her legs as she arched her spine to raise and tuck her fleshy quota of hips and butt. She could feel everyone's eyes on her, and it didn't make her want to flip inside out, or divert all attention to the nearest prom-queen as the prom-queen had always expected her to do. She gave the throttle another wrench, owning it, and this time the cool wave hit somewhere soul-deep and droughty.

"Are you sure you're *good?*" Brooks called over her wild vrooms.

Sadie let her hair down. Shook it out. "Not one bit." And after switching gears, made off into the expanse of badlands, wide open and playful, just waiting for her to feel it's elbowroom.

The whizzing grew louder as the speedometer climbed, and soon Sadie was intuitively half-standing with her knees bent, to absorb any shockwaves from unpredictable terrain. Sunshine harshly roasted her back with natural vitamins. The wind and sky and forest blurred to different shades of bayou wildlife. It was the closest she'd ever gotten to flying, almost like she'd had wings this entire time.

Caleb streaked past then, slinging a shower of black muck until her arms and face were covered in it. He'd expected a distressed rise out of her; he'd only meant to cast a few drops of mud. But before he could offer assistance, she took off again, looping back around to give him a taste of his own medicine, and with this adventurous laugh living declaratively across her cheeks.

They raced down parallel trails, catching fickle glimpses of each other through the greenery, until Caleb lost her track... and discovered her waiting for him triumphantly at the dead end clearing.

"Well, well!" He cheered completely out of breath, clapping and whistling, almost falling out of his seat with the hysterics. "Fuckin' finally!"

This compelled from her a wry, confused scoff. "What? You've been *waiting* for me to smoke you?"

"No, princess. I've been waitin' for you to have the guts to try." With a few figure eights resulting in more mud hail, he banged his chest like Tarzan and raved at the sun, before leaving her alone to her real-time metamorphosis.

The group of friends spent the next hour tossing bags of corn kernels into the platforms Colton had sitting in his truck, on a less-wet area of grass by the snack shack selling sodas, cheese straws and fireworks year-round.

Sadie was nestled between Brooks' legs, turning her fingers

into highways for a ladybug on a mission to cross them. Everything is a sign, when things are going right. Everything is free, when you've never seen the tab.

Brooks kissed the sensitive area of skin under her ear, and rested his face on her small bony shoulder. "You sure you've never done this before? That didn't look like a city-girl out there."

"Well don't forget, I used to visit."

"Oh, I could never forget." He split into a complete grin, taunting and flirty. "By the way, your dad told me about Chives. So it was spiders... *and* toads?"

Pasting a smile over her real reaction, she turned to look at him, and he stilled at once, as if standing at attention was his chosen tactic of courtship. Sadie imagined them in a different era, with sun umbrellas and gloves, chaperones and vintage times, *going steady*. It was fairly hilarious to think, considering Caleb and Sterling were currently grinding their groins on a tree for no apparent reason, and yet fairytale was exactly what it was. "Thank you for bringing me," Sadie shared her gratitude into his brown eyes. "I mean, not that I had much of a *choice*."

They leaned into brushing kiss at that, ensnared once there, only stopping because Caleb's sack of corn accidentally hit Sadie's elbow.

"I'm really glad you came," Brooks said. "You fit in my world pretty nicely, you know."

"You think?"

"Maybe next weekend we go get you some boots."

"Let's not get ahead of ourselves." Sadie laughed and observed the sound as it departed her lips, only then realizing how many of her own laughs she'd never even heard, or felt, or let follow through to the very end. What a simple yet pivotal luxury, to laugh a full laugh.

Brooks took great credit in deactivating those brakes, though he shouldn't take all of it. "Can I ask you somethin'?"

Her body subtly hunched. "Of course."

"How well do you know my brother? I mean... are you two... like friends?"

Sadie felt her face fall white, knowing she was basically see-

through when it came to her emotions. "Oh, um… we're…
yeah… friends." It wasn't a lie. She did *not* lie. "We have English
together." Also, not a lie.

"English. That explains it."

It, Sadie thought.

They silently watched Colton and Tanner sink a few more
cornhole bags.

"You wanna go for a walk?" Brooks suggested, and helped
her up. "I feel like bein' alone with you."

With an appetent nod, Sadie's gold untidy ringlets followed
him down a densely wooded path of tupelo gum and one
heavenly late-blooming magnolia tree with highly scented, big
white petals in the shape of pretty teacups. They stayed in the
shade and cloud of fragrance, hugging and kissing, and half-
dancing as their bodies responded to the breeze. The sweat above
his brow glistened and he had traces of soil scattered across his
skin, making him feel as if an extension of their earthly
surroundings, so biologic and honest. He, on the other hand, saw
her as something too light and enchanting to be shrouded under
the moss, and yet kind enough to embrace it anyway. An earth
boy and a cloud girl, hopefully, meeting in the middle.

The two teenagers were completely there, completely under
the magnolia tree, completely enraptured and recipient to the
moment at present. At that age it's easy to be, when it all matters.
The enchantment, the craze, the pain of young love. Of first
love. It only happens once, after all. Unless of course, it happens
two at once.

Brooks pushed a strand of gold behind her ear, the way guys
do in movies before they say something life-changing. "I want to
do right by you."

"Okay." She wasn't quite sure what it meant, but it hardly
sounded anything less than she'd hoped for.

"I guess I just… I *really* like you."

"I really like you too."

His Adam's apple wriggled restlessly and his mouth tightened
to one stern line as he strung the words together. "I don't trust a
lot of things, or people. I trust the ball in my hand that I control,

I trust my feet that I tell to move, and sometimes I trust the ground I'm standin' on. But I don't trust that my left tackles got my blind side, or that the receiver will be anywhere near to where I throw the ball, or that the goal posts won't close in on an impulse. I dunno why, but that's how I am. I think it's from my dad, maybe, I dunno. But I trust you, Sadie. Okay? I trust you."

Her neck was craned so precisely into his brown eyes, it'd started to hurt. She didn't dare move now. "You should," she vowed. "You can." *I think.*

The layered warbles and whines of the swamp turned on another percussion instrument, and Sadie hummed pleasantly along to the tune.

"We should go back," Brooks instructed, and chuckled wisely, but first kissed her once more, and with a sort of passion and torment that left that tasty pressure on her pelvic bone again.

"Why do we have to leave?"

"Well… that extra jingle is what we swamp kids like to call a rattlesnake, and it's usually their polite way of tellin' us to get the hell out."

Sadie's eyes bugged, but instead of fleeing, she reached up to pick a white flower. "My grandparents used to have a fresh wreath on the front door every summer. Grandpa would bring them home from the chicken feed store, because the owner Gus had a tree in his yard, and grandpa and Gus both agreed that wives should get fresh flowers every Saturday." She twirled this one in her hand, before cushioning it to her nose. "I want to give it to my mom."

"Chicken feed, huh? You almost sound like you're from here." He admired her attention to life. "My dad used to go to Gus too, Gus Moore."

"Did your mom get fresh magnolias, too?"

His eyes flickered away, stoic, or perhaps sad, before he stretched his farmer's tan high and picked the finest one. "She will now."

Sadie nodded, extra matter-of-fact. "It is Saturday, after all."

"Yes." And he fretfully glanced down to size up his shoes, and all the room to fill. "Saturday, it is."

The lovebirds took their time getting back, where half their friends were engaged in a good ol' hands-and-knees mud fight. Brooks' competitive nature couldn't resist joining, so Sadie watched him use a tailgate like a diving board and start hurling gooey balls of roots and slush. Then, he went to assist an unconventional squad of bachelorette party-girls whose tube float had been stranded on a cypress knee. Sadie had watched one of them throw it on the wood protrusion just to have a reason to get his attention, but she wasn't jealous. The usual frail voice in her head had altered after she'd gone forty miles an hour on open wheels. It said *back off, he's all mine.* Then deeper and more hushed, *his brother might be too.*

Sadie set off across the countrified theme park to find herself a refreshment from the cooler. It took some rigorous trudging, with every step suction-cupping her feet to the ground, and she was plastered in sweat and pink as a lingonberry by the time she reached the box of ice.

"Excuse me." Sadie did a sarcastic curtsy at Shelby, who was using it as her personal throne.

Despite having witnessed her entire backbreaking trek over, Shelby simply said, "You're excused."

Sadie demanded, "Get up, now."

"I'm—I'm *sorry?*"

"No, you are not. You never are. Now get up so I can get a water before I pass out."

"No 'please'?" Shelby appeared suddenly fulfilled. "I knew it."

"Knew what?"

The freckly shoulders shrugged. "That your whole poptart-poppy-princess thing was an act."

"Yeah, um, I don't follow. But I *am* still thirsty."

"No one is that nice *all* the time, so your second face was bound to melt off at some point. Did Brooks think it was cute how you drove off all 'southern girl' into the woods? Did you have a fun time being country for five seconds? Aren't you just itching to go tell your Kardashian wannabe friends all about it, that you're a total cowgirl now? This is just some aesthetic to you, isn't it? What's next, Sadie? Dirt bikes and monster trucks? Tell me: would you *ever* willingly hang out in a place like this, with people like us, if you weren't *forced* into it?"

Shelby clearly didn't know about her connection to a dear earthly friend named Chives, or the mud soups, or the Black Widow in her picnic basket, or that she'd never felt much alive until today. And yet Sadie found it more satisfying to confirm, "Probably not."

"Exactly," Shelby scoffed. "God, you're so fake."

Here, Sadie fitted herself for a new kind of smile, tweaking and modifying so it stung just right. Her darker green eyes batted at Shelby's pink nail color. "I was wrong. Your skin tone completely washes you out. What's next, Shelby? Girl clothes and a hair brush? God, you're so fake."

Shelby immediately shot up to shove her into a tree, but she was too stunned. Meanwhile, Sadie happily grabbed her refreshment from the now available cooler, shoulders back, taking one sip and lusciously pouring the rest of the cool liquid down her hair. To flaunt it, to waste it, to wash away the dying and detaching of her *first petal*...

We rarely notice the first one go, only realizing we've been shedding the day we're holding tightly to our last.

Again, Shelby reaffirmed for her own sanity. "Bitch."

"*Bitch*," Sadie repeated the word quietly to herself. And then said, "Thank you." She fluffed her feathery hair and waffled her light tone, dug her heels in the ground like the southern girls do. "Can you tell Brooks I'll be waiting for him in his truck?" She trudged off, ignoring Caleb who'd been close enough to keep score.

Once the F-150 door slammed, Sadie screamed her head off for a good long while.

"Hey." Duke had been casually lounging in the back. "I was sleeping."

"I'm sorry?" Her tone spasmed angrily, backwashed from Shelby and the fact that this was the second time today he'd surprised her this way. "You didn't get a good night's sleep?"

"Probably better than the rest of you." He cracked a hardly

humorous face, before shaking his head. "But no. Hung up on a lyric. Couldn't fall asleep until I got it right."

"Right. Your music." Sadie softened. "Can I hear something one day?"

"One day. Sure."

"Have you ever played anywhere?"

"In front of people? No."

"That's too bad. I'll bet you're good. You have that face."

"A face?"

"Yeah, you know—like the lovable, anguished one you see singing in a pie shop with books and classic movie posters, that makes you want to be the girl he sings about, just so you can know how it feels for someone to think such magical things about you."

He turned all the way so his reaction stayed classified. "That's awfully... specific."

"There was a spot in LA with coconut cream pie and a 'take-one leave-one' book shelf that did open mics every Friday. The best ones were the guys with those faces. Granted, they usually ended up making gross passes at the baristas, but that's probably because they'd just had their heart shattered, and they just didn't know that wouldn't make it better."

Duke studied Sadie, like perhaps the formula was somewhere disguised on her face. "You have a funny way of lookin' at the world, don't you?"

"The wrong way?"

"I don't think so. Just yours."

She sighed with labor. "It's been harder to see it that way lately."

He got the impression she wanted to say more, but also, he wasn't the assigned confidante for these kinds of jobs, or any job that didn't pertain to the common 'friend', as verbally established. Even just being there could be considered a crime; an intimately enclosed space, unofficial and undeclared, no nearby listeners, a freedom to speak their minds. It was entirely, radically, riskily out of bounds. Naturally, they made no effort to return inside them.

"Why did you come, anyway?" Sadie breathed, finding herself flushed. "If you don't want to ride?"

He chewed the loose skin on his lip. "My dad suggested it, and by 'suggested', I mean basically locked the front door so he wouldn't be forced to awkwardly sit in a house and pretend he's interested in talkin' to me."

Sadie was positive that wasn't true, but she knew not to belittle his feelings, from others belittling hers. She leaned in closer. "Your mom tells me your neighbors, Jenny and Mike, they patch up your pool screen in a jiff and with no extra charge, in case you wanted to break it down."

His kind brown eyes lifted, and without overthinking, laughed ever so winningly in this light-hearted timber, so she laughed too, until neither knew why they were laughing, only that it came so easily in present company. "You're amazing," Duke let slip.

Out of bounds. Out of bounds.

"Er—I should—I should find Brooks," Sadie swiftly redirected.

"Yup."

"'Kay." But before she opened the door, she gave him an extra silly face and whispered, "You too," as if simplifying it to a joke dignified the mistake.

As if she had no idea he was falling *in love with her*.

In the eye of the sunbeams, Brooks and Caleb were being reckless on the jump ramps, roasting each other with no holding back, like they had since peewee, only with curiously thinner-skinned egos that made each fiber of their necks cross-grained and nodular. Their friendship hadn't been the same lately; for-life and unconditional; there were *definite* conditions, but neither knew them.

Truthfully, Brooks had never minded Caleb's uncouth mouth or self-seeking ventures, mostly because it was highly entertaining to watch. He'd never protested, not even when his best friend had been inappropriate with a girl Brooks had taken out, like Crista with the belly-ring and StubHub hook-up. It was Valentine's Day, and they'd been in line at the Orville Cinema 10 concessions. Crista had just told them that her pet pygmy pig had died, to which Caleb had toyed with her belt loop and sympathized with, "If you're feeling down, I can feel you up." Brooks had bought her a large popcorn and three bags of candy, yet she'd ended up spending the climax of the movie doing just that in the back of Caleb's truck.

"You didn't mind, did you?" Caleb had mumbled with a yap full of McDonalds fries later, and Brooks answered, "Nah," because he truly hadn't. But Sadie wasn't some crochet-bra wearing, leggy phone number he'd picked up in line at the Rustic Bull teen night. She wasn't like Crista, unsurprising and common and sharable—especially not sharable.

"Yo." Brooks braked harshly on the floodplain trail to cut Caleb off.

"Sup?" He turned the key to quiet the engine, leaned back and dug a totally lax heel on the tire.

"I was just thinkin'... do you still remember that one night we egged the old man who used to live in the Bexley house? Cause we thought he had a glass eye or some shit."

Caleb's heel slapped down on the footrest. That, he had *not* expected. "Glass eye? Nope, sure can't recall." He implored him to drop it.

But Brooks only got more bound and determined about it. "It was Halloween, in like seventh grade or somethin'. You, me and Levi hit Lake Josey, then rode all the way down Paddock on our bikes. Ida—or whatever her name was, the crazy old lady—she started eggin' us back with rotten stink bombs, and they invited us in for cokes after. You really don't r'member?"

Sobersided for once, Caleb squinted as if his eyes had been slashed with one of the wooden twigs lying about. "Ah, shit! Sure!" He mimed churning a handle adjacent to his brain. "Ex-army guy, fat glasses, showed us his cool guns. That guy?"

"Yeah," Brooks said.

"Sure, I remember him." Caleb reached over to pick a cable of sawgrass, then tying a knot, he fashioned a pipe and puffed on it. He pretended to blow big 'O's of smoke up at the bushy clouds. "Why is this important again?"

"That was Sadie's grandfather."

"And?"

Brooks shifted atop the ATV, sunburn impaling through his shirt, as he considered how to explain it. That since that night, he hadn't stopped thinking about the girl in the photograph, and now she was here, and she was even prettier in person, and surreally easy to talk to, and he was sleeping better, and thinking clearer, and all the ugly moss and algae ponds and sagging oaks in their little green purgatory, now with her smile, had transformed into a haven that put heaven to shame, and this life had meaning, for she was it. How could he get Caleb to understand that, when he didn't understand it himself?

Caleb might've had the words to illuminate: *You're falling in love with her, dude.* To which he'd surely add: *Don't.* "Well?"

"I guess I… I just don't want you being a dick all the time to scare her off."

Caleb chuckled with a trough-like bounce back, as if something was fermenting beneath. "You really think she scares that easy?"

"Well, yeah. She's not like us. She's good."

"And may she forever hold her peace," Caleb muttered under a short covert breath, before putting his hand up to take a serious vow. "I, Caleb Lindley, promise to back off Sadie Bexley, for you two shall live happily ever after. Happy?"

Brooks' chin dipped gratefully. "I mean… yeah."

"Cool," Caleb snapped. "Oh, and they were cherry cokes, by the way."

"Huh?"

"The cokes Lance gave us. They were cherry." With a criminally loud rev of the engine, he thumbed the clutch as far as it would go, and finally disappeared into the colorful marshland textures without another word.

"Lance," Brooks repeated as he suspiciously watched him zipper away, because he hadn't reminded Caleb of the old man's name, meaning he hadn't needed to remind him of anything at all.

Another hour later, the sun was slanting into late afternoon and everyone's bug bites were bleeding from the scratching.

While some were packing up, the last two sets of tires emerged from the lush—Sterling leading, Grace and Mallory behind.

As they got closer, it appeared Mallory's head was unconsciously bobbing on Grace's back. Then, she fell off the four-wheeler.

"Guys! We need help!" Grace cried out at them, and they took her with as much severity as the girl who cried wolf. "No, seriously—HELP!" She flashed desperate eye-codes to her brother, and he at least, immediately understood.

Caleb rushed to the side of the four-wheeler, already knowing what to do though he acted like he didn't. The cheerleader's arms and legs were wilted and lifeless as he carefully set her on the ground and propped her against the vehicle. He left to get something edible from his truck glove compartment, but by the time he returned, Mallory's almond-shaped eyes had rolled all the way back, and she was retching neon bile on an ant pile. Grace covered her eyes and held her friend's hair back, half-thinking: *See? I do things for you too, bitch.*

"What the hell happened?" Brooks took some steps back.

"I—I don't know," Grace lied. "She was fine, and then just… passed out."

"Hangover?" Levi suggested.

"Food poisoning?" Duke said, who'd gotten out of the F-150 to check on all the commotion.

"Someone get this girl a water." Sterling plugged his nose.

Shelby caught Sadie's eyes, before volunteering, "I'll do it!"

All the while, Mallory was heaving from her knees, both arms up in a crumbling push-up, spitting up the last of her liquids, as her closest friends slowly increased their distance and didn't say aloud what all of them were thinking.

Sadie's mind was bending in shock, not from the puke, but from witnessing something so glamorous, inch-perfect, self-assured, prove no more immune to the debits of being human, as the rest of them. Becks too, had known just how to dress herself in distracting credit; with enough spray tans and jojoba oil, soul cycle and keto cups, the edited photo she'd posted of herself at the Beverly Hills Hotel pool cabana, who cares if her parents had been up screaming at each other until 4am, or that her dyslexia had held her back a year, or that she'd landed herself in the ER with hypokalemia after weeks of diuretics—

Sadie eyed Mallory's lantern-thin ribcage, while Caleb tried to force-feed her Rice Krispies Treats. "That won't work," she said plainly.

"Oh? You got any better ideas, princess?"

"She needs electrolytes, that's just sugar. With what she's... coming up with... it looks like she hasn't eaten in days."

"Actually she had a bagel this morning, so you can just back off." Grace lashed at her with a twiddling wave of fingers, which was exactly what Tenley had said to the nurse, right before she'd basically saved Becks' life.

Before she'd had time to practice it in her head, Sadie ran full-speed to the snack shack, cut the long line of bachelorette partiers and their wanderlust tube float, grabbed a Gatorade and banana while explaining, "It's an emergency," to the tweenish boy at the counter, who ended up ringing some alarm when she took off, probably to signal the mud hole police to swoop in on their alligators.

"This'll work faster." She handed Caleb the stolen cargo, who gave her an impressed glance, and actually took them without any further snide remarks.

Fifteen minutes and three bites of banana later, Mallory was well enough to stand up.

"We need to get her home," Grace signaled to Sterling. "Babe?"

"Fine," Sterling moped but eventually agreed. "Mrs. Jordan can buy me one of those fancy Porsches if she upchucks all up on my interior." A salvage yard treasure trove pre-stained with a plethora of rainbow substances. "Ah, shit." He checked his pockets and fingered through his stash of loose change, no paper. "Hey Colton, toss me a couple bucks for gas. I'll pay you back."

"Again?" Colton announced, for everyone.

"I forgot my wallet." Sterling's scrawny shoulders shrugged. "But I'll pay you back t'morrow." In odd little jerks, his eyelids squeezed.

Colton sucked his tongue and stuck out his lips. "Uhhuh. Sure you will."

And though Sterling would do his best to fight it, the incoming shakes he'd contended with his whole life, they would take him under for a brief intermission. As a child, it was more complex. Repeating observed movements, tapping objects and people, the throwing of pencils he got suspended for time and time again; bare rump later belt-spanked over the sofa armrest by one of his mother's many air mattress companions who'd steal his Frosted Flakes. Sterling had never been diagnosed—seeing a specialist was *expensive*—but he'd read about it on the Internet after Samantha Wagner told him her new dog from the pound had Tourette Syndrome. That it would twitch a lot and it really freaked her out. Sterling had learned to control it with great effort and practice, the funny swarming sensation no one could understand, and slowly, people started to forget, called him quirky instead. But with all eyes on him, even practice couldn't contain it, and soon his limbs were in crawling rippling flames. "I promise I'll—I'll—I'll pay you back."

"I dunno man." Colton sighed to reiterate his annoyance. "You moochin' off us is gettin' real old."

Sterling's blinks and breaths continued to happen in shaken snatches. "D—dude, what's the big deal? I—I forgot it. It—it's just a few bucks." Sterling hated himself, hated that he was as incompetent as Samantha Wagner's defective dog, which turns out a week later, they'd given back to the pound. "D—daddy cut you off or somethin'?"

"Soon probably, since we're all gon' get sucked dry by free loaders like you. What do your parents even do all day long?" He flicked the rim of the dirty wife beater. "Bet it ain't laundry."

"Colton!" Shelby interjected, because this wasn't like him.

"Shut up, Shelbs. You're not my mom," he snarled back.

And there the life-long friends stood silently in a gawkish circle, centimeters away from budding flowers at their feet, and yet unlearned on how roots work.

"What are y'all lookin' at? You know it's true!" Colton hungered for a fight with dark rancor inking over his eyes. Not installed or taught, but a curse that'd been surfacing for quite some time, advancing to fruition, belonging to him just as rightly as the family butt-chin and freckles and impending inheritance. A gift from his father.

"Fine!" Grace threw up flustered arms. "Yes, it's all *my* fault. Sterling is just covering for me being a total spoiled brat." She lifted her Tiffany heart necklace. "I made him buy me the whole mall for our anniversary, so it's on me, I'll get the gas babe." Her familiar sweep of thumb tucked inside their held hands, like she'd done in Mrs. Harris' fourth grade class closet during a lockdown drill, when he'd panicked and twitched and she'd known how to stop it. "Let's get our Mal gal home, safe and sound."

The wild teens gathered the last of their things. Shelby and Tanner put the cornhole in the back. Caleb and Brooks hooked up the ATVs. And Colton remained in his locked angry stance, imagining the violence he could inflict, wanting to. He remained here for a few more minutes, and when he finally moved on, he barely remembered any of it.

Back in the soft shotgun of the F-150, flying down Paddock Road, Sadie stared up at the unfathomable teal sky, letting her head fall leaden as she stroked the velvety petals of her Magnolia, like it were the last drop of hope in the world that she was holding in her hands. Why do you think, she had the sudden urge to rip it?

· There was a patter on tin, falling gullies on the windows, before the pungent scent of ozone and plant oils penetrated the truck air vents. Then came the wet pavement, which smelled different each time. A typical Florida afternoon sun shower followed them down that principle backroad, and Sadie rolled down the glass and draped an arm in the liquid sunshine, wondering how that was possible; rain and light coexisting at once, and how together it was something entirely new and precious. Perhaps there was a lesson in that, like yin and yang, inappreciable and unbridled without the other. It never rained in LA and people rejoiced in that, later complaining that everything was dead and sand-colored. Maybe it was unhealthy to be perfect all the time. Maybe there was something worthwhile in the woebegone and wretched. Maybe it was important, necessary, to *blossom.*

Behind them, a complete rainbow jeweled across the teal beyond, though they never turned around to notice.

At the Holden house, Brooks helped Sadie rinse off with a garden hose around back. He grinned sideways at the gunks fossilized in her armpits when he said, "You know, this is a hot look on you." To which she giggled and struck a pose like the models in Italian Vogue, except with the world in her eyes. A better one; Brooks could attest.

He hadn't been kidding about his mom and the marigolds; the entire perimeter of the yard was filled with cheerful yellows and saffron oranges, several systems of inflorescence resembling a candy shop for bees and alike.

Just then, Mrs. Holden poked her energetic gumption through the screen door and handed Sadie an old Tampa Bay Ray's tee and joggers, fresh from the drier and still toasty to the touch. Then, she requested Sadie stay for dinner.

Despite Brooks shaking his head and mouthing *no*, Sadie answered, "I'd love to."

"Mom, I got you somethin'." The magnolia flower was crumpled from being in his pocket, but she didn't seem to mind.

Around the kitchen island, Sadie helped Kelly plate the side dishes while the counselor detailed the same story about her dad that Mrs. Dunn had shared her first day: with Betty and the whopping plate of buttermilk biscuits. Apparently, that was a local favorite, but one that made people sad. Kelly, much like Elaine, strayed off into a melancholic state by the end. "Your father, he was this medicine to the whole town. This place has been in a horrible bellyache ever since."

Sadie asked, "What do you mean by that?"

But Kelly just ruffled Sadie's sweet ringlets, and answered with her own questions. "Has he ever mentioned why he left? Better yet, why he decided so out of the blue to come back?" She smoothed a placemat with curious fuss. "Is he... planning on staying for good?"

Sadie's mouth opened and froze, because she didn't really

know. Aren't these things she should know? "The chicken smells really lovely." Though, there wasn't any.

With umph, Duke's bedroom door swung open down the hall. He was shirtless and ripped, freshly showered and succulent, sauntering past Sadie to where they kept their clean laundry and pulling a gray hoodie over his head. Once Kelly had dashed to pick the neighbor's lemon tree, and before Brooks was done helping his dad unjam the garage hatch, Duke approached Sadie by the drip-drip-dripping sink, just the two of them again, and with a pleased quip twinkling from the pair of carbon copy brown eyes, he whispered in her ear, "You're wearing my clothes."

"Oh!" Sadie's entire body flushed the shade of flamingo, now actively fixated on the fact her panties had been too drenched from the hose, and that currently, she wasn't wearing any. "Your mom gave them to me. They're... really soft." She complimented as if in interview. "The cotton feels really good." Her breath caught. "On my *legs!*"

"You can keep them if you want."

"What?" She scoffed, or coughed, something inbetween. "Um, no. That's—that's like a relationship thing."

"Right." He stared immorally at her lips. "Then probably not."

The Holden household functioned very differently than her own, the dining table set up like a Golden Corral buffet, leading to the couch sectional and foldable lap trays, where the flat screen and surround-sound were already set up. They inhaled platters of green beans and brisket, mint chip ice cream for dessert, until the poker-themed wall clock struck 7, and Mr. Holden suggested Brooks 'take the girl home'.

Sadie wandered the hallway of richly ornate photo frames and Hobby Lobby medallion hangings with phrases like 'God Gave Me You' and 'Born To Sparkle', while Brooks relieved himself of the liter of sweet tea he'd washed down with dinner. She marveled longest at the hung capsule of time-snippets, Brooks and Duke with outrageous baby-fat grins, showing off their missing front teeth, tiny and indicating every feeling felt, and still with that football tucked under their arms.

"This one's my favorite." Brant's crisp voice caught her off guard, especially because he'd been anything but sociable the whole evening. "That was the day Brooks made his first touchdown. Of course, opposin' teams defense wasn't but a field of sprightly sticks at that age, but still… it was a big day."

Sadie stood straight and latched her hands behind her back, like in elementary school lunch lines. "Wow."

"Yep, big day. Hasn't been the same since his hands touched that first ball."

"I can tell it means a lot to him."

"Mhm." Brant's lips pursed and pouched with askant air, manipulating it around, before very slowly releasing. "It's hard to understand just how much, and I've been there—big dreams, big head—it's fragile, you see. It's a fragile place to be in life. I know just how easy it is to lose sight of those dreams, when say…" He seemed to sift through a registry of unsatisfactory adjectives, "A more *whimsical* gamble comes along."

She politely smiled at him, and assured, "I'll make sure to keep my eye out for him, in case something dangerous and… whimsical comes our way."

And now, deservedly so, it was him who was caught off guard. He should've known. "You really are Henri's daughter, no doubt about that." Brant chuckled, but crestfallen. "Bexley blood, through and through."

Except, Sadie didn't understand the significance, nor did she understand what happened twenty years ago, or why everyone loved bringing it up. "Thank you for having me over, Mr. Holden."

"Sure, sure. Tell your father to keep me posted."

She certainly didn't understand that.

Sadie found her dad with black car fluids on his laugh lines, in the shed under a 1969 Chevy Camaro that might've been scrap metal, if Henri hadn't been the type to care about the bottom dogs and long shots. He offered the suffering car words of encouragement, saying aloud what he was doing as he did it, shaking passionately his silver wrench. Being a dad.

He radiated at her arrival, doing that marchy walk over and giving her a kiss on the forehead, before sliding back under the rusty carriage. Sadie sat with him for over an hour, giving small tidbits of her day as the tidbits naturally came up, guiding conversation to what she wanted to come up.

"It was crazy, dad. I went like—so fast! *Way* faster than Caleb. I think we should get one, a four-tire thingy. I could ride it in the orange groves." She mindlessly re-braided her hair.

"Caleb? That Stacy and David's son?"

"Yeah." She made a face and went on. "He's not important."

"Okay." He smacked a dirty towel around his deeply reddened neck, and leaned back to get a complete look at the new lights he'd just put in. "What do you think darlin'? Found her with a 'for sale' sign in front of Gus Moore's feed stand just this mornin'. You remember Gus. There's a photo somewhere of you and him, with black olives loaded on all ten fingers, in the stands of the San Ann gopher tortoise races. You always did love the Rattlesnake Festival, I would hear. Maybe we'll go together this year."

Which only begged the question: Why hadn't they been able to go in previous years? Why hadn't he been here? "What were you doing at Gus' place?" Sadie wondered if the chicken feed merchant's ears had been burning today, being such a trending topic.

"It's Saturday, darlin'." And he pointed to a bouquet of pure white florals wrapped in brown craft paper. "Thought I'd make a wreath for your mom, continue the tradition. I think your grandpa would appreciate that."

Sadie's shoulders danced in thrill as they did over incidence of romance, before all of her slumped. "I miss him, dad. I miss them both."

"Me too, honey." He sighed. "Me too." And his arms crossed, eyes fell to the floor, rubbing up and down the strain in his neck, as though undecided on whether or not to impart news. "There's um… well, it seems like maybe someone else misses 'em too."

Sadie drew hearts in a bag of soil, as she waited for him to elaborate.

"I stopped by the cemetery today, figured I'd go and clean up the stone, whack down those dandelions before your gram comes hauntin' me with a stirrup hoe in my sleep. But somehow, by some*one*, it'd already been done, and with a basketful of blue hydrangeas, like gram liked to sew, left right there on the plot. I asked the groundskeeper if he'd seen anyone, but he wasn't any help." Henri paused to dwell, more worried than heartened. "It's just… concerning."

"For grandpa and grandma to have friends leave flowers at their grave?"

"That's the thing, sweetie. They didn't have many friends. They were private. And even if they did have some buddies from bingo nights, I doubt someone would keep it up after all these years. It's been consistently cared for, most polished rock out there." His stress levels aged him years in minutes. "You remember, how they were private."

"They were, or *you* were?" Her confident grownupness was back, and it'd matured a frightening amount since the time she'd left the house that morning.

Putting down his wrench and propping a knee, Henri smiled with that heroic sense of humor she'd regularly found safety in. It looked different now. "Oh darlin, what's that about? Somethin' on your mind?" Like he expected the quandary to be a shortage of apple juice or pink tutus.

"*Private*," she enunciated with her feet firmly grounded to gravity.

"Well, they sure weren't social—"

"But it was *you* who didn't want me playing at the Orville Woods park with the other kids my age, or to sit inside at Pizzahut, or go to a movie, or walk inside the SunTrust bank. Grandpa only took me in that one time because it was a hundred degrees out, and there was a line, and he didn't want to leave me in the car to cook like candle wax. *Of course* I loved the stupid Rattlesnake Festival, dad. It was far enough away from people who knew you, wasn't it? That's why it was the only place I was allowed to go."

The expression he wore now made him almost unrecognizable. Sadie was positive the one she wore, did too. "I don't know what you're gettin' at here. Look, I'm sorry if you hated it here so dang much—"

"No, dad. That's not the point at all." Sadie kicked off from where she'd been leaning on his workbench, pacing and purging the pent-up belief that *her* parents were tamper-proof. "The *point* is, you shipped me off to this green fantastical estate and I never thought to ask—just as you never cared to explain—*why* didn't you come with me?"

The sweltry climate was obnoxiously ceaseless, even through the evenings. Henri wondered if maybe he should build them a pool, and a barn with some ponies Sadie could ride before jumping in that pool. She mentioned four-wheelers; he'd get her three. "I had work."

"Work? You had *work*? No offense dad, but it's not like we would've lost our house or gone hungry if you took some time off your freelance moving-big-objects-for-movies job. You could've visited, seen your friends. Did you think people would've judged you for leaving? Because I don't think they do. They really, really love you dad."

They who? Who had she been talking to? Through the ajar garage door, he rationalized into the flat horizon, before finally coming up with, "Ah, darlin'. You're still so young."

"I'm not that young."

"You're sixteen. There's so much you don't understand."

"Then *make* me understand. Just try to explain it to me."

"I'd rather you enjoy this time and not have to think about the tangly stuff just yet. You know, go shopping for skirts, make those homemade forts like you used to."

"Yeah, because a wall of sheets and pillows will make it all go away."

"Just trust me, you'll understand when you're older."

"What does that even mean?"

"Means you're too young."

"STOP CALLING ME YOUNG!"

"DAMMIT SADIE, YOU ARE YOUNG! AND THAT'S

EXACTLY WHAT YOU SHOULD BE UNTIL YOU JUST CAN'T BE ANYMORE!"

Sadie furiously glared at her father's doused pores in the sunset light, either from sweat or humidity or the tears getting creative in escape route, since real men would never allow them from their eyes. She instantly wiped away the soil hearts she'd drawn, feeling the same fading away in her chest. Furious is what she was, that her father had raised his voice at her after going strong for this long, the many spared years of never doing so, of her believing he never would. Those years all seemed wasted now. Sadie undid her braids, and with them, obliterated any youthful sentiment they held. Just a frizzy, adult, air-dampened mess, and one irreversible step… away.

"Sadie, honey…"

"You're right, I don't understand why Bambi's mom had to die, or why you weren't in that photo with me and Gus, or why you need a stupid shoehorn every time you put on your big hideous boots when you could just as easily use your hands!" Her forehead tightened and cheeks sucked in. "But you want to know the part that really gets me?"

"What, darlin'?" The back of his nose burned with remnants of the past, becoming present.

"That whenever someone talks about you moving away, they say it like something really bad happened. Almost like… like…"

"Like what?"

"Like someone *died*."

Henri froze.

"Whatever. I'm going to bed." She said it as if their relationship hadn't just been permanently altered, and on her way out, she noticed a small carving in the door frame. It looked like initials. DL? Maybe CI? *Probably just meaningless cracks in the wood*, Sadie decided, and continued from the yard into the kitchen where her mother was listening to Celine Dion with a bottle of Pinot instead of her usual herbal tea.

Sadie stole a glass and went upstairs.

CHAPTER THIRTEEN

The Flower Room

The main church sat at the corner of 14th and Church Street, gleaming and dictatorial in all it's red brick glory. The building was blockish like an old schoolhouse, with three deluxe pillars in front and tiny stiff tulips planted under the windows. Composed townies dawdled around in their Sunday clothes, parents giving the occasional brow raise to their children with uninhibited energy who were poking each other with Y-shaped seed heads of bahiagrass.

Ringleader Stacy was overjoyed to see Henri, Margot and a hungover Sadie (turns out her mom's wine had been a neat cognac) walking up the white steps. She greeted them with judicious hugs and a wealth of passive judgement.

"What a marvelous surprise! You finally made it! Get in, get in, we're just about to start. You couldn't have picked a better day. It'll be an *extra* long service this mornin'!" Eggshell stained teeth flashed at Henri, before her umpiring eyes swam Margot up and down. "Oh dear, I believe your dress is torn." She pointed to her unclad leg.

"Actually, it's a slit. On purpose." Margot smiled, and lowered her pashmina to reveal even more skin.

"Mhm." Stacy pivoted at Sadie. "And you, young lady, are you ready to become all that God has called you to be?"

"Me? I'm… fine." She peeked to her dad for backup, who was finding this all quite humorous.

"Here, let me help." A diplomatic boy voice oozed, like an

infected scab, from behind Sadie, making her knees lock in the yellow sundress Maia had likened to a gumdrop. And her parents just left her there as if he were harmless, as if this wasn't teenage Lucifer himself.

When she turned to face Caleb, she had to muffle a hiccuping laugh, because *this* was next level misleading. His beach blonde shags were slicked back in a classic combover, and he was wearing a pressed white button-down and ironed navy pants. The backs of his ears and palm creases were soaped and scrubbed, and it almost looked like he was wearing clear nail polish. The same iron he'd used to wrinkle-free his clothes, he must've used on his eyes, because the naughty blue coils were also absent today. Nonetheless, the fake saint grazed her inner thigh. "Here to confess your sins, princess? Or make more of 'em?"

Sadie jammed her wedge heel in his foot. "Aw, Caleb," she hummed as he hunched over in front of her. "I know you think I'm a princess, but you don't have to bow at my feet. Actually, no, carry on."

"I think you just broke my toe," he moaned.

"There, there." She patted his crunchy scalp in slaps.

"Man, you're mean today." He appeared psyched by this, entirely electrified with each vicious response. "What changed?"

"I got in a fight with my dad."

"I'm sorry to hear that." Again he touched her leg, but he'd actually gone for her hand; she just moved at a bad time.

Sadie spotted a small spider on his sock, when she said, "I don't believe you." And before she'd had time to put a hole in his other piggy, or name that spider, the second swindling Lindley twin hopped up the steps towards them.

Grace sang, "I think I hear father beginning the service. Shall we go inside?" And so they did, all three of them with their arms hooked and Sadie sandwiched between; like two truths and a lie, only it was two lies and a truth. Maybe, even three lies.

By now, just about every face in town was crowded inside and Henri scrutinized each one in a scrambling paranoia. From the hypochondriac Ferrel parents squirting hand sanitizer on little Johnny's elbows, to the neutrally reputationed Patels passing out coupons to their restaurant, to smiley Joe who worked the Lake Josey gate with his bolo tie and wife Pam, and even the Sinclair couple in their matching wheelchairs bouncing their great grandkids on their laps. Henri felt the goji-superfood-parfait Margot prepared for breakfast swirl in his upset tank. He loosened his tie, which he probably shouldn't have worn because he never wore ties. Why did he wear a tie? Would people notice? Ask questions? *Shit.*

"Hey." Brant nudged his arm. "You look like you're about to lose your stack there."

"My mind is more like it. No, no. I'm fine. Let's just keep an eye out, yea?"

"Do we know what for?"

"Nope, but figured the best way to catch a sinner is to follow the saints."

"How do you figure that?"

Henri took a beat. He winced. "We're here, aren't we?"

They shared a brief harrowing ache over it, before the manly constitutions kicked in again, machine-like and militant, and those constitutions can be like antibiotics in how they wipe out the bad feelings as effectively as the acceptable ones. Infirmity and fear might leave the premises, but so do looks of love, joy, appreciation.

Loyal to that very cure-all, Brant nodded, "Let's get to it then." And then he returned to where his family was standing at the front, silently making a deal with God that if he did him this favor, he'd finally go to marriage counseling, donate to charity, clean the garage if that's what it took; suddenly wishing he'd done all those things a long time ago.

Before it started, Brooks turned to give Sadie a small wave. All her hopes and dreams seemed contingent on that wave. Then Duke waved too, and once again she didn't know what to do.

Pastor David took his place behind the podium, and in an instant, the room struck mute and regardful. During an opening prayer, a flume of light erupted from a gorgeous stained glass window of indigo and currant, as if a divine spout had been opened, because soon enough the entire sanctuary was consumed with these bright natural effusions of elixir.

In rhythms, the pastor taught magnific histories with a bible as his guide, each sentence with a brief delay at the end, the added spaces laboring his lessons and massaging them in the listeners' chests like alleviating VapoRub. He moved in large gestures, eyes so upgraded and blissed out, it made you envious of what he was seeing, or *not* seeing.

Sadie was a little skeptical, which was a newfound capability, but decided it was pointless to dwell since none of it can be proven, which made her wonder how David and the others in the room could be so sure. Then she remembered when *she* had been sure, and reflected if that might be similar. If maybe religion could be simplified to playing pretend as a grownup. No, she sincerely prayed not.

She closed the bible in her lap and put it back in the seat pouch, now with teardrop stains on Proverbs 4:23.

"Psst." Caleb persuaded from the side door, the hand in his pocket with a finger out, calling her in inchworm kinks. Sadie frowned at him, but got up. Neither of her parents asked or worried, and she wasn't sure if she should be grateful or disappointed for that.

Brooks was puzzled to turn and see Sadie dashing into the hall, because the bathrooms were the other way. He checked, and Duke was still sitting next to him, so it was nothing to get worked up about.

Sadie hadn't breathed as to not make a sound, and by the top of the stairs, she was faint enough to stumble into the railing. She tapped Caleb's back, jolted and concerned that she'd willingly touched *it*.

He spun swiftly, back to his real defiling self again, noticing how her slight eye bags in conjunction with the dareful actions made the rest of the pieces less barred as a brooch. She was making progress. She was giving in. "Why'd you follow me?"

"What?" Sadie gasped in a squeak. "Didn't you... want me to?"

"I did," he answered fast, lips curling, eye coils lighting, before the steep height leaned down extra low. "But I hardly think you did it to appease me."

"You're right. Actually, I was just bored."

"Really? Cause you looked pretty into it." His gaze dipped to her wet cheeks.

"You... you saw." Her instinct told her to be embarrassed, but she wasn't really.

He nodded minimally, and suddenly grabbed her hand and pulled her down the passageway, into the dim rooms with an urgency and imminence of cavorting kids playing hide and seek. Most were filled with soft rugs and floor pillows, shelves of old books and craft supplies, but one was larger with a music stage, drums and keyboard set up for youth band nights, and Sadie giggled deep down when Caleb told her he'd always gotten stuck playing the triangle.

Finally, he led her into the prop room in the very corner of the upstairs. It was attic-like and filled with oversized bouquets of tissue paper flowers, cardboard Noah's Ark cutouts, amongst piles and piles of biblical costumes. A small square window let in a few rays of morning light, but other than that, it was dark.

Sadie didn't know how she'd ended up there, and she didn't just mean in a cluttered church closet. "Do you believe in any of it? God?" she asked him. "Sure, you do a scary good job of acting like you do... but do you?"

He was glad she'd finally spoken her mind, another part of him equally glad for her to hear his answer. "I used to. Never thought twice about it when I was a tot, goin' to camps every summer, singin' the songs. But then I turned twelve and my mom started timin' my showers, allottin' me a certain number of socks per week, and it didn't matter what I did right, or what I didn't do wrong. The more forgiveness I asked for, the more shame they somehow found. You can't just wake up one day and tell your kid they're full of sin and not expect them to be a little fucked up over it." He stared at the Joseph costume on the floor. "You can't, and yet they've found a way to make it a sacred tradition."

Sadie hadn't ever considered that side of it: only heaven, not the hell. "So, what? You just stopped caring?"

"I stopped lettin' other people tell me who I am."

"Sounds like an excuse to just do whatever you want without consequences."

He smirked in spite of himself, how well he'd worn his own mask. "Not without consequences, just not the ones you think. Life ain't black and white, Sadie. Good or bad. *We're* not."

Hearing him group both him and her in the same category felt mishandled. "I just... I don't think I've ever seen someone as genuinely happy as your dad. He was so alive up there."

"Alive? You think that man is *alive*? Striving for some redemption he'll never achieve, killin' himself over any human urge he might have, stayin' in an unhappy marriage and calling it devotion. You know, he's almost forty and he's never watched porn, not even on accident. Sure, self-deny if you want, just know what you're denying first."

"That's like saying you should take drugs, to know not to take them."

"Because then you don't have to wonder, no spiraling what-ifs, no building it up in your head to make it better than it is. You know a little somethin' about that, don't you?"

She surprised herself when she confessed, "A lot."

"Yeah, I can tell."

"But if your dad is happier that way, does it matter? And the church does a lot of good for people, right? Like, for other families—"

"Yeah," Caleb cut her off, unraveling some more. "It does. He's so damn busy carin' about every other kids' problems, can't even remember his own son's birthday. Not now, not when I was seven and we were supposed to go to The Kennedy Space Center —sun will probably burn up before I get to a damn telescope— but he did remember twelve, cause that's the year they took the lock off my door."

Sadie had grown too accustomed to responding to him with flyswatter slaps, that she had no idea what to say next. This Caleb, the one with a heart, was the most unnerving Caleb of them all. She peeled into a blindsiding smile, because it almost felt like they were friends in that moment. "The beast has feelings after all."

"Does that make you the beauty? If I'm the beast?"

"No, I think I'm just a singing teacup."

"You would," he snapped brusquely like he'd somehow been expecting that answer, and was angry to be right. "Tell me, Sadie: at what age did you stop being the heroine in your own story?"

Had he read her mind? Were the pages of her journal stamped across her face? Where were all these coincidences coming from?

"When you're a kid," he went on, "you watch movies and claim which character you are, even fighting with your friends who gets to be the coolest one. Then *you* get to the part in life where you're actually living the movie, and here you are, casting yourself as an extra and making some other girl the lead. Stop it."

Sadie was speechless, and after letting him simmer in the upper hand far too long, she mustered, "I don't... do that."

Caleb smirked. "Okay."

"Or *so what* if I do? Being the heroine is stressful. There's pressure and expectation and drama, and a chance none of it will work out, and this is such a stupid metaphor by the way." She was visibly worked up. "What does that make *you*? The sidekick to Brooks?"

It'd been aimed to hurt him, but it couldn't be done. "No, I've always been the villain. No expectation there." He sauntered around the small scope of closet, picking up things just to put them back down. "You know, this is what they call the *flower* room."

"Let me guess... because there's flowers?" Sadie flapped at a faux hydrangea, like gram used to sew.

"The *de*-flower room."

Her basil eyes widened. "You're lying. In *church*?"

"Well, that's what it's called. Typically it's just first base. People sneak in here whenever the bands having an off night, or they're pissed off at mommy and daddy." He took three slow steps towards her, then two more, relaxing his mouth so his lips parted and protruded, and she could smell that same cinnamon gum. "It is awfully romantic." For the third time that morning, his fingers touched her thigh.

Sadie's blood turned hot and boiling, before rushing to her face like she was living upside down. How could she be so naive? She'd become his very own personal sucker. She was so shook up with a mixture of reactions, she couldn't even slap him away. "You're an ass," Sadie eventually quivered out. "You're supposed to be Brooks' *friend*!"

He ordered her, "Don't yell, or they'll hear you."

So Sadie jumped up and down to shake the floor, knocked her wedges on the wood as hard as she could, and ripped the tissue flowers before stuffing some in her fist for later. "Was any of it true? Your missed childhood birthday? The philosophical bullshit?"

He clapped for her defiance. "Keep going. You're on a roll."

"It was all strategy, wasn't it? To *de-flower* me? You really are a miserable person, who just wants everyone to be as miserable as you!" The yellow dress stormed from the closet, but stopped at the door. "You're right, you are the villain, and you always will be."

Caleb stilled and smiled at the image of the ringlets swinging wind-swept and ungoverned down the hall. From where he was standing, there was a tiara, too.

Sadie apologized to the knees she bumped as she ushered back to her seat, quickly checking her phone: nine messages from Brooks. He was staring at her now. She typed and sent '*food poisoning*'. She also had an unopened message from Maia, who hadn't been replying all weekend. Her excuse: '*food poisoning*'.

Pastor David asked them to bow their heads a final time.

Brant sensed a vibrating thrum in his pocket, and despite Kelly's scolds, he checked it. A text from a blocked number read: *For with the heart one believes and is justified, and with the mouth one confesses and is saved. What about you? Will you be saved, Brant?*

He strangled the small screen and jammed the delete key, but it slipped and smacked flat on the floor. He scanned the heads frantically, but each friendly neighbor had their eyes down and hidden, unfazed by the burst of noise, so he couldn't read which one of them was spitting in their potluck pies. Only Henri had his eyes open, permanently so, watching Brant get hit with the same ticking time bomb with the power to change their lives forever.

All they knew was this: they were being watched, and it was someone in this room.

CHAPTER FOURTEEN
Voyeurs

October promised crisper mornings of hot-hands bags and girls in Uggs, pumpkin spices and the jittery glees of homecoming looming around the corner. Lovebug season had come and gone. The football team had upheld their undefeated streak after playing against two of the most competitive teams in the county, one of which Orville had lost to the week prior. The town's businesses were booming, The Elks Lodge had been renovated and installed with a new karaoke machine, they'd finally finished paving that rutted Clayton Heights dirt road, and the Main Street square gazebo had been lathered in fresh paint. Even Otis had landed a job bussing tables at the Backdoor Brewery and bought himself a fresh stack of Sports Illustrated reading material. There were more people out than usual chatting on the sidewalks, perhaps because of the tolerable weather but almost certainly because the vibration had started to change. The team was flourishing, the town was thriving; two separate things and yet always riding on the same trend.

As for Sadie, sixteen days had passed since that morning in the church, and she'd decided speaking of the incident would only be a tragic waste of her breath. And Brooks hadn't asked anyway, so it would forever remain their dirty secret—no. Clean secret. A super sanitary, explainable, insignificant, not-her-fault secret she didn't even want. Who? What? Secret? She knew of no such thing.

Her and Brooks had been spending more time together,

which collaterally meant spending more time with Duke. They'd gone to the movies and the bowling alley, and that was pretty much the extent of available date places in town, so a lot of the times they'd end up on the Holden house couch. But on weekends they'd venture farther to Tampa, eating out at a chain restaurant, later walking around a Dicks or a Petco or a ToysRus, holding hands, soaking up time since they had plenty, and later making out in his truck. Whatever the plan, it always ended with making out in his truck.

Sadie had only seen Maia at school—kind of, for she was always running on some impulsive schedule Sadie knew nothing about. She'd laughed convincing circles around her when Sadie asked about the conundrum she'd seen: Maia's raven hair, dead of night, school office. After thinking it over, Sadie decided she must be right. With the deviative party games, a brawl with some coonhounds, almost-car-accident; she must've imagined it. This made sense.

Today, just another, Sadie hugged her knees on the chilly Ogilbee Park bleachers, and watched Books hit baseballs in the diamond area of rust sand. Caleb and Levi were there as well. It was a little before 7am, with fog and sun mingling in cinematic affair.

"You askin' Sadie to homecomin' soon?" Levi said to Brooks, pulling his Polar Pop straw up and down with his mouth so it emitted a rancid screech.

The quarterback glanced at the compact, shivery, sweet girl through the chain link. "I don't know. Maybe." He swung the bat smoothly; as long as he stuck to taking three triple strength Tylenol with breakfast, lunch, dinner, smoothly things would stay. The bruising had at least healed, so he no longer had to pretend being insecure of his nipples in the locker rooms, and flee to a closed stall just to change his shirt.

Levi, wearing an interesting outfit of a turtleneck knit with Jordans, snorted loudly. "Man stop playin', actin' all cool and shit. You know you whipped as hell!"

"We're just hanging out."

"Mmmm." He blew jet bubbles into his cup. "I don't think

so."

Brooks grabbed the repugnant straw and hurled it on the ground. "We're just *hanging out.*"

"So why is she here then?" Caleb's tone was incorrectly hoarse and grainy, probably because it was early. "And at lunch, and watchin' practice, and in your truck at the LJ dock 'til who knows how late every damn night?"

Brooks just looked at him. "Because that's where we hang out. Didn't realize you've been payin' such close attention. Is she *botherin'* you, Caleb?"

"Not at all. In fact"—he cupped his hands as a voice amplifying device, as if he needed one—"Aye princess! You wanna hit a few balls?"

Sadie flinched in her tights and white-as-snow dress, met with an inappropriately entertaining thought. "Yours? Sure."

She'd dabbled in many hobbies, but somehow managed to avoid all the ones involving a ball. Ballet, swim, checkers even though she called it chess, speed reading, flower pressing, karate for half an afternoon, and gymnastics minus the balance beam. Her lack of athleticism became obnoxiously apparent with the first swing. The bat slipped from her hand, flung over the fence, and rolled down the mist-tipped grass. Sadie frowned. "I give up."

"You just need a little form." Brooks suggested, and wrapped his arms around hers from behind so they were basically spooning standing up. Here, their bodies swayed.

"Can I try one?" A female voice called from between the two oak trees where Brooks and Sadie officially met, but where Shelby and him had spent years lying in the shade, eating bags of Gushers, planning how they'd carve their pumpkin lanterns that weekend.

The new and evolved Sadie didn't give Shelby a muffin, just yelled back, "Sorry, I'm not done." She swiveled to Brooks. "Again."

"Yikes." Shelby inhaled a condescending slip of air. "Should we duck? Remember, you use the *bat* to hit the *ball*—"

"Yeah, I got it." She imagined it going well; hearing the

immaculate echo clobber their eardrums, watching as the white ball soared over their heads, so far out they'd never find it, and the boys would guffaw with their jaws gaping, Shelby would be forced to swallow her underestimations, and soon the whole school would be talking about her awesomeness. That didn't *exactly* happen.

"Three strikes, you're out." Shelby's back trampolined against the bendy fence and launched her to home base. "I'll take that." Just between them, she whispered, "You finally found something you can't fake."

Another petal loosened, and slipped into the wind. "It *is* pretty difficult trying to be a guy when I'm a *girl*." Sadie handed Shelby the bat. "You're a natural, though." High from the moxie, she skipped to give Brooks a kiss before grabbing her things and heading for the beaten path towards school.

"Wait—where are you going?" Brooks hollered.

"Dukes waiting for me in the quad." Her words evasively tossed, and yet he caught them on the money.

"So you're ditchin' me to hang out with my little brother?" He chuckled ironically like it were an impossible scenario, which really backfired when she established this, in fact, was exactly what she was doing.

"We have an English project together." Once again, not a lie. "The partners were assigned." Okay, white lie. "But I'll see you after second!" Sadie added merrily to hopefully cure whatever horrible neck scratching attack had overcome him. She curtsied to remind of her upstanding moral character. *I'm Sadie. Don't fret. I'm a good girl.*

It worked. Brooks just nodded.

On the bumpy tree-lined path to the school, Sadie kicked rocks to dirty up her new white Converse, because they looked better that way; puddle stains, grayed laces, indie-movie quote calligraphy on the soles. It distracted her from her excitement to see Duke. Still, she imagined the miniscule gap in his teeth, generous hunter eyes, bookish demeanor, how comfortable it made her that he wasn't obsessed or even slightly interested in being immersed with the minutia and commotions of the town.

With Brooks, Sadie was a main focus of the kingdom. With Duke, the kingdom was just the two of them. Both had their upsides, but which did she prefer?

Maia's yellow bug was missing from it's parking spot, so she stopped to call her but it went straight to voicemail. Maia followed the decline with a text. '*Sick. I think your mom's green juice is coming out of my nose. Bleh*'. Sadie sighed and dropped her phone in her bag. She'd been learning to ask less questions. Only, she hadn't yet learned when.

A black truck with hardened mud on the tires was positioned an outlier from the rest of the trucks with hardened mud on the tires, by the far gate no one ever used. Sadie swore she saw it moving as she passed, shaking, like a remote earthquake specific to that coordinate. As she got closer, she *knew* it was shaking, and suddenly a girl's naked upper body flung up in the backseat, oscillating in an unmistakably vigorous motion.

Sadie's face crimsoned as her brain came to terms with the explicit act she'd unwittingly surveyed, and yet she didn't move. She just glaciated and stared like when she'd stumbled on a TV channel as a kid with actors making taboo noises and faces and gestures she knew were strictly banned to her still-preserved eyes. The same rabid curiosity stunted her judgement now and lit inferno to her senses. She watched a hand, clearly a boy's, tug at the dirty blonde hair and pull the mystery vixen back down, then up, before she flipped her hair out of her sweaty face, and that sweaty face was Grace's.

Instantly, Sadie's feet were lurching her away like a wind-up toy wound nine times over, squirming in her own skin, mentally screaming undo, delete, erase! Grace had seen her peeping. She was sure of it. *Oh god, oh god—*

Sadie accidentally slammed into a bony boy in a wife beater, and soon both her and Sterling were maimed on the asphalt. Her and... Sterling. Grace's boyfriend Sterling. Who wasn't in the black truck venue of bodily acts because he was here, and you can't be in two places at once, and Sterling was in this place, and the boy in *that* place...

"We've gotta stop doing this," Sadie breathed edgily as she

rubbed her pebbly knees and elbows, thinking at least this time she wasn't mooning half the school.

"We've done this before?" He helped her up.

"Um, yeah, nevermind."

"Alrighty then." Sterling picked up the football he'd dropped. "Hey, have you seen Grace? She's supposed to copy Paola's Spanish homework before I gotta give it back to her. I keep tellin' her she can't wait for that Dunkin' every mornin' and expect to get an 'A'."

Sadie gasped. "You—you know—about—'Duncan'?"

He squinted as if the last light bulb in her brain had popped. "You *don't*?"

"Well, I… I just saw…" It felt like a cheese grater was sawing her heart to a pile of tartare. "Are you okay?"

"Sure, I'm alright. I mean, I myself wouldn't wait thirty minutes for a glazed doughnut and bean juice, but I feel like it's an accessory for some girls. Like, they got their shoulder bags and their fuzzy boots and the rose-gold keychain, then they have their coffee cup—"

Sadie pursed her lips. "Aha. Right. *Dunkin'*. Got it."

"Got what?"

"I have to go."

Sterling watched her head for the quad stairs. "Hey, wait!" He caught up and stooped awkwardly. "I uhh, I wanted to apologize if I acted cruddy to you when you first got here. Truth is, we don't get a lot of new people. Sort of assumed you were lookin' down on us. People do that… sometimes."

"Oh." Sadie shifted, and for the first time really looked past the dirty wife beater at the pasty skittish boy with noble intentions in his eyes. "I'm sorry too, for questionin' your *American sports*." She grinned, and they bonded over the reference.

His chin wrinkles bunched seriously. "You and Grace should hang out sometime. Go to Panera, or somethun'."

"You know Mallory would have my throat on a stick, right?"

"Hah, yeah." He went even paler. "Just think about it, okay? She wasn't always such a challenge to get to know. I think you'd be… good for her."

"We don't have much in common."

"Actually, you do. Or... you did. Listen, just think about it."

It was obvious how much he loved her, and that he had absolutely no clue of the betraying film Sadie was still seeing every time she blinked. "I will." Turning around, she unconsciously chewed on the inside of her cheeks until something spongy broke off and she tasted blood.

After wandering sullenly amongst the caffeinated teenagers, she situated by the marigolds that were beginning to wilt, and admired a bluebird hopping on it's hairline legs. She texted Duke to let him know where she'd be waiting, then took out a compact mirror and softly brushed strokes of Bare Minerals 'warmth' bronzer where her face had begun to lack color. Today, that was everywhere.

The brown powder showered in her lap as a hand grabbed hold of her loose pony and yanked, dragging down the hall and into a girl's bathroom. Grace kicked open the stalls one by one to make sure they were vacant.

"You snooping little hypocritical tart!" The tiny girl screamed at her face, desensitized and yet hoarding desperation. "I saw you! I saw you talking to Sterling! What did you say to him? Huh? Maybe I should go tell Brooks about you and Caleb and your seven-minutes-in-heaven vanishing act!"

A bulldozer slammed in Sadie's chest, and took a chunk out. "You—you can't. It wasn't like that!"

"Not yet," she sang very softly, with an eerie inflection. "But that's how it starts."

"You're wrong. Maybe with you, but *I'm* not like that."

"*That*," Grace repeated. "How extravagantly pretentious of you. You really think because you live in the pretty house where your parents still kiss each other goodnight that you're exempt? That *you specifically* have been chosen for some sparkly life, and that if you spend all of it trying to glow in the dark, all the pieces will just fall into place? Because you *deserve* it?"

Sadie ignored her almost mathematical accuracy. "You said the rumors about you weren't true, but clearly they are."

"I hate to break it to you, but you're *just* like me. It just hasn't hit you yet."

Sadie had never been more sure of Caleb and Grace's shared DNA; equally as miserable. "I won't say anything to Sterling. But, why cheat? Why don't you just break up with him? If you don't love him anymore."

"I *do* love him." Somehow, it sounded truthful.

The still golden girl shook her head. "It's just not fair."

A suppressed tide welled behind Grace's marine eyes, taking her back to a time when she'd said the same. She backed away, opened the door, looked back once more at her former-reality. "It doesn't matter if you glow brighter than the sun, Sadie. It won't matter."

It made no sense for Sadie to feel devastated and want to follow. She started to, but stopped. She'd been learning to ask less questions. Only, she hadn't yet learned when.

Margot dallied at her classroom sink, moving her hips to her wellness meditation music as she made preparations for their chapter on watercolors. She sipped from the matcha latte in a mason jar she'd brought from home, before catching and pinning her ruby-glossed hair in an aventurine crystal clip. Harmony, balance, compassion were all locked inside that aventurine, but just weren't coming *out*.

· Fortunately, Margot had decided not to let a few trifling qualms about her husband's past get to her, because that's exactly where they were; in the past. She didn't need to know, what she didn't know. After all, nothing had changed besides the scenery in which they were living. Instead of French bistros there were diners; instead of cocktail dresses there were rain boots; instead of early morning call-times there were—

"Knock knock!" Stacy's shoulders hinged back and forth excitedly at the door, voice as sing-songy as ever. "Aha! Finally found ya!"

"Was it hard?" Margot asked.

"I made a few wrong turns searchin' for the right classroom. Honestly, didn't think this even was one. I reckoned it was a closet of some sort." Her face dried up at the new age spiritual accents around the room: chakra poster, lunar calendar, singing bowl, a turkey feather on the desk. "What's that smell?"

"It's palo santo, a tree native to Peru."

"And what is Peru doing in Florida?"

"I burn it to clear negative energy from the space."

"Oooh," Stacy mouthed like the spooky women in Hocus Pocus. "Witchy." And gingered to such degree, her eyes almost leapt from their sockets.

Margot lit three more sticks. "Oh definitely, this is where I cast all my magic charms."

Stacy's happy spike dropped ten floors. "How is Sadie doin'?"

"I'm sorry—why are you here again?"

"Did you two talk yet about her makin' better choices? Sometimes all a young girl needs is someone to listen. Might even be a cry for help."

Margot didn't actually know any witchcraft, but she was about to hex the living bejesus out of this woman. "We're doing alright, thank you for your concern."

"Right, yes. Of course." Stacy's pitch changed, and her intent staring was indicative of meddling. "Anyhoo! I have some leftover art supplies from the church, so just thought I'd bring it over. It was sittin' collectin' dust upstairs in the prop room." She handed her a heavy cardboard box. "Oh! I don't know what on earth happened to these poor tissue flowers!"

"That seems like a lot of trouble, going out of your way to bring this here."

"Oh, nonsense! Ain't nothin' in this world we southerners wouldn't do for a friend. Especially old friends like Henri, and *you're* his wife, so that hitches you to the same privileges!" Her features puckered to an unflattering prune.

"Lucky me." Margot exercised breathing deeply to her belly. "You can just set it on the table there. I'm a little busy getting ready for—"

"How's Henri with Sadie?" Stacy hovered.

Margot was thrown by the question, momentarily losing her way with kind words. "Excuse me?"

"I'm sorry, it's just… so strange seein' how he was back then, comparin' it to him now. With a whole daughter, and all."

"And why exactly is that strange?"

"Probably because I was under the impression he never wanted kids."

"And where *exactly* did you get that impression?"

Stacy scrunched her nose, like Margot was being scatterbrained. "Because he told me, of course."

Margot was suddenly on fire, with Stacy the iron rod poking about, tossing some kindling, a few daffy squirts of provoking gasoline. She could be lying, but if she wasn't, Margot had a hard time imagining a casual conversation where that would've come up. "I didn't realize you two had been so close."

"Well, you sure get to know a person after *two years* of dating them!" Her hysterical laughter made her busy-printed waistline jiggle and chunky bob cut bangs catch in her eyebrow. "I'm sure he told you *all* about that."

With her breath vacuumed from her throat, Margot agreed. "All about it."

"Oof—would you look at the time! I'll get out of your way now. But dearie, you have to send me this CD! Super zen!" Stacy rammed up her thumbs, smoothed her dress, and went about her business, of being in people's business.

Margot clutched the watercolor spackled sink. She'd really much preferred her French bistros.

Continuing their investigation, Henri and Brant had been frequenting the abandoned basketball courts on Church Street, to no avail. It wasn't logical to keep coming back, but they did, usually late at night, but sometimes in the mornings when the only people out were senior couples with impaired hearing, and nannies with tandem-strollers and broken English. Being there felt boring and familiar, and it was paradise.

Through the protest in their backs and the crunch in their hips, Henri and Brant shot some free throws and played a game of 1-on-1. They were getting really into it today, relying on the physical activity to renew them as it had when they were budding bucks, letting the lactic acid numb, the fresh blood cleanse their conscience, but sadly it only had an effect in cleaning up their cholesterol.

Back then, problems were assigned to days, and even if the problem made it a bad day, tomorrow was a new day. The problem didn't roll over; it had no business crossing the threshold of midnight, where it would simply expire and fade away. Then there were the problems that took a lifetime to fade, in the meantime leaving you to wonder if it'd follow you even then…

The manly men took a seat on the shaded bench, panting with their elbows rested on their knees. Brant fixed his New Balance sneaker as Henri undressed down to his drenched undershirt, then they both tilted their creased necks back over the seat in an auditory stretch.

"You know, I had one of those bulged discs in my spine some months back. Hurt like hell." Henri drew in his bottom lip because he liked the salt. "The doc told me I needed surgery to push it back. Then Margot tricked me into a few of her pilates classes, and by my next appointment, I was good as new. Healthy as a work horse. Can you believe that? Think I'm gonna need a class or two after today. Phew, we ain't teenagers no more. You never think it'll happen to you, gettin' older, until it does."

Brant stared warily at the tree branches tapping each other. "Or doesn't."

Henri gave it a respectful moment of silence, before asking, "You ever do stuff like that with Kelly?"

"What stuff?"

"I don't know. Out-of-the-usual stuff. Like dates."

The wind whistled it's own opera tune and sailed a plastic bag that'd been littered on the cobblestone.

"We went to a show in downtown Tampa a few weeks ago."

"Oh yeah? Like dancers and music? That sort of thing?"

"Well it was more of a game than a show. Stamkos ripped a flawless one-timer."

"Hockey? Kelly into that?"

"We do other stuff too, sometimes. Picked up Cheesecake

Factory on the way home. She likes the shrimp and the piña coladas."

"Uhhuh."

"Don't do that. I know what you're thinkin'." Brant dug for a container in his pocket. He wedged a pouch of smokeless tobacco to just the right spot. "I know what you're thinkin.'"

"What am I thinkin'?" Henri asked, bemused.

"You're thinkin' I'm a bad husband. You're thinkin' whatever problems we got at home are all my fault, and Kelly would be better off with one of those Tate brothers from the dealership, or Tex with the speedboat and a timeshare at Summer Haven. Well I got news for you, Henri. I love my wife. And I sure as hell ain't losin' her to a speedboat."

Henri pulled out a pocketknife, lifted a stocky piece of twig from under the bench, and began hacking it down. "Huh."

"What?"

"Well… Margot is used to dressin' up on the weekends, so I've been wantin' to take her somewhere nice. Somewhere the wine glasses sing if you lick your finger and rub the edges. I was just askin' in case you had any ideas. That's all."

"Oh."

"Yeah." Henri closed his eyes, held his breath, counted to ten. "You ever feel like the stress is just seepin' out of you? Like if people come close enough, they'll see it on your skin?"

"You can't tell a thing. It's in your head."

"I yelled at Sadie the other weekend. She came in while I was workin' on a car, my little girl just wantin' to tell me about her day. How precious is that?" Henri broke down, hacked and hacked at the wood. "And I blew up on her."

"Kids are resilient with those types of things. You know how many times I've yelled at my boys? If I had a nickel for every time…" Brant realized the sound of it, and stopped there. "Well, I'd have a lot of nickels."

"But they're boys. It's different with girls."

"That might be true." The edges of Brant's mouth slowly curved upward, and he relished in the comment before he'd even made it. "At least your daughters got my son's shoulder to cry on when she needs it."

"You bastard." Henri laughed. "Didn't see that comin', did we?"

"No, we did *not*."

Nappy rounds of clouds wallowed over the treetops, dark and dense as if a downpour was due.

"What happened the day of?" Henri's tone lowered.

"Day of what?" But from his friend's haunted expression, Brant knew exactly the station they'd arrived at. "An elderly woman—had a horse boardin' business few miles past the drive-in, think her name was Claire—was on a sunrise walk in the neighborhood when she saw him. Apparently an ambulance came, but course, that didn't do no good." He watched Henri keep slicing at the branch where little branch was left. "There was blood, a lot of it. You can still see it in the asphalt if you stare long enough."

"Did you? Stare?"

"For days."

"What then?"

"The media showed up, with police, detectives, relatives. Took all but twenty minutes for the whole town to get a whiff of news and come down here with their sleep clothes and camera phones. Did you know he hadn't been home for a week? His mom, Teresa, had already filed a missin' person's report at the station. I don't know why. He was with us at Betty's Biscuits that mornin'. Sure he skipped graduation, but it's not like he was hidin' out. But Teresa did say he'd been gettin' messages, visits even, from some of the boys with Lane Street."

"Lane." The nuances of that one sinister syllable caused a landmine to explode against Henri's ribs. It was a label used by a malevolent street gang; *The Lane Street Lunatics*; widely infamous for attracting drugs into the county.

"Did you know Manny was using?" Brant asked.

"I never saw it, if he was. He was one of the rare good kids."

"Apparently he was also takin' drugs, Henri. Hard stuff. That night in particular, he'd taken a brutal dose. Since there were no witnesses—none that they found—detectives figured he'd been shootin' hoops juiced up, stumbled, hit his head. They ruled it an accident."

"An accident? They just figured that?" Henri was outraged to hear it, and absolutely certain they would've had a much lengthier investigation had Manny been from a more 'low-risk' part of town.

"Don't get mad at it now. We were involved. We should be thankin' our lucky stars they didn't ask more questions, dig deeper into his personal life, get word one of the victim's best friends skipped town less than twelve hours later."

Henri closed his eyes, held his breath, counted to ten. "It ain't right. It just ain't right!" He sliced the knife again—"Shit!" The twig was gone, and he'd just cut a pumping red line of blood down his finger.

"Stop your yellin' and get yourself to Urgent Care." Brant handed him his shirt from the ground so he might wrap it in a tourniquet, but Henri just tossed it on the Chevy bed, swung open the door, and found the single-use tube of Krazy Glue he keeps close by for emergencies like these. Biting off the cap, he applied the adhesive all over his bloody finger, and it worked right enough. "I don't need no damn Urgent Care." He turned the key and left to go buy more Krazy Glue.

The vehicle convulsed and the tires suffered on the cobblestones. "It was an accident. It was an accident. It was an accident." Henri punched his skull again and again and again, and it was true; for the worst crime he'd committed that night was running away, and how dandy, that he'd run *all* the way across the country. It hadn't gotten him very far.

With the car flying, speeding triple the limit, he floored it even more. Then, he calmly closed his eyes, held his breath, counted to...

A slideshow appeared in his mind: a grieving Margot with her ruby hair graying, a teary-eyed Sadie setting the table for only two, his dinner chair empty...

Henri's eyes shot open, foot slammed the brake, and only the left headlight was pulverized on the cement wall he'd almost just crashed into.

Meanwhile, Brant was still parked by the basketball court, deforming over a newly arrived black mail, hot and searing off the press. It read: *Keep the Golden Holden off the field on Friday, or your secrets out, coach.* A second followed, just to make the game more intimate and sick. *It's a good thing you have two, huh?*

But all Brant heard was: it's a good thing you still have two.

Nearing mid-day, Elaine glided through the door of the front office in a ruffly top and pencil skirt, hair freshly blown-out and full of flirty bouncy gloss. She greeted the admin ladies at the desk who were on their lunch break, and they lit up over their half-eaten sandwiches. Her presence was affecting that way, a rejuvenating tonic, like she was Daisy Buchanan in a roaring fur collar, come to whisk them somewhere far and brilliant; one of those people who should always be in white clothes, because black looked funny on her personality.

She stopped to gift Mabel Daughhill a care-basket of snickerdoodles, a box of chai, and a 'thinking of you' card made of caramel-scented stationary. Her husband, Ezra, had recently been diagnosed with prostate cancer, and Mabel had been having a really rough time. Snickerdoodles were Ezra's favorite, Elaine recalled, from the party she'd catered when they'd renewed their vows in the backyard.

"You're not alone," Elaine whispered to Mabel in her gentle voice that made you believe it, and Mabel burst into tears before hugging the baker.

Next, Elaine made her way to the principal's door, but it was jammed. She used her body to slam against it, but it still wouldn't budge. She patiently knocked and waited.

"Would you just *look* at this sensational woman I've found at my door?" Which nearly blast off the hinges as a towering Jay lifted his trophy into a spinning embrace, and the admins sighed with sore jealous hearts, aspiring to be just like them. "Boy oh boy, am I glad to see you," he said hungrily, and planted a wet smooch on her blush so it actually sucked off the varnish. He went back to his state-of-the-art desk chair, closing a few drawers, putting away a few papers.

Elaine trailed behind and handed him a grilled cheese. "Since you couldn't make lunch at the café." She smiled in her pearls. "Dear, I think there's something wrong with your door. I couldn't open it."

"I installed a lock," he explained.

"You did? What for?"

"What *for*?" Jay repeated, running an infernal tongue up and down the roof of his mouth. "Why, let me show you, Mrs. Mayor's Wife." He journeyed to where she was primed for him, detaching her hand from the other, padlocking them to his and coaxing them over her head. He trained her up against the wall, pinned and puny, and entered into frenzy from her sheer purity and warmth.

Elaine hummed along at first, allowing him access to what he'd take regardless of her say, sensing his body flex in that precursor way. "Honey?"

Jay's beady eyes locked on her with possession, and he kept going, the bulging tendons of his fingers sinking in her thigh like it was his own special grade of Play-Doh. They rerouted upwards, all the way to her dainty underthings. Perhaps, if she were allowed to wear jeans, he'd be more controlled. "Honey… honey!" Elaine tried not to sound panicked as he kept pawing at her gates. "Not *here*."

Jay pulled away so sharply, she ducked. But of course, he could've moved in slow motion, and she still would've ducked. "Your skirt is too short." He was a different person now; he was himself.

"Wh—what?" Elaine fixed her hem. "I'm fairly certain I'm in dress code, Mr. Principal. Would you like to use a ruler to check?" It was then that she spied his undone zipper, a few elongated strands of womanly black hair stuck to his arm, those same skipped-over belt loops.

"Then it's *too tight*." His voice raised. "Take it back to the store. I want the see the receipt when you do."

Elaine shrunk at the sound of the hole puncher his fist kept smashing, and couldn't help but feel sister to that tattered sheet of paper. "Don't you think… you're overreacting just a little bit?"

"Overreacting? I'm... overreacting?" The hole puncher became a dart, their glass-framed wedding photo his target board. "I would say I'm *underreacting* considerin' the message your skanky clothes are sendin' to the young ladies of this school! For our own *daughter!*" His barking had such mass, Elaine expected Mabel and the others to come rushing through the door, and they surely would have, had the room not been recently sound proofed.

Elaine built up the courage, and finally asked, "Has someone else been in here today?"

One can imagine this was not the salve to moderate an outraged narcissistic husband. "Someone... *else?*"

"That is what I asked," she said.

Jay's libido was still drumming in his provinces, more so now that she was shaking like a leaf. He started to throw things—stapler, paperweight, binder, chair—until one of those disposable belongings was his wife. He plunged her against the bookshelf so all it's materials rained down, and one of his many plaques shattered and nicked her ankles.

Elaine made a break for it, dodging under his toxic perennial arms, and when she was out of the room, she again fixed her pearls. From private to public, she jumped oceans across her two differing lives. It's amazing no one could see how much she traveled daily.

Soon her heels were clicking past the koi pond bridge, pushing down her 'skanky' knee-length hem, shaping up her hair, stitching in her elbows, softening her forehead, repairing her smile, compromising any happiness in the careful management of her virtue. *Be a lady Elaine Elizabeth,* her mother sternly caroled from heaven. *And stop running! It's unruly for a girl!* But she only ran faster with the autumn breezes beside her, the coolness of them soothing the inflamed cuts and bruises. A wanted angel on the loose is what she was, but with a knife in her side; keeping sealed the very wounds it produced. The knife had grown so deeply into her, it would certainly end her if she ever pulled it out.

Elaine didn't know where she was headed to anymore, and before she could decide, she slammed headfirst into Margot.

"Oh! I'm so sorry! Please forgive me for—"

The holistic beauty simply rubbed Elaine's frazzled arms. "Aren't you cold out here?"

"I—I hadn't realized the temperature."

Margot bent and retrieved the aventurine clip that'd fallen, and informed Elaine, "Your ankles are bleeding."

"I—I hadn't realized that either."

"Did you *know*," Margot teased lovingly behind his back, "Henri sometimes uses super glue to stopper his cuts? Absolutely ridiculous, does it even when there's a perfectly usable band-aid right next to him!"

"I—I'm late for a cake tasting."

Margot wondered if Elaine was aware her blush was horribly uneven; one side a stellar coral, the other a red rouge. Then, a gut feeling somersaulted her out of sorts like a ghost had passed straight through her, and Margot suspected a celestial movement was to blame. Probably Uranus, wreaking it's usual havoc. "Please, don't let me make you late."

Elaine graciously took a few mousey steps, but spun. "Do you think a man can change?"

"A man?"

"Yes, a man. Such as a husband." Like they become something else when the gold band hits their finger. "Do they ever... change?"

Margot revised; must be Venus playing the tricks instead. "For better or for worse?"

In sickness and in health. "Either," Elaine responded.

"I think the longer people are married, the more cemented our behaviors become." Margot was honest, not buttered and veneered with so much southern charm, that speaking turns into a feigned recital. "Does that help?"

Elaine nodded slightly. "You are such a delight, Margot. Can I ask you: did your mother ever teach you about how to be a lady?"

She reminisced quickly on her childhood. "She taught me how to be a 'thoughtful woman', as she called it, which I'm sure is pretty much the same thing."

Except, the marriage books had many discouraging laws about that; wives with too many thoughts. Elaine bid her a goodbye, before retreating to her car to sob and wipe away the evidence of blood, prepare for the next time. Elaine knew in her barely beating heart, with the knife simultaneously churning and keeping her at bay, there would always be a *next time*.

Sadie was watching the football practice after school with algebraic expressions in her lap, when Mrs. Holden approached her in the stands. She'd wondered if Sadie had plans to see Maia by chance, because she'd missed some important homework and needed a way to get it to her. Sadie offered to drop it off on their way home, as Kelly handed her a paper-clipped packet with a sticky note address on top.

Before she took off, she added, "I hope my boys are bein' good to you!"

And Sadie stiffened at another haphazard plural, people dropping 'S's like a rampant game of pick-up-sticks. "*He* is, yes." But as she peered down at the strip of football field, Sadie tried to make her eyes split off in two different directions.

Thirty minutes later, Sadie and Margot were in the car with the AC on full blast, because even if the mornings were nipping, it was back to hyperthermia by noon.

Turns out, the drive to Maia's was far from 'on their way home'. They rolled south on a main road for a while, later several jagged short ones. They crossed train tracks and a water tower, a kind of one-story motel you often see in documentaries, and gradually the cultural style of homes transfigured to straight carmine roofs, white stucco walls, pops of bright colored huts that'd faded in the tropic heat. Some windows had old Día de los Muertos stickers and candles in the windows, while others had bars.

Batches of children ran unsupervised in the neighborhoods. Two girls in mustard babydoll dresses played patty cake in a driveway, one boy in a diaper dragged a toy elephant on a string, shirtless brothers with spiky black hair kicked a deflated soccer ball, and a youngest clinked a rainbow xylophone with expressive faces of concentration.

Sadie smiled at a spindly weathered fella flipping tortillas on a taco cart and dancing to mariachi music, also the big-bellied one in a plastic chair with a cigar puffing from his beard. They both returned the gesture with exclamation and suspense, as if she'd been a good omen to them.

Counting the stray cats on trashcans, cars, and piles of yard supplies, Sadie devised a plan to rescue them all to her bedroom, before being distracted by a group of male youth, idling by a rusty swing set. They were all in a uniform of khaki-colored pants and a plain white tee-shirt, black bandanas linked to their wrists, heavy rope chain necklaces. Something about their penetrant gazes made her sink deeper in the seat as the car passed, and turn around to see if they'd followed.

They drove past an especially weedgrown and shaded aisle named Lane Street, and finally, turned left at a hairpin curve, onto Siesta Drive.

Maia's house was teal and cube-shaped. It had a riven wooden porch with a grill, dusty couch, hanging shell wind-chime, and a corner designated to brooms and rakes. And while the other yards on Siesta had Pitbulls or Rottweilers in pronged gothic collars, Maia's yard was guarded by a giant shaggy Golden Doodle, who was leaping on all fours with his tape-measure tongue flapping kookily in the wind.

Sadie expressed a thank you for the slobber as she shut the door of her mom's Cadillac, bending down and greeting— "Winnie," she read from his bowtie necklace. "Winnie the pooch, huh? It's very nice to meet you sir. May I come in?" She pointed to the gate, and he approved and pushed it open, giving a few more walloping licks before leading her to the front door. Sadie knocked on it.

"What are you *doing here?*" Maia hissed when she saw her, and kept the door cracked.

"I brought soup." Sadie held the chicken noodle they'd picked up at Publix on the way. "And homework, sadly. I took a peek and I think it's pretty easy, just basic multiplying and dividing polynomials. I got stuck on number seven for a while, but there's a Kahn video that breaks down all the steps—"

Reluctantly, Maia let the door open all the way.

Sadie stared numbly at her running shoes. "You... you look pretty healthy for someone who has green juice coming out of her nose." And after Maia disappeared inside, Sadie waited ten seconds, before inferring she was meant to follow.

The house was slightly more neglected on the inside: floors gray cement without a rug to comfort one's toes, walls a bland sand color, and the kitchen area was a realm of soppy soup cans and used dishes. Maia sulked with embarrassment as she pulled out two chairs from a closet, because there were none otherwise, and set them down by the only window of the house.

Sadie took a seat, crossed her hands and ankles, chewed on her cheek until she'd bit off the same rubbery portion that had just started to grow back.

"My parents are undocumented," Maia fessed in a sprint, and draped her curtain of dark hair over her trembles.

"Hmm. That's okay," Sadie answered, with unfiltered childlike candor. "My parents are over-documented. It's ridiculous, the amount of filing cabinet space."

Maia was in the middle of taking a sip of water, and she had to hold back from spattering it out. "You do know what that means though, right?"

"I think so. But I don't understand why it's keeping you from coming to school."

She sighed burdensomely, and it didn't take long for a 90-pound Winnie, deputized with sloppy licks at the ready, to somehow jump in her lap like one of those ridiculously-sized teddy bears. "We get by. Mamá cleans houses and papá works any labor job he can get his hands on, mostly picking oranges or tomatoes for fifteen hours a day. But neither of those are consistent. Mamá gets fired all the time, because they think she's stealing, or mocking them in Spanish, or planning on seducing the husband; the same husband who comes and puts his gross hands on her ass while she's scrubbing his piss marks from under the toilet seat. So I help, whenever I can. Whatever I can... I do."

Maia had so much sorry in her eyes. Even after what she'd been through, *she* was sorry for *Sadie*, for having to be the one to tell her these poverties exist.

"Maia..."

She was weeping in waterfalls now, with Winnie's matted curls her box of tissues, and Sadie stood up and hugged her from behind so she had two extra sleeves to drench. Maia wept and wept over the table, with complete abandonment for once, emptying out, replaying the cursed series of events that'd led her there. Her emotions streamed from humiliation to rage to love, and with Sadie's innocent locks hanging down her broken chest, she swore to never let the same impurities of life touch her Anastasia. Maybe she could do so, bare it, protect her; like how she did for Luca.

"I want you to meet someone." Maia's head lifted in that moment, giving Winnie a marrow-soaked bone from the freezer before fleeing mysteriously to a back room. When she returned, she was pushing a pediatric wheelchair carrying a brittle-bodied boy, holding a box of Nilla Wafers.

He was in a ninja turtles outfit and looked around eight-years-old. His complexion and hair were a soft blended shade of mocha, still he was much paler than Maia, which could've been from a lack of outdoors, but Sadie didn't think so. The boy's fully-open eyes wandered the room like he was discovering it for the first time. He was able to plop a cookie in his mouth, before something confusing happened: all of his limbs entwined and criss-crossed, like it was fun to be a human-pretzel, and also it frustrated him to a scream.

Maia stroked his head affectionately. "This is Luca, my little brother." Any evidence of her bouts of violent crying dissolved from her face, and she seemed peaceful now.

Sadie introduced herself to Luca, but he didn't take her hand or know how to acknowledge her at all. So, instead she curtsied, and he appeared enthralled by that.

"He has epilepsy," Maia explained, and Sadie instantly felt guilt for not being more informed on the condition. "It's a nerve disorder. In his case, severe. Mostly it's seizures, and when it's not, he sometimes has trouble controlling his arms and legs. Luca panics if he's alone. He wakes up with episodes of fear that might last for days. And on top of all that, there's an intellectual disability the doctors haven't yet given a name. They seem pretty useless, so I'm not holding my breath." Her stance toughened, but her heart was clearly severed by this. "We give him stuff to relax his muscles, which usually just knocks him out." She massaged his tiny shoulders as his eyes draped closed.

"He's so special. There's no one in this world like him. I like to tell him he was sent to the wrong planet, that he actually has superpowers, and that they just don't work here." She was crying again. "I don't know how else to help him."

Sadie kneeled to Luca's level, right as he woke, and he jolted in surprise then broke into the best grin she'd ever seen in her whole life. It was so exceptional that he should be a model for it. If they ever needed a picture for the word 'grin' in the dictionary, it should be a picture of Luca.

"We had a nurse coming to look after him during the day, but we can't afford it anymore. So now if both mamá and papá have work, I stay. That's why I haven't been at school."

Sadie suspected there was more she wasn't telling her, but she'd been learning to ask less questions, and for her own sake, she chose to not know when. She traced little words of encouragement on Luca's knee, and he danced in the seat to say *More! More!* "I think he likes me."

"I know he does. Granted, he doesn't meet a lot of people so he doesn't have much to compare."

Sadie was glad for the joke, because it meant she was feeling more herself again. She went to rewarm the chicken noodle in the microwave, positive that Maia hadn't eaten all day. "Sit," she demanded, until she did.

The three of them planted at the table, rolling the Nilla Wafers across like coins, trying to keep them from falling over. Maia sipped her broth while Sadie admired her first true friend. A gladiolus flower with sword-shaped leaves and a symbol of strength, half-hippie, half-hipster, and totally a badass with the best comedic timing. And if all of these qualities didn't make her one of Sadie's favorite people on earth, she was now also a gold-medalist big sister.

"I've decided something," Sadie said.

"That you'll do my math homework?" Maia answered.

Sadie laughed *you wish*, before sitting up straight and confident. "I've decided I want to be just like you when I grow up. I want to be just like Maia. What do we think?" She tickled Luca, and his happy squeals endorsed, while the crumbling girl with raven hair swore to never let that happen.

CHAPTER FIFTEEN
Natural Sweeteners

The quilt on Sadie's walnut sleigh bed was, by miles, the most valuable item in her room. Grandma Ida had spent months on the patchwork, rocking in grandpa Lance's chair, waiting for him to be relieved of his duties at war. It was a wedding-cake-white with tessellations of blue hydrangeas. Blue hydrangeas had been her specialty.

Ida was born and raised in a wealthy community in West Palm Beach with her Nordic-origin parents. They'd gone to a spa resort in Naples one weekend, to celebrate her eighteenth birthday. Lance was on leave, driving up and down state-lines for two weeks, before eventually heading back to the salt marsh of Parris Island, North Carolina. First hour in, his truck had a hissy fit and broke down right in front of the resort, where Ida was already peering at him curiously through the window in her high-waist bikini and floppy sunhat. She brought him an iced tea refreshment while he worked on the engine—*pretending* to work by then—and later they'd snuck out to Paradise Coast and gone skinny-dipping alongside the currents of the gulf stream. Grandpa had once mentioned them also making love in a lifeguard tower, to which grandma, with a peach hue all over, had explained away with, "That's what old people call hugging."

The next morning Lance had to leave for the salt marsh, and two weeks later he was sent overseas to Vietnam. But they'd fallen in love that night by the gulf stream, meaning from then on, they were each other's no matter the distance.

So, they'd written.

Years later, they'd saved everything. Ida used to read to Sadie from the important box of love letters, rocking in the same creaking chair, with Sadie of course doing her puzzles on the floor. She was just two years past toddler at the time, and couldn't rightfully comprehend and appreciate what she was hearing to the capacity it deserved, but it still gave her goosebumps, a sense of marvel, and eventually consecrated her finer rules of life. *Her* family tree was a premier Crepe Myrtle, an ultimate canopy of long-lasting passion, heaps and heaps that would never run out. Right? It would never run out?

That evening after Maia's house, Sadie dwelled with a pinky outlining the dainty hydrangeas, debating whether it was possible that the Lake Josey dock had been her Paradise Coast. Then, with her thighs suddenly moistened, if a white F-150 might become her *lifeguard tower...*

A knock sounded at her balcony door—wait, balcony? She didn't have a balcony.

Sadie jumped from the bed and ran to the window, where Brooks was unstably perched on an overhanging plank in the darkness, waving.

"Ohmigod," she inhaled too harshly and choked, then plopped it back up like a lodged grape, before trying again with more tact. "Oh... my... god." Smoothing the tops of her troll-humid hair, wiping the outworn concealer under her eyes, she was suddenly hit with an obscenely upsetting fact: she was in the magenta giraffe jammies, and yes they were swallowing her whole, and no she hadn't shaved anything for a week, and—

"Crap." Clunkily, Sadie kicked off the giraffes, stumbled, and crammed into her smallish 8th grade yoga pants that constrained her butt to a bubble.

All the while, she'd apparently forgotten the function of a window, and Brooks had very nearly fallen to his death at the sight of her undressing.

Sadie opened the latch and the boy with brown eyes climbed inside her bedroom; an attendance of orange tree viewers saving it all, on leafy hard discs, for now, and later.

"Hi." His demeanor was ecstatic and craving, moving around like he'd chugged three Monsters. When he kissed her, he put a soulful pressure on her lips so it almost knocked her over; like he'd really needed it.

"Hi." Sadie giggled in giddy bewilderment. "How did you get up here?"

"I climbed the tree." And he pointed to said tree.

"Oh... okay. Well, you shouldn't be here. If my parents see you, I'll get in trouble."

Brooks refuted that with an arching brow, and instead of doing the smart thing and fleeing, put it up for discussion. "How do you know?"

"What do you mean how do I know?"

"Have you ever *been* in trouble?" he challenged, eyes lifting triumphantly because he knew he had her hands tied. Indulgently, Sadie enjoyed having her hands tied. She enjoyed it *very* much, and maybe she'd said so with her face, because in the spur of the moment his steely hands found her full cheekbones, kissing them again, admiring the green irises and embracing her girlish consonance the way two leaves embrace a rose bud. "It's late. They're asleep. So I'm staying."

"Fine," she happily complied, noting how even chinstrap acne looked profoundly handsome on him.

Brooks re-pictured the sight of her jewel-toned thong, the sensual upside down heart wearing it, and spoke his mind. "I wouldn't have been able to sleep without seeing you."

Sadie's pulse accelerated like the beat of a song. "We can't have that, now can we?"

They rested on the edge of the bed, on the hydrangeas.

"So... how was the project?" he asked.

"Hm? Project?" Her body was still thumping down low with delight.

"With Duke."

"Oh!" The thumping returned to her chest, unfortunately. "It was fun," she answered without thinking. "I mean, as fun as homework *can* be, so really kind of boring. He's doing Hamlet, I'm doing Ophelia—it's a whole 'act it out' thing. We're working our way through Shakespeare's themes. Just tragedy after tragedy, ya know? Really the theme is that everyone dies, so what's the point of even reading it?"

Brooks eyed a special hardcover of *The Complete Works of William Shakespeare* on top of a stack of Italian magazines. "I thought you liked that stuff."

"Oh—I do. Just annoying that I have to do it with Duke."

Brooks really disliked that sentence, that *It*. He just wished she'd be normal about it. "Why is that annoying?"

"Isn't it to you?"

"It wasn't." *But it sure as hell is now.* "Whatever. It's just homework. Not a big deal, right?"

"Exactly!" Sadie sighed, a little too relieved. "Just a few weeks of rehearsing the play—"

"A few weeks?"

"Um, yeah. Did I not mention that?"

Brooks shook his head, fighting the urge to hurl himself out the window and act like he never cared, but then he looked at her again, and knew he was far too deep to get away with something like that. *I trust you,* Brooks reminded himself, with a longing to feel whatever the English ginger singer with the math-symbol albums sings about on the radio.

"You wanna cuddle?" Brooks broke his silence, and from the cute dance in her shoulders, knew for certain it was the most right thing he could've said.

Together they curled up under the quilt—but not the sheets because of the lustful entrapments that could cause—with her head fitting perfectly on the smooth muscle of his chest.

Their conversations were first relaxing and frivolous; talking about the seasonal Dairy Queen flavors, how nothing will ever beat Reese's, before Brooks went on and on about a family-owned ice cream shop called *Shakers* that used to exist across the movies, in a 50's theme of black, white and pink and an old-western ceiling train suspended from the ceiling. The owners, Norman and Blanche and their Labrador Biscuit, would put on holiday skits with roller skates and hot fudge. One year, during a Polar Express skit, they even got it to fake snow. There'd been a whole big news story about it, folks driving all the way from Polks County to see it. Still, it'd closed down shortly after a DQ and Twistee Treat opened in town, and Norman and Blanche and Biscuit packed up the freezers and ceiling train and moved to nowhere Montana to try again.

Sadie stared into space, just listening, until the story mined a memory loose. "Wait! I've been there!" she yelped, then covered her mouth with his bicep. Her green eyes flickered to visions of malt balls. "Did they have a Whoppers sunday? And did Norman call his mustache a moo-stache?"

Brooks smiled at the girl from the photograph. "You went there after the fruit stand on Eiland."

"Okay, stalker. Clearly you've been obsessed with me for years."

"Eh, maybe a little," he teased, noticing how she was changing. "You said you ended up with ice creams that day, and that was the only place to go back then. At least for the good stuff."

"Mhm. Obsessed."

"Yeah, yeah." He leaned in for an impactful amount of time; long enough for Sadie's toes to fondle his, a leg to cross over on top, if only to have more of them touching. Maybe it had to do with being in an *actual* bed, with movability and pillows, and the awareness that the accommodation was typical to such… 'hugging' sprees… but she found the uprising of affectivities strenuous to keep coy.

He pulled back, and once again, neutralized her hot beating. "Has Caleb been bothering you?"

"Caleb? No." Sadie half groaned. "Well—yes. But it's fine. I can handle him." She waited for him to lean in again, but it seemed the moment of doing something rash had passed. It's okay, she'd simply wait for the next one.

He let his chagrin occupy him, which he'd prove to do often. "I'm sorry about that."

"Really, it's fine—"

"He's been such an idiot lately."

"Yeah, well I'm sure it's nothing new—"

"Do you want me to say somethin' to him?"

Sadie exhaled, huffier and disappointed, accepting the detour and that there was no U-turn in sight. Maddening, how Caleb had somehow managed to dissemble the expressway, even in absence. "You don't have to say anything. Trust me it wouldn't help, only provoke him more," she explained, as if more expert in Caleb tendencies than his best friend. "Might I suggest getting better friends?"

Brooks smiled like he'd heard that once or twice before. "Summer right before middle school, Caleb's mom took us to Universal Studios," he started. "We were there late, and apparently they give out glow sticks to the likes of harebrained boys, because they gave me twelve. So, on the drive home, I kept crackin' the sticks in the backseat because I thought it'd make them glow brighter, until one of them squirt all it's flashy neon goo in my eye. Just straight up in my eyeball like a squirt gun, and I swear, that liquid stuff they put in 'em might just be lemon juice cause it burned more than I can tell you. We stopped at a gas station to try to wash it out in the bathroom, which did nothin', and I ended up havin' to wear an eye-patch my first three weeks of school, bumpin' into walls and gettin' called Hook."

"No!" Sadie whined and shrunk into the quilt. "Poor baby Brooks."

He laughed unexpectedly, knowing if anyone else had reacted that way, his inner man would be greatly insulted. "Yep. Tough times of the youth."

She mulled it over again, and as she bunched herself closer to him with sleepier eyes, he mistakenly saw right down her shirt. "Not that I don't love the stories, but what does this have to do with Caleb?"

"Oh—uh." He recouped from the disruption; now it was him who was thumping. "After people started sayin' stuff, Caleb went home and cut a hole in one of the other eleven sticks, poured the goo right in his eye so he'd have to wear an eye-patch too. We were friends before, but after those eye patches... we were best friends."

Sadie couldn't imagine it, Caleb doing a good deed. "I'll take your word for it."

He chuckled for a staggering fifth time that night, and she adored how his body vibrated against her. "Just thought you should have some back story. Now, what about you? You've never told me about your friends in LA."

All light in her eyes flatlined. "Oh, right. They're fun."

"That's it? That's all I get?"

"What do you want to know?" Sadie shrugged out of the blanket; it'd suddenly become scratchy. Then, the trust funds of minimizing remarks afflicted her heartstrings like root rot.

"Are they like you? I'll bet they are." He nudged her kissable arm, flirted with the pink tips of her ear. "I'll bet their names are ones like Daffodil and Daisy, in those same frilly tea-party dresses. I'll bet they ask for way too much Parmesan on their gluten free pasta, talk old-timey, and read Perks of Being a Couch Potato just like you." He'd expected a smile, at the least.

"They'd definitely dump their iced Americanos on you for saying that," Sadie snapped in a somber note, and glanced around, as if they could be prying from the closet; come to punish her for drinking that inaugural cappuccino. "And no, their names were Tenley, Emma and Becks. They had fake IDs, wore bottom eyeliner and had gross full-frontal crushes on Mark Ruffalo, made even weirder by Mark being buddies with Becks' dad."

"The Hulk?"

"Don't get me started," she warned. "I met them in fourth grade, or I guess I always *knew* them, but they didn't really pick me until freshman year."

"Are you an orange?" Brooks asked, to which her big cheeks just pouted in daze. "You said pick, like you're an orange."

"You don't get it!" Sadie dismantled. "You didn't know them, so you can't talk about them like that." Why, she wondered, was she still defending the satiny tyrants? Why did it still affect her so? Why did it still hurt? Why, ten years down the line, would she still feel like a fraud for ordering a *goddamn cappuccino*?

Whether intuitively or selfishly, Brooks drew her in closer to his musky gray sweatshirt, inhaling her rosewater like a personal diffuser. More gently, he asked, "Well… do you think this 'Tenley, Emma and Becks' would like *me* if I met them?"

"*Like* you? You're asking if they would *like* you? If you met them, you'd already be dating Becks instead of me. Trust me, they'd like you just fine."

Needy and fault-finding, Sadie turned away with testy elbows as though she had reason to be mad, which in turn made him slightly mad too. Brooks flopped bluntly on his back, untying them. "Is that what you think of me? Of us?"

Sadie simply shrugged a 'such is life' shrug, a heartbreaking detachedness numbing her overcast. To decongest, the stuck gunk has to come out eventually: resentments, angers, the feeling of being fooled. It's never pretty; it's never easy. "Becks is everyone's type. It wouldn't even be up to you," she strained out in whisper because her voice was, all over again, nowhere to be found.

"Not up to me?" Brooks echoed with a vivid bother. "What does that mean?"

"You haven't *met* her."

"*So?*"

He waited for her to turn back, but Sadie stayed miles distant, slipping very close to her holding-back-tears limit. She spiraled—seeing Becks' natural-corset-waist and hips galore pivoting against his lap, seeing him revivify against her, because *she* went for things and that was exciting. Sexy, irresistible, every guy's saucy dream girl, and Sadie was just 'frilly'. How long would it take for him to realize it? Sadie imagined those loan shark girls, her ex-friends, rolling on the floor with laughter in seeing her with the quarterback. She could hear it so blaringly in her ears.

"No," Brooks said heavy-handedly, understanding it better now. "You don't get to decide what this is, dismiss it to somethin' vain and surface simply because that's the kind of guys you've dealt with in the past. Maybe your wanna-be crossfit boys would do that, but not me. You're like color in a black and white world, and I've never—I could never—I just—I'm not lookin' to do this with just anyone. Do you understand that? This means somethin' to me, *this*…" he gestured to their mirrored chests, "means

somethin'. I want you, only you. I will *always* pick you, Sadie."
He'd never be a man of many words, only life-changing ones.

Brooks took off his sweatshirt and vaulted to her other side in
a heavenly motion, before his fingers attentively sunk to the fleshy
upside-down heart and cupped it into him. He pressed his lips on
hers to the fullest extent, enough to finally make his point: *Becks
didn't have a damn thing on her.*

Sadie's cheekbones lifted so high, they were in danger of
displacing her eyeballs. "Am I an orange?" She leaned into her
wit, now that in her mind, no one was holding it hostage. "You
said you'd 'pick' me."

"Yes," the boy with brown eyes said. "You're *my* orange."

Sadie braced herself, because the moment had finally arrived,
and as sure as the thumping inclining them both under the
sheets... she wasn't going to lose it this time.

With the dim glow of the chandelier above, Brooks' and
Sadie's toppling figures were, by *no fault* of their own, begging to
do something rash. Thumping in unison, falling victim to an
innate messy humanness, and in doing so, the mess becoming
more necessitous than breathing. Brooks and Sadie breathed each
other, losing track of time, losing track of where his tongue
started and hers began. His heart, her heart.

Sadie had expected some of it to feel wrong, scary even,
being so young in adult predicaments. That's what they tell you,
that it's wrong. Only, nothing had ever felt less wrong. Nothing
had ever felt more natural. Have you ever considered how flowers
are fetching not to please our eyes, but to seed, to flower, to fruit,
to reproduce in exquisite meadows, and despite their flirtatious
engagements, we applaud their purity.

I've always been envious of flowers; no one condemns them.

Brooks felt lightly on her breasts, which he'd done before, but
this time there was no bra. He played with the part that counted
and Sadie felt that whole part of her body instantly change,
become something more interesting and accomplished from then
on, and in need of constant attention. Her head pressed back in
the pillow, back arching. The more he swirled, the more it
trickled like dripping water to other eventful places. She levered

her hips upward, because it twinged and pushing it upward was clearly what it wanted.

They moved to other positions that allowed them better anchorage, constancy in pace, the right friction against their bodies and clothes. As he tested kissing new regions; collarbone, ears, breasts, naval territory; Brooks panned fingertips up and down the spot between her legs, where the energy had all trickled and collected, bringing her warmer to tipping point. He tried to travel beneath her clothes, but keeping in mind her not-shaving dilemma, Sadie gave a little shake of her head, and he thoughtfully continued feeling over the fabric.

She tried to multi-task by reaching for his pant drawstrings, but he admirably interlaced his free hand in hers, and pressed it into the bed. She had no choice but to lie there, to focus only on the rhythmic clenching, his smell, his brown eyes absorbed and on-task, *on her*. Nerves and anxieties evaporated away, as she watched him. Then, as she squirmed and pooled, Sadie had the foggy realization these were the same leggings she'd worn in the car on the day she'd arrived, when they first saw one another... the ones that were basically... *Sadie tensed*... tights.

The entire earth shook on it's axis, maybe even slipped off it entirely. At first, the slowly building charge felt like a disorienting, pleasurable, charley horse in her stomach, before summiting in an explosive surge of flying colors, coursing and lathering her up in tingles until clamping the sheets and biting her lip were her only means to not whimper in place. Her whole body trembled and folded, and finally fell back. She was euphoric and spent and dramatically enlightened, there under Brooks' chiseled bare chest. It was incomparable, those exhilarating free-falling seconds, and perhaps most exciting: there was more where that came from.

Winded, Sadie opened her eyes. She'd never loved the color brown more. Picking up on a meekness in his posture, she almost got the impression he didn't do this often, but that of course, would be false.

"Have you ever..." Brooks started, reddening. "I mean, was that your—"

"No, I haven't," she admitted, half-embarrassed in knowing many girls her age were skilled drivers in this 'self-care' arena. She'd just always had the idea that it negated the romantic value of it; she'd never wanted these things to feel casual.

He nodded and tried not to look smug. "Okay."

She was still coming down; eyes starry like when she'd underwent too many camera flashes. He rubbed her shoulder, before resting his chin on it. "Can I ask you one more thing?"

Sadie smiled. "After that, you can ask me anything you want."

Brooks whispered, "Will you be my girlfriend?"

Sadie's neck swiveled, bunching a posy of blue hydrangeas in her fist. "See? I knew it. Totally... *obsessed.*"

The amber pendant lights in *Elaine's Coffee* reflected off Sadie's well-endowed locks, as if bringing attention to her amended womanliness. Even under cloak of a raucous Tuesday morning rush, Sadie waited until they'd sat down in the corner to tell Maia.

"He did *what?*" she yelped and knocked into the table, as her hazelnut coffee jumped from the cup.

Sadie quickly shushed her, knowing her normal speaking voice was more or less miles-reaching, and today she was even louder than that. "I am this close to stuffing that bagel in you. *This.*" She pinched a centimeter of air.

Maia's fingers tap-tapped her thigh suggestively, to go along with her scandalous grin. "Good work my frisky petunia."

"Maia!"

"Okay, okay. I'll stop. Just because I'm worried about how red you're turning!" She managed it about six seconds. "Did he have different modes or was it more of a steady cruise control?"

Sadie shot her a flustered frown, and as if to prove her worries valid, Mr. Dawson snailed by just then with a cane and funk of an old folks home. He told Sadie and Maia about a sinkhole in Shelby County from '72 called the Golly Hole, and they entertained him with inquisitive faces, before he concluded with, "Say, anyone ever tell ya you look just like young Geena

Davis? Must be from your momma, cause your daddy sure don't look like a Geena Davis." He guffawed and winked, and then his orthopedic shoes were scuffing away.

"You think he heard you?" Sadie stress sucked on a packet of honey. "He definitely heard you. He so did!"

Maia just shrugged and took a bite from her bagel, but at least the chewing shut her up. Though, with a mouth-full, she did quietly repeat, "Golly Hole."

At the register, all three Dunn kids were juggling the line of antsy customers, which they sometimes did before school when their mom was backed up with cake orders. Colton slipped away once the Lilly Pulitzer clique approached, because their pumpkin spice was never 'pumpkiny' enough, and Tanner had a thing for McKenna anyway, so really he was doing him a favor.

Lately, Colton couldn't decide if he was just going through an introvert phase, or suddenly hated people, and as he thought more about that, going around table to table and topping off already-full mugs, he spotted two joyful girls in the corner who never triggered any aversions. "Hey, you guys need anythin'?"

"Ah, yes! Please, replenish me good sir!"

Sadie wasn't sure what provincial Irish region Maia's accent was from, but wherever it was, Colton had been there too.

"But 'af course!" He poured with flair.

"I don't know if you knew this, but you've always been my favorite Dunn," Maia told him. "Sure, Tanners got the Einstein thing and Shelbys mastered the death stare, but you know what you've got, Colton?"

"Mmm, well, I got that top-ten spot in the national soccer ranking, and I'm pretty decent at darts."

Maia leaned back in her chair, checking him out. "I was gonna say you know how to rock an apron, but I guess those other things are cool too."

It put a glee on his face that suited him much better than the fury at Bandit Bog. "By the way, I heard you were a big help to our dad this summer. He said his office had never been so organized before you came in."

Maia paled. "It'll be good for the resume."

"Definitely! And hey, if you're ever lookin' for an internship in that line of work, I'm sure he'd take you in a heartbeat—"

"I'm not," her words trampled out, "in that line of work." Then she was busy with spiking her latte with an undrinkable amount of sugar.

"Sure, alright... well anyway, enjoy your topped off cups. Might wanna sip it from the table first. Let me know if you need some napkins."

"Thank you," Sadie said, because Maia wasn't able to.

Colton backed away with awkward footing, just in time to be royally waved down by Delilah and Mallory, finger-snapped at when he wasn't quick enough.

Sadie overdrew her fall sweater sleeves to give herself muppet hands, and cupped her mug. "I didn't know you worked for Daddy Dunn."

Something in Maia flipped with physical force. "What did you just say?"

"It's what all the girls in my Bio class call Mr. Jay, daring each other to flash him in the hall. They also say he's got 'buns like Beckham' and have several theories on why his chin stubble always looks so dewy. "

"That's disgusting," Maia lashed back with a truly repulsed look, one Sadie wasn't used to getting, as if it'd been her who'd come up with the name, and she'd completely gone off the deep end. Like her recent womanly doings had made her just that: *disgusting*. "You're right. I can't believe I said that." Her skin went hot with shame.

"No." Maia realized she'd been a bad friend again. "I didn't mean that. It's just... I guess I just don't see it."

"I think that's the whole point, it's innocent really," Sadie explained. "It's easy to say things like that when you know it would *never* happen. They're not *actually* going to flash the principal. Can you imagine how much trouble they'd get into?"

"Yeah. I can."

Sadie snuggled some more with her tea, pulling her knees up on the chair like she was a seven-year-old who'd just gotten yelled at by the teacher.

Maia knew exactly what she was thinking. "Are you okay?"

"I'm fine—"

"You know what I mean." Maia paused. "I'm talking about last night. You don't feel any... regret, do you?"

Regret wasn't the right word for it; it felt more like her young state of comfort had been dumped on by ice cold water. If she'd had her journal, she'd write that it's like she'd left on a one-way ticket to cloud nine, only she'd forgotten to pack something. She didn't remember what it was, only that she'd never get it back. Unsteadily situated on the fence of pre and post, dawn and dusk, girlhood and maturity. Sadie wished to be up in the air, for just a moment longer. "No," Sadie answered, "I don't regret it."

"It doesn't have to be sad." Maia went to the vulnerable place with her. "It doesn't have to feel like you're 'losing' something— when you start to do those things with a guy—even if the word is quite literally built into the terminology. It's supposed to be... fun, right?" Or so, she'd heard.

Sadie ran her top lip along the edge of the porcelain, before very faintly breathing, "It *was* fun. Is that... bad?" Her cheeks were red again, thinking that if angels did exist, they might be reading her indecent thoughts.

"Did you know dolphins are one of the only animals that copulate for fun?"

"You mean make love," Sadie corrected.

Maia grinned. "I mean... *do it*."

And just like that, they were back to two uninterrupted high school girls squawking in the corner, in no hurry. Comparing their horoscopes on phone apps and updating each other on which Gossip Girl episode they'd just finished. Sadie asked about Luca, and Maia caught her up on his recent Jungle Book obsession. They planned to go shopping in Tampa that weekend for Halloween costumes and vanilla cookie candles and those T-string thongs that feel like they're slicing you in half after a full day of wear, but are a total rite of passage. Two blossoming girls, drinking ordinary coffee, at an ordinary table, amongst ordinary people—together an extraordinary pastime, indeed.

The sweet bell on the door rang suddenly, and Duke stepped

in under it, in boat shoes and that army green henley he wore at least once a week. Upon spotting Sadie, his features nudged up, as she unwisely wondered how he'd feel about her new relationship status... wondered how he'd feel about Brooks' fingers running up and down the ravine of her legs... wondered how different it would be, if the fingers were *his*.

"Still can't believe he asked you to be his actual *girlfriend*!" Off Sadie's horror, and with cream cheese chives on her nose, Maia grimaced, "Sorry, was I too loud again?"

Slow and stiff, Sadie's neck rotated as the press release spilled to every corner of the café's busy square footage. Foam-milk jaws in laps, whispers like lawnmowers, glares in the shape of bow and arrows, and texting tantrums ignited across a line of dominos. Honestly, she may as well have put it on a blimp. She may as well have held a huge announcement sign right in Duke's face. She may as well have passed him a silent note. The delivery didn't matter; it wouldn't change the pain it caused him.

But Duke did well at hiding his reaction; he just strode past her without a look, the same way she'd left him in the Lake Josey thickets.

Outside on Main Street, Sadie and Maia caught a ride to school in Sterling's truck—*Danger Ranger* as Sterling preferred to call it—which screeched at stop signs, veered on traffic cones, and had a distinct swing like the backseat wasn't entirely attached to the rest. Sadie asked if they'd be picking up Grace, to which Sterling replied, "No, she went to Dunkin'."

Sadie's phone dinged in her sweaty hand. *'Good morning beautiful. Did you sleep well?'* Already knowing she most certainly had. *'By the way, we're skipping today.'*

The Danger Ranger continued neighing fumes up Stadium Drive, under the awnings of skunk vine, past the preschool sign of Carolina Jasmine, all the way up to the stretch of parking lot where they discovered police cars flanked where Britney and Whitney would normally be tanning. The first bell rang, but the whole school stayed gathered out front where the football team and a tomato-faced Brant punched fists in the ground, kicked backpacks, cursed, spit, and cried for revenge.

"What is *happening?*" Sadie hurried to where Brooks kneeled and fumed, but he was mute. She looked up at Caleb and Levi to say *start explaining, busters.* They weren't any help either, and she was seriously beginning to worry something dreadful had occurred. That's when she saw the graffiti.

"They're gon' pay." The boy with brown eyes finally murmured. "Cameron, Dustin, Dakota, every last one of 'em."

Caleb put a hand on his injured back, and since they had quite an audience, played angel's advocate. "We'll pray on it, God will know what to do." At Sadie, he winked.

Levi hung his head. "Windows smashed, equipment stolen, and that shitty orange jail paint dumped all over the stands. Man, they had to have been at it all night."

Although the policemen attempted a barricade, the Weston Hills High student body trooped up the quad stairs to see it for themselves, pure heartrending gloom settling when they did. More students chanted for vengeance, and even stony Brant, with a gibbous forehead vein the size of Texas, appeared to consider it. He made himself large atop a picnic table. "We'll settle this on the field. End of season." He fixated solely on Brooks. "*End* of discussion."

Kelly joined him, balancing in a bright pin-up dress with poodles on it. "Classes are canceled until further notice. Enjoy your surprise break."

Then the adults scattered to figure out how to break the news to the Orville admin, and the legal logistics of what it meant. Later on surveillance video, they'd make out hoarier faces that almost looked like some of the offenders were the coaches themselves, but that couldn't be right. That would be utter anarchy.

Brooks box-jumped atop the same table once they were gone, flashing that laid-back, lone-wolf, stoical smile that made him such a star. Sadie admired her muse, before her muse reached out his arm to pull her up with him.

"PARTY AT THE LAKE JOSEY DOCK!" Brooks declared.

It was sure to be one for the... *books.*

CHAPTER SIXTEEN
Growing Pains And Other Prickly Things

It was a second-chance summer, that random Tuesday at the lake. Teenage kids with John Deere hats and Johnny Cash attitudes rolled in by a string of tires, ready to take it too far; far enough to never come back, to never grow up, to be the bad-news LJ dock crew until that dock was nothing but a cock-and-bull story told derogatorily in the news. That *one* thing that happened somewhere in the south. The Weston Hills kids were happy being that thing.

Sadie found the dock to look different in daylight: wooden planks riddled with slimy green coatings, water vapidly muted, opinionated cicadas overpowering her cricket friends. She was horrified at the number of snails she murdered just walking down the herbage, how instantly yucky she could be with sweat, the summer-day pops of color in the trees—gone. It disenchanted her previous folklore image, until Brooks scooped up her arms and legs like one of the many weightless critters in the grasses, ran them to the front of the swarm, and mumbled in her hair, "What are all these people doin' in our home?"

"Home," Sadie echoed with a hand on his warm beating, noting how she'd never before, imagined to find it in a person.

Sterling decided the Danger Ranger looked best at the water's edge, working and tucking a blue tarp into the bed, duct-taping it down and using dirty buckets to fill it with water. "I'm on some innovative shit today!" A patent had been filed in his name. The excess length of tarp was rolled down the hill, and once drizzled with some Dollar Tree soap, became the perfect miscreant slip 'n slide—"How our ancestors used to do it."

In the water, blow-up tables levitated Dixie cups and different flavors of beer. Colton, Tanner, Ali and Duke—for once taking part in the indecencies—played a drinking game Ali had picked up on Adult Swim.

Mallory and Grace oiled their legs and boobs on pop-art towels on the dock, setting heart charms one inch inward of their hipbones, so once they were sun-stamped they'd be left with baby tattoos.

Shelby was nearby the cloud of smelly BananaBoat, in running shorts and a sports bra, eating goldfish crackers, contemplating body image. She'd never understood all the hoopla and fuss they feed to girls her age, that is, until Brooks had fallen for a shiny girl with an appearance draped and wringing-wet in all of her shortcomings. Truthfully, Shelby didn't want to hate Sadie. But it was her fault Shelby despised her durable wrists, rectangular stance, all the muscle in her thighs that used to be strong and promising and beautiful like Serena. Now, all she had was strong. No one ever told her the boys wouldn't like strong.

Sipping on wide-mouthed mason jars of Sangria, Britney and Whitney waded joblessly in the shallow shore in matching red bikinis. Caleb had invited them because he normally would; get them tipsy, get him inebriate, take one or both to the private mowed cove of turf just behind the trees. But today he'd taken one look at their jejune pretty legs, and ended up comfortably squatted behind his best friend and his best friend's lovething, detailing the time he caught a largemouth bass with his bare hands, chewing on venison jerky and chasing it obnoxiously with canned spray cheese.

Sadie flinched with each aerosol sound.

The sun blazed, and since Sterling had prioritized the money he'd had for Screwdrivers instead of the waters he'd been assigned, the barefoot teens drifted astutely wasted.

Sadie, the lightest of those weights, hopped up to shake it for the young bucks, like Luke Bryan was instructing from the speakers, tipping to and fro over the ledge.

Brooks, in his black Hurley board shorts, eyed her with concern. On the other hand, Caleb, in his showier pineapple trunks, sang and gyrated along.

It was no secret Brooks had been economic with his drinking, because ever since he'd met Sadie, he didn't have a need to comatose his brains away, act stupid in his free time. He'd rather be present, better, for her. Not to mention he was downing a full pain med bottle a week, and you're not supposed to drink with those.

The quarterback assisted his wayward little flower back to a crouched position, so Sadie could go back to supervising the baby tadpoles swimming around in the lake. He pushed back sticky gold strands from her neck as he said, "I'm gonna fetch you somethin' a bit more hydratin'."

Her pouty frown hinted noncompliance, but then she noticed a patch of dandelions growing through the wood planks, and urgently started cupping water as though it were a solid, pouring empty fists upon them.

"Whatcha doin' there?" Caleb knelt and coddled her elbow.

Sadie was in a floral one piece, which she might've sensed could use some adjusting had she not shown off how chugging four gulps of vodka *didn't* make her gag; her slightly cheeky coverage was now much more micro. "They were thirsty," she informed. "They told me."

"Sorry to tell ya, but… they're gonna stay thirsty at that pace." He tried aiding with a Dixie cup but she didn't want it.

Sadie confidently slurred, "In case of fire, do not use elevator. Use stairs."

Damn, she was gone. Caleb grinned, and while leaning closer, "Objects in mirror are closer than they appear."

Then she whipped around sharply, and with a clever air as if she was totally super with-it, "I had it wrong. In case of fire, *break glass*"—Sadie rammed her elbow in his gut, and it flung his chiseled bare body far into the murky surface. She giggled and celebrated and clapped for herself, all without any overthinking.

Caleb was moved to amazement that she'd taken action. A

good sport about it, he slurped and fountained water from his mouth, approaching in shark form, intimidating with 'dadums'. Then suddenly, he pounced for her toes flailing sky-high over her head. "I'm gon' get you!"

"No! No! Stop it! Let go of me!" she screamed, and Brooks came running back over with half a mind to punch his best friend out.

"What is wrong with you?" He threw a bottle cap at the blonde head. "She said let go!"

Caleb eventually did, but made sure Brooks knew it wasn't by his ordering. "As you wish, princess."

"Anyone want?" Ali swam over to them with what looked like a fully wrapped Tootsie Roll shooting from her lips.

"I do! I do!" Sadie shouted with her tongue out, as though she might be inclined to feed it to her.

"Uh, no you don't," Brooks notified lovingly. "It's weed."

"Well how do *you* know I don't want the weed? I'll take a few whiffs." She placed two hands on her hips, and offered Ali a star-shaped stone she'd found as currency. "One weed, please." Everyone cracked up over it, and Sadie thought it about time she be appreciated for her rich comedic gifts—though, had she given a joke? Whatever; take that Emma. I'm funny, *too*.

Brooks said, "Sorry, your rock money has been declined."

"Aw, darn it. I'll get 'em next time."

He kissed the top of her silly head. "You sure will, babe."

Sadie blinked up at him with slow-moving eyes full of snowglobe liquid. "You're really hot."

"And you're beautiful."

"Psh." On his hunky body she rested her heavy head, shifting her posture to have a clear shot at another hunky body, mentally singing *eenie meenie minie mo*. "You know who else is hot?"

Brooks stiffened, because what the hell? "No, I don't." A fingernail scraped on his neck until it'd scarred. "You wanna tell me?"

' Sadie's booziness bubbled over, and she fell completely on her back. "Nope! It's a secret!"

"But we don't have secrets."

"Maybe I do. Don't you remember what you said the last time we were here? *You* called me a wild card." She got up on her feet, twirling and floating and spiraling into the shadows. "You said I'm *one hell of a mystery to you.*"

He tickled small drawings on her belly. "That's because I'd never met someone as good as you."

Sadie sulked with an energetic packing box taping shut around her, and aggressively tore out the dandelions she'd only just attempted to water. "What if the secret is that I don't *want* to be good?"

So strongly it amused him; so reducing that felt. "You don't have to *want*, you just are, and there's nothing that can change that."

Brooks coaxed her in the lake with him, and Sadie sensed him worship every part of her he could see. As she dove under to wash her hair in the refreshing cool murk, she considered how he might feel about all the parts he *couldn't.*

Drunker now, Sadie frog-swam to ask Britney and Whitney if they preferred cauliflower or broccoli. And Brooks watched Duke, as Duke watched Brooks, as Caleb watched them both and secretly ran the whole show.

The afternoon continued lulling on in distorted acoustic snapshots.

"Comin' through!" Sterling cannoned down the homemade slide, but then he rolled off to the side and almost dislocated some knees.

"Watch it, Nascar!" Colton threatened.

Sterling, anemic skin tone stained with hick greens and browns, fixed his checkered hat as he stood. "Sorry, man—"

"You should be! Got mud all over my damn shorts!" Colton shouted back at him.

Sterling glanced down at the damage. "You're right. Sure hope I didn't get my poor person disease on your snazzy new threads. Patagonia? Damn, what are those, like fifty Big Macs worth?" His twang was well-supplied with sarcasm. "It's a good thing they're made for swimmin', cause did you know, that mud'll come right off in the water, bud. It tends to do that."

Colton was now minted with a very scary frown, and Sadie only wished Maia could be there to make him light and joyful again. "That supposed to be funny?"

"I am the jester, aren't I?" Sterling skipped with high-knees in a circle, arms swinging. "Hey Colton, pull my finger—"

Colton threw his first punch, which activated the violent arm into an automated weapon of beating and scraping and possible skull cracking. Sterling backed away with his forearms up in defense, but his nutrition came mostly from Chef Boyardee so he didn't have the same boxing stamina, or will power to fight, or lust for blood as the slugger going at him. Colton was *really* going at him. He hit, and hit, and hit, and hit, and he didn't care that Sterling wasn't hitting back, though that would've been more satisfying.

"STOP!" Shelby rushed to her brother, but was boomeranged by his elbow in the throat. When he turned to growl at her, Shelby noted: *that wasn't her brother.* Tanner forced himself between the gladiator and the lizard-like boy who was bleeding from both his nose and ears, but that didn't help either. Brooks, Caleb and Levi ran down the dock, but were stalled over the game of hopscotch it took to get across the broken boards.

Meanwhile, Grace was begging for desist in a frantic storm of tears, coughing over her terrified screams. Her boyfriend's entire face had been shuffled around now, and she couldn't bear to watch stupid boys do stupid things. "Colton, you idiot! Stop hurting him! *Please*, stop hurting him!" Even the roughest of necks wouldn't keep kicking someone already etched into the ground. What was his *problem*? "I'm gon' kill you for this! STOP IT, PLEASE!"

Sadie wanted to cover her eyes, but she didn't know how to anymore.

Without another option, Grace grabbed the nearest bottle and hurled it at them, not caring who it hit as long as it didn't kill them. It worked.

At the break in fighting, Colton's tired muscles relaxed, and he simply peered around at the spindles of red bloodshed infusing in the mud and water around them. He noticed it was silent. He noticed people were getting farther from him. "Wh—what happened?" There was a strange gap in his memory. Then, he spotted the pasty disfigured boy heaving out his organs and snot in the sawgrass, and Colton looked down at his own knuckles. "I didn't mean to—"

"You monster!" Grace hurried to wrap Sterling with a towel. "You about killed him for no damn reason!"

"I—I didn't—"

"Come on, let's go." Shelby grabbed Colton's shaking arm, and led them away. Tanner followed with their things, first making sure Sterling hadn't busted anything serious; like teeth or a spleen; and luckily for him, he was surprisingly shatterproof for a lizard-boy on a regimen of canned ravioli.

It was just a short walk up the wooded hill to their house.

"Wait!" Shelby called after her brother, or someone that looked like him, as he sprinted up the driveway. "Where are you going?"

"I want to be alone," he said.

"Dammit Colton! You can't attack someone and expect us to act normal, and give me that look like I'm just your annoying big sister." She exhaled, really trying to get through. "What happened back there? That... that wasn't *you*."

"Maybe it is now," he mumbled.

Tanner fidgeted with his ten-gallon hat, which was short on luck today. "Look man, if you want to... I don't know... talk to someone—"

Colton cackled oafishly in their faces. "Oh sure! Let's get Mrs. Holden over here right away so I can tell her how anytime a teacher says 'the bell doesn't dismiss you, *I* dismiss you' I spend the rest of the day fantasizing pushing a pen in their arm. And how sometimes I just get so mad from people bumping me in the hallway, or passing me on the road, or looking away when I talk to them—that *really* bothers me—that I think I might push 'em down the stairs." His gray eyes didn't show any signs of these maniacal moods, but they were frightened. "You think her and that clipboard can fix me right up?"

Shelby didn't know what to say, so she tried to hug him.

"We're here."

"Don't you dare make me some pitiful charity case to distract you from what's really going on."

"I'm worried about you," she defended with strawberry frizz distraught over her eyes. "That's all that's going on."

"Nah." Colton laughed again, because he knew it would injure her more. "You're just in love."

Shelby's brows knitted to one line and she stopped talking then; forced to simmer in all that she'd told herself she was too heavy-duty to feel. "You know?" Her voice cracked.

"I know," Colton said, and this time hurt with her instead of at her. "But he isn't in love with you. And you're so crabby about that, that you act like you can't stand being a girl, and you *really* can't stand anyone who's *good* at being a girl. Before Sadie it was Crista. Before Crista it was that waitress who waved at Brooks at the Outback. But you and him have been friends since preschool, Shelbs. Other girls aren't your problem, and you know, maybe you'd actually be friends with those girls if you didn't keep making them the enemy. Maybe then everyone could see how cool you are."

Little bursts of emotion showed themselves on her face, and she hated how they did, because remember—being strong was all she had. "Does *he* know?"

"I don't think so."

Tanner came up and put one arm around her, then Colton enlisted the same on the other side, and together the three siblings continued in the house where they'd grab the salted caramel and extra big spoons, light the fireplace, throw on the matching sweaters they'd outgrown years ago, watch Beetlejuice on the big TV, under piles of blankets with the fan on too high. And here, with her family, Shelby realized this was perhaps the best thing of hers that Sadie would never have: brothers.

Back at the dock, the rest of the crew cleaned up the aftermath.

Sadie, coming down as far as her impractical senses allowed, dwelled with her feet swinging over the lily pads and tadpoles. She'd swaddled herself in Brooks' gray hoodie and tied her filthy lake hair in a droopy loose bun.

"The oranges will be ripe soon," Caleb thought aloud, picking up cups and lingering where she sat.

Sadie sensed there might be some larger thematic premise to that, but she didn't have the energy to put the pieces together today. "Great, I'll make juice." She waited for his footsteps to disappear, but that was unlikely.

"I heard what you were sayin' earlier, and you should pick Duke."

Sadie's lips churned furiously at the horizon, mostly at how he seemed to always know things he shouldn't. "He's not an orange."

"What?"

"You said pick, like he's an orange."

"Well, you know what I mean."

"Actually I don't, because I'm Brooks Holden's girlfriend, and we're *very* happy together in case you haven't noticed."

Caleb had a hard time not pointing out the desperate way she'd articulated his full name, as if the attachment was to an idea and not the person. "You do remember how Brooks spoke to you your first day at school, right? You do know he let everyone think you had sex on this very dock for two straight weeks before doing anything about it?"

Sadie didn't answer him, but she didn't need to; he already knew she didn't know.

Insolent as usual, Caleb sat down next to her, which made her cross her arms and turn away with an annoyed vent of air. Her flyaway baby hairs flurried at the nape of her neck like thin yellow silks. He touched a few, but she didn't notice. "Did you ever think maybe... just *maybe*... I'm actually tryin' to help you out? That I could be someone who does the right thing?

Her pillowy mouth parted in a scowl, and for once, not a drop of her was tolerant, or obliging, or fearful of the outcome. Her words had a tendancy to come out swayable, as if preparing to be retracted. This time, they were irrevocable. "Never."

Caleb heard it, truly. "Really? Never?"

"Not for one second."

And now he'd lost the humorous glaze in the eyes; that is to say, somewhere in the world, pigs were flying. "Fine, I accept that. But did you ever stop to think maybe Brooks doesn't deserve to be on some pedestal either?"

"Maybe *I* don't deserve to be on the pedestal," she declared, and her tense temples let go of their ethereal elevation, like it'd been a relieving confession to make.

"Aha, *now* you're getting it. It's just a shame he never will."

"Seriously, you don't ever make any sense."

"It's not about makin' sense, it's about makin' sense of it."

She flipped him off; he was stoked. "Whatever, Caleb."

"I like this side of you, princess," he said.

"What side?"she asked.

He shrugged and smirked, and Sadie hated it, and in that moment she was all of her.

Mallory and Grace opted out of clean up duty, traveling on foot down clean Lake Josey sidewalks under the sunshades of moss, wet friendship anklets turning gross and incompatible.

Gel nails scrolled down a contact list, looking for a male with a license who lived close by. Mallory was sure anyone with those credentials wouldn't turn down picking up two bronzed tipsy hitchhikers with asses and majesties like theirs. It only took reaching the end of the 'A' names to secure a ride.

"Giddy up cowgirl, you're takin' forever." Mallory wrapped her arms around her shivering friend. "Waddle waddle, there we go. We'll get to the front gate by next week."

Grace smiled with her eyes closed, trusting that she wouldn't accidentally lead her into a fire hydrant like last time. "Mal, I love you."

The best belle in town bit down and slurped up a stripe of meat on Grace's arm, like they'd done at age thirteen during an intense fascination with the art of hickeys. "Mwah! I love you too!" She tossed back an anklet and kicked her burnt butt cheeks.

Grace observed Mallory's creamy skin, copiously overlaid in cold beauty creams, and the invisible blackheads she stressed over daily. Then it was Mallory's turn to look closely at Grace and see her invisible bits, but she picked at her cuticles instead.

Their platform flip flops flapped loudly on their feet.

Grace asked, "Can we go back to your house and watch all the Olsen twin movies like we used to? I promise I won't fall asleep." Though it appeared she was already on her way.

"We can do that any time," Mallory replied, which meant they probably never would.

Still hopeful, Grace agreed. "Your bed is so soft and smells like Hawaii." Then she cursed at a middle-aged man watching them closely from his lawn, hosing down his garden roses. Instinctively, she pulled up her towel over her chest.

Oppositely, Mallory turned winsome and glad and struck him a burlesque showgirl leg to make his day, because she'd been trained to get her daily serotonin from reinforcements of that nature.

"You don't need that," Grace breathed, but Mallory didn't hear it; she never heard the important stuff.

"Have you lost weight?" Mallory inspected her friend's petite figure.

"What? I don't know. Maybe I—"

"You should totally come work out with Dale and me! With the collagen bone broth cleanse and the cardio circuits he has me on, I'll definitely be a zero by pageant."

"You already are a zero."

"But like a *sure* zero. Come, I'll show you. Dale says I have really good form."

Grace caught the devious emphasis on his name, as if *Dale* was just the most arousing name on the entire planet. Fun fact: it also rhymed with jail. "Isn't he like thirty-five?"

"Thirty-six." Off her face, she squealed flagrantly. "Oh come on Gracie! It's not like we're doing it between mountain climbers and Quest bars! Who do you think I *am*?"

"Doesn't mean he's not thinking it."

Mallory made herself all mature and cosmopolitan, sipping from a phantom martini and gobbling up the olive. "I'd be offended if he wasn't."

With that, Grace distracted herself by spying two poofy

squirrels playfully chasing each other in the hedges, safe and sound and wholesome, until the tinier one emit a horrid crying noise, and Grace realized they weren't playing at all. "Can I tell you something?" She put a sallow hand on her stomach.

"Oh god no." Mallory made a face. "If you're gonna yak, can you please try to do it in the woods and not in Avery's Jag? He gets pissy about the interior…"

Her glossy mouth was still saying words, but they only passed through Grace like a heart-stopping breeze. "Avery?" Just saying the name aloud put pollution in the air. "Avery… Owens?"

"Yeah, he lives right down the road."

"He's… he's coming here?"

"Would you rather call your parents to pick our drunk asses up?"

Grace ripped hysterically at her stick-straight hair; the crystallized fear in her eyes pathologically panicked. "We can't get in that car with him!"

Mallory only responded with a rascally smirk. "And *why* not?"

Grace almost clawed the immaculate skin off Mallory's shoulders. *"We can't! We can't! We CAN'T!"*

She covered her gaping mouth. "Stop screaming! Jesus Christ, you psycho!"

Grace wiped away the dripping under her eyes. "So you'll call someone else?"

"Well obviously since you're being such a brat about it."

"Thank you."

"Whatever." Mallory strutted faster ahead. "Next time you can find your own ride home. I'm done being passenger on this train wreck."

The afternoon wind resumed in a much wintrier temperature. Grace's eardrums were still clogged with lake water, now also freezing, and yet mercilessly receptive to the sinister sweet nothings coming from the leaves. As if he were there, stalking, listening, readying… for seconds. Grace began puking in the rain gutters, just as a silver Subaru slowed on the road.

"What on God's green earth are you two doin' lookin' like that?! Get in this car this instant! GRACE ABIGAIL LINDLEY, have you been DRINKING?'"

Grace collapsed into the grass and let the juicy crocodile tears fall. "I'm so sorry, mom! I didn't want to!"

For a split second, Mallory was shocked by how sincere she sounded, but then she ripped into a painful hangnail and had quickly forgotten all about it.

The Holden family went to Bucks for family dinner that night; the place they went to when Kelly suggested they 'do something special', and Brant found it wasteful to drive over twenty minutes for a meal. Brooks and Duke bandied about the defaced stadium, while Kelly asked Brant what he thought about making a weekend escape to the St. Pete Don Cesar. They hadn't been back to the pink palace since their honeymoon, and they'd recently announced a new restaurant.

"That's expensive honey. Maybe another time."

With her extra controlled chewing of iceberg lettuce, Kelly implored him to recall the basic principles of marriage while there was still use to do so. "So!" She focused on her more chivalrous men. "Who are you boys takin' to homecoming? And is it safe to assume one of you will be askin' that darlin' doll Bexley girl?" Both sets of brown eyes squeezed her from across the table, and she simply sipped her sweet tea in a joyous wingding, laughing with a pressing need for them to laugh too. "That's right. I'm clued-up on the dramas, plugged in, if you will."

Duke ate half his chicken burger in one bite. "You're absolutely right, mother. Perfectly safe to assume *one* of us will be takin' her." He cleared his gums with a loud suck and shot his brother a campy wink. "Which one? Who knows. As I see it, the games wide open."

"That right, Hamlet?" Brooks capsulized his knuckles under his basketball shorts. "As I see it, you're fixin' to have a big ol' dent in your neck."

"Brooks Ethan!"

"Okay, listen. Before you take his side, let me ask you this, mom. If Uncle Lee had said somethin' like that about *you* when you and dad got together in high school, wouldn't you want dad to put a dent in his neck too?"

"You don't have an Uncle Lee."

"But say we did, say he was like dad but a… dorkier, less-attractive, sort of a cream puff rendition. With a peanut allergy." He returned the wink. "What would you say then?"

"I'd say let the better man win." This struck both lovesick boys' faces like a flashlight to the eyes, and she bopped their dusty noses to reset. "A lady can never have too many options."

Brant put down his own grease bun, wiped his hands, set them neatly on the table. "Well now you've done it. You've gone and made me jealous over some brother Lee that don't exist!" He chuckled and reached for her, fondling her wheat-pony.

"Careful now," Kelly quipped, just happy to find something that worked. "Never know when I might run off with him."

Brooks found absolutely zilch of this helpful. "Well, she's *my* girlfriend so you have fun with that."

"Girlfriend?" Brant echoed in seizing an opportunity, because he'd been needing an inciting factor to fulfill the orders of the text—*Keep the Golden Holden off the field, or your secrets out*—a believable one that wouldn't spark questions. Him acting intolerably dictating: no questions.

"Yeah." Brooks shrugged. "Sadie is my girlfriend."

"Were you plannin' on mentionin' it?"

"I… thought I just did."

"Don't smart-mouth me, son. You know what I told you about girls takin' away from your practice schedule. I don't want you seein' her." Brant heard his unfairness now how they must've always.

"Are you kidding me? Dad, we're undefeated!" Brooks upreared in the booth. "I don't do nuthin' *but* football! I'm the one bustin' my ass while you just sit in your office with your coach's cap, tellin' me what I do and don't have time for." His vocal chords sounded sat on. "You can't let me breathe just this once?"

His mother softly touched his arm in hopes he'd understand the message: *I'm proud of you.*

For an abating moment, it seemed the Holden family had hashed and patched up their dysfunctions, until the head coach adjusted in the seat and pointedly declared, "Benched."

For the quarterback, the room went a swallowing white, and if Sadie hadn't entered through the door just then with her hilly upper lip and novelistic means of continuing through the bullshit, Brooks might've lost it. His brown eyes trailed her rosy glow around the room, to keep steady as he underwent the rest...

"Yeah, that's right," Brant improvised along, "if Brooks thinks girls are more important than his athletic career, he'll sit Friday out and think about that. He can explain to the team why he won't be on the field. He can explain how he let them down." Did he lay it on too thick? Was it too much? No, it was exactly the course they'd expected.

"You think this town is still yours, but it's not. I don't *need* you," Brooks spoke roughly, turning red.

"Son, I only hope that's true." The coach wavered with an authenticity rock hearts weren't known for, in seeing his depressed wife and two terrific boys finally fizzle out; the family he'd distanced from emotionally out of fear of loving all three of their perfect heads too much to bear it when he lost them. For twenty long years, he'd been preparing to lose them. "I do hope you're right."

"I hope you get fired," Brooks lashed back with foam in his teeth.

Kelly intervened by gently pushing into her husband's ear. She whispered, "One day that boy's gonna have to learn there's more to life than football." In hindsight, she'd wished she could take it back, to never have to hear his response.

Straight into his wife's eyes Brant barked, "Then how come I never did?" Then louder across the table, "Duke you're startin' Friday."

"No way! Thanks pops!" Duke made a faux show of pride and thrill, before becoming just as stoic and Holden as the other two. "Always happy to be your backup son." And he thundered from the restaurant without finishing his chicken.

Duke hid in the back of the building where there weren't any eyes or windows or Sadie, kicking at the brick wall, muttering to himself over and over, "Nice guys finish last."

"You done?" Colton leaned from his truck, jeering. "What'd that poor wall ever do to you?"

"I was pretendin' it was Brooks."

"Well Brooks is about to split your big toe open if you don't hop up in this seat and come talk it out." The locks clicked free.

"I'm fine," Duke argued.

"You don't look fine," Colton replied.

"Neither do you nowadays." He froze, backtracking. "I—I didn't mean it like that."

"Yeah you did. But it's cool." And he meant it.

Eventually Duke climbed up the passenger door, wary of Colton's chilled-out decorum in the reclined chair; considering he'd almost ripped Sterling's head off just six hours prior. Fixing the air vent, he spilled Pepsi on his jacket and phone, and that didn't seem to bother him in the slightest, just casually bobbing his head to bad vibey EDM music with shades on at 9pm. "Hey, Sadie will come around," Colton finally said.

Duke played dumb and stared out the window, realizing they were about ten feet from the spot where she'd draped on his runners, clover-eyes and sepia beauty mark right there in reach, and he'd called her a *friend* when she clearly didn't want him to. "I don't know what you're talkin' about."

"You don't have to admit you love that girl, your googly eyes say it for you. Does seem like your type."

Duke drew in a lamented breath. "Can someone get that memo to her then?"

"You've gotta be the one to tell her, champ."

"Tell her what? That her bad-boy beau with the reputation and body count is nothin' but a coward and liar and *virgin*? The notorious 'dock'—ha! You know that's just a sad sham that started his sophomore year? He took some Crystal River girl there on a date. Nothin' happened, didn't even kiss her. But he thought it'd be funny to leave girl's underwear in the paddleboat for Caleb and Levi to find the next morning."

"No effin' way—"

"It was just a dumb joke, and now he's a legend. Didn't you ever wonder why the girls he takes there are always from some other school? They either don't exist, or they're just far enough out to not blab about how scared he was to touch them below the shoulder. He's a fraud, and Sadie will just end up a collateral casualty to his clout and whatever it takes to keep it, and I'll be the 'friend' who picks up the pieces, fixes her up and sends her right back into his careless arms. Brooks will have all the chances, and I won't have one. Feel free to spread the word." He opened the window and yelled it at some unassuming starling birds. "Spread the word folks! Brooks Holden is a vir—"

Colton yanked him back inside before he woke poor Otis sleeping peacefully in the bushes. "Even if that is true, you can't convince me Brooks doesn't love that girl. He hijacked a damn pep rally for her."

"Sure, maybe. But that doesn't change the fact he likes feelin' like a better person for gettin' Sadie, straight up usin' her like a" — *drug.*

Colton had uncovered a tin can from his pocket, dumping elongated white pills on Duke's navy blue sweats.

He writhed around like they were stinkbugs. "What the—"

"Calm your squirmy nips, Holden! Sheesh, it's just a kind donation. Be thankful, cause not everyone gets hand-outs."

"Since when did you become some closet junkie? Don't you have a couple hundred or so soccer scholarships on the line?"

Colton lit a joint right after ingesting one of the stinkbugs. "You know my theory on how Weston Hills was born?" He puffed dense gray rings in the air. "I think one day God spit, and *we're* that spit. Why else do you think the whole state of Florida looks like it's drippin' off? We're slush, and we sure as hell ain't favored slush, so we do what we have to do to survive out here. Hence, the survival kit."

What a creative justification for taking benzos; Duke pictured how that would fly at a police station. Reluctantly, mostly to put an end to the backwards lecture, he poured the pills in a discreet Tylenol bottle and stuffed it back in the pouch of his hoodie. "Though, if *any* of us are favored, it's gotta be you Mr. Gated

Living."

"That's true." Colton exhaled some more smoke. "King of the spit!"

"So where'd you get the kit?"

The middle Dunn kid chuckled a nefarious opener. "Get this: my dad has a whole stash in his study. No wonder we're never allowed in there. Trust me, he won't miss 'em. Just save it for a rainy day, that day you send Sadie back into Brooks' arms, or whatever you said."

Duke wondered where the time had gone, the part of puberty where they're still just dorky boys counting each other's armpits hairs. "You know, I think I liked you better when you were into Yu-Gi-Oh."

Colton laughed again, but it dwindled at the end. "Me too."

Under the sports screens, Sadie was dipping curly fries in her honey barbecue, stress eating a few 'Million Bucks' buckets. Brooks had just raised his voice across the room, then Mr. Holden raised his voice louder, then Duke stomped out the door. What happened? Was everything okay? Did it have to do with her? Now *that* was a ridiculous notion. *But did it?* Sadie was still a little bit drunk.

Therefore, it was the least optimal time for her mother to avidly request, "Tell me everything that's been going on."

"Everything?" Sadie repeated in dread.

"Well not all at once. How's Brooks? What did you two do today?"

She gave the clean version. "We went swimming." Pointing to her lake weed topknot to prove it. "And then we watched a movie on his couch."

"And are you... well have you..." Margot struggled with a sudden bout of bashful blushing. "You are being... responsible?" She finally stickered some words together, careful to avoid any operative phrasing that might paint too clear a picture and cause Henri a stroke.

"Holy smokes!" Expectedly, Henri turned his head from max slants of side to side. "I don't like this. I don't like this one bit. Is it hot in here?" He flagged down Karigan for some ice water, but when it came out, "May I have seven beers please?"

"Dad—"

"Okay, I'm ready. Skin me alive."

"I'm an angel nun, remember?" She mimed tuning up her halo.

Henri peered at the Holden table. "You mean to tell me you've just been huggin' with that boy?"

"Well, not *just*—"

"La la la la!" Henri plugged both pinkies in his ears, but wore a grand smile, so despite the sensitive themes, it was okay for them to arrive. "You know I'm just kiddin'. Even if it does give me the jim-jams, you're growin' up, and I want you to be able to talk to us about it. Your mother is right about bein' responsible, because sometimes," he gagged, "*things* start to happen and before you know it—"

"Yoohoo friends!" Stacy's arm fat waved in her matronly silhouette and sensible shoes, before meeting them at their booth. "Howdy howdy, Bexleys."

Margot's head felt immediately pounding. "Hi Stacy, we're actually just having a dinner—"

"And by heavens, don't you let me interrupt Margot!" She wagged a finger with peeling skin. "Right after I tell you the wrenching news. Ah, it's just hard. You see, some of the kids have been tied to an inappropriate party at the Lake Josey dock just earlier today—and Henri, I *know* you know the merrymakings teenagers get into down there. I understand they were upset about the vandalism at the school, but it's really no excuse to lollygag into temptations."

Merrymakings; Margot would need upwards of ten selenite wands and a whole bucket of burning herbs to shuck those vibrations.

Stacy crouched to meet Sadie, her perfume a powerhouse of patchouli. "Is there anythin' you'd like to tell us, dear?"

"Oh, um. I was there?"

"Mhm. Mhm. Very good."

"And so were Caleb and Grace."

Now Stacy was distraught to tears. "Oh my poor Gracie girl!

She went down there, she *sure* did, from the guidance of Jesus no doubt, to convince her friends not to engage in the activities, but was peer pressured and *threatened*! I'm just grateful Caleb got there in time before anyone got hurt."

Sadie hiccupped in a laugh, all prudence and discretion aside, before muffling it into her water straw. Her blood baked as she eyed the blonde con-artists order praline shakes from the bar— the innocent lamb, the prodigal saint—and then for a flicker of a second, she imagined how hard it must be having Stacy as a mom, and felt glad they were the way they were, for their sake. *Free*.

"I haven't seen you at any youth nights, Sadie. We carpool every Wednesday if you could make it." Stacy smiled with croissant wrinkles on her massive neck. "It'd be very beneficial for a girl like you."

"Oh yes. Very beneficial." Locked on the blue sapphire solar systems in Caleb's eyes, the ones that held her to no standard at all, Sadie spoke loud enough for him to hear. "Especially the de-flower room."

The Abercrombie boy was throwing her a figurative party from the jukebox, as Stacy lost her overwhelming amount of cool.

"I'm just gon' jump in here right quick," Henri charmed up at the chatty pain in the neck. "It's actually my fault Sadie's been too busy to attend. Wednesday nights are the nights we take out all the guns in my safe and polish 'em up. She's my best assistant, and it's very grueling work. You do understand?"

The abstinence advocate appeared tongue-tied. "I... think so."

"And it's supposedly fantastic for the chakras! At least that's what my wife tells me. Isn't that what you said about the chakras, dear?"

Margot gave an impervious smile, like the real movie star she was. "Fantastic."

Henri summed up, "And there you have it."

Finally, Stacy was fed up with their antics and retreated to her husband and his measly ginger-ale, and together Henri, Margot and Sadie relished in the highs of what could only be seen as a victorious 'Bexley vs. Lindley' showdown. Their hearty laughter rang across the room, shaking it down, cleansing the whole little green town and it's intricate net of well-kept secrets, until everyone could feel it coming—a good ol' down-home rinsing.

Did you clean out those gutters, yet?

Down Paddock Road and up the beaten path of orange groves, Henri and Margot nestled between the rumpled covers, traces of ecstasy still evident in the saturated nature of their faces.

"Why didn't you ever tell me about you and Stacy?" Margot asked her husband while still chasing down her breath.

Henri furrowed with amused disbelief. "Is that what you were thinkin' about just now?"

Margot giggled in realizing her moronic timing. "Well, no. Not just *now*. But don't you change the subject. You put me in a very awkward position. Why didn't you tell me that you two dated? That woman was in our house the first day that we arrived."

Henri adored all the lovely bits and pieces of his red-hot woman, rubbing her knee and down to her toes, which were stubby by her standards, and a big insecurity when they'd first started dating. Naturally, he kissed each one now. "Margot, you are the love of my life. I didn't tell you because anyone and everything before you is just so monumentally irrelevant! I dated Stacy in *high school*, and bringin' it up would feel silly, like... like... like tellin' you what kind of sandwich I had for lunch on labor day 1993, which by the way was bologna."

Margot covered her embarrassed face with a pillow, but Henri moved it aside, because her light show of expressions had always been a vital sustenance of sort, and it was rather mean of her to rob him of it.

"Darlin', this is where I grew up. This is my history. I wish I could change that to make you more comfortable—"

"Shhh." She waved her long piano fingers, and they tapped

the air is if playing floating keys, before looking up at him intently. "Henri Bexley, you are one of the good ones."

This made him transfixed and troubled, because the incredible belief she had in him was more than he could afford. "I don't always know what that means."

"But you'll always figure it out, won't you?"

"I hope so." He nodded, hugging tightly his undeserved salvation, one of his two very reasons for even existing at all. "Let's go out tomorrow night. Just you and me."

"Really?"

"Yeah. We'll go somewhere fancy for my lady, so you can wear that new dress I got you."

"You got me five," she reminded. It was how she knew he was in his merriest of moods (or trying to be); throwing cash at boutique store owners who'd drape her in fine feminine linens, tickling up her thigh as she tried on tens of short and long gowns, putting on a fashion show.

"Then bring 'em all, and we can do outfit changes throughout the night. You know what—wear whatever you want! A dress, those hippie harems you like to garden in, a trash bag, anythin'! Long as I got that beautiful smile, I'm happy." He scattered little kisses across her shoulder. "You can even wear nothin' if you're feelin' frisky."

Margot's youthful joy engrossed them both, romantic and radiant and restorative for the soul, not unlike another little lady they knew.

"Where will we go?" she asked.

"To the city, we'll go for a nice dinner," Henri decreed valiantly. "Let's leave this rut for a few hours."

"I was planning on doing some shopping in Tampa. I'll meet you after."

"And I'll be waiting for you," he whispered. "Very, very impatiently."

Unfortunately, Henri would never make it to that dinner.

CHAPTER SEVENTEEN
Forget-Me-Not

The tires of Delilah's Porsche created a smooth rapping sound against the wet gravel as the pitter-patter of rain leapt in stride. The storm was coming down hard that early morning. According to channel 9, the rest of the week would be just as submersed.

June to November is hurricane season, and the way Florida juts off the country like a fishing line, makes it a sort of magnet lure for those tropical blusters ready to rip up entire trailer suburbs from their anchors and steel straps. The only friendly thing about hurricanes: you can see them coming. That predicting vision would be less clear, this year.

The flashy Jordan car crossed through the gates of Thompson Farms, passing views of a small-scale ranch conspicuous with perceivable wealth; Mallory's resplendent kingdom and exile.

With homecoming week approaching rapidly, Delilah, in head-to-toe LuLu Lemon, felt it imperative they talk logistics, specifically Mallory's lack of date prospects and court campaigning efforts.

"Mom, I win every year. I don't need to bake cupcakes and pass out tacky posters to get votes." She shrugged, texting. "The people love me. Go ask them."

"Things are different this year." She glanced at her Dooney and Bourke, not her daughter, when talking. "There's certain variables we need to take into account."

"What? You mean *Sadie?*" Mallory's gloss scoffed and returned her attention to her phone, before recovering a half-eaten Snickers bar from her bag. Last time Mr. Edwards had taken attendance, he'd had to pause because the gurgling in her stomach was that distracting, and after what happened at Bandit Bog, she didn't need more chubby-ankled softball girls expressing their mimicked concerns.

Growing impatient, Delilah pushed up the Swarovski diamonds on her arm, but really just mimed doing it, and Mallory noted how legitimately stupid that was; how women were expected to be so dainty and slight that their every movement was only an appealing enactment. It wasn't sexy to roll up your sleeves, but it *was* to weakly graze a feminine hand up the article of clothing, just so it entrancingly slipped back down. It wasn't sexy to walk at a normal speed and get to where you're going—absolutely *not*—one must unhurriedly mosey at a leisurely pace. How were they ever expected to get anything done?

"Baby doll, do you really think you should be eatin' that?" Her mother interrupted her thoughts. "It might help to think about how much time it takes on the treadmill to burn off those calories. Don't forget what Dale says about morning metabolism."

Mallory's face flushed hot under the Dior foundation, a perfectly blended mixture of shame and warped agreement. "But... I..."

"It's your choice. I know what *I* would do, but it's *your* choice."

Mallory watched her mother make the same face as she had when she'd instructed her to 'suck in' while standing in line for an Adventure Island waterslide. When she was just a kid in line for a slide, and her mother had ridiculed her for having baby fat, and traumatized her so she'd made herself throw up the chicken fingers and fries and Dippin' Dots from lunch. Then she remembered the digitals for the Miami modeling agency when she was fifteen, and how she'd dieted so hard before the meeting, she'd lost her period for six months. Mallory had cried on her bedroom floor about being scared she couldn't have kids, and her mother had rubbed her back and said, "At least you don't have to worry about stretch marks," though she hadn't ever thought of that before. What did families talk about at the dinner table if not simple carbs and scales? What did little girls obsess over if not thigh gaps and showy wrist veins and remarkable clavicles? Had she even wanted to be a Pussycat Doll for Halloween in second grade?

"No."

"I'm sorry?" Delilah again nudged up her diamonds, and again they stayed where they were.

Mallory shoved all the chocolate in her mouth, encrusting her teeth with the caramel and calories and high fructose corn syrup. "No, it isn't my choice, mom. It's never been. And you *really* wanna know what Dale says about 'morning metabolism'? He says he's worried about me. He says I don't eat enough. Are you going to fire him now?"

As if her complex wasn't deep-rooted enough, Delilah airily replied, "Maybe that right there is why Brooks Holden will be taking Sadie to the dance instead of you." Her tweaked contours were unfeeling, and it wasn't from the botox.

Why was she never good enough? What more did she want? "Brooks is my friend," Mallory was barely able to whisper, before her mother shot her an alarming dose of disdain.

"Men aren't your friend, sweetie. You'll realize that when you grow up." But she knew as soon as she'd said it: there was one man in her life, recently reappeared, who'd always make that statement untrue.

Mallory observed her mother glimmer with something humble, though it snapped back to supremacy pretty quickly. Her hunger manifested to anger. "Well? Any advice for the chemistry test I have today? Maybe 'nothing tastes as good as skinny feels' because that's always been your answer to everything else!" She smeared off her 'plumping' lip gloss that burned them raw and swollen; a tube made of bee venom and chili peppers, probably. "Have a great day in your big empty house, mom! Promise to not come home too early and catch you with the tall, dark and handsome stable worker with the tight jeans and hairy chest. Love ya."

Mallory dashed from the Porsche, but not before dropping the Snickers wrapper on the seat so the melty side stained it. After regaining herself in the pouring rain; letting the cutting water drops wash away her cold creams; the beautiful aristocrat took off up the quad steps in a spinning vortex of scheme, locating Sadie and Maia who were lounging in the grass.

"Hi," Mallory said to them with a smile.

"Umm." Maia's raven scrolls sat up, huge eyes squinting. "Are you lost? Cheerleaders are about thirty squat jumps that a way."

"I actually wanted to apologize for how I've acted," Mallory lied.

"We forgive you," Sadie sang like she was in *The Sound of Music*, words rippling out like a seismic auto response. She was relieved for some harmony amongst the lands.

"We do?" Maia was more skeptical.

"Great," Mallory, unblinking as if in a staring contest with life, concluded quickly so it held the terms of a business deal. "I'd really love it if we could be friends." And before they could digest this unimaginable idea, she'd already made her way to the picnic tables to tell Grace to stop sucking on a blue ring pop because *it made her look like she just made out with a Smurf.*

Sadie was jarred, but pleased nonetheless. "Should we be... scared?"

"Probably," Maia fretted. "But... why do I feel kind of bad for her?"

"I don't know... but same."

"Huh, well that's unsettling."

Once Maia elusively vanished at her usual time, Sadie found Brooks leaning against their pole; the one that still had 'reserved for Sadie Bexley' carved into the paint. Brooks had tried to scratch it out with a car key, but it was still readable.

They spent their ten minutes before the bell completely bound in enamored lip-lock, heads tilted just right, fingers cosseting whatever vicinity of their body they felt drawn to in the moment. Sadie enjoyed running her fingertips down the strength of his neck, meanwhile Brooks melted at the swimming dips in her waist. No one ever dared bother them, not even the teachers, but they did watch.

Thunder rumbled overhead when he said, "Meet me at the stadium after the last bell?"

"Don't I always?"

"Yes, but... today is special."

"Every day is special."

He shook his reckless crew cut hair, grinning. "Not like this."

She smiled with an inquiring tug at the corner. "But what could that mean, since I've already cashed out all my muffins?"

And did you know; he'd started to believe in her lovely castles in the air, too. "I'll see you then, weirdo."

After one last lustful peck, they stayed hips to hips as had become a safe routine, until Brooks had deactivated from having her breasts pushed up on his body, and he could go about his way without openly publicizing just how *much* of him she'd woken up. Sadie found it all a little humorous, but she kept that thought to herself. Today, it took almost two whole minutes.

The day dragged on just as drearily as the weather and by the last bell, the school campus had flooded. Sadie tip-toed around the puddles, quickly giving up and letting the dirt water submerge her socks and Converse, but at least now they were just as grungy and rad as the ones Tenley had worn to that scary festival called Warped Tour. She sighted Maia's Red Hot Chili Peppers tee waiting by her locker.

"Are we in a hurricane right now?" Sadie made a wry face at the sideways palm trees with aggressively whipping fronds in the nearby neighborhoods. The rain gutters above oozed gray glop so it spattered on cheerleaders trying to maneuver by.

Maia stomped in puddles to make it worse for them as bubbles flew from her socks. "Hurricane? This is an afternoon sprinkle!"

"I'm supposed to meet Brooks at the stadium, but I'll melt by the time I get there," Sadie groaned at the black sky, but wholeheartedly relied on every element of the universe having her best interest in mind, so she needn't fret. Even her worry and dread sounded like sea in a conch shell, was the hue of orchid pink, manifested a sanguine expectant look on her face like she was simply playing out a scene in her fairytale, and this is the big conflict she must overcome, to achieve the happy ending.

Suddenly, Maia grabbed her by the shoulders and shook melodramatically. "Run to him, Sadie! Run to your man and *leap* into his arms!" She seemed to enjoy her one-woman skit, before adding, "Ooh! You can have one of those scrapbook kisses in the rain!"

Sadie just blinked, perplexed by what that meant. "Do you mean... *Notebook* kisses?"

"Eh, I dunno. I haven't seen it."

Sadie dwelled on Maia's deficiency in cinematic Ryan Gosling as she figured out her driest bet to the football field. Skipping at full-speed past the math portables, she turned left into the electives hall, and stopped; someone was playing a guitar.

More than curious, her shuffling feet followed the sedative country ballad into an empty band room she'd never seen before, where she discovered a removed boy with uncombed brown hair and chiseled squared-off shoulders, a singing voice that was detrimental to her mental and physical health. Gritty yet consoling, drowsy yet guttural, and hypnotically bittersweet. Sadie lingered secretly at the door and listened to Duke's lyrics about a girl who could change the world, according to him. He stopped a few times to scribble lyrics into his red notebook.

"Keep going," she whispered, and he heard her.

Duke spun around so fast, the guitar fell from his lap and he jammed his elbow against the metal leg of a chair. "You're you, here, listening to me—ow."

"I didn't hear much," Sadie fibbed to spare him the embarrassment, though embarrassed is the last thing he should be, considering this exact scenario was written in short-story form somewhere in her journal. If she weren't unavailable, she might actually think this a prophecy. She sort of did, still.

"You're not supposed to be here." Duke sighed as he glanced at the sterile wall clock.

"You really don't want me to hear your music, do you?"

"It's not that. It's just… you're supposed to be at the stadium by now. At least… at least that's what I overheard." He seemed somehow saddened by her schedule.

"I was on my way there," she justified while sitting down next to him on the carpet, criss-cross-apple-sauce. "But I took a detour." She looked into his brown maple eyes like she could look into them forever. "Is that alright? Or are you going to tell on me?"

Duke swallowed. "N—no, I would never tell."

"Then no one will ever know. And what's the harm, if no one knows?" She sipped one felonious lace of breath, pushed out the warm slip, passed it to him.

He played along gloriously. "I guess there is none."

Sadie smiled, like someone who'd gotten exactly what they wanted. "None at all."

And here the impractical girl and the brother indulged in an igniting silence trembled with tension, sustaining the throbbing energy between them that had begun to feel like a real living thing. Which also, by the laws of nature and free will, made it uncontrollable.

Sadie's darling gaze peered wondrously around. "I've never been in the band room before."

His captivated ones stayed put on her. "I'm honored your first time is with me."

Pins and needles badgered her sweet spot, which caused her to flutter to jiggle it away. "Uhhuh." It didn't go away.

Admittedly, Duke took a tremendous amount of satisfaction in what she was missing to instead be here with him, even if she didn't know it. Even if Brooks would assume he kidnapped her on purpose and made good on that neck-denting promise, it was worth it.

Sadie was in a cropped aqua sweater that brought out her irises, with layered Forever 21 necklaces and a push-up bra that made the straight stria in her smashed-together bust secure enough to prop a quarter. Duke observed that she'd started shaving her arms, a metallic glitzy shimmer was brushed on the cherry summits of her cheeks, and there were dark smudges of liner in her lashes that made him want to lick a thumb and swipe it across. She was a luxury delicacy in cheap generic wrapping, and he didn't understand why a vased lily would want to be a garden weed.

But isn't it obvious?

Sadie gently stroked the smooth wood of the instrument, fingering at a string and half-jumping at the sound. Gold flumes of hair fluctuated from her chest to his, back and forth. "I didn't realize you could sing like *that*," she mumbled with depression.

"Well, there's a lot you don't know about me." Duke was actively less smiley today, and it launched her to reach further for it.

Sadie adjusted to her knees, bouncing. "Oh yeah? Like what?"

"Mmmm, I hate black olives."

"I love black olives, but I hate the green ones."

"I love the green ones."

"Interesting." She leaned back competitively, like this was her favorite sport. "Okay, I have another question."

Duke took a second to hedge his bets on what it was, before tenderly drawling, "Shoot."

"Who is your song about?"

He won the bet. "How do you know it's about anyone?"

Her back straightened and temples scrunched, because *this* was one of those few things she felt strongly about. "I would hope it is. Art has to have a story to make it meaningful, otherwise it's a setup. Like... paintings, poems, songs... if they're all just made up words or random brush strokes about nothing, I'd feel tricked."

"Tricked?" he repeated, taking notes. "How so?"

Sadie detected Duke's white cottony long sleeve was just thin enough to vaguely show his nipples. She cleared her clumped throat and focused on other things: the drying raindrops glistening down his arms, the masculine size of his fingers and hands turning the delicate tuning pegs, the lack of slack in his blue joggers in the intimate gulf between his thighs that was now swelling in real time. Her eyes quickly went back to circling his nipples. "Um, well, art makes me feel a lot, and that would make my feelings exploited. Say, you connect to a really heartbreaking song, and you listen to it over and over, but in reality the songwriter has never felt a broken heart and was thinking about a grilled cheese when they wrote it. It's fraudulent art. It's manipulative." She expected he might walk out after that one, but then remembered who she was talking to. "Wouldn't you feel like a fool, too?"

"I don't know. Maybe." He rubbed hard around the firm architecture of his jaw. "Or maybe those people are the best ones to write the song, maybe they can still make it feel beautiful *because* of the ignorance."

Sadie felt personally attacked, though she knew he hadn't meant it that way. "Do you feel that way? Is that what you do?" Hands clamped tightly in her lap, she couldn't manage to face him directly, but she did hear him twist up in long ragged breath.

Duke spoke in a voice dyed of both scowl and sympathy. "That your way of suggestin' I'm inexperienced?"

"No," Sadie defended her indiscretion quickly, before blurting, "but are you?"

He got up and angled the guitar against a skinny black stand. With his delivery turned, he answered truthfully, "No less experienced than your boyfriend."

Sadie stared with ferocious emotion at his sinuous lower back, athlete glutes, fit calves. Her eyes fluctuated in these rounds, waiting for him to turn, mouth to creep into a smile, make it a joke. "I doubt that's true."

His non-boat shoes took a wide stance, a definitive stance. "It *is* true."

"That—that you've been with as many girls as Brooks?" She'd gained a sudden stutter on both her parched lips and racing heart. "No—no you haven't."

Duke crouched to one knee to confirm it straight at her. "Yes, I have."

"You... you...." Her rapid blinking was all over the place, working it out across the gray sooty carpet. "But you and

Brooks... you're different..."

He actually laughed from the torture of it all. "Are you mad to hear that?"

"Of course I'm mad!"

He provoked further, grilled harder, aroused the situation until the sparks were like real fireflies zipping in a creamy cloud around them. "Why are you mad, Sadie? If Brooks is so great, if you'll always choose him, what's wrong with me being like him?"

She finally rammed both hands into his pecks, perhaps from needing a reason to make physical contact. "Because now you're just the fraudulent artist I was talking about! I *did* hear your lyrics, and they're about a girl, but if you treat girls like Brooks treats girls—"

"Your boyfriend," he corrected pointedly, "how your boyfriend treats girls!"

"At least he was honest!"

"*Honest?*" Duke was hunched on hands and knees now, crawling closer with powerful hind legs in launch position like a hungry animal. "Notice how you assume, Sadie. You didn't even think about what I just said! You didn't for one second step back to see the bigger picture! We've been with the *same* amount of girls, think about it—"

"I *am* thinking about it! And I heard you the first time!" She copied his prowl position as the slight aperture between them ailed. "I thought I knew you, but I don't!" Lightning seemed to strike her through the ceiling. His unfamiliar hand tightened desperately atop hers. Their shallow breaths aligned in one fickle slip. The lordly lines of right and wrong went blurrier, harshness dial of pouring rain turned up, drowning all reason, washing away what happened as it happened, like it wanted to be their shield, a cover, just to see... one... *thing...*

But Duke didn't want her this way. She wouldn't have, anyway.

Or would she have?

Would you have?

"You're actually killin' me, you know that?" Duke's kind eyes were wild and begging yet whisper gentle, then suddenly his spine shuddered as though something heavy collapsed inside him. He groaned from the sheer pain of keeping this control, of counting the feebly many reasons why he shouldn't hike his hand around her small thigh, hoist her body against the Mozart wallpaper, unleash every arrested want stifled inside him like pendulum swords swinging lesions across his ribcage. It hurt Duke so greatly to want her like this, but more than that, it hurt to see that she wanted him too.

He needed to know, "So if I *am* just like Brooks, what's the difference? What's gon' make you walk out that door and run to him instead?"

Sadie did have an answer, even if she didn't believe in it with the same fixed endurance anymore. "Fate."

"Fate," Duke echoed with a mournful misshapen expression. "And do you really think you'd have to fight this hard, go through so much, if it were fate?" He paused. "Do you think fate would let you end up here, when Brooks has a whole homecoming proposal waitin' for you at the stadium… at this very moment?"

Sadie's basil eyes opened to the maximum extent. "He… oh my god." She grabbed her phone that had been buzzing nonstop, but she hadn't heard it until now. There were fourteen unread messages. *Where are you? Did you forget? Is everything okay? Babe, did you get lost in the marigolds again? This sucks. Hurry.*

Stumbling, she grabbed her bag and scurried for the door, but remembered he'd never given an answer to her question. She turned back, accidentally imagined them in bed with teas and books on a Sunday morning, before softly breathing, "Who is the song about, Duke?"

He tossed his mini-pencil in a trashcan; it bounced off the rim and rolled on the floor—figures. "Mallory," he answered.

Then, she was gone.

Spinning down the sidewalk, stairs, and undersea parking lot, Sadie tried to come up with an excuse for being late. Eighteen minutes late, to be exact. She could say she lost track of time searching for a poetry piece in the library, or had to save a baby dove that'd fallen from a tree, or tripped. Brooks was far more likely to believe any version of those than what'd really happened. She imagined saying it: *I almost kissed your brother.* Then laughed outlandishly aloud because even she didn't believe it, before the laugh caught stiff in her lungs, and she deemed herself the most selfish person on the planet for wanting them both, needing them both...

With every step, tiny aquatic sinkholes tugged at her dismal soles, and the puree of earthworms and snails would definitely hurt her soul later. But looking up, she realized the rain *had* miraculously cleared, so that must be why she'd been diverted on the roundabout route. Obviously, the universe distracted her with Duke, to save her from showing up a sopping wet golden retriever. Yes, that was it. That was the reason.

Sadie was both smiling and crying; getting closer to one, farther from the other; as she thought about the saying *be careful what you wish for.* Hadn't she craved to be torn to pieces? Hadn't she pursued life to the fullest? Hadn't she begged, pleaded, ached for love? She should've been more specific, because she'd meant a different kind, one without so much suffering. One day she'd come to terms: there is only this kind.

Nursling petals dispersed from the footloose girl like leaking pennies from a childhood piggy bank.

The sun slanted on the football field so the grass glittered to life as Sadie, much more hot mess than angelic, emerged from under the stands. Then, Mallory's toned arm yanked her by the necklace, dragging her up the stairs. The pretty cheerleader smoothed the tangled ringlets and urged Sadie to listen. "I'm not even going to ask where you were, but girl, word to the not wise, he *doesn't* do this. You got the quarterback, don't be numb now. Don't hurt him, okay?"

Sadie nodded, and requested the same. "I won't, if you don't."

But Mallory didn't hear her, only twirled her around by the waist to show her the dream come true she'd almost stood up.

It was a modern fairytale. The entire varsity football team had lined up on the cold jellied field (minus Duke), each holding a hand-painted life-size letter spelling out *homecoming*, and a question mark at the end. In front of the formation, Brooks held a magnificent bouquet of swan-white magnolias, wearing his typical nonchalant smile, but hands shaking more than they had at his first freshman kickoff.

Birds sang, sun shined, small charming winds brushed Sadie's body and whisked her up like a vision of all lovely things. It was incredible. It was perfect. It was for sure, hands down, most likely… *fate*.

With an encore of messy smiling and crying, Sadie hopped up and down, before whimsically plunging down the stairs with such parlous speed, it'd be impossible to steer anywhere but his waiting arms. They spun her round and round, eyes meeting as one, hot mouths open in young glee and possibility, until their heads got dizzy and their backs hit the ground. She wrapped her legs around him, clung fantastically tight until he coughed and chuckled from her grip, and she clung tighter.

"You like to keep a guy waiting, huh?" Brooks, relieved and impassioned, kissed her forehead and took out his phone to document with a photo.

"I… I guess I do." Sadie blushed a vineyard's worth of grape, smiled shyly for the camera, and peeked over her shoulder just in time to see Duke watching from under the stands.

I love you, deep down inside, she said to them both.

Acknowledgements

Thank you to my incredible parents, Henri and Nina, for leading by example and showing me what it means to live a meaningful life. Thank you for protecting, preparing and pushing me. Thank you for teaching me about hard work, resilience, and compassion. Every triumph and success of mine is a direct reflection of both of you. I will cherish every opportunity to make you proud.

Thank you to my first reader and fierce friend Sabrina Wrabley. Without your excitement, support and hand-written letters of encouragement, Blossoming wouldn't have—well, *blossomed*—as confidently as she did. Thank you for believing in me when I was still learning to believe in myself.

Thank you to Summer Vaughan; my greatest advocate, soul sister and favorite matcha date. It's hard to imagine a time in my life when I didn't have you by my side, and it's an invaluable richness to know I will never have to again. Thank you for helping me grow into the person younger me dreamed of being.

Thank you to the extraordinary producer and wonderful human being, Susan Cooper, who gave me the idea to write this novel. Thank you for being open to having lunch with a hopeful young woman and her vast ideas, and allowing her the space to learn from you.

Thank you to my coffee shop companion, Harry Thomason, for the kind smiles and chats during months of long writing days. You have made this process all the more delightful.

Thank you to Monica Virgen and Caralyne Jahns; those rollercoaster teenage years weren't easy, but you two sure made them fun. Thank you for making me laugh until I cried, and for making every cry end with a laugh.

Thank you to my elementary school teacher, Barbara Pittman, who in my fourth-grade year took my hand and with a gentle fierceness said, "Never stop writing." You may not have known it at the time, but this small gesture made a world of a difference for the quiet girl making up stories in the corner.

Finally, thank you to the rambunctious small town that raised me; you both shattered my heart and healed it back stronger. It was a heck of a ride.